W9-BKK-270

"Do you want to be kissed by me?"

"Purely as part of our business contract," Richard added, his voice deepening.

"Of course. I understand that," Tina said. "And yes, I think perhaps I do want to be kissed by you."

Richard stood up and reached out his hand. He drew her toward him slowly, giving her time to change her mind, although he had no intention of changing his. Her breath was a little uneven, her lips parted in anticipation, and then he pressed his lips to hers.

Soft, just as he'd imagined. Her skin was scented like orange blossom, and he breathed her in as his lips coaxed hers, gently but firmly, into responding. Until finally, with a little sigh of pleasure, she began to kiss him back.

This was no longer a lesson.

Like a bolt of lightning it came to him that, given half the chance, he'd lay her down on the sofa and undress her until she was pale and naked under his touch.

There was nothing cool and measured about this. Richard wanted her.

By Sara Bennett

ATTENTION: ORGANIZATIONS AND CORPORATIONS
Most Avon Books paperbacks are available at special quantity discounts for bulk purchases for sales promotions, premiums, or fund raising. For information, please call or write:

**Special Markets Department, HarperCollins Publishers,
10 East 53rd Street, New York, New York 10022-5299.
Telephone: (212) 207-7528.   Fax: (212) 207-7222.**

SARA BENNETT

Sin With a Scoundrel

The Husband Hunters Club

PAPL
DISCARDED

AVON

An Imprint of HarperCollinsPublishers

This is a work of fiction. Names, characters, places, and incidents are products of the author's imagination or are used fictitiously and are not to be construed as real. Any resemblance to actual events, locales, organizations, or persons, living or dead, is entirely coincidental.

AVON BOOKS
An Imprint of HarperCollins*Publishers*
10 East 53rd Street
New York, New York 10022-5299

Copyright © 2012 by Sara Bennett
ISBN 978-0-06-133919-6
www.avonromance.com

All rights reserved. No part of this book may be used or reproduced in any manner whatsoever without written permission, except in the case of brief quotations embodied in critical articles and reviews. For information address Avon Books, an Imprint of HarperCollins Publishers.

First Avon Books mass market printing: November 2012

Avon Trademark Reg. U.S. Pat. Off. and in Other Countries, Marca Registrada, Hecho en U.S.A.
HarperCollins® is a registered trademark of HarperCollins Publishers.

Printed in the U.S.A.

10 9 8 7 6 5 4 3 2 1

If you purchased this book without a cover, you should be aware that this book is stolen property. It was reported as "unsold and destroyed" to the publisher, and neither the author nor the publisher has received any payment for this "stripped book."

There were times when this book looked like it would never get written. And the fact that it is finished and, hopefully by the time you read this, in bookstores and on e-readers everywhere, is in large part due to the help given to me by my friend and fellow writer Christine Gardner. Thank you, Chris. I owe you!

Prologue

Miss Debenham's Finishing School
Graduating Ball of 1837

The fuss over Eugenie and her duke had died down. Miss Clementina Smythe—Tina to her friends—found her heart beating a little more quickly than it usually did. Which was odd because she was not the sort of girl to indulge in palpitations.

Practical, that was how Tina saw herself. Not coldhearted, not at all. She was warm and generous, but there was always that little part of her that sat back and considered the situation before it rushed in. And it was rarely she changed her mind once she'd made it up to do a thing.

"I don't think my choice of husband will come as a surprise to any of you," she said, with a smile at the flushed, excited faces of her friends. "I have spoken of him a great deal to all of you."

"Lord Horace Gilfoyle!" they cried in unison, and then fell about in laughter.

Tina laughed, too, and if it was slightly strained, then no one noticed.

"He doesn't sound terribly exciting," Olivia ventured, when they had recovered themselves.

"Or dashing," Marissa added.

"Nonsense, he's both," Tina retorted. "And he has quite a rakish reputation, I'll have you know!"

Eugenie widened her eyes. "Goodness, I can't imagine you with a rake, Tina. Do you plan to re-habilitate him?"

Tina raised an eyebrow. "Of course. Once I have him. The thing is . . ." She pulled a face. "He is an old family friend, and he looks upon me more as a little sister than a woman he might fall in love with and marry. I have to change his mind."

Averil was thoughtful. "It may be difficult, Tina. You may need a seduction plan, a way to jolt him into the realization that you are a beautiful young woman in your own right."

After that ideas came thick and fast.

"Speak in a breathless voice and lean on his arm as if you're about to faint! There's nothing like a fainting woman to bring out the protective-ness in a man."

"Flirt with him. He will be astonished and then intrigued."

"No, no. Why prevaricate? Invite him into your boudoir."

This last had them all in stitches again.

"But why do you want to marry Lord Horace Gilfoyle?" Olivia said. "Are you so madly in love with him, Tina?"

Yes, of course I am! I've known Horace all my life, and he's the only man I've ever wanted to marry. The only man I can ever imagine marrying.

But as she opened her mouth to speak the words, she found herself hesitating. The truth wasn't as simple as a yes or a no. Despite the fact that Horace was almost like another son to her mother and father, another brother to Charles, and Tina knew they wanted her to marry him just as much as she wanted to marry him herself. Despite all that there were far colder and more pragmatic reasons for such an alliance.

Horace was a very wealthy man.

Tina's father had lost most of their fortune in a disastrous speculation.

Put the two facts together, and that was why she needed to marry Horace. No one had put pressure on her to do so—not yet—but in her heart Tina knew it was the right thing to do. The only thing to do. She must marry Horace—which she told herself she wanted to do anyway—and save her family from disaster and ruin.

It was the logical choice. The *practical* choice.

But she felt an aversion to telling her friends the truth. She didn't want their pitying smiles and reassuring hugs. Tina had too much pride for that. Besides, they might try to talk her out of it.

"I am madly in love with Horace," she said firmly. "He is the only possible man for me."

The glasses were filled and raised once more.

"To Tina and Horace! May they be very happy! Good husband hunting!"

Oh, Tina knew she would need to be very good

to win over Horace. Horace who never gave her a second glance except to tease her—if she'd had pigtails she was certain he would have pulled them. But somehow she must make him fall deeply in love with her. Enough to propose. Because surely, if he loved her and she loved him, then the marriage would succeed?

But a man like Horace . . . if only she knew how to begin. If only there was someone who could give her instructions in what to do and say.

Chapter 1

Summer 1838
Mayfair, London

Miss Clementina Smythe inspected the brass plate. Number Five. Mr. Eversham lived at Number Five Jasmine Square. She looked up at the narrow building, its long windows blindly gazing across the square, and wondered which of those windows belonged to Mr. Eversham.

Perhaps they all did, perhaps he was wealthy enough to own the entire building, but she didn't think so. The word was Mr. Eversham had wasted his fortune on the gambling tables and betting on the races, not to mention ladies of loose morals, and now he was obliged to work for a living. How his blue-blooded ancestors must shudder at that— and the gossip was that he was very well connected indeed although society tended to shun him these days. To make matters worse the work he was currently engaged in was advising gentlemen on winning the ladies of their dreams.

In other words, Tina decided cynically, he was a seducer who taught other men the art of seduction.

His reputation was rumored to be very bad and in other circumstances, Tina would have taken care not to recognize him in the street, let alone visit his address without a chaperone. But she had no choice. She was here for his help. She needed him to teach her how to win the tricky heart of Lord Horace Gilfoyle.

"You're a dear girl, Tina, but really, you are such an innocent. And innocents are a dead bore."

The words were emblazoned into her mind.

She'd thought everything was going along so very well, that Horace was finally beginning to see that she was the one and only woman for him, and then he'd spoken those shattering words. Her plans were thrown into chaos, and for a time, a very dark time, she'd contemplated abandoning them altogether.

But what alternative did she have? There were holes in her petticoats for goodness' sake! They'd had pigs' trotters for last night's supper, and all the while pretending to their friends and the world that nothing was wrong. Her family was living on the edge of a precipice. Constantly teetering on the verge of financial disaster. It was only a matter of time until they slid into the abyss. Truly, it was unbearable, and the only way Tina could see to save them was for her to make a wealthy marriage.

And Horace was the wealthiest man she knew,

the only man with whom she could imagine spending the rest of her life.

Her practical mind worked on the problem, and came up with a solution. She must contrive to no longer be a bore.

That was where Mr. Eversham came in. Presumably, if he was as good at teaching men to seduce women as she had heard, then he would be equally as good at teaching women to seduce men. The socially unacceptable Mr. Eversham was just what she needed.

Tina lifted her hand to the door knocker.

There was a moment, a brief moment, when doubt threatened to turn her about and send her home. But Tina was not a woman to be thwarted by such a thing as a little doubt. No, she had already made up her mind, and this was her only way forward.

She knocked loudly, several times, stood back, and waited.

And pretended her heart was not beating just a little bit faster.

Richard Eversham rustled his newspaper and read down the column in the engagement section. There were several names he recognized. Pupils of his who had benefited—clearly—from his tuition. His gray eyes narrowed as he read the final name, and then he gave a chuckle.

Well, who would have thought it! Barrington finally got his girl! This was a time for celebration. Where was that bottle of '11 he'd been saving?

"Archie!" he shouted for his butler, valet, and

manservant combined. "Archie, where the devil are you?"

Archie popped his curly head around the door frame. "You bellowed, sir?"

"Don't be lippy," his master retorted, setting the newspaper aside. "I have come into funds. I think we should celebrate."

Archie's face lit up, and he was about to answer when the door knocker sounded from the street door below.

"Who the devil is that?" Richard Eversham barked, and rose to go to the window, which gave a view directly down onto the square. "I haven't any appointments today, have I?"

"Not to my knowledge, sir. Should I go and see who it is, or will we pretend not to be at home?"

"Wait a moment . . . Good heavens, it's a woman. A lady, I should say. She looks like a lady, at any rate. Bonnet, pelisse, walking dress, gloves. Yes, definitely a lady. And . . . oh yes." The lady had glanced up at the window. The bonnet framed a very pretty face although at the moment she was frowning.

Suddenly he realized she was about to walk away.

"What the devil are you waiting for, Archie?" he said. "Go and let her in!"

Archie scurried down the stairs.

Richard returned to his chair and sat down, arms resting on the leather armrests, fingers steepled beneath his chin. He assumed his approachable and trustworthy gentleman expression; he'd found it invaluable when it came to persuading his clients to believe every word he spoke.

And why shouldn't they believe him, he mockingly reminded himself, with a reputation like his? He was Richard Eversham, grand seducer of women and rake extraordinaire. No one could bring a woman to heel like he could.

And while no gentleman would recognize him in a social situation, in private they were desperate to pick his brains. So desperate that Richard's business was doing very well indeed.

Archie was returning up the stairs, and with him came the swish of silk skirts and petticoats and the tap-tap of a lady's shoes. As much as he'd been looking forward to that bottle of '11, he was curious as to what someone who looked very much like a gentlewoman wanted with him this fine summer morning.

Tina turned left at the landing, following the curly-haired servant, and waited as he tapped discreetly on a half-open door.

"Enter!" called a deep, masculine voice.

The room was flooded with sunlight from the long windows on the other side, and for a moment Tina was quite dazzled. She blinked and took another step, and the glare was reduced somewhat. Enough for her to see that she was in a large and untidy sitting room, and a gentleman was just now rising from his leather chair.

"Mr. Eversham?" she said, before he could speak, although she was already certain that that was who was facing her now. Who else could this be but the most disreputable gentleman in London, Mr. Richard Eversham?

"I am indeed," he said in an amiable sort of voice. "And who are you, madam, if I may be so bold?"

Before she answered Tina took a moment to consider him. His broad shoulders were framed by a brown jacket, which he wore over a rather rumpled white shirt. His necktie was undone, and the V of skin disclosed was tanned and dappled with dark hairs. Tina wondered if the rest of him was just as fascinating, as her gaze slid down over his trim waist and long legs encased in riding breeches, finishing on boots that needed a polish.

Perhaps he had been out riding? That would explain the untidy, windblown air to him. He appeared to be the sort of man who enjoyed a good gallop on the heath, thighs clamped to his horse's sides—in fact that was possibly how he obtained those muscles she could see beneath the tight cloth.

Mr. Eversham cleared his throat.

Tina's gaze returned to his amused one. She smiled up at him; she couldn't help it. He had the sort of eyes that were so warm they made her want to smile. It was as if at any moment he might burst into laughter, just from the sheer joy of being alive.

"Do you have a name, madam? Perhaps you are a spy, sent by the government, to beg me to hunt down a dangerous criminal?" Something about that odd comment made him chuckle to himself.

Tina cocked her head to one side to consider him. His gray eyes were still smiling at her. She drew herself up and held out her hand toward him. "I am Miss Clementina Smythe, Mr. Eversham."

He took her hand carefully in his. Indeed, his was so much bigger it swallowed her white-gloved fingers entirely although his grip was very gentle. "How do you do, Miss Smythe?" he said automatically. "What can I do for you?"

"I am come to engage your services," she told him. No point in beating around the bush.

A line appeared between his slashing dark brows. "You have a gentleman who needs my assistance in matters of the, uhm, heart, Miss Smythe? A brother or cousin perhaps?"

"I have heard you are very accomplished in your chosen work, Mr. Eversham."

He released her hand, and she felt the loss of the warmth. With a gesture toward the sofa opposite his chair, he waited until she had seated herself before he made himself comfortable.

"I have never been known to fail," he said mildly.

"Then I have come to the right place," Tina murmured. She looked down at her purse, twisting the plaited loop handles in her gloved fingers. It was proving to be extraordinarily difficult to explain to him what she wanted. Normally she was perfectly lucid when it came to outlining her requirements, but for some reason Mr. Eversham had her tongue-tied.

Tina looked up. Perhaps it was his warm gray gaze that was making her dumb? Or his large, engaging presence. He was very manly, very good-looking, very . . . very . . .

"Miss Smythe, you need not be afraid our conversation will go any farther than this room. I am a master of discretion."

"As well as of seduction," she said, and then wished she hadn't as surprised laughter lit his eyes. Hurriedly, she moved on.

"Mr. Eversham, I have a confession to make."

He leaned forward. "I am all ears, Miss Smythe."

"I am here for myself, not for any gentleman who might require your services. I wish to marry, and the man I wish to marry does not value propriety and innocence in a woman. He finds it tedious. Boring. Therefore I must become the sort of woman he finds interesting."

She had surprised him. For a moment he said nothing, considering her as if he were turning over a particularly delicious fruit, deciding whether or not to take a bite, and then, reluctantly, it seemed, he put it aside and shook his head.

"I fear I must decline, Miss Smythe. My business is only with gentlemen. Ladies are rather more complicated."

"But surely, Mr. Eversham, to understand how a gentleman must behave to win the lady of his dreams, you must also understand the lady? Or am I misinformed, Mr. Eversham? I was told you were a master of the art of seduction. Is that not so?"

A painful expression crossed his face. "That is so, Miss Smythe."

"Then you *must* help me. I can pay, if that is what troubles you. I-I am a wealthy young woman." She lifted her chin at the lie. "I am able to have anything I desire."

"And you desire me?" he broke into her words, his eyes quizzical and his smile teasing.

Tina felt a little breathless. How odd, she

thought. Her practical soul did not normally respond to flirtatious word games.

"I desire Lord H—that is, the gentleman I wish to marry, and I desire you to make me into the sort of woman he wishes to marry," she corrected him primly.

He bowed his head, his fingers steepled once more under his chin. He seemed to be considering her proposal from all angles. After a time he lifted his head and again met her gaze. For the first time since she'd met him, the smile had gone from Mr. Eversham's gray eyes.

"Before I agree you must be very certain of what you're asking me, Miss Smythe," he said quietly. "You wish me to teach you to be a woman of the world. You do not want to appear as an innocent. In short, you require that I teach you the art of seduction by, eh, seducing you, at least verbally if not physically? Is that correct? Is that what you want? Are you entirely certain?"

From his lips it sounded improper. Risqué.

But Tina had made up her mind this was what she must do if she ever wanted to marry her childhood sweetheart, so she said firmly, "Yes, that is what I want, Mr. Eversham."

"May I inquire as to the name of your intended husband? It would help me if I understood his preferences."

Tina thought a moment, but she knew the name must be spoken eventually. Better do it now. "Lord Horace Gilfoyle."

There did not appear to be any change in his expression, and yet Tina had the odd sense that he tensed—like a dog on a scent. He nodded again, watching her. "You are a surprising young woman, Miss Smythe. I am inclined to take you up on your offer. I charge a set fee for my consultations and a bonus if you achieve the desired result. But because your case is rather unusual, I will only ask for payment if we succeed."

He named the fee, and Tina managed not to flinch.

"Is it agreed?" he added softly.

"Of course," she said briskly, as if she had that sum of money about her person right now, and stood up, holding out her hand to shake on the deal. Horace would pay him, she told herself. He would be glad to do so.

He took her hand, his smile back. "We will start on Friday morning at eleven o'clock. Tea and seduction, Miss Smythe."

"Friday at eleven, Mr. Eversham. I shall be here."

Richard watched her leave from his sitting-room window. He didn't glance around when he heard Archie enter the room. In fact he watched Miss Smythe until she was no longer in sight, and that was a very rare thing for a man who found most respectable ladies dull indeed.

He resembled Miss Smythe's intended in that regard. He preferred women who knew what they were about and didn't pretend they must love a man before they could countenance him kissing and caressing them. But respectable as she undoubtedly was, this lady was different. She certainly knew her mind.

But even so Richard admitted he never would

have taken on the job if she hadn't named her intended as Lord Horace Gilfoyle.

And there lay another problem. How could he justify being party to marrying Miss Smythe, with her vivid green eyes, to a man like Gilfoyle?

"I know what you're thinking, Archie."

"Added mind reading to your skills now, sir?" Richard chuckled.

"There was a message for you while Miss Smythe was here. You're to go to headquarters as soon as possible."

Back to work! Richard sighed and turned from the window, putting the lovely Miss Smythe from his mind.

Chapter 2

As she entered her home in Mallory Street, Tina breathed a sigh of relief. The subtle scent of lavender and lemon furniture polish hung in the air. Her mother's longcase clock, with the delightful paintings on its face of the moon, sun, and the stars, was ticking the moments away. A bowl of blooms sat perfectly centered on an oval table. She felt relieved to be home. Safe.

Safe? she asked herself. Had her visit to Mr. Eversham really been so life-threatening? It had gone well, hadn't it? Then why did she feel the need to find sanctuary as if she was under threat from some mysterious and unspecified danger?

"Master Charles has a visitor in the drawing room, Miss Tina."

James, their butler, was hovering about her. As usual he sounded as if any visitor was a personal affront to him. Tina couldn't help but contrast his manner to Mr. Eversham's man, with his curly hair and twinkling eyes.

"Thank you, James."

As she approached the drawing room she could

hear two male voices, interspersed with chuckles.

Tina opened the door and peeped inside.

The two men, their faces flushed with laughter, turned toward her.

"Tina, we have a visitor!" Charles cried with his usual exuberance and completely unnecessarily. "Horace is here!"

Horace Gilfoyle shrugged his broad shoulders as Tina came toward him. Her hand was swallowed by his larger hand, and a whispering, treacherous thought told her it was not quite as overwhelming a sensation as it had been this morning when her hand was taken by Richard Eversham.

She dismissed the thought. She had known Horace forever, and they would make the ideal couple. His blond hair was a perfect contrast to her own dark tresses, and his tall, compact body and broad shoulders were just right for her smaller stature and soft curves. The thought of marrying anyone else was unthinkable. Ridiculous. Thank goodness she'd grasped her courage in both hands and approached Mr. Eversham.

And she had no doubt she had chosen the right man to teach her all she needed to know to go husband hunting. Horace was fond of her—in fact she could tell he was by the smile that was in his eyes right now as he gazed down at her—but that wasn't enough. He had to love her passionately, enough to give up his free-and-easy ways and marry her.

Tina slipped off her gloves. "I must go and freshen up. I'll be down in a minute. Will you stay for tea, Horace?"

"Of course he will!" said the irrepressible Charles. "Or maybe a whiskey?"

Horace smiled at Tina's frown. "Tea would be delightful. Although I must be on my way soon. I have an appointment I mustn't miss."

"Will you ring then, Charles? I'll be down shortly."

Charles pulled the bell rope, and Tina gave Horace a little smile before she turned away.

Horace watched her leave, thinking she was becoming a fine figure of a woman. No longer the little girl he used to tease. He was surprised at her curves, nicely on display in her blue silk gown. Why hadn't he noticed them before? Probably because she'd always been like a sister to him. If things were different, he might have thought about bedding her. As it was, she'd be saving her virtue for a suitable husband. The Smythes were very right and proper about things like that—something Horace found secretly amusing.

Maybe when she was married he might think of a dalliance with her. She'd be more worldly then and probably bored with her husband, up for some lustful dalliance with an old friend. Horace had always found married women far more grateful for one's efforts.

"**M**aria?"

A maid in her early thirties, the same height as Tina but considerably more buxom, turned from tidying the room. "Yes, miss."

"Master Charles and Lord Horace are taking tea in the drawing room. Help me with my hair, will you, before I join them?"

She sat at her dressing table and Maria removed her bonnet and began to slip the pins from her long ebony hair.

"Do you know when my parents will be back, Maria?"

Maria hid a smile. "Not for some time, miss," she answered. "Lady Carol said they would be back for dinner, but cook is to keep it warm if they are late and not to keep you and Master Charles waiting."

She knew her mistress was hoping they wouldn't be back too soon. When they were younger, Miss Tina and Master Charles had always found some mischief or other to get into when their mother and father were busy. And Lord Horace had been their companion a good many times in that mischief. Of course, Miss Tina thought herself far too grown-up now for childish mischief although she still enjoyed the company of both her brother and Lord Horace. And lately, Maria had begun to realize that Miss Tina's interest in Lord Horace was changing. Deepening. Turning toward thoughts of marriage.

And that had Maria worried. Despite his outwardly affable and easygoing nature, Lord Horace reminded her of a man she'd known once, who had a darker side when he was opposed. Miss Tina was a strong-willed young woman with a great zest for life. She needed a companion to complement her rather than go head-to-head with her, as she feared would be the case with Lord Horace.

And then there was the time when Lord Horace had found Maria alone in a corridor and attempted to touch her in places no gentleman should touch.

He had been rather drunk, and Maria had escaped without harm, but she'd never forgotten the angry twist to his mouth and the ugly look in his eyes when he'd been thwarted.

Maria had traveled from Spain to England as a very young girl, and yet she had vivid memories of the home she'd left behind. The first position she had held in England was as a scullery maid in a big house in the country. She considered herself very fortunate to have had the opportunity to train as a lady's maid, but that lady was now long dead, and Maria had been with Tina's family for over ten years, first looking after Lady Carol, Tina's mother, and now Tina herself. Maria was comfortable here, protective of her young mistress, and she loved being in London although she did still long for her childhood home.

Perhaps, she mused, if Miss Tina married, she would travel—perhaps even to Spain— and Maria would travel with her. But not to Lord Horace, she decided firmly. No, not him.

"There. All done, miss," Maria exclaimed.

Tina gave a final glance at her reflection and hurried to the staircase, stopping there to catch her breath before she walked sedately down to the drawing room. The tea had already arrived, and Tina poured for them all. She knew very well how Horace liked his tea and made sure to add one lump of sugar with oodles of milk.

"So where have you been today, Tina?" asked Horace as he sipped his tea with evident enjoyment.

"Just visiting a friend." Tina gave her prepared answer. "An old school friend," she added firmly.

She'd decided on the old-school-friend story on

her way home. She knew that her brother would not be particularly interested in her activities, but if her parents were at home, they would have asked questions. If they knew where she'd really been . . . well, it was just best if they didn't. Tina told herself she wasn't lying, not exactly, just keeping her own counsel. Mr. Eversham was a means to an end, and once she and Horace were wed her parents would be too ecstatic to care about the twists and turns of just how it had all come about.

Now, she watched Horace furtively, trying to imagine them together in their own house. She'd be curled up by the fire with a book, while Horace sat nearby in his armchair, reading aloud to her snippets of daily news from the newspaper. It was a very cozy scene, but for some reason just as she had it fixed in her mind the man in the armchair changed, became more muscular, his hair darker, his eyes with a warm, teasing look that brought a flush to her cheeks.

"Oh!"

It was Mr. Eversham!

"Did you say something, Tina?"

Charles was giving her an odd look, and Tina realized she'd spoken aloud. She really had to stop this living in her head. Time to concentrate on the here and now. On hunting Horace, her future husband.

Chapter 3

Richard climbed the narrow staircase to the heavy door at the top and entered the dark, smoky room. There was a large table in the middle of what were somewhat austere surroundings. The windows were opaque with dust, and lit candles threw flickering shadows. The five men who called themselves the Guardians sat, all but one of them puffing on cigars; all but one looked up as he entered. Sir Henry Arlington, the gentleman at the head of the table, shuffled his pile of papers and spoke in a quiet but commanding voice.

"Ah, Richard. Lock the door. We are all now in attendance."

Richard bolted the door and sat down at the far end of the table, as far from the smoke cloud as he could. For a moment no one spoke, and there was some important throat clearing.

Here in this room were some of the most influential men in the government. They dealt with the shadowy issues, matters the British public were completely unaware of, matters that could undermine society and potentially bring down the Prime Minister and his cabinet. That was the reason they were called the Guardians. They were faceless, nameless, beavering away in secret. And that was how they liked it.

Richard's father and Sir Henry had been in the same regiment during their army days, but Richard had known nothing of the Guardians until a family tragedy drew him into their shadowy realm. In the aftermath of that tragedy Sir Henry had asked him to join, to take his dead brother's place.

Now Sir Henry cleared his throat one last time. "Any further unrest in the East End?" he demanded.

"All quiet at the moment," he was reassured by one man. "I'm keeping an eye on things."

"Sir Henry, we should discuss the Bossenden Wood riot," another of the men spoke up, younger than the rest.

"Oh nonsense, Jackson, surely that's all done with!" butted in an older man, with a large white mustache, lush enough to draw attention from his completely bald head. "They've shot the chap—a lunatic—and put the rest of them away. It's over with."

But young as he was, Will Jackson was not easily crushed by his more important companions. "I hardly think it's completely done with, Lord Montague. Eleven men died. The fact that it happened at all is something I think we need to consider. And was Thom really the organ grinder or merely the monkey? Sir Henry?"

Richard watched Sir Henry lean back in his chair and prepared himself for the usual wait while their commander considered the matter. He tended to agree with Lord Montague—the small riot that took place in Kent in May was over and done with. John Thom, a Cornishman, had styled himself as Sir Thomas Courtney and claimed to be the Messiah. He drew people to him with his speeches and even displayed evidence of stigmata. When the authorities began to show an interest in him, he led a rising against them and was shot dead, although not before he'd killed Lieutenant Bennett, who was politely asking him to surrender. Those who didn't die in the ensuing battle were arrested.

Sir Henry interrupted his musings. "What Lord Montague says makes sense, Will. I think it was more a problem with this particular chap's brain than any real civil unrest. An aberration. Besides, there's always discontent among the peasants, what? Surely that can be dealt with at a local level? Richard, you have connections in Kent, what do you think of this Bossenden Wood business?"

All the men turned toward him.

Richard's life was currently in London, but his family was originally from Kent, where Eversham Manor had been home to generations of Evershams. The house belonged to him now but he rarely visited. He had made a solemn promise to himself when his brother died that he would not live in the family home, he would not claim his rightful place, until his brother's death was avenged. He meant to honor it.

"Richard?"

Richard roused himself. These men expected him to know what was happening in Kent, and he took his position at this table seriously.

"It's true Thom was considered an imposter and a lunatic, but there must be a considerable amount of dissatisfaction for him to have gained such a following. These were men who were willing to die for him. Was there someone else behind him, pulling the strings? I don't know. But I can find out if that is what you want me to do."

Sir Henry nodded with sudden decision. "Yes, we need to be sure. Remember the Captain?"

A shudder went around the table. Richard felt a pain deep in his chest.

The Captain had been a mysterious figure who had set about causing dissension among the laboring classes in Suffolk and worked his way up to the minor gentry. By the time Sir Henry and his men made the connection between the numerous riots and bouts of lawbreaking, the mysterious Captain had slipped through their net and disappeared. But not before one of their own had died. They'd been made to look like incompetent fools, and they still didn't understand the Captain's motive for what he did, or even if he had a motive. It was a very sore point with Sir Henry Arlington and his men.

"Richard, I think any answers you could find to our questions would be helpful. For now we will treat Bossenden Wood as possibly linked to the Suffolk riots. Yes, yes, Montague, I know it's tenuous, but we can't be too careful. All agreed? Can we have a show of hands?"

All of the Guardians but Lord Montague raised their hands and agreed with the motion.

"Anything else to discuss, gentlemen?"

Richard shifted in his chair. "I have some information of sorts on Lord Horace Gilfoyle. You are all aware of my . . . more public occupation." Several men guffawed. "Yes, I see that you are. Well, a young lady has asked for my assistance in gaining the attention of Gilfoyle."

It had been purely accidental that Richard fell into the game of teaching seduction. A friend had asked for his help with a difficult lady, and soon afterward he was swamped with requests. When he explained the situation to the Guardians, Sir Henry had decided it was as good a cover as any for a spy, and besides, what better way to hear all the latest gossip about town?

"An introduction, do you mean?" asked Sir Henry now. "Surely you're not that well acquainted with Gilfoyle?"

"No, no, not an introduction. In fact the young lady is well acquainted with Gilfoyle herself. It's more that she wishes to attract his attention in a romantic way. In fact she imagines she wishes to marry him." He ended with a serious note in his voice.

There was a moment's silence as they all considered the possibilities. Horace Gilfoyle had been a man of interest to the Guardians for some time, for although he was from a respectable and wealthy family himself, he had a penchant for living on the edge of society and rubbing shoulders with rascals. They had been following his exploits and noting his friends and contacts. And of particular interest was the news that he'd been in Suffolk during one of the Captain riots.

"I take it this young lady is an unattractive piece?" Sir Henry's eyes narrowed through the smoke, but there was a twinkle in them that made Richard uncomfortable. The other man had always been adept at reading his mind.

"No, she's far from unattractive, but that isn't the point, is it?" He hesitated but decided to keep his indecision to himself—it was none of their business that after a long night wrestling with his conscience, he wasn't sure whether he could abet Miss Smythe in her plan to marry a man who might be a murderer. "I've accepted her commission. It will give me a chance to discover more about Gilfoyle. The lady's brother is a longtime close friend of Gilfoyle's, apparently, so she sees quite a bit of him."

"So the brother may be of interest as well?"

"That's a possibility."

"Good. You may have some things to tell us the next time we meet, Richard. Gentlemen!" He looked about the table. "I think we are done."

They began to leave, but catching a meaningful glance from Sir Henry, Richard lingered until they were alone.

"How long since you've been back to your home in Kent, Richard?" his superior asked in an even tone. "Your brother has been dead for years. The house is yours, is it not?"

"Yes, it is. My sister-in-law lives there."

"And yet you stay away?"

"There's nothing for me to go back for."

"I understand how keenly you feel the need to find your brother's killer, whether or not it was this Captain. But surely you don't still blame yourself? Anthony knew what sort of work he was involved in. Just as we all do. You cannot blame yourself for what happened to him."

"I have always believed I could have pre-

vented his death. If I hadn't fallen out with him.
If I'd been there for him. He might have spoken to
me—come to me for help."

"Romantic nonsense. You were not your brother's keeper!"

When Richard didn't say any more, Sir Henry
shrugged his burly shoulders. "Well, keep your
secrets if you must. As long as you do your job.
You must remember that the work we do here is
far more important than any personal considerations, Richard. It is vital. Sometimes we are all
that stands between order and anarchy. We are
the guardians at the gates."

"I will do my job, sir," Richard said quietly. "I
always do."

Sir Henry nodded and finally released him.
Outside, Richard took several deep breaths. He
hadn't planned to return to Kent. Not yet. Sir
Henry was right; Richard had a promise to keep
before he resumed his life as a country gentleman. He had to find Anthony's murderer. He had
to put the restless spirit of his brother to rest.

Chapter 4

Tina spent some time shopping before going to Number Five Jasmine Square to keep her appointment. Horace was holding a soiree on the following Saturday evening, and then he was taking a coachload of his particular friends to the theater. Tina was one of his particular friends, and she meant to make the most of the opportunity to put her husband-hunting plans in motion.

In short she needed something to wear that would catch his eye.

Horace was so complacent where she was concerned; he needed to be jolted out of that complacency. Tina wasn't quite ready to invite him to her boudoir, but neither did she want him thinking of her as the little girl who had chastised him for stealing eggs from birds' nests for his collection. Tina knew they were perfectly matched, and they would make a perfect couple. If he would just open his eyes and look at her afresh!

Then *all* her problems would be solved.

"Miss?"

With a sigh she shook her head at the roll of

crushed velvet the hopeful shop assistant was displaying for her. It was no good. She couldn't decide. A new dress was an expense she shouldn't even be contemplating, but her father had insisted, and she hadn't the heart to tell him she knew the truth. That her mother had told her in tearful whispers that the Smythe family was as close to penniless as made no difference.

This dress was probably the last new garment she would ever have, the last chance for Horace to see her in something new and pretty, at least until she married. But if she didn't marry Horace, then she'd soon be going about in rags—matters at home were becoming desperate. So much was dependent upon a construction of cloth and thread that suddenly the dress assumed monumental proportions, and Tina felt she must get it right. She must. Her usual practical coolheadedness deserted her.

Feverishly her gaze darted from greens to blues to reds. Choose the right one and all would be well; choose the wrong one, and the Smythes would sink without trace into the murky mire of bankruptcy. She'd known a family that had happened to, a child who had been a friend of hers many years ago when Tina was young. One day that child was there, the next she and her family were gone in a gust of scandal, and Tina's parents spoke of them in hushed tones.

Was that what would happen to Tina? Would she become the girl people spoke of in murmurs?

But then she remembered she wasn't alone in this.

She had Mr. Eversham.

A sense of relief filled her. Yes, she would leave the choice of the cloth for her new dress to Mr. Eversham. He would know what a man like Horace would prefer. He would know what she must wear to win his heart.

Tina was just gathering the samples the shop assistant had prepared for her when a church clock struck the hour. She was late! With a gasp she flew out of the shop and set off along Bond Street, clutching her bonnet to her head with one hand and holding her parcel close with the other, avoiding the people strolling along the exclusive thoroughfare. By the time she reached Jasmine Square, she was out of breath and had to recover herself a moment before using the knocker.

"Miss Smythe?"

Mr. Eversham's man answered so promptly she gave a start of surprise. She watched him for some knowing glance or smirk, which would show he was in his master's confidence, but he was perfectly polite as he showed her up the stairs.

"Should I take your parcel, miss?" he asked her, as they paused on the threshold of the sitting room.

Tina glanced down at her samples, wrapped in brown paper, once more caught in a maelstrom of indecision, and then shook her head. "No. I need to ask Mr. Eversham's opinion, thank you."

He showed no surprise and immediately tapped on the door and then opened it for her.

Tina found that today the blinds were drawn down and the sun did not beam into her eyes. In fact the room was much tidier, and so was Mr. Eversham. He wore a brown jacket and trousers, his waistcoat a bright teal color. There was a watch chain dangling from one pocket, and his necktie was neatly arranged above a pristine white shirt. His face was closely shaved, his brows dark slashes above his gray eyes, and his brown hair brushed becomingly.

He looked like a gentleman.

She was somewhat relieved—secretly she'd half expected him to be lounging shirtless, smoking a hookah. But of course that was ridiculous. He *was* a gentleman, just one who'd lost his way.

Tina sat down.

So did he.

He watched her a moment, observing her posture, the way she held herself. "You went to a finishing school," he guessed. "Which one?"

"Miss Debenham's."

"Ah. Yes, you have the Debenham look."

Tina preened a little, but his next words dented her pleasure in his praise.

"The neatly-folded-hands-and-knees-together look."

He was blunt. Tina wasn't used to men who were blunt—apart from her brother Charles, and he didn't count.

"Is there something wrong with folding my hands and holding my, uh, knees, together?"

"Not at all. If you are in church or attending a vicarage tea party. But you, my dear Miss Smythe, are seducing a gentleman."

She gave him her direct look and considered the matter. "Yes, I can see that might be different. What should I do differently?"

It was his turn to consider. He let his gaze travel

over her in a manner she would have thought insulting and disturbing in other circumstances, but now, alone with Mr. Eversham's expertise, she felt neither. His manner was so unfamiliar she found herself captivated, constantly wondering what he would say next.

"I think if you reach up and brush that lock of hair back, perhaps tuck it behind your ear . . . Yes, that's it."

Tina complied.

"Slowly, slowly, as if you enjoy the sensation."

Again Tina did as he asked, this time winding a tendril of hair about her fingertip, smiling at him shyly through her lashes. His face stilled, and for a moment she feared she'd done something wrong.

"I feel a little foolish," she admitted.

"You shouldn't." He leaned forward, his gray eyes alight. "You are trying to attract the attention of the man you want to marry. There is nothing foolish about that. Not if you're certain this is what you want."

Her own eyes widened. Did he know about her family circumstances? No, how could he! She was imagining nuances where there weren't any. Tina made herself smile.

"It is. *He* is."

But instead of beaming back at her, Mr. Eversham gave her a look that was insultingly kind, as if he were a thousand years older than she. In experience, she expected he was. Suddenly she didn't want him to look at her like that.

"I know this is difficult for a well-brought-up young lady, Miss Smythe. I am asking you to do the opposite of all you have been taught by your mother and your governess and your finishing school. But believe me, if you want to ensnare a man of the world like Lord Horace Gilfoyle, you have no option."

Tina blushed. "Is 'ensnare' the right word?"

"Semantics, Miss Smythe." He eyed her kindly again. "Do you want me to help you or not? If so, then you will have to harden yourself to what I say and act with your emotions, with passion, with your *heart* rather than your mind. Perhaps this is something you cannot do?"

But I have to, Tina thought anxiously. *My future is with Horace, the fate of my family depends upon it, and if winning him means I must act in a manner more suited to a courtesan than a lady, then so I shall.*

Determinedly she put her embarrassment behind her. "I think what you want me to do," she said clearly, "is draw attention to my feminine attributes."

"That would be a start," he agreed mildly. "You could touch the lace on your décolletage, draw the eye, eh, downward. You are a beautiful woman, Miss Smythe, and there is nothing to be ashamed of in wishing others to notice."

Dear God, did he say that? Tina swallowed and nodded.

Stiffly and self-consciously she brushed her hand across her décolletage. She tried again, and this time felt more comfortable with the gesture. A brief touch of the lace, a movement designed to draw male eyes. Certainly it drew Mr. Eversham's.

Her heart was beating rather quickly, but she told herself that was because she was overturning years of ladylike teaching. It had nothing at all to do with being alone with Richard Eversham.

In spite of her modest dress—the style was in fact some years out of date—Richard was surprised at his gut reaction to her timid gesture. The sudden surge of desire. The urge to undo those buttons where her hand rested and discover for himself, inch by inch, the pale swell of her breasts. She was a client, he told himself, nothing more, and a means to an end where that shady character Gilfoyle was concerned.

He had no intention of becoming romantically involved. Once bitten, as the saying went. And Richard had been well and truly bitten.

However, he had a part to play and forced himself to carry on. "That is a very good start, Miss Smythe," he said, as if he felt nothing. As if this were merely business.

"Do you think so?" she asked with an anxious glance. "Should I place my hand here? Or here?"

"I have no doubt Lord Horace's attention will be drawn by either positioning."

What a waste! was what he was really thinking. *To think I am wrapping up this luscious morsel for that bastard! But perhaps her education with me will give her a little more wisdom in her choice of men. When this is over and done, I can help her to choose a better man than Gilfoyle. I'm sure I can think of someone who will suit. Will Jackson perhaps? He's a fine young man with a nice inheritance waiting for him. No title of course, but is she the sort who is set on having a title?*

Richard realized he didn't know anything

about Miss Clementina Smythe apart from what she'd told him. In the interest of doing a thorough job he really should do some digging about.

"Mr. Eversham? The fabric?" Tina interrupted his thoughts.

"Fabric, Miss Smythe?"

"For my dress for the theater. Horace has invited a group of friends." She looked puzzled, and he realized he hadn't heard a word she'd said. Hardly the behavior of a professional seducer, a man who knew how to charm and woo the most difficult of women. He pulled himself back into the moment and assumed a serious expression.

"Ah, yes. Of course. The fabric." He brushed his fingers over the samples she'd laid out on the table in front of him. "The crimson is the obvious choice of course. That will certainly attract his notice. But I do think that dark green would be more effective with your coloring. With your eyes. And it would be all to the good if you could ask the dressmaker to lower the décolletage."

"Lower the décolletage?" she repeated faintly. "How low?"

"As far as your modesty will allow," he said firmly.

In his years on the town Richard had discovered that the most hardened rakes were often repelled by forward behavior in their nearest and dearest. They were like dogs with bones in that regard. Richard was hoping that seeing Tina behaving in such a manner would cause Gilfoyle to form a dislike for her.

Unfortunately Richard was discovering that watching Miss Smythe play her part was having the opposite effect on him. There was something very seductive about instructing her in the arts of seduction.

"Perhaps a little lace might draw his attention?" she suggested tentatively, and lifted her chin as if to draw courage in what must seem to her a very strange conversation.

"Indeed. A creamy lace with the dark green velvet would be exquisite. What is the occasion again?"

She gave him an odd look but answered politely enough. "Lord Horace is having a small soiree at his residence and then taking a few friends to the theater afterward. My brother and I have been invited to both events."

"How exciting for you." He stifled a yawn.

Her eyes flashed.

"Oh yes, I like that. You must do that more often, Miss Smythe."

"Do what?"

"The way you looked at me then. Eyes glittering, the flush on your cheeks. Most attractive, and captivating, too."

"I-I don't know if I can do it again. You made me cross when you yawned."

"You could always remember this moment. There! That's the look I want."

Tina sighed. "This is getting rather complicated. You want me to glare at Horace for no reason? Are you sure that will appeal to him? In my experience Horace has never been one for bad-tempered females."

"Oh no, you won't be trying to appeal to Lord Horace. Not at this stage. I want you to concentrate on every other man there, with the exception of your brother, of course."

"But I have no desire to attract any other man!"

"My dear Miss Smythe, obviously you are very ignorant of the male mind."

Her green eyes gave him that attractive flash again, but this time he managed to ignore it and the effect it had on his senses, and carry on instructing her.

"We men are creatures who invariably want what attracts other men. If you flutter your eyelashes at some chap and laugh at the bad jokes of another, you'll soon have them all eating out of your hand. When Gilfoyle sees every other man lusting after you, you can be quite sure he will suddenly see you, not as a little sister, but as the object of his own desire."

Richard wondered whether he'd spoken too freely. Was she shocked, or did she realize he was talking nonsense? In actual fact he was expecting Gilfoyle to be livid when she played off the other men in his party against him.

But although Tina seemed slightly bemused, she didn't argue. For a moment, she gazed questioningly into his eyes and then lowered her lashes in that charming manner she had and composed herself once more. He felt almost ashamed of himself then for using her for his own ends—she really was the most valiant girl.

"So you think I should act like a courtesan at Horace's soiree, Mr. Eversham?" she said primly, as if she were discussing the weather.

"Do you know many courtesans, Miss Smythe?" he answered in amusement. "Stand up. Let's pretend we're at this little soiree."

Clearly unwilling, still she obeyed him and stood up. He could see she was wondering what he would do next, eyeing him sideways as if he were a dangerous animal at the zoo. Her head only came to his shoulder, and he resisted the temptation to kiss the top of it and tell her that everything would be all right and did she really want to marry a chap like Horace Gilfoyle?

Instead he took her hand and rested it on his arm. "When you're standing beside a gentleman, chatting about whatever it is you would like to chat about—the theater, perhaps—touch his arm, just gently. And smile. Look into his eyes. Widen your own, just a little."

Tina's fingers tightened, and she felt his hard muscles through his clothing and suddenly wondered how he would look without it. Her thoughts made her cheeks feel hot, and she knew she was blushing. She really needed to stop blushing. That was hardly the behavior required of a woman trying to attract a man like Horace. It would only prove to him what he already thought of her: She was too innocent to be of any interest.

Did courtesans blush?

Stop it. Concentrate. Tina took a deep breath and looked up into his gray eyes and smiled.

"Oh yes," he breathed. "That's very good, Miss Smythe. Try again."

She didn't really need to do it again, but he was enjoying it so very much he couldn't resist. His praise drew a smile that dazzled him.

"Very good indeed. You're a fast learner."

"Perhaps you're a good teacher, Mr. Eversham."

"Well, we'll be able to see whether that's true or not from the results, won't we? Do you think we can dispense with the formalities now? I prefer to be on first-name terms with my clients. There are no lords or ladies here; we are simply client and teacher." He held out his hand. "Richard, at your service."

"Clementina. That is . . . my friends call me Tina."

He lifted her hand to his lips and kissed it gently. "Tina."

His voice was deep and quiet, and it made her shiver inside. His lips were warm and intimate, and that shiver intensified. Despite their being nearly strangers, she felt close to him, as if they shared a secret.

Which of course they did.

Although for the moment Tina wasn't certain she completely understood just what that secret was.

Chapter 5

"**A**rchie, I have to go out. Business."

The accompanying lift of Richard's eyebrows spoke volumes about the nature of his business. *Guardian business.*

"Very good, sir. Would you like me to accompany you?"

"No, I won't need you this time. I'm just doing a little reconnoitering. I don't expect to find out anything of importance. Or get into any trouble."

"If you say so, sir."

"Have Samson saddled."

Richard caught Archie's smile as he left the room. It was true there had been times when his work with the Guardians had resulted in a black eye or a bloody nose. And one memorable evening he'd sustained a blow to his head that had laid him low for days. Anthony had died on a mission.

He tended to be more careful now. Although he wanted to avenge Anthony's murder, he also wanted to live to experience the satisfaction of the moment.

His thoughts drifted into more pleasant realms.

While he didn't expect to be out of town for long, he'd written a note to Tina Smythe for Archie to deliver to Mallory Street. He pictured her now in the clothing they had planned together, the dark green dress with the cream lace and the low décolletage, clinging to her sweetly rounded bosom. Why, he wondered idly, hadn't he thought of employing his skills with young ladies before? They were considerably more stimulating than the gentlemen he usually dealt with. But then again was stimulation necessarily a good thing?

Richard also remembered he'd decided on an extra pair of eyes to keep watch in the Smythe household.

When Archie returned to tell him that Samson was ready, Richard said, "Archie, I have a job for you. Well, two actually. I want you to deliver this note to Miss Smythe."

"Yes, sir."

"And there is something more while you're at it. A little mission."

"A mission, sir?" Archie's eyes twinkled. "I hoped you might find something for me. What is it?"

Richard explained the situation.

"Ah. You think there might be a pretty maidservant I can win over to our side?"

"That did cross my mind, Archie. Do you think you're up to it?"

Archie grinned. "I may not be as young as I used to be, sir, but I'm not in my dotage yet. I'm told that now I have turned forty years of age I have a certain gravitas."

"I'll leave it to you then."

Samson was saddled and ready, and Richard lost no time in setting off. He was heading out of London, going southeast, on the road that then turned into the major coaching route to Kent. However, Richard wasn't intending to travel far. His destination was a popular inn situated where the city turned to country and was frequented by coaches, public and private, and run by an acquaintance of his. If there was anything to be learned about mysterious travelers coming and going at the time of the Bossenden Wood incident, then Gareth was the man to ask.

The Great Southern Inn was as busy as he remembered, and Richard settled into the parlor with a tankard of ale, amusing himself by watching the antics of a large family who'd broken their journey for food and drink. The children were overexcited, the mother at the end of her tether, and the father pretending they didn't belong to him. While the young nursemaid looked as if she was about to hand in her notice.

His own family, he mused, had been very different.

Richard and Anthony had been born two years apart, and a younger sister had died as a baby. Their father was a traditionalist, stern and distant, but their mother was warm and loving, the heart of the family. She had died when her sons were still children, and afterward, their father only grew sterner and more distant. It was his decision to send the brothers away to school rather than deal with their grief himself.

Richard had a difficult time at school. Anthony,

for whom the whole notion of boarding school was far easier, became his protector and, more importantly, his friend. They'd been very close, and remembering those days now only made what happened later all the more painful and regrettable.

"Mr. Eversham! Setting out for Eversham Manor, are ye?"

Gareth's jolly voice broke through his reverie, and Richard stood up with a smile of greeting. He was used to Gareth's battered face, but one of the children gave a little squeak of fright before she was hushed by the nursemaid.

"Not today, Gareth. I wondered if I might have a word." He glanced about him at the family, now all agog. "Privately."

Gareth didn't ask questions but led Richard into his inner sanctum—a small officelike room—and closed the door. A fire was burning comfortably in the hearth, and there were a number of cups and trophies set on the mantel, mementos from Gareth's boxing days. Fame had come at the price of Gareth's good looks, but he'd done well enough out of it to purchase this inn.

Richard seated himself in one of the battered old leather armchairs and after some brief chitchat, Gareth said, "You're here on business then, Mr. Eversham?"

"I am. Have you had any interesting guests through here, Gareth? Around May, the time of the Bossenden Wood riots? I'm interested in quality rather than riffraff."

Gareth considered the question, rubbing his thumb along a scar on his cheekbone. "May, eh?

Well there was a few gents passin' through here. Don't rightly remember their names, but after you was here the last time, I took your advice and starting keepin' a little book."

With a grin he went to the desk and opened a drawer, removing a battered notebook and holding it up.

"Now, May . . ."

After much page turning and some frowning, he came up with a list of names. Among them were two gentlemen who had been traveling to Kent at the same time. One of them was unknown to Richard, but the other was very familiar. Lord Horace Gilfoyle. Now what on earth was Tina's intended doing passing through the Great Southern Inn just before the Bossenden Wood riots?

Archie had been waiting outside the house in Mallory Street for what seemed ages, trying not to look too obvious. Now and again he would stroll off and back again, pretending he was enjoying the sunshine. Luckily there was a small garden square at the end of the street, and he was able to lurk by the iron railings, gazing up at the plane trees and generally pretending he was waiting for someone.

Richard Eversham might be his employer, but Archie much preferred these little jobs for the Guardians. It reminded him of his younger, more carefree days, and although he willingly accepted his current role of middle-aged butler, there were times when he still hankered for adventure.

Eventually his wait was rewarded.

A woman left the house, her modest outfit proclaiming her a servant although something about the way she set out, her walk confident, her chin up as she gazed about, told Archie she wasn't just any servant. No, indeed. She was a superior sort of servant. He waited by the railings—she was heading his way—pretending to do up his shoelace.

As she reached him he stood up, timing it just right, and bumped into her. It was perfect. The woman cried out, dropping her reticule, and Archie stumbled, offering a barrage of apologies.

She took a breath, stepping back, and brushed herself down as if the contact had disarranged her. He stooped to pick up her reticule and held it out to her. She looked up.

Archie just managed to hold on to his dignity and not gasp out loud at the vision. She was older than he'd expected, not a young woman, in her thirties perhaps. Definitely a superior servant. Her hair was very dark, almost black, with bouncy curls escaping her straw bonnet. Her eyes were almost black, too, and he felt her gaze like a punch in his stomach.

"Ma'am? Please, accept my apologies. I am shattered by my clumsiness. I don't know what I was thinking."

She considered him a moment more and then nodded, her full mouth softening into a smile. "I accept your apologies, sir. I will not let your clumsiness spoil my afternoon off."

She had a faint accent. Spanish, Italian? He wasn't certain of its origin.

As she moved past him, he fell into step beside

her. She glanced up at him beneath her brim—she was small in stature, although curvaceous in all the right places—and there was a curious gleam in her eyes. She wasn't afraid of him, just amused by his clumsiness, and he found himself wrong footed in a way unusual for a confident man of his years.

"My name is Archie Jones," he offered with suitable humility. "I am a butler in Jasmine Street. It is my day off, too. May I walk with you, Mrs. . . . ?"

Another of those direct looks from her snapping black eyes. "Senorita," she corrected him. "Or Miss, if you prefer. Miss Maria Baez. And yes, you may walk with me, Mr. Jones. I am taking a trolley bus to Camden. I often do so on my afternoons off. There is a tea shop there that serves turron." She noticed his blank look. "It is a Spanish sweet, for Christmas, but at this tea shop they have it always. Delicious."

Better and better, thought Archie. "Because of my clumsiness, Miss Baez, I feel I should buy you tea. And some of this turron? Please, do me this honor."

He'd amused her again, he could tell by her smile, but he didn't mind. As long as she agreed it didn't really matter if she thought him a buffoon, or just a lonely butler seeking love. He had a job to do, but this job looked like being more like a pleasurable interlude than the missions on which Mr. Eversham usually sent him.

Senorita Maria Baez was attractive and exotic, and suddenly he wanted to know all about her.

Maria was enjoying herself.

Mr. Archie Jones the butler was a charming fellow, there was no doubt about it. She stole a glance over her prettily patterned teacup and found him gazing back at her.

"Do you like the turron, Mr. Jones? It is made of honey and almonds, and sometimes a little chocolate or vanilla or coffee." She popped a square of the sweet into her mouth and smiled in childlike delight. "Delicious!"

He appeared bemused, as if she wasn't at all what he'd expected. She wondered what he *had* been expecting when he pretended to bump into her. Oh yes, she knew it was all make-believe. Maria had been watching him from the window at Mallory Street, wondering what on earth the trim, neatly dressed gentleman was up to, strolling back and forth, sending furtive glances up at the Smythe's residence.

She'd decided to find out.

"Have you ever been to Spain, Mr. Jones?"

"I have indeed, Miss Baez. When I was much younger and much more foolish I enlisted in the army and went to fight Napoleon. The war was all but over by the time I got there so I didn't have much to do but enjoy the scenery. I actually have very fond memories of my days in Spain and always hoped to return."

Maria smiled, thinking, *That makes him forty or so. A nice age for a man.*

"Perhaps you could persuade your employer to go for a holiday and for you to accompany him, Mr. Jones. I have longed for my own employers to travel, but at the moment it is out of the question."

His gaze sharpened.

Ah, just as she'd thought. It was the Smythes he was interested in. They were the prize, and she was merely the conduit.

"I would enjoy a trip to Spain, Miss Baez, but unfortunately while I was there last time I got myself into a bit of bother, and they threatened to put me in prison if I ever came back. The country is out of bounds to me."

"A shame, Mr. Jones. What sort of bother?"

"We captured some bandits in the hills, and my captain ordered them shot. Turned out later they were favorites of the local Spanish commander. He swore his revenge on our company, however long that might take. The commander is now high in the Spanish government so I'm not sure I want to risk it."

"Oh."

"Can I persuade you to call me Archie, Miss Baez? I know we are barely acquainted, but I feel as though we are already friends."

She sipped her tea and thought for a minute. "Very well, Archie. And you may call me Maria."

They smiled. Maria decided then and there that when Archie asked to meet her again—and he would—she was going to say yes. Whatever he was up to she wanted to know about it, for her young mistress's sake as much as the other members of the family.

Perhaps he was a debt collector?

Maria knew that the Smythes were in debt up to their well-bred necks. It was in their interest, and hers as their employee, to make certain Archie wasn't planning any mischief.

Yes, it was her duty to play his game.

But if she was honest, that wasn't the only reason she wanted to meet him again. She was enjoying his company. He was a man who was old enough to be comfortable in his own skin, and he had seen the world—even if he couldn't go back to Spain. She was interested in what he had to say, and she liked his smiling eyes.

It was a long time since Maria had met a man whose company she enjoyed quite this much. She hoped, she really did, that he wasn't a debt collector. It was a mystery what else he could be, but she could wait. The truth would reveal itself in time, and Maria was looking forward to making the discovery.

Chapter 6

Tina was resting. At least, she was supposed to be resting, but she was a healthy young woman, and in reality she was reclining on her bed thinking about the future.

Her future. With Horace.

She'd already decided that they would have two children—a boy and a girl—named Gideon and Penelope—and they would spend their time between Horace's country estate and his London town house. He would go hunting in the country, of course, and as she was not much of a rider to hounds, she would busy herself with . . . with . . .

Tina sat up. What *would* she do to occupy herself? Walking? Embroidery? She shuddered. Embroidery was not her strong suit at all. Perhaps she could take up watercolors. Tina had been well grounded in the running of a household and expected to be busy with that—and children. In fact she was a homebody who loved her family and wanted the same sort of warm relationships with her own husband and children. But surely the important thing was that she and Horace would be happy? Yes, that was the important thing.

Satisfied, she lay down again.

But her thoughts had brought forth a question, and she realized she had no answer. What *did* Horace do with his time? He had no close family and didn't have to earn a living, of course, so she imagined he spent his time in much the same way as her brother, who didn't seem to do much at all. Charles went to a gentlemen's club, where one had to be a member, but as far as she knew all they actually did there was drink whiskey and smoke cigars and make wagers. She must remember to ask Horace what else he found to occupy himself.

But not tonight.

Tonight was about practicing her skills of seduction at Horace's soiree. She giggled. Her finishing-school friends would be all agog if they knew what she was up to. She wished they were here right now so that she could tell them all about the disreputable Mr. Eversham. And of course about Horace, she reminded herself hastily. After all, this was all about marrying Horace, whom she'd loved forever, and saving the family from penury.

She remembered some years ago a family friend had gazed fondly upon her and Horace and predicted they would marry. Of course, they had burst themselves laughing at the very idea! And now here she was contemplating that very thing.

Just then her mother's head appeared around the door. "Are you asleep, darling?"

Tina sat up. "No, Mama. Just resting. We may be very late tonight."

Lady Carol Smythe sat on the edge of the bed.

"Yes. It's quite an occasion, going to the theater with a Lord of the Realm," she said, a twinkle in her eye.

"Oh, Mama, it's just Horace. We've known each other for years. And it's not as if it's just us; Charles and other people will be there."

"That's as well, too." Her mother fiddled with the pearl trim that edged her sleeve, and Tina noticed she looked anxious. Her own heartbeat quickened as she wondered what new secret she was about to share. "But you do like Horace, don't you, darling?"

"Of course I do, Mama. He's a good friend."

"And a handsome man. You're not children anymore." She fiddled with her sleeve some more, and Tina, growing more anxious herself, watched and waited.

"You know that your father is in difficult straits, Tina. I told you so."

"Yes, Mama, I remember." How could she forget? The shock she'd felt when her mother had whispered the truth about their appalling situation! And although Lady Carol had said nothing since then, it was obvious to Tina that matters were getting worse. Although appearances were still kept up when they had visitors or went out socializing, when they were at home with just the family the meals consisted of the cheapest ingredients possible—more gristle than meat—and Tina had noticed a growing number of empty spaces on the walls, where paintings used to hang.

Slowly but surely, their once-comfortable life was being eroded away by debt.

And it wasn't just the material changes: Tina

had also noticed a change in her parents' behavior toward each other—particularly Lady Carol. There was a bitterness in her manner that had never been there before. She was obviously finding it difficult to forgive Sir Thomas his financial blunder, and who could blame her? It was Lady Carol's money he had lost, after all.

Lady Carol interrupted her thoughts, her voice high and trembling. "I fear we cannot keep pretending everything is as it was, Tina. So many unpaid bills! Your father has managed to stave off some of the larger ones by promising to pay— promises we cannot possibly keep! But at least it keeps the bailiffs from the door. We just cannot go on for much longer."

Tina was sure her face was just as white as her mother's, and she suddenly noticed there were new lines about Lady Carol's mouth and eyes, and the line between her brows was deeper. Worry was taking its toll on the once-renowned beauty.

"But is there nothing we can do?" Tina said. "Is there no way father can get the money back?"

"I'm afraid not. It is gone. His friend took it all and then lost it. Your father trusted him completely, Tina, and see what has happened. We are ruined." Her mother looked away, her eyes shining with tears. "Your father is thinking of applying to his brother Harold for a loan. Although it is in no way certain. Harold is not the most generous of men, and your father and he have never been close."

She turned back to Tina, her eyes still bright, and spoke in an agitated way. "Do not tell Charles. He is not levelheaded like you. He wouldn't be able to cope. I want to keep this awful news from him for as long as possible."

"Father should not have told me to get a new dress for the theater. We cannot afford it, I see that now. I will take it back."

She made as if to get up, but her mother put a hand on her arm to prevent her. "No, Tina. You must have *one* new dress for the summer, and who knows, perhaps you will find a wealthy husband to fall in love with you." She laughed shakily, as if she were making a joke, but there was no humor in it. "You are a lovely girl, and beauty has been enough to bring men to the altar before."

"Mama—"

"Horace is a very wealthy young man."

"Yes. Mama—"

But Lady Carol was not to be stopped. "If Horace were to propose to you, then your father and I would approve of the marriage. There is no question that we would be very happy indeed with such a match."

"Marry Horace?" For a moment Tina wondered whether her mother had read her mind. "But—"

However Lady Carol was resolved to say her piece.

"It is our hope, Tina, that you and Horace . . . and of course it would solve all our problems . . ." She bit her lip. "Oh listen to me! This mess is not of your making, and you should not be asked to fix it. Please, Tina, forget what I said. I'm sure we will find some other way to escape the Fleet."

The name hung over them like a monstrous black cloud. The Fleet, London's debtors' prison.

Tina tried to order her scattered thoughts.

She knew now what her mother wanted to hear, needed to hear. Should she tell her the truth? That she'd already begun a scheme to marry Horace? But no. Lady Carol had enough to worry about, and despite their desperate straits she wasn't convinced her mother would approve of the infamous Mr. Eversham and his lessons in love.

No, reassurance was what was needed here.

"I want to marry Horace more than anything in the world, Mama. I've always loved him."

Lady Carol clasped her hands and gave a shaky little laugh. "But that is marvelous, Tina!" But her obvious relief and excitement quickly faded. "But does Horace feel the same way? Perhaps we shouldn't get our hopes up too high?"

"No, he doesn't feel the same way. He thinks of me as a friend." She saw her mother's face fall even further, and hastened to add, "But I am trying my best to persuade him otherwise, Mama. Believe me, if it is at all possible, Horace and I will be husband and wife before . . ." Before the bailiffs arrived to toss them out of Mallory Street. "Before too long."

Lady Carol gave her a searching look while Tina attempted to appear innocent of any whiff of scandalous behavior.

"Tina, when you say you are trying to *persuade* him to marry you, I do hope you are not being reckless? It is vital that you keep him at arm's length. By all means give him a glimpse of what you have to offer, but do not let him touch. A man will not buy what he can have for free."

"Mama, really!" Tina cried, taken aback by her

mother's uncharacteristic bluntness. This was not the sort of conversation they had ever had together.

"I'm sorry if I've shocked you, darling, but there are some things you don't learn at finishing school, and I'd rather you hear them from me than have to experience the hard facts for yourself. More than one young woman has ruined herself by trusting the wrong man with her virtue. And frankly, Tina, without the dowry you might have had, your looks and your virtue are all you have to bargain with."

"I can assure you, Mama, I have no intention of allowing Horace to take liberties with me," Tina said self-righteously, while the voice in her head was whispering, *Liar.*

Her mother continued in that awful earnest, worried tone until Tina felt like squirming. "You are such an innocent."

"Horace would never—"

Lady Carol's smile was forced. "Would he not? Well, you know him best, I suppose. I'm sorry to worry. I can't seem to help it these days."

Affectionately, she leaned to kiss her daughter's cheek. "Just be careful, darling. I'll leave you to your rest now."

Tina wondered how she was supposed to rest.

Her mind was turning in circles.

What if she was making a terrible mistake? Was she going too far with her plans to make Horace notice her? Perhaps her mother was right, and he wasn't the sort of man to be trusted with a pretty girl. There had been some talk about a shopkeeper's daughter although until now Tina had dismissed that as mere gossip. Would Horace wantonly ruin a girl's reputation?

She jumped up and went to the wardrobe, where her new dress hung. The cloth was beautiful, the fit perfect, but the neckline was *very* low. What if Horace thought she was ripe for the picking? It was all very well to flutter one's eyelashes like a courtesan, but Tina didn't want to give the impression she would like to *be* one!

If Horace believed he could have her without the wedding vows, would he let any gentlemanly concerns prevent him? And yet she could not believe Horace was the sort of man to treat a friend with such contempt. Even as she protested, she found herself with a doubt. She'd just been telling herself she didn't know what Horace did with his time, that she didn't know him as well as she'd thought. Could she really trust him with her virtue?

And yet what choice did she have but to carry on with her husband hunting? Horace was the only man she'd ever wanted to marry, and marrying him would be the perfect solution to the Smythes' troubles. No, she had no choice, but perhaps there was something she could do to calm her nerves where the dress was concerned.

Rummaging through her wardrobe she found what she wanted—a silk shawl in a paisley pattern, mostly cream in color, which matched the cream lace on the green dress. She draped it about her shoulders and bosom and peered anxiously at her reflection.

She couldn't help worrying about this evening. She had enjoyed the scene she had acted out with Richard Eversham, but now she wasn't sure she could behave like that with Horace and his friends. Charles would make fun of her, and she would be mortified if Horace thought it funny to see his "little sister" make such a spectacle of herself. It was different with Richard Eversham—she'd known him such a short time, and yet she felt very comfortable in his presence. She trusted him.

That is because it is a business arrangement.

Well, whatever it was, he made her feel safe—that she could do whatever she wanted, and he would still not think badly of her.

So what would she do at the soiree? Would she go through with her plans or not?

Tina smiled a little grimly. Of course she would. The simple truth was she had no choice.

*"**W**hy, Mr. Eversham, I didn't expect to see you here!"*

All about them the theater hummed with excited patrons. He bowed over her hand, his breath warm through the thin evening glove. For some reason she was wearing a diamond headpiece, almost a crown, and diamonds swung from her earlobes and glittered from her fingers. She was quite awash with them.

"I needed to see you, Miss Smythe. I could not wait."

He was holding her hand for far too long, and yet when he moved closer, almost embracing her, Tina did not push him away. His lips brushed her temple, and she gasped. Several people around her gasped, too. She heard them begin to gossip, and yet she didn't care.

"You are far too beautiful to marry Horace Gilfoyle," *Richard Eversham declared, his deep voice vibrating*

within her in places she'd never paid much attention to before.

Tina placed a trembling hand on his shoulder. "But I must. I love Horace."

"I can make you love me," Mr. Eversham said with an arrogance her dream self found breathlessly exciting. His mouth hovered over hers, his lips so close that if she swayed just a fraction, they would be kissing.

"Oh," she said, although it was more like a moan. "Oh, Richard . . ."

"Miss Tina, it's time to get ready!"

Reluctantly and somewhat ashamed of her dream self, Tina woke up.

Chapter 7

"**M**iss Tina, it's time to get up. And you have a letter—hand delivered!"

Tina opened her eyes, yawned, and stretched. "Maria," she said with a smile. After finding the shawl, she'd lain down again on her bed and actually fallen asleep. And she'd been dreaming. Her smile wavered and disappeared altogether. She'd been dreaming of flirting outrageously with Richard Eversham!

The dream was fading, but the feelings it had engendered remained.

Uncomfortable with the direction of her thoughts she sought to cast Mr. Eversham from her mind, but almost immediately he was back again.

"Your letter, miss."

She took the letter from Maria and broke the seal. A single sheet of paper covered in bold black script, and signed *"Eversham."* Tina felt a little frisson of shock and, seeing Maria watching her, turned away for more privacy.

"Are you quite sure this is the dress you want to wear, miss?" Maria said doubtfully.

"Yes," Tina answered firmly, and returned to her letter.

Miss Smythe, I wish you the best with your venture at the theater; be assured I will be thinking of you. If it helps, I want you to imagine me standing at your shoulder, whispering encouragement in your ear. I have set aside some time for another appointment tomorrow at 2 o'clock, if that is acceptable to you. I look forward to our next encounter. Eversham.

Tina felt a shiver run over her skin, as if Mr. Eversham really was standing at her shoulder, whispering in her ear. She wasn't sure if she wanted to imagine him doing that. She certainly wasn't sure she wanted to have him in her dreams. In fact she wasn't sure if she wanted to be doing any of this at all.

But when she saw herself in the floor-length mirror in her new dress, with her hair pinned up and the loose curls Maria had created framing her face, her confidence returned. Horace would not dare to laugh at this woman. Maria fastened her jade necklace around her neck, and she felt beautiful, for the first time happy with herself. She had frequently wished herself to be taller and slimmer, but she could see now that she had grown into an attractive woman. She told herself in her practical way that she would wear the shawl, but only until she was comfortable enough to remove it.

This was not the time for false modesty or coy missishness.

Her family's future, as well as her own happiness, rested on her actions tonight.

"You look beautiful, miss," Maria said quietly

from the shadows behind her. "I am sure *all* the gentlemen will think so."

Tina tried to read her maid's expression in her reflection. Did Maria know about Horace? Did Maria know about her father's financial catastrophe? How could the servants not realize how dire the situation was becoming—they must be afraid of losing their positions in the Smythe household.

Perhaps tonight would see all that change.

Downstairs in the sitting room her mother admired her new dress, and to Tina's relief said nothing about the shawl she was wearing. "You look lovely, darling. Doesn't she, Thomas?" Carol turned to her husband, who was reading his newspaper.

Sir Thomas looked over the rims of his glasses and grunted. "Hmm. Too good for that lot."

"Thomas!"

"You know it's true. Most of those young wasters come by their wealth far too easily. They should be doing something constructive with their lives. Put them into my old regiment—give them some discipline. That would keep them occupied usefully instead of spending their days gambling and worse."

It was so unfair that this disaster had happened to her father through his being too trusting. He'd believed the investment his friend had convinced him to undertake was foolproof, and this was the result. Now he'd grown suspicious and bitter of all wealthy men.

"Thomas, you like Horace, you know you do."

"Humph."

"Tina is waiting."

"Yes, yes, you look beautiful, Tina. Just like

your mother." He stood up and kissed her cheek. "Enjoy the theater," he added for good measure.

Tina could see that the poor man was trying very hard to be cheerful for her sake.

"Thank you, Father. I'm glad you like Horace," she added, with a sideways glance at her mother.

Tina couldn't help but wonder what her father's opinion would be of a man like Richard Eversham and the way he made his living. Best not to think of it, she decided with a shudder. They would never meet so the problem would never arise.

Just then Charles came running down the stairs and barely glanced at her. "Ready, Tina?" He noted the time on the longcase clock. "We should get a move on."

"Yes, Charles. I'm ready."

They walked out together to the waiting coach. Tina found herself considering how much the vehicle was worth, and at what point that, too, would have to be sold, and then she told herself to stop it. Tonight she must concentrate on her quest for Horace and forget about everything else.

Charles was shuffling about impatiently in his seat, and it wasn't long before they arrived at Horace's Bell Street town house. Tonight there was a wash of light from the windows and open door, welcoming his guests inside.

It was a tall, grand building and had belonged to the Gilfoyles for many years. Horace, having inherited his fortune so early—his parents had died in a boating accident when he was a child— had lived here most of his life.

Tina took a deep breath—as deep as her corset would allow—and stepped over the threshold. Tentatively she imagined Richard Eversham at her side, and it helped, so she kept him there. Horace was nowhere to be seen, but there were several familiar faces, and she drifted toward a group of young women with whom she was acquainted.

"Clementina!" said Anne Burgess. "There you are, at last."

"Charles made us late," Tina said, with a teasing grin in her brother's direction.

Charles pretended to frown. "Humph. How do you do, Anne? Looking as beautiful as ever."

Anne smiled back at him. She was a very attractive blonde. Tall and slim and elegant, she wore a royal blue dress that matched her eyes. She attracted the attention of a great many males, without, it seemed to Tina, any deliberate effort at all. Tina and Charles had known her almost as long as they had Horace, and she was always so nice, it was impossible to dislike her.

Unless, of course, she was here because Horace had a special interest in her, thought Tina. How cruel that would be, when she had gone to so much trouble and expense to try to capture that interest for herself.

At her shoulder Richard Eversham told her to show more confidence in her own abilities, and she immediately felt better.

A moment later Horace arrived through a side door, alone, and looking flustered and upset. She had never seen him like that and was so surprised she said nothing, simply watching as he straightened his waistcoat and brushed back a lock of fair hair. An expression of delighted welcome settled over his face, almost as if he had put on a mask, and he strode into the room to greet his guests.

There was a group of young men nearby, and he

was soon laughing with them and slapping their backs as if he hadn't seen them for years. Then he went to the pianoforte and spoke to the pianist, after which, to Tina's surprise, Horace began to sing, a ditty about the life of a beggar being an easier one than that of a workingman. He sang it with a great deal of gusto.

"Horace is in good voice tonight," Anne murmured, as Charles and another friend joined him, roaring the words in a less-than-tuneful fashion.

Tina thought Horace was behaving very oddly tonight, but she merely smiled.

Others were taking their turn at singing around the pianoforte, and Horace made his way over to Tina and Anne although, to Tina's dismay, his gaze *did* seem to linger on her lovely friend.

"What do you think, ladies? The life of a beggar might be far simpler than working for a living, might it not?"

Tina gave him a doubtful look. "Do you actually know anyone who works for a living, Horace?"

"Hmm, my servants work. Some of them better than others," he added darkly.

"And do you suppose that they would be better off as beggars?" Tina asked, unable to keep the annoyance out of her voice. What did Horace know of poverty? It was all a game to him. He'd never experienced it, not even a little bit. At least Tina could tell herself she now knew something of the misery of doing without.

Anne added her calming influence to the conversation. "It's just a silly song and mustn't be taken seriously. We should always remember the poor and do what we can to help. Don't you agree, Tina?"

"Yes, of course," Tina said, but she felt a little

sad. She had changed. Her circumstances had changed her. She would never be able to have a lighthearted conversation again without this feeling inside her of being apart from her friends.

What would they say if they knew she was about to become one of the poor they were speaking about? What if they were to find out that beneath her lovely and fashionable new dress her petticoat was darned because it had holes in it, and she couldn't afford to buy another? Or that her slippers were scuffed at the toes, and Maria had colored in the bare spots to disguise them?

"My family often attends charity events," Anne said earnestly. "I think everyone should consider those less fortunate than themselves."

The conversation had clearly become too earnest for Horace. "Now, ladies. Champagne!" He summoned a passing servant, and both Tina and Anne accepted a glass. "You both look exceptionally lovely tonight."

Anne smiled and accepted the compliment as her due and although Tina did likewise, she was certain Horace was simply mouthing words to be polite. He did not mean them. There was no special glint to his eye or smile to his lips when he looked at her; there was nothing to say he found her any more attractive than he had when they were five years old.

Tina drank another glass of champagne, frustrated by the turn the evening and her own feelings were taking. She had imagined having Horace to herself and instead she was sharing him with everyone else.

Richard Eversham, at her shoulder, chose that moment to whisper in her ear.

Why not see if you can turn his attention back to you?

How will I do that? You can tell he's far more interested in Anne than me.

You know how. Do as I told you.

As she sipped from her glass she allowed her shawl to slowly slip farther down her shoulders until her décolletage was no longer hidden. If her bosom was her only attribute, then she must take Mr. Eversham's advice and show it off as much as possible.

And Horace certainly noticed.

He looked and then turned away and looked back again as if he couldn't believe what he was seeing. Was he interested or embarrassed? She couldn't tell, but now she'd begun she could hardly go back. It was time to try her charms on some of the other guests. Why not? What had she to lose now? By next week she might be inhabiting a small room at the Fleet Prison.

With all the confidence born of two glasses of champagne—and Richard at her shoulder—Tina excused herself from the small group that included the object of her heart's desire and joined the boisterous assembly around the pianoforte. She bent over the pianist to look at the words, giving all those present an extra good view of her attributes, and then joined in the singing. She found she was thoroughly enjoying herself and the company she was in. It was amusing to flutter her eyelashes and touch gentlemen's arms, and she soon became the life of the party, or at least the small section gathered around the pianoforte.

So what if several of the ladies were staring

at her disapprovingly and whispering about her behind their gloved hands? They were jealous, that was all. In fact she was having such a good time that she was a little disappointed when it was time to leave for the theater although it was quite gratifying when several young men asked her to accompany them in their carriages.

Fortunately she had Charles to escort her, as she had no desire to single out any of the young men and have him think she might have any real interest. She was interested in one man only, the husband she was hunting, Lord Horace Gilfoyle.

Actually the theater was a trifle dull after the excitement of the soiree, and she found herself sitting beside her brother and a rather timid gentleman who introduced himself as John Little, a business acquaintance of Horace's. There were refreshments in the interval, and more champagne. Tina knew she really shouldn't, but the drinks she had had at Horace's town house were wearing off, and with them her sense of invincibility where her reputation was concerned.

Of what use is a reputation when you are poor? Let those with money worry about their reputations. You need to marry a wealthy husband.

"You're still here!" she cried with pleasure. She had thought Richard was gone, but now he was back, whispering in her ear.

"Miss Smythe? Are you well?" Mr. Little was looking at her with some concern, and Tina realized she'd spoken aloud.

She laughed gaily. "Mr. Little, I do apologize. A thought just popped into my head, and I spoke it without considering I was in company."

"Tina, do be quiet, the play is starting again."
Charles was giving her a disapproving look,
which she found amusing considering the number
of times he'd overindulged with champagne and
become noisy.

She was tempted to tell him so but as she opened
her mouth, he leaned toward her and said, "If you
don't shut up, I'll tell Mama you were drunk."

Tina subsided into silence, brooding upon the
difficulty of having a brother who only noticed
one's behavior when one didn't want him to. But
it was pleasing when Mr. Little gave her a sympathetic smile, as if he understood completely.

As the play drew to a close Tina found herself
feeling very sleepy, and Charles kept nudging her.
As they were leaving to go home Mr. Little took
her hand and asked if he might pay her a visit
and, without any real thought, she said of course
he could and, after brief good-byes to the other
guests, she and Charles departed.

"What on earth got into you?" Charles hissed,
as they jolted along London's dark streets. "I was
embarrassed, Tina."

"Don't be ridiculous," she said, stifling a yawn.
"I had a wonderful time."

Charles subsided, and Tina was left with her
own thoughts.

Congratulations! Richard was still there at her
side. *You put your mark on tonight's proceedings,
Tina. Mark my words, only good can come of this.*

Tina smiled at the passing night beyond the
coach window. Yes, it had been a success. She'd
started her husband hunting tonight, and surely,
very soon, Horace would be hers.

Chapter 8

Richard returned to Five Jasmine Street late in the evening and slept well and rose eager to begin the day. Miss Smythe's visit was for two o'clock, and he was looking forward to it. In fact his level of anticipation surprised him and made him uneasy. As did his growing urge to warn her about Lord Horace Gilfoyle.

But that was impossible.

Knowing Archie now had a foot in the Smythe household would just have to be enough. Good God, she might already be engaged! And even if she did believe what Richard had to say and not storm out of his house, she might let slip to Gilfoyle the Guardians' suspicions of him, and that would ruin everything.

Because if Gilfoyle was the Captain, then Richard knew he would stop at nothing to bring him to justice for his brother's death. Spoiling Miss Smythe's wedding plans was hardly going to prevent him from taking his revenge; in fact it might make him even more determined to deal with the brute.

After a late breakfast Richard made his way to see Sir Henry Arlington at Whitehall. He entered the building of the Metropolitan Police, using the back entrance from Great Scotland Yard. His superior had a small office tucked away in a corner of the labyrinthine building where he sat frowning over numerous dispatches and snippets of intelligence received from all over the country. Not unlike a spider at the center of its web.

"Richard. You have something for me?"

"I believe so." Richard explained about his visit to Gareth. "Lord Horace was there at the right time to have had a hand in the riot in Kent."

"Interesting. And he had no reason to be journeying to Kent, no estate to visit, no family?"

"Not as far as I know."

Sir Henry mulled over this latest intelligence.

After a moment Richard went on. "The other man, the one who was traveling with him, I've never heard of. He's a businessman, an importer, who calls himself John Little."

"And as we know, Lord Horace has some rather shady friends. I will discover as much as I can about this Mr. Little. In the meantime, keep a close watch on your Miss Smythe. She may be our way into Gilfoyle's inner circle."

"I'm seeing her today at two o'clock."

Sir Henry gave him a knowing smile.

"In a purely business capacity," Richard added stiffly, and wondered why he felt the need to justify himself. His relationship with Miss Smythe, business or otherwise, was none of Sir Henry's affair. But then again, if they discovered Gilfoyle was the Captain, then perhaps it was.

"My brother's final mission," he began.

Sir Henry's smile vanished. "We've spoken of this, Richard, and I've told you all I know. Your brother had a bad habit of keeping things to himself. All very well to play it alone, but when he was killed, all his secrets died with him. I know he was on the trail of the Captain because he'd told me so several days before, but he died in Kent, near his home. The Captain might have followed him there, or perhaps it was just a coincidence, and he had nothing to do with his death."

"But it is likely," Richard said quietly. "It is more than likely that if Anthony was onto the Captain, then the Captain was onto him. If Anthony knew enough to ensure that the Captain hanged, then that villain would feel he had no choice but to silence him."

Sir Henry nodded, his mouth turned down. "Yes, that is a fair assumption. But it is only an assumption. You need to concentrate on the here and now, Richard. Do your job. Don't make the same mistake as Anthony and go off on your own tangent. The Guardians are here to help you, don't shut them out."

"I don't intend to," Richard assured him. And yet, in his heart, he wondered. If he were to discover for certain that Gilfoyle was the Captain, would he really go to the others? Or would he head off alone to take vengeance on the man who'd murdered his brother before he had a chance to set aside their differences and repair their relationship?

Even if it meant his own demise.

On the way back from seeing Sir Henry, he

stopped off at Gilfoyle's town house, strolling past as if he hadn't a care in the world. It was a wealthy man's house, ostentatious, with a liveried servant at the door. Why would a man with so much to lose involve himself in sedition and a possible date with a hangman's noose?

"**M**iss Tina. You have a visitor."

Tina stretched and then grimaced as the lingering effects of the champagne shot pain right through her head. She decided that was the first and last time she overindulged like that. How on earth could Horace and Charles do it night after night? Clearly they were both very silly.

"A visitor? What on earth is the time, Maria?"

"It's after ten, miss. Lady Carol had said to let you sleep, but now there's a gentleman here to see you, and she wants me to wake you up at once."

Tina sighed. "A gentleman?" Not Horace then. Had she really expected Horace to come rushing to her side? She admitted that she had hoped he might, despite its being most unlike Horace to be so impulsive. "Who is this gentleman?"

"A Mr. Little, miss."

Tina forgot about her head and sat up. "Oh no! I did tell him he could call, but I didn't expect him so soon."

"Lady Carol and Sir Thomas are entertaining him in the drawing room, but you are to hurry."

"Help me to get dressed, and I'll go and rescue them."

Tina washed, and Maria helped her into a modest day dress.

"I've let it down," she said, with a critical glance. "I don't think it shows, miss. Anyway Mr. Little won't be looking at your hem, will he?"

Tina eyed the darker color around the bottom of her skirt. "Well, it can't be helped."

"No, miss."

Maria met her eyes and looked away as quickly. She did know then, Tina thought. How could she not? They were like a sinking ship, all going down together.

However, there was no sign of gloom when she reached the drawing room; in fact, laughter greeted her as she opened the door.

"Tina," cried Lady Carol, looking flushed. "Mr. Little has just been regaling us with tales from his travels. Some of the things he's seen!"

Bewildered, Tina looked at her father, whose face was red from laughter, and at Mr. Little, who had risen to his feet and was smiling at her. Could this possibly be the same man whose company she'd endured last night? He was almost attractive when he smiled, she realized, although he was still barely an inch taller than she, and his shoulders were stooped like a man twice his age.

A comparison with Mr. Eversham popped into her head, but she pushed it firmly out again.

"I had no idea you meant to pay me a visit so soon, Mr. Little," she said coolly, meaning to disconcert him.

"I was in the vicinity and took a chance," he replied with his smile undimmed.

"How did you enjoy the theater, Mr. Little?"

Comically, he turned down the corners of his mouth. "It was a very dull play, Miss Smythe. I could barely stay awake." He gave her a sideways glance, as if inviting her to share the joke, but Tina couldn't help but feel the joke was at her expense.

Lady Carol laughed; clearly she was charmed by Mr. Little even if Tina was not.

"I was rather surprised to be invited. I'm not a close friend of Lord Horace. We have done some business together, and I happened to run into him a few days ago, so perhaps he felt obliged to ask me to his soiree. I felt a little like an imposter and was rather uncomfortable with all his . . . uh . . . noble company."

"Ha!" scoffed Sir Thomas. "A perfectly worthless lot! It's nice to meet a young man who works for his living."

Tina's father had become very opposed to the upper classes since his money troubles. Tina couldn't remember him being so egalitarian before; in fact he'd been rather indifferent to the struggles of the poorer classes, avowing more than once that they brought their misery upon themselves through idleness. Now that he was well on the way to joining them, he'd suddenly become a strident socialist, and it could be embarrassing in company.

However, to Tina's relief, Mr. Little didn't seem to mind at all. In fact, he seemed similarly inclined. "I am most gratified that you think so, Sir Thomas. It is refreshing not to be looked down upon because I am in trade."

"What is it that you do exactly, Mr. Little?" asked Tina.

"Mr. Little is in the manufacturing business. Tobacco," said her father enthusiastically. "One of the most useful products of our times, I believe. The doctor put me onto it to help ease my nerves, and it has done wonders for me."

John smiled. "I don't actually manufacture tobacco. It grows in the Americas, and I import it and refine it locally in my factory—make it a little more palatable for the British market."

"I wonder you can't make it smell any better, then," said Tina, who abhorred her father's addiction to smoking.

John chuckled. "Believe me we do our best, Miss Smythe. Do you know, it isn't just men who smoke tobacco, there are many women, too."

"I have often thought of taking it up myself," Lady Carol said, and earned herself a beaming smile from Mr. Little. "Ring for some tea, darling," Lady Carol instructed her daughter. "You're not in a rush are you, Mr. Little?"

Tina hoped he was, but he leaned back in the chair, completely at home in their drawing room. "Not at all, Lady Carol. I'd be delighted to join you for tea."

John Little had been to most of the exotic places Tina had read about as well as quite a few she'd never heard of, and despite herself, she was swept up in his tales. If only Horace would call in and see her enjoying the company of another man, her morning would be complete.

Lady Carol was sipping her tea and seemed to be deep in thought. She had been rather subdued ever since she discovered just how wealthy Mr. Little was. Tina watched her uneasily, only half listening to her father speaking enthusiastically with Mr. Little. Mama was up to something, and it didn't take long for her to discover what it was.

"We should have a dinner party! It has been such a long time. We could invite the Thompsons, Horace, Mr. Little of course and perhaps Sir Henry and Lady Isabelle? What do you think?"

Sir Thomas looked momentarily as if he'd been stuffed, as well he might. They had been dining on pigs' trotters and cabbage all week, and his best brandy had been watered down until it hardly tasted like brandy at all. But something urgent in his wife's fixed expression must have impressed upon him the importance of his reply, and at this point Sir Thomas would do anything in his power to please his wife.

"As you wish, my dear. A dinner party. Yes, hmm, good idea."

"Mama," Tina murmured, anxious to catch her mother's attention. "Mama, there is no need—"

But Lady Carol was well away with her plans, and even Sir Thomas was becoming quite caught up in the idea.

Tina noticed that Mr. Little was entranced by her mother. Was it the fact Lady Carol had decided upon a dinner party, just because she liked him, that had won him over? And to be fair, Lady Carol did like him—Sir Thomas certainly did—but her mother also liked the fact that John Little was a wealthy man, and he'd called promptly upon her daughter after one meeting.

Mr. Little finally made his excuses and left, pressing a gallant kiss to Lady Carol's hand and promising to be present at the dinner party. He'd stayed well over the allotted time for first calls,

Tina noted, but no one but herself seemed to notice or care.

"Tina, we must have some more ladies," her mother burbled. "We have too many men. Are there any young ladies you would like to invite?"

Tina had lost touch with her London acquaintances while she'd been away at finishing school. For a moment she wondered whether she could ask Olivia or Marissa or Averil or Eugenia, but of course they would be busy with their own husband-hunting plans. No, she would have to think of someone else. But the only name that came readily to mind was Anne Burgess. As soon as she said it she wished she hadn't. Anne was far too attractive and would take Horace's attention away from her. So she hastily added Margaret Allsop, who wasn't quite so attractive and rather more dull than Anne.

This afternoon Richard Eversham must help her with her plans; she needed to know how to behave during the dinner. Surely, he would be able to practice a little dinner flirtation with her. At the thought of it she experienced a frisson of excitement. She was beginning to enjoy her meetings with Mr. Eversham. She smiled a secret smile and allowed her mother's words to wash over her while she indulged in far more interesting thoughts.

Chapter 9

Tina was relieved to reach Jasmine Square only slightly late. She'd had great difficulty escaping Lady Carol, now deep into the particulars of planning the dinner party. It seemed no expense was to be spared. Sir Thomas, too, was completely caught up in it, especially on the subject of which drinks were to be available to their guests—"My dear, champagne and brandy are most important. We cannot have enough of either."

It was as if they both didn't have a care in the world.

Suspecting this was all in her honor, no matter how they tried to pretend otherwise, gave Tina a squirmy feeling in her stomach. Lady Carol might say that her daughter's happiness was more important than the family debts, but Tina wondered what her decision must be if it came to a choice between her happiness and Mr. Little's tempting fortune.

Although her parents seemed to like him very much, Mr. Little as a prospective husband did not fill her with joy. Horace was her first and only option. The pressure for him to propose was mounting with each passing moment.

By the time Tina entered Richard Eversham's sitting room she could feel emotion roiling inside her, like a great whirlpool, and keeping it hidden was becoming more and more difficult. Practical, levelheaded Tina was feeling very shaky indeed, and as she removed her gloves she was shocked to see her normally steady hands trembling like leaves in the wind.

"Mr. Eversham."

"Miss Smythe." He was watching her with his usual warm and charming smile, and in a moment of madness she longed for him to put his arms about her and hold her close.

Tina took a deep, calming breath, but her voice was anything but calm. "I am so glad to see you, Mr. Eversham."

The expression in his gray eyes appeared a little startled, but his smile remained. "Are you? Are you so in need of my guidance, Tina?"

She meant to give an insignificant answer but instead heard herself saying, "You are the only one I can speak to plainly. Without subterfuge." She glanced up at him doubtfully. "At least I hope so."

Richard waited for her to sit down before he followed suit. "Of course you can speak plainly to me. That is because I am of no consequence."

Tina was startled into a laugh.

Richard leaned forward, still a hint of a smile in his eyes although his manner had become serious.

"No, don't laugh. It is the truth. At the moment

I am your teacher. A mentor. Once your object is attained you will no longer need my services. You can tell me all your secrets, and I promise not to betray your confidences. I have a good many secrets myself."

Tina decided he probably did. Richard Eversham must be privy to all sorts of concealments by his clients, but if he told tales, then people would soon stop coming to him for help.

And yet she hesitated, her emotional whirlpool growing wilder and even threatening to capsize her.

He merely waited until the words came tumbling from her.

"My mother is planning a dinner party. It is very important that Horace notice me. More important than I can possibly explain, Mr. Eversham."

"Didn't he notice you at the theater?"

She considered. "Others certainly did." And she smiled at the memory.

"Then things are progressing well, Clementina."

She looked up, into his gray eyes, and knew he could read the confusion in her face. "Why is it so much fun *not* to obey the rules, Mr. Eversham?"

"What do you mean?"

"When I was good and proper, as I was taught to be, I am sure I did not have nearly as much fun as I did last night, being bad and I think rather *im*proper."

He grinned. "Sweetheart, I think you are exaggerating! I can't imagine you were improper. Perhaps a little risqué, that is all."

Sweetheart? Tina swallowed and put the word aside for later examination, concentrating on his other words. She supposed that he, being an expert, knew what he was talking about.

"Well risqué or improper, it makes no difference. Rather than draw the attention of the one man I want to marry I drew the attention of the wrong men . . . man."

"And did you think of me there, at your shoulder?"

A warm heat washed through her as she remembered her imaginings of last night and her earlier flirtatious dream. Oh yes, Richard had very much been with her. "I did," she said a little stiffly, hoping he wouldn't ask any more.

"And it helped?"

"A little."

"Did Lord Horace kiss you?" he asked her abruptly, once again throwing her heart into a wild rhythm. The only man she'd been dreaming of kissing was the one right here in front of her.

"Kiss me? Goodness, no! We weren't even alone, and if we had been . . . well, I didn't get the impression he wanted to kiss me. He seemed more interested in my friend, Anne, and besides, he was in a very odd mood. Agitated about something or other."

"Agitated?"

"Or upset."

Richard considered her, his fingers steepled under his chin. "Forgive me for being blunt but did you *want* him to kiss you?"

Tina opened her mouth to tell him that yes, of course she did! But the words wouldn't come. An image of herself, clasped in Horace's arms, suddenly poured into her brain. It was vivid, very real, and strangely unsettling. Horace's cologne, which she wasn't particularly fond of, his mouth on hers, his hands grasping her. It made her feel uncomfortable, almost revolted. No, perhaps that was too strong a word. Rather it was how she might feel if Horace were Charles and Charles had suddenly decided to kiss her in a very unbrotherly fashion.

She took a ragged breath. This was completely ridiculous! Horace was definitely not her brother. No, he was the love of her life and the answer to all her troubles. She was absolutely positive that once Horace kissed her it would all be simply wonderful. Yes, one passionate embrace, and all these silly doubts would disappear like smoke on the wind.

"I want Horace to kiss me very much," she said decisively. "I do. It is just that"—she lifted her chin to hide her sudden sense of vulnerability—"I have never been kissed by a gentleman, so I am uncertain how to proceed."

Never been kissed?

It was too good to be true, and far too tempting a prospect for Richard to pass up. Oh, he knew what he should do. He *should* tell her to use her instincts and all would be well. Then he *should* change the subject.

But the words refused to be uttered.

Tina's lips were there in front of him, soft and pink and gorgeously lush. He desperately wanted to kiss her, to make her remember this kiss forever, and he was damned if he'd give the privilege of her first kiss to a man like Gilfoyle.

"Perhaps you need me to give you a lesson or two in the art of kissing. So that you feel more comfortable about the whole process." He spoke as if he was doing her a favor, as if he cared for her peace of mind.

He did care, he told himself. Of course he did. He cared so much that he was willing to bear the brunt of her anger by undermining her chances of marrying a brute like Gilfoyle. Surely that was because he cared about her? Certainly not because he was a greedy fool who was lusting after a woman he could never have, no indeed!

She was looking at him in that serious way she had, as if she were weighing up the pros and cons. As if the decision she was about to make would be one of life or death.

"Tina, do you want to be kissed by me?" he said, his voice deepening. "Purely as part of our business contract."

"Of course. I understand that. And yes, I think perhaps I do want to be kissed by you."

Richard stood up and reached out his hand, and she placed hers trustingly into it. He drew her toward him, slowly, giving her time to change her mind although he had no intention of changing his. Her breath was a little uneven, her lips parted in anticipation, and then he pressed his lips to hers.

Soft, just as he'd imagined. He brushed his mouth against hers, but she didn't respond, simply allowing him to kiss her. Clearly she had been telling the truth when she said she'd never been kissed. Never mind, he had plenty of time, and it wasn't as if this was a hardship.

Her skin was scented like orange blossom, sweet and fresh, and he breathed her in as his lips coaxed hers, gently but firmly, into responding. Until finally, with a little sigh of pleasure, she began to kiss him back.

Tina's cheeks were warm. Her arms were heavy where they rested about his neck, her fingers catching in the hair at his nape with a tug that was more pleasure than pain. Her sleepy green eyes were almost closed, shielded by her lashes.

This was no longer a lesson.

There was nothing cool and measured about this. Richard wanted her. Like a bolt of lightning it came to him that, given half the chance, he'd lay her down on the sofa and undress her until she was pale and naked under his touch.

But he couldn't do that.

If he did, he'd be risking everything, and certainly destroying any trust she had in him. He simply couldn't.

He lifted his head and gave her a friendly smile to disguise what he very much feared was the expression of blatant lust on his face. Gently, with a hint of regret, he set her at a distance.

"You kiss very well, Miss Smythe," he said, his voice light and teasing.

She appeared a little dazed and turned away, reaching to tuck a curl of dark hair behind her ear. "Do I?" she said, her voice husky. She cleared her throat. "Perhaps it is just that you are an expert, Mr. Eversham."

Richard bit his lip. He could start to boast about all the women he'd kissed, but he didn't think she'd want to hear that, and suddenly he didn't want to hear it either. Something about having Tina in his arms, her lips opening under his, had stirred surprisingly tender feelings in him.

"I'm certain Lord Horace will find nothing amiss in your kisses, Miss Smythe. He might be a man of the world, but he'd be a fool to let you slip from his grasp."

The words were heartfelt, and she looked up in surprise before quickly veiling her eyes. But not before he saw something in them that made him long to step forward and take her in his arms again.

And kiss her swollen lips until she surrendered entirely to him.

Had she really been kissing Mr. Eversham? Mr. Eversham, the rogue whom gentlemen paid to show them how to win the women of their dreams? And yet, as he had held her in his arms, he hadn't felt like a rogue. And if she was honest, rogue or not, she'd enjoyed his kisses very much indeed.

Was that another example of improper behavior being so much more fun? That must be it, for surely there could be no other reason for Tina to be suddenly longing to throw herself into Mr. Eversham's arms and kiss him forever.

Instead she half turned away, and said, "My mother is planning a dinner party. She is inviting a large number of people, including Lord Horace.

I may be able to tease him into kissing me if we have a moment alone."

"He will make certain you are alone."

He said it with such certainty she was tempted to stare at him but she stopped herself because too much gazing into Mr. Eversham's eyes was dangerous. She took a little breath to try to calm herself. For Tina, the cool and practical girl, who considered herself a thinker rather than ruled by emotion, this was a revelation indeed. Goodness, who would have thought a kiss would have such an effect on her? For a moment there, in Richard's arms, she'd been all passion, and her thoughts had grown so unsteady that they'd been flying about like shooting stars.

Still trying to calm herself, she moved to the window and gazed out at the street below.

Get a grip, she told herself. *This is a lesson to capture Horace into proposing marriage, it has nothing to do with Mr. Eversham. If he thought you were imagining his kiss as something more than part of your business contract, he would probably show you the door.*

And she really couldn't do without him at this juncture.

When she thought she was ready, she turned with a smile. "It is a pity you cannot come to the dinner party and tell me what to do, Mr. Eversham." Then her face colored as she remembered why he could not, why he would never be invited to her home.

He read her dismay perfectly but chose not to acknowledge it. "I'm afraid I am otherwise engaged," he said dryly.

Mr. Eversham was a scoundrel. How could she have forgotten even for a moment that they were members of two completely different strata of society? Although, it occurred to her, if her family's fortune kept declining, then perhaps she would eventually fall far enough to enter his realm. To her dismay, instead of being shocked, the idea gave her a glimmer of hope.

"You will manage very well at the dinner party," he said with polite finality. "I have complete faith in you."

Their lesson was at an end.

"You can always flirt with the other men. Horace will notice, believe me. He's probably noticed already."

"I can practice on Sir Henry Arlington. He's one of my father's old army friends. He's always the complete gentleman."

"Sir Henry . . . ? Oh. Yes."

"Or I can flirt with Mr. Little," she added with a wry smile.

His smile remained, but there was a stillness about him she'd noticed before. "Mr. Little?" he asked lightly.

"I met him at Horace's soiree. He is the wrong man I spoke of attracting. Anyway he called upon me this morning. Rather bold of him, I thought, and to tell the truth I barely remembered him, but he's made quite a hit with my parents, for different reasons. He is a wealthy importer of tobacco, you see. A self-made man. My father is very admiring of self-made men these days, and my mother is on the lookout for a wealthy son-in-law."

He was listening attentively, and yet she had the feeling his thoughts were far away. "So he's not a gentleman," he said mildly.

"No," she agreed. "My father does not seem

to be as strict about such conventions as he used to be."

She was glad he didn't ask why. She'd already said too much, and she didn't want him to start asking about her financial woes and perhaps begin to pity her. Or ask for her fees to be paid immediately instead of later.

"Next time you can tell me how things went."

Tina nodded. Now that it was time to go she suddenly felt lost and alone. She didn't want to go. She wasn't sure she was ready. What if she tried to kiss Horace, and he laughed at her?

Impulsively she said, "Do you mind if we do it again? Just to be sure I have it right?"

Amusement flickered in his eyes, but he inclined his head gravely. "Of course, Miss Smythe, it is important to get these things right. Perhaps if you were to approach me this time, if you were to kiss me?"

"That is rather bold, is it not?" she ventured.

"But you must be bold. Take the bull by the horns, or in this case, take Horace by the lips."

She straightened her back and approached him, purposely resting her hands upon his shoulders, taking a moment to gather herself before she lifted her face toward him and gently brushed her lips against his. He did not respond; he dared not. She did the same again and then, perhaps frustrated by his lack of response, took his lower lip between her teeth and nipped it gently.

Desire skewered him.

His hands went round her waist, holding her against him, not caring if she could feel his obvious erection. He was responding now, and she kissed him with a lack of self-consciousness, totally immersed in the moment.

This time it was Tina who broke away, breathless, flushed, her lips swollen. "My goodness," she gasped, green eyes shining. "That was . . . was very instructive. Thank you, Mr. Eversham! I am sure I have the hang of it now."

He thought he might smash something, but instead he smiled his polite smile and put on his charming face, disguising how he really felt. If she knew how much he wanted to lay her on the sofa, she'd be frightened of him. He almost frightened himself. Lack of control was not something Richard was used to feeling—he'd trained himself to be cold and heartless.

"Good, Miss Smythe. I shall see you next time."

She was saying something about the time and place, hurrying to the door as if she couldn't wait to escape him, and he let her go. With the door closed he told himself he was back in control, that there was nothing underhanded about what he was doing, it was simply his job, and if Miss Smythe led him to his brother's killer, then that was all that mattered.

Then why did he have to go to the window to stare down at her, to watch her hurry away?

After a moment his thoughts calmed, and he remembered what she'd said about Little. That was the second time that name had cropped up recently. He wondered just what Mr. Little had to do with Horace Gilfoyle; why was he at his soiree? They didn't seem to be cut from the same cloth, and yet here they were together.

Tina was right, it was a pity he could not go to

her dinner party. He would have liked to observe the main suspects interacting. He would have liked to know just what they were planning next.

And then he remembered that Sir Henry Arlington was also going to dinner. Sir Henry could pull some strings, surely?

It was an audacious idea. Richard wondered if he dared, and what would Tina say if he did? It would move their relationship into a completely different sphere if their kissing practice hadn't already done that.

Did he dare?

Richard smiled. Of course he dared.

Tina felt light-headed, a most unusual sensation for her. And she felt warm, very warm. Her body was one warm glow. Who would have thought a kiss would have such an effect on her? And would being kissed by Horace be as pleasurable?

She hoped so, but deep in her heart she feared that it was kissing Mr. Eversham and not the kiss itself that had made her ache and glow all over.

And if that was the case, then she was in quite serious trouble.

Chapter 10

Archie had arranged to meet with Maria on her next free afternoon, and he found himself looking forward to it far more than he'd expected. Not that he'd tell Richard Eversham that; after all this was meant to be work, prying information from the woman, not gadding about enjoying himself.

But who said he couldn't do both?

Archie had taken more pains than usual with his appearance, plastering his unruly curls down on his head, brushing down his jacket and trousers, and shining his shoes. He felt he was looking his very best when he arrived at the park opposite the Smythe residence.

Not long afterward he saw the very alluring Maria Baez walking toward him, her head tilted to one side, her mouth curved in a smile.

"Mr. Jones," she said with her charming accent. "You are early I think."

"I may be a little early, Miss Baez." He found himself simply looking at her, enjoying the curve of her cheek and the dark shine to her hair beneath the straw bonnet. Archie had never found it difficult to chat to women—he'd once regarded himself as a bit of a ladies' man—but suddenly he felt as gauche as a boy. What if she discovered the truth about their "accidental" meeting? Perhaps he should simply tell her.

At first she returned his look, and then she laughed. "Mr. Jones, it's not polite to stare."

"I am sorry, Miss Baez. I was just . . . thinking."

"Would you care to share your thoughts?"

For a moment he thought he might do just that, but common sense reasserted itself. He was cultivating Maria's company so that he could spy upon her household for his employer. Such information was not likely to endear him to her, and it certainly wouldn't get the job done.

"I was wondering whether you might have been too busy to meet me today, Miss Baez. I believe the Smythes are having a dinner party."

"And how did you know of that?"

She gave him a sharp look, and Archie wondered whether he'd stuck his foot in it. Richard had told him about the dinner party, after the visit by Miss Smythe, but he could hardly explain to Maria how he came to hear of it. Miss Smythe's visits were a secret, and he'd been sworn to silence. Perhaps he wasn't very good at this game of spying after all, or perhaps it was being in Maria's company that was scrambling his brains.

Luckily she didn't wait for an answer. "Actually you are right, there is a dinner party, but they will not miss me for an hour."

They strolled along in companionable silence.

"Are you happy in your current position?" Archie asked her at last.

"I am very happy," she said firmly. "They are very kind to me. I worry sometimes that . . ." She glanced at him. "There are money problems, you understand, but they will rise above them. I know they will."

Archie tucked that piece of information away for later.

"What of you, Mr. Jones? Are you happy in your position?"

Archie chuckled. "Oh yes, very happy. My household is not a conventional one by any means. I never know what will happen next or who will come calling. Life is never dull in Jasmine Square, Miss Baez."

Maria smiled, putting aside that address for future reference.

For herself she'd prefer dullness if it meant Miss Tina would forget about her plan to marry Lord Horace. Several times it had been on the tip of her tongue to tell her young mistress exactly what sort of man he was, but she didn't feel she could—it was not her place—not unless Tina asked for her advice.

But there was more to Miss Tina's secretiveness than Lord Horace. She was up to something, and Maria was determined to discover what it was. Just as she was going to find out what Archie Jones's game was, sniffing around.

And yet she was enjoying his company. Where was the harm in it? And he didn't seem to be a debt collector. If he had been, she was certain he would have quizzed her after she mentioned the Smythe's financial troubles instead of simply letting it pass.

So what was he? Who was he?

Maria glanced sideways at him and bit her lip on a smile. He had tried to flatten his curls, but they were already springing up irrepressibly all over his head. She didn't know why he bothered. She liked his curls.

She liked him.

He caught her eye and smiled at her. Maria slipped her hand through the crook of his arm, and they strolled on. It was such a lovely day, and suddenly she didn't care what his real agenda was, she was determined to enjoy it.

Chapter 11

Tina stood in front of her mirror. She could not, of course, wear anything too revealing for a family dinner, and she thought the pink dress from last season, though a trifle insipid, suited her coloring well enough. She and Maria had worked on it, altering the hem and sleeves, adding some ribbons and lace. At least the neckline was high enough to appease her mother and Maria had done wonders with her hair, as usual.

Outside she could hear the coaches arriving as their guests made their way to Mallory Street. Earlier, seeing the crates and boxes being carried into the kitchen, full of the finest food and wine, Tina couldn't stop herself wondering how much money this was all costing and how her father could pay the bills.

Well, he couldn't. It was a tribute to his previous standing that he'd managed to extend his already overstretched credit.

And as if that wasn't bad enough, Tina had the uncomfortable feeling that she, too, was being treated like one of the dinner dishes. Prepared and primped and laid out on a silver platter for the highest bidder. Horace or Mr. Little? They were both wealthy men. If she were to put the question to her parents, then she was sure either of them would do.

But that was unkind. They weren't really going to force her into a miserable marriage, but at the same time they would be hoping that she could bring herself to take one of them to husband. Horace's fortune would chase away all their problems, and of course it wasn't such a hardship, marrying him. She'd known him all her life, dreamed of marrying him all her life.

Why then was she feeling so glum?

Determinedly she pinched her cheeks until they were pink, her green eyes returning her desperate stare from the mirror. If she could manage to get Horace alone, if she could kiss him, then at least she would have given this her best shot. Even if he rejected her—laughed at her—she could say she had tried. And if Horace did laugh at her, then she was confident Mr. Little wouldn't.

Once upon a time her father would have locked her in her room rather than allow her to contemplate marriage with a merchant.

How times had changed!

Tina forced a smile, forced herself to appear happy in her role of the good and dutiful daughter, and with her head high set off to make her own history.

As Richard followed Sir Henry and Lady Isabelle into the Smythes' house, he was well aware that tonight he would be the most unwelcome guest at this dinner party. Although Sir Henry had agreed that his being here was a splendid idea, Richard doubted anyone else would think so.

Richard had also taxed Sir Henry with the fact that he was a friend of Tina's father and had never mentioned it to him, but his superior grew evasive.

"Personal business and Guardian business, Richard. I try not to muddy the two."

"But when I mentioned I was meeting with Miss Smythe, you said nothing."

"I didn't want to make it awkward for you."

Richard suspected that was true, but realizing Sir Henry knew more than he'd expected made him uneasy. He didn't like surprises. Now he was wondering if Tina was the woman he thought her or if perhaps she was in league with Gilfoyle.

He stopped himself. No, Tina was exactly as she seemed. A beautiful young woman who had her innocent heart set on a man who wasn't good enough for her. Although if Archie was right, and the parents were in financial difficulties, then they might have an ulterior motive for throwing their daughter at one of the wealthiest men in the country.

The house was large and rather fine, the sort of place he would have expected Sir Thomas Smythe to settle his family in, but the lack of knickknacks and the curious absence of paintings made it obvious to him—but only because he was looking—that Archie was right. The Smythes had money troubles.

His hostess, Lady Carol, an older version of her

daughter, was very regal, and her manner made it abundantly clear that his invitation had only been issued because of Sir Henry's intervention. She wasn't rude. She smiled and received him— she was too well-bred to do otherwise—but he couldn't miss the steely glitter to her eyes.

What had Sir Henry told her to force her hand like this? Or rather what had he told Sir Thomas? Whatever it was, Richard wasn't here to make friends. He had a job to do. Little and Gilfoyle could well be dangerous characters, involved in riots at the very least, and at the most . . . murder. If the Smythes wanted to invite such men into their home, then they must take the consequences.

So he gave Lady Carol a smile that was charming and totally unrepentant, and strolled into the drawing room to join the other guests.

Tina wasn't here.

He knew it at once although he looked about, just to be sure. Because how *could* he know? How *could* he be so sure? And yet he was. Absolutely. As if he was already so attuned to her scent and the timbre of her voice that he would instinctively have found her in any crowd.

A few of the guests glanced at him uneasily, but for a moment he was alone, and he remembered why it was he hadn't been to anything like this for almost two years. He was almost relieved when Sir Henry caught his eye and came to stand beside him.

"Over there." His superior gave a discreet nod toward a group of gentlemen by a marble bust of a Roman emperor on a plinth.

"Who am I meant to be observing?"

"Charles Smythe, in the green waistcoat, and John Little done up like a dog's dinner."

Charles stood with a couple of others who were immediately recognizable as young blades about town, and a slight gentleman who looked uncomfortable in his immaculate evening wear. The tobacco importer—the new player in the game.

Richard decided he looked harmless enough.

As if he'd heard his name spoken, despite that's being impossible, John Little looked at them across the drawing room. It was only a brief moment, but Richard sensed a stirring in the air, a soft whisper of warning.

Perhaps appearances were deceiving.

" . . . Had a devil of a job getting you invited," Sir Henry was saying, oblivious to Little's glance. "Don't do anything to make me regret it."

"Like telling off-color jokes at dinner?"

Sir Henry's eyes narrowed. "Not funny, Richard."

"Well, you know I am unaccustomed to dining in the company of quality, Sir Henry. I hardly know which fork to use."

"You know perfectly well how to behave," he retorted gruffly. "You know better than most of them."

Did he? He knew he should reassure his superior, but there was a devil in Richard that liked to behave outrageously. Which was probably why he enjoyed his current work so much. Oh there were times when it was difficult to be the man no one wanted to be seen with in public, never more so than right at this moment. But Richard knew it was important to his work and revenging his brother's death to place himself in a position where he was considered not quite a gentleman, a bit of a rake perhaps, and a wastrel. People were inclined to tell such a man things they wouldn't have told someone respectable.

Because he didn't matter, he learned so much more.

A nearby group of ladies were sending glances his way, and he was tempted to flirt a little, cause a few blushes, give them something to tell their friends. He was, after all, the notorious Mr. Eversham, and wasn't that just the sort of behavior society expected of him?

But Richard wasn't really interested in those ladies; he was interested in one particular lady.

Then a movement near the door caused him to turn, and there she was, pink-cheeked and smiling, her dark curls swept up onto her crown, pearl earrings matching the necklace about her creamy throat. She was quite ravishing, and why Gilfoyle hadn't already snapped her up was beyond Richard's comprehension.

She'd only taken a few steps when she saw him.

Her green eyes widened. Her soft mouth fell open. She froze.

Inwardly Richard sighed. If Miss Smythe was such a poor actress, she would never capture Lord Horace. Clearly she needed a great many more lessons.

"Tina?" Lady Carol had noticed and slipped an arm about her daughter's waist. She shot Richard an unwelcoming glare. "Are you all right?"

"I . . . that is, yes. Yes, of course I am."

Good, he thought admiringly. She'd recovered herself well and now turned away from Richard to greet her friends. Lady Carol sent him another withering look, as if it was all his fault. And of course it was.

A moment later Lord Horace breezed into the room, laughing, shaking hands, completely secure in his place in society and particularly the Smythe household.

Richard felt his hackles rise.

Sir Henry was quick to introduce them.

"Mr. Eversham!" Gilfoyle said in delight. "You are a man I could have a very interesting conversation with. I believe you helped Peterson to the altar. Saved him from the Fleet just in the nick of time by marrying him to that ugly heiress."

"It was Peterson who did the proposing, not I," Richard said politely.

"That wasn't how I heard it," Horace retorted, and his blue eyes gleamed with malice.

"Heard what?" Charles Smythe had joined them, clearly eager to support his friend. He cast a look at Richard that was coolly disapproving. "I'm rather surprised you are here, Eversham. My mother wasn't particularly pleased to know someone of your reputation was coming, I can tell you. You'd better not go near my sister."

"Now, Charles, mind your manners," Gilfoyle said with quiet authority.

Charles flushed and cleared his throat, like a puppy that's been reprimanded. Obviously, Gilfoyle was the stronger personality in that friendship but not for much longer if Richard guessed right. Young Charles was finding his feet.

"I can always eat in the kitchen," Richard suggested mildly. "If you prefer?"

Charles chose to make a joke of it, laughing

with some relief, and a moment later it was time
to go in to dinner.

Tina was very much aware that although she had
greeted their guests, she hadn't spoken to everyone. There was one person she hadn't been able to
bring herself to approach.

"Mr. Eversham is your father's guest," Lady
Carol said dourly, when she'd whispered the
shocked question after she first saw him. "Just
ignore him. That's what I intend to do."

So she had. Trying to understand why he was
here, in her house, was too difficult for her just
now, and really she couldn't deal with it.

Anne and Margaret gathered about her, perhaps sensing her inner turmoil. Anne was wearing a pale lemon dress with white lace, which
suited her pale coloring beautifully, while Margaret wore a pale green gown, which contrasted
nicely with her red curls. Indeed Margaret looked
far more attractive than Tina had expected, and
suddenly she was anxious about Horace's wandering attention. But he didn't seem to notice
Margaret or Anne, and once he'd greeted her, he
barely glanced at Tina either although she saw
him laughing with Mr. Eversham.

What was he *doing* here?

When she first saw him, she thought she was
seeing a ghost. Indeed, she'd been struck dumb
by the sight of him in her familiar surroundings.
It was all very well to imagine him by her side,
but for him to be here, in flesh and blood . . . She
was still shaken by his presence. Had he come to
help her win over Horace? Did he really think she

could remember any of his instructions, let alone put them into practice, while he was observing her with those warm gray eyes?

It was a nightmare.

If only she could get him alone, to question him, but her mother was watching her like a hawk.

His being here is going to ruin everything.

Lady Carol led them in to dinner, where they all took their places around the long, mahogany table. Tina found herself seated between Horace and John Little while Anne was between Horace and Charles, and Margaret sat on John's other side. She was surrounded by friends, she reminded herself, and Richard Eversham was far, far away at the other end of the table.

But she was aware of him. No matter how she tried to pretend he wasn't there, his presence colored everything around her.

He had kissed her. And she had asked him to do it again! What if her mother were to find out? What if he were to tell her? What if people could see it just from looking at the two of them?

She closed her eyes briefly and took a deep breath. This was getting ridiculous. He would never tell, and neither would she. No one would know, no one *could* know. Her connection with him was a secret between him and her.

"Miss Smythe, are you feeling faint? You are very pale this evening." It was John Little, wearing a worried frown as he peered into her face.

Mr. Little seemed determined to claim her attention. He was a nice enough man, but she wasn't attracted to him; if anything, she felt a little sorry for him.

Tina gave a nervous laugh. "Actually I am famished. Should a well-brought-up lady admit to such a thing?"

He smiled back, his blue eyes twinkling, as if he found her completely captivating.

"Didn't finishing school teach you the answer to that?" Horace put in. He'd obviously been listening. "'Though I'd be sorry if it polished too much of the old Tina from you. Girls are all the same these days, and you are refreshingly different."

Had Horace offered her a compliment?

"I doubt anyone could change our plainspoken Tina," Anne teased. "And like Horace I would hate to think she had become like all the other young ladies in London society."

Charles laughed, too, and something about the way he was looking at Anne tugged at Tina's attention, but then Lady Isabelle Arlington interrupted, and she forgot it.

"The notion that a girl needs to be 'finished' before she is of marriageable material is quite absurd."

There was a hush, as there usually was when the eccentric Lady Isabelle expressed her opinion in company. She had insulted so many people that it was only her aristocratic family connections and her wealth that ensured her continued welcome in society.

"I'm sure 'absurd' is too harsh a word," Lady Carol said, her face stiff with disapproval. "Tina has learned a great deal from attending Miss Debenham's. The establishment has a fine reputation, and many of its young ladies have risen high in society."

"You might as well put a placard on them. Sold to the highest bidder."

Tina choked back a giggle. Because Lady Isabelle really had gone too far this time, and she could see her mother was almost bursting to say aloud the unflattering things she was thinking. Lady Carol cast a glance at Sir Thomas that promised "words" later on. It was he who had invited Sir Henry and Lady Isabelle. And Mr. Eversham as well!

As if the thought of him had made the sight of him irresistible, Tina found her gaze seeking him out, way down the table. She had to know what Mr. Eversham thought of this conversation.

Chapter 12

He was looking right back at her, his gray eyes warm and smiling, his handsome face alight with enjoyment. She realized then, with a leap of her heart, that he had sought her out, too, and they were sharing a special moment. Tina relished it, knowing that for this fraction of time she and Mr. Eversham were in perfect harmony. But a heartbeat later she came to her senses and looked down at her soup, the color rising to her cheeks, her fingers trembling slightly as she lifted the spoon.

"My dear." Sir Henry, with his deep, measured tones, was used to calming the agitated atmosphere around his wife. "We all know your views on the marriage mart, but there have been some very happy marriages made without the participants feeling more than a modicum of affection for each other."

"But without love," Lady Isabelle declared dramatically, "we never truly live."

There were some hastily disguised sniggers around the table.

"My dear," her husband insisted, a warning in his eyes.

"I agree with Lady Isabelle," Horace murmured at Tina's side. "It would be the very devil to marry a woman one didn't like, just for her fortune or her connections. How would one ever go home, knowing she was there?"

She flashed him a smile, feeling too shaken up to say anything. What would Horace think of her if he knew what she was planning? Suddenly, she wished she could sink beneath the table and vanish completely.

"What do you think, Mr. Eversham?" Horace raised his voice. He must have known he was causing mischief, but he didn't care. As Tina well knew, Horace had always enjoyed causing mischief.

Richard Eversham smiled politely, but his eyes were no longer warm. "I think if marriages always began smoothly, then I would have a great deal of spare time on my hands."

There was a ripple of shocked laughter, and Lady Carol grew even more stony faced. To have Mr. Eversham to dinner was bad enough, but to discuss his scandalous occupation was worse. Tina shot Horace a quelling glance, but he deliberately ignored it.

"I do not think all the gentlemen you help to their happy event are madly in love with their ladies, Mr. Eversham. I think they often have far more pragmatic considerations at play."

"Perhaps they do, but I've yet to see a marriage I had some small part in making fail to thrive."

The dinner guests were agog. Rattled, Lady

Carol began a conversation about the weather, but Horace only spoke more loudly.

"Do you mean to tell me that everyone you've dealt with is deliriously happy? Come now, Eversham, you must have some failures. Admit it, some gentlemen are simply lacking in the ability, or more likely the will, to make any lady happy."

Richard considered. Tina held her breath, appalled and yet eager to hear what was said next. Horace was being awful, but Richard wasn't a man to be easily browbeaten.

"I don't consider anyone beyond my help. I make it a point never to turn away a potential client." His gaze slid briefly to Tina. "Please feel free to make an appointment, Lord Gilfoyle."

There was a murmur of shocked amusement.

Horace flushed angrily. "I wasn't speaking about myself."

"Oh? You seem so interested in my, eh, vocation, I thought you must be having difficulty persuading your chosen lady to marry you."

"You are mistaken," Horace spoke coldly. "I have no need to use you. I think anyone who does must be a poor sort of fellow indeed."

Richard smiled and said nothing, and his lack of answer seemed to infuriate Horace even more. Horace didn't like to be bested, and he'd been bested tonight.

Sir Henry frowned, glancing between the two men, but Lady Isabelle was enthralled. "My goodness!" She clapped her hands like a child. "How generous of you to help others to find love and happiness, Mr. Eversham."

"My dear, this is not a subject for dinner conversation," Sir Henry said. "Mr. Eversham's personal life is his own business, and we have no business interrogating him in this manner."

"I don't mind answering," Richard spoke evenly, as if he responded to such intimate questions all the time. "No, Lady Isabelle, it is not entirely generosity that drives me to help others to the altar, but it is kind of you to think so."

Another ripple of shocked laughter. This was certainly a night the guests would remember, and not for the reasons Lady Carol wanted it remembered. She forced her way into the conversation, her cheeks flushed with anger.

"It is the parents who must make decisions in regard to marriage, not the young lady or gentleman. And certainly not you, Mr. Eversham," she snapped. "I cannot imagine any parent willingly handing over a child to an unsuitable partner, no matter how much the word 'love' is bandied about. An ill-judged match could taint an entire family, and that would never do. Love is all very well, Lady Isabelle, but there are limits."

Lady Isabelle looked mutinous, but Sir Henry's frown prevented a hasty retort.

A second wife, Lady Isabelle was some twenty and more years younger than Sir Henry, and Tina wondered whether Isabelle had married him for love. Or did she have a lover somewhere, a man more her own age and opinions, someone she hurried to in the dark of the night, when Sir Henry was at his club.

And would Tina do the same, in her position, if she were married to a man she didn't love? She gave a little shudder. She didn't want to live a secret life; she didn't want to have to.

Mr. Little was watching her again. Tina was

beginning to find his constant regard irritating. When he leaned toward her to speak, only politeness prevented her from turning her head away. "Has Lord Horace some grudge against Mr. Eversham?"

Unfortunately Horace overheard. "The man is a rogue who has no place in civilized company," he said, at least lowering his voice. "And I do not like the way he has been ogling Miss Smythe."

Shocked, Tina stared at him. Ogling her? She had not noticed him ogling her, but then she'd been keeping her gaze firmly away from him, apart from that one moment when . . . Had Horace seen that? Was he anxious for her reputation?

Or could he possibly be jealous?

The main course arrived to interrupt her cogitations, and roast pigeon, perfectly cooked, with all the trimmings, was sufficiently distracting to halt the guests' conversation. By the time it began again the topic had drifted to more mundane matters.

Over the meringues and trifle, Tina noticed how well Charles and Anne seemed to be getting along, lost as they were in each other's eyes. She was surprised and then wondered why she should be. Just because Charles was her brother didn't mean he couldn't be of interest to a beautiful heiress like Anne. He was rather handsome, and he had an engaging way of smiling and turning a joke upon himself.

Lady Carol was watching them, too, an acquisitive gleam in her eye. Did her mother hope for a match there? It would certainly be a wonderful thing if Charles were to bring a large dowry into the family—and it would solve a great many of their problems. Perhaps then, Tina wouldn't need to marry Horace. Or Mr. Little.

Immediately she felt guilty.

Hadn't she already decided it was her duty to marry, to save her family and make a good match? And of course Horace was her childhood sweetheart—although he'd never known it. What was the matter with her that she could so easily be turned from her chosen course?

Tina had never considered herself flighty. She was practical, levelheaded, and here she was behaving like a silly debutante. And it was all the fault of Richard Eversham.

The meal finished, Lady Carol rose to her feet. "Ladies, shall we leave the gentlemen to their cigars and brandy?"

They followed her into the drawing room. Tina found herself hemmed in by her two friends, eager to hear why the scandalous Mr. Eversham had been invited to dinner.

"I didn't think he was welcome in polite society," Margaret said prissily. "His reputation!"

"But he's very handsome." Anne had a twinkle in her eye. "Don't you think so, Tina?"

Tina did think so but was not about to say it aloud, not when she noticed her mother listening avidly as she commanded the pouring of the tea. "Mr. Eversham's invitation was none of my doing," Lady Carol said firmly, "and so you should tell your mother, Anne, if she makes a fuss."

Anne didn't appear perturbed. "My mother makes a great deal of fuss over nothing. It is because I am an heiress, Lady Carol. But I think it is interesting and exciting to meet people who are so different from oneself."

"No, my dear," reprimanded Lady Carol. "It is neither interesting nor exciting, and there is a very good reason why men like Mr. Eversham are kept away from young ladies such as you. They are not to be trusted." She hesitated, finished pouring a cup, and handed it to a servant to carry to one of the guests. "Not like my Charles," she went on with a fond smile. "He is a dear boy, not an untrustworthy bone in his body."

Anne smiled back, eyes lowered, a flush in her cheeks.

The signs were there, Tina thought wryly, and her mother knew it. She only hoped she would be subtle and not upset the budding romance before it could begin to blossom.

"Mr. Little is an interesting gentleman." Margaret took a studied sip of her tea. "He was telling me about his tobacco. It is all very complicated, you know." Something in the way Margaret avoided their eyes made it obvious the girl was infatuated.

Oh dear, thought Tina, secretly relieved. *I've lost Mr. Little. Well, Mr. Eversham or no Mr. Eversham, somehow I must get Horace alone tonight and kiss him.*

Richard spent an uncomfortable twenty minutes in the library, with Lord Horace making pointed remarks about gentlemen who were not gentlemen, Sir Thomas looking embarrassed, and Sir Henry enjoying it all immensely.

"You wanted to come," he murmured to Richard, when the conversation had finally taken another turn.

"I didn't expect to be such a hit," Richard said wryly.

Sir Henry chuckled and puffed on his cigar before he replied. "I think it has worked out very well. Gilfoyle loathes you, and we've seen he is the sort of chap who doesn't bother hiding his feelings. Hotheaded I'd say. As for Little, he is a bit of a mystery man, isn't he? I'm not sure I believe the meek-and-mild act. Do you?"

"I think he is here because he has an interest in Miss Smythe," Richard said coolly.

"Oh?" Sir Henry was watching him, but Richard refused to meet his eyes. "And do you think that interest is reciprocated?"

Did he? Instinctively Richard decided he didn't, but perhaps that was just wishful thinking. When Tina had met his eyes over dinner, while Sir Henry's wife was rattling Lady Carol, he'd felt as if he'd found a kindred spirit. Someone who was enjoying the ridiculous humor in the situation as much as he, someone he could always rely on to understand perfectly how he was feeling, just as he understood how she was feeling.

Dangerous, very dangerous. Thinking like that could only get him into trouble.

"Anyway, at least we have a clearer picture of the men we're dealing with," Sir Henry went on without expecting an answer. "If one of them turned out to be the Captain, then I'd put my money on Gilfoyle."

Despite his dislike of the man Richard wasn't so certain. Gilfoyle was certainly a hothead, but it was men like Little, quiet and unobtrusive, who needed to be watched.

When they joined the ladies, he was amused to see Tina reluctantly seat herself at the pianoforte at her mother's prompting. Lady Carol was smiling at her daughter fondly, looking very different from the cold-eyed creature who had greeted him. But then he couldn't blame her for wanting to keep her daughter well away from the scandalous rogue who'd weaseled his way into her home.

Although Tina was a competent if not brilliant pianist, it was clear her heart wasn't in it. Richard watched narrow-eyed as Gilfoyle sauntered over to claim the spot next to her, launching into a song in a pleasing tenor. Tina and Gilfoyle exchanged smiles as he turned the pages for her. Little wandered over and stood behind them, waving away their invitations to join in, claiming his voice was unfit for such illustrious company.

"Your singing has much improved while you've been away," Horace said to Tina with unflattering candor. "It was dreadful at one stage—like a cat screeching."

"Thank you, Horace," she said with grave humor.

"Was singing one of the accomplishments taught at your finishing school?" asked Little.

"One of many," Tina teased.

Neither of them seemed to know how to respond.

Richard would have known; if she'd given him that provocative look, he'd have known exactly what to do. She was a lovely woman. Far too good for Gilfoyle or Little. Whether they were villains or innocents made no difference; she deserved better.

Eventually someone else was persuaded to display her piano playing, and Horace rose with Tina, while the young lady with the red hair led Little away. Tina lingered by the doors onto the terrace, engaging Horace in conversation.

Richard could see what she was up to. She had it in her mind to take Horace outside. It was a mild enough evening, and with everyone else busy, this was the perfect opportunity. Half of him was urging her on, but the other half . . . the other half didn't like it at all.

Soft music was drifting on the evening air, and there was a strong scent of lilies from the garden. Tina was well aware that Lady Carol had had to let the gardener go, but as yet there was no sign that the area was untended. No doubt it would soon take on the appearance of a jungle, and Horace would gasp in shock, but for the moment he seemed more interested in her.

There was something in his expression. A mixture of puzzlement and curiosity, as if she had changed in some way, and he couldn't fathom what it was. Or perhaps it was his perception of her that had changed.

Her heartbeat quickened. Were Richard Eversham's lessons working? Had Horace begun to see her as the desirable and passionate woman she longed to be? And, perhaps more importantly, as a future wife?

"Tina," he said, his voice dropping lower, as he moved toward her.

Breathlessly, she waited.

He took her gloved hand in his and placed it in the crook of his elbow. "There," he said, with satisfaction, "the path looks a little uneven. Shall we walk a little?"

"If you like."

He spoiled it by patting her hand in a paternal fashion and led her down the stairs onto the path that wound into the garden. The air was cooler here, and Tina could hear the voices from the open windows behind them. Lady Isabelle was speaking loudly again, this time about a ball she'd attended where two of the guests had eloped, while Sir Henry attempted to moderate her enthusiasm for the idea.

"I do not think that was a good match," Horace spoke abruptly. "Lady Isabelle and Sir Henry Arlington. I don't know how he puts up with her."

Tina had wondered, too, but perversely, on hearing Horace say it, she wanted to stick up for Isabelle. "She has strong beliefs, Horace, there's nothing wrong with that."

"Isn't there? I prefer my women less strong in their beliefs, and certainly a bit more biddable. I can't imagine Lady Isabelle ever being very easy company, can you, Tina?"

"Perhaps they get on very well together when they are alone."

"I think they probably go to opposite ends of the house and stay there."

"That does not sound like a recipe for a happy marriage."

Horace laughed at her glum tone. "I don't know. If it suits them, then it might be a very good recipe. Not everyone is the same, Tina, you should know that. Not everyone is going to end up in a nursery-tale romance." He smiled down at her. "I remember that when you were a little girl you were determined to find the frog who was a prince. Do you remember?"

Tina tried not to, and she shuddered now. "No," she said stubbornly.

He laughed again. "Yes, you do." He paused and turned to face her. "You know you do."

Tina realized he'd led her just far enough along the path so that they were out of sight of the windows. Clever Horace. He took her hands in his and gave them a squeeze. "Warmer now?"

"Yes." Her heart beat faster.

"I always enjoy your company, Tina."

"Do you? I wonder if you do, Horace. We have known each other so long, and yet there is always more to discover, don't you think?"

He smiled. He bent closer.

Was he about to kiss her? Then why was he taking so long.

Suddenly she couldn't bear to wait any longer. Horace was too slow and if she was going to kiss him, then it must be now, before her practical mind argued her out of it. Tina reached up and placed her hands on his shoulders, gazing up at his face in the moonlight.

"Horace," she murmured, "what if I were to pretend you were a frog now?"

He stared at her a moment as she looked up at him with shining eyes, her lips softly parted. And then he burst out laughing.

"Tina," he gasped, "you are priceless!"

She backed away from him, stumbling on the

path. Now he was doubled over and to her chagrin incapable of speaking.

She turned and began to hurry away. Behind her she could hear him still laughing, and it only added fuel to her anger and humiliation. Tears sprang to her eyes—tears of fury, she told herself—and rolled down her cheeks. She couldn't see where she was going, everything was a blur, and when she blundered into the hard masculine body in front of her, she thought at first it must be Horace.

"Let me go," her voice wobbled as she struggled in his grip. "I don't want to speak to you ever again."

"Miss Smythe . . . Tina?"

That warm, deep voice could only belong to one man: Richard Eversham.

She stopped struggling and peered up at him, blinking to clear her gaze. He was a silhouette against the pale lights from the house, and then he'd drawn her off the path and into the foliage, sitting her down on a stone bench placed beneath a fragrant honeysuckle arch. The air was damp and cool, enclosing her, and she wanted to sob against his shoulder and be held in his arms.

"What is it?" he commanded. "Tell me."

He was holding her hands, and she could feel his hard grip through her gloves, while his thigh brushed hers on the seat—it wasn't really made for two. "I'd rather not," she faltered miserably.

"Did he hurt you?" he demanded, bending his head to see her face. He let go of one hand and used his fingertip to smooth away her tears. He was so gentle, it eased her aching heart amazingly.

"No," she said huskily. "At least, not in the way you're thinking."

"Then tell me," he insisted, tipping up her chin so that she had no choice but to look into his face, into his eyes.

She licked her lips. It was a relief to let the words spill out. "I did everything you said. I rested my hands on his shoulders and stepped close to him. I could feel the-the heat from his body. He was looking at me as if he wanted to kiss me. I'm sure he *did* want to kiss me. But he was taking so long!"

A frown creased between his slashing black brows. "What do you mean?"

"I didn't want to wait, in case I changed my mind, I just wanted him to kiss me and make everything all right, so I decided I would kiss him instead of waiting for him to kiss me. Only it all went wrong," she ended, her voice catching.

"How did it go wrong?" he insisted, and she knew he wasn't going to let her off without hearing the entire truth.

So, reluctantly, but with a certain sense of relief, she told him.

Chapter 13

❦

Richard bit his lip, struggling with laughter. And delight. Serve Horace Gilfoyle right, he *was* a frog. But now definitely wasn't the time to say so to Tina.

He took a steadying breath and softened his tone. "Oh dear, Tina."

She tried to pull away, but he held her, gently but implacably. He sensed that if she got away now, he'd never catch her. She gave a choking sob, her body resting trustingly against his.

"I'll never be able to convince him that I'm the woman he wants to marry. Not now. He'll never let me forget what I said. I know him. He will d-delight in reminding me at every o-opportunity."

"Hush, stop it, Tina."

After a moment, she did, giving a decisive sniff. He handed her his handkerchief and she dabbed at her eyes.

"Actually I think it was rather endearing."

"Endearing?" She looked up at him in astonishment. "Would *you* have laughed?"

He told her the truth. "Yes, but I would have

kissed you, too. He's a fool to have let the opportunity pass. You must make him suffer for it, you do know that, don't you? You can't forgive him too easily. You must make him work for the privilege of kissing you now."

She liked that idea; he could see it in the curve of her sweet mouth.

Richard shifted a little uncomfortably on his seat as desire dug its claws into him. Just as well it was so dark here, although she was too innocent to know what the bulge in his trousers meant. Increasingly he became aware of the brush of her skirt against his thigh and fantasized that it was her skin. Imagined laying her back over his arm, while his mouth was busy on her breasts. Licking, tugging, kissing. And she would be sighing and moaning and begging him for more.

"Show me how you put your hands on his shoulders," he heard himself saying in a husky voice. "Show me how you were going to kiss him."

She hesitated, and for a moment he thought she was going to show good sense and refuse, but no, she was turning toward him. She reached up to smooth her palms across his broad shoulders, settling them to her satisfaction, and then she gazed up into his face from the shadow of the honeysuckle arch. Her green eyes gleamed.

"Like this," she whispered.

"And what did you plan to do?" he said, knowing he was mad to persist with this and unable to stop himself.

She wriggled a little closer. "I planned to brush my mouth over his, just gently, just to see what he would do." Again she followed her words with actions. He tried not to groan aloud. "And kiss the corners of his lips, and perhaps lick him with my tongue, to taste him."

This time he did groan. He couldn't help it. As she teased him with her lips, he followed her mouth with his. Capturing it. Kissing her with a deepening passion. Although he was far gone, a part of his brain still expected her to reject him, push him away. But Tina responded instantly, clinging to him, her breasts hard against his chest while he lightly caressed her throat and bare shoulders, skipping the dress sleeves to run his fingers over her arms to the edges of her long evening gloves.

There wasn't enough bare skin to find and touch, and he wanted more.

Much more.

She tried to pull away, and for a moment he thought he'd finally frightened her with his desire, but as he opened his mouth to apologize, she put her fingertips against his lips. Then he heard it, too. The sound of footsteps quickly approaching down the path. He drew her back into his arms, so that she rested against him, feeling her quickening breath against the hollow of his throat, the clutch of her hand on his lapel.

It was Horace Gilfoyle.

They could see him through the shielding screen of shrubs. He was walking with his head down, and as they watched, he paused and gave a chuckle. The next moment it was as if he felt their gazes upon him because he lifted his head, suddenly alert, and peered into the shadows.

"Tina?" he called softly. "Tina, where are you?

Do come out. I didn't mean to laugh, but you have to admit, it was very-very funny."

He could hardly keep his continence at the memory, and Richard felt her stiffen and held her tighter in case she decided to fly out of cover and attack her future husband. But then Horace gave a sigh and moved on toward the house, and they were alone again.

He stroked her silky back. "It's all right. He's gone. And he's already regretting what he did."

"No he's not," she retorted, keeping her voice low with an effort. "He thinks it's all so hilarious. He will tell everyone, particularly Charles. They'll giggle every time they see me. They're like schoolboys when it comes to something like this."

"Tina, stop it." He pulled her to her feet and turned her to him. "Listen to me. Are you listening?"

Startled, she stared up at him. "I'm listening," she whispered.

"You will ignore them because you are above all that. Above them. Believe me, Lord Horace will regret what he did. Think a moment, ask yourself why he lured you out here? Alone? He's interested. He isn't completely yours, not yet, but he will be soon."

She stared at him a moment longer, and then she asked, "Why are you here tonight? I don't understand why you are here."

Awkward question. Richard did his best to answer it without actually answering it.

"I thought you wanted me here. That's what you told me."

"Yes"—she eyed him suspiciously—"but I

didn't think you could make it happen. My mother is furious. You are-you are . . ."

"Not suitable for polite society? A rogue? A rake? A scoundrel without conscience? A seducer? Someone not to be trusted with a lady's virtue? A man about town? Come, Tina, what am I?"

He was angry, and he couldn't hide it. He knew he was called all of those things, and perhaps long ago as a boy he had been such a creature, but now it was all a game, a necessary role he was playing. The real Richard Eversham was someone else, someone dangerous, someone who lived in the shadows, someone Tina would be better off not knowing.

Suddenly he felt a wave of despair wash over him. It seemed ages since he'd had a normal conversation with someone without thinking about the Guardians and how best to get information for them. Every situation he found himself in these days had something to do with his work. With hunting his brother's killer. How would he ever return to normal once Anthony's killer was brought to justice? *If* he was brought to justice.

Because Richard had made a vow to continue the hunt for as long as it took, and until then his entire life, his entire future, was in limbo.

He came to himself with a start. Tina was touching his face, her gloved finger stroking the corner of his mouth. "Don't be angry," she whispered. "I didn't mean to hurt your feelings. I don't think of you like that at all. It was just that your being here made it more difficult for me to play my part, to remember what you'd told me to do. I kept thinking about you instead."

He struggled to regain his usual charm—

although he was so good at playing *his part* she would never have known that his smile was forced. He captured her hand and kissed her palm, folding her fingers inside his. "I'm not angry with you, Tina."

She smiled, glancing at him through her lashes in that innocent-provocative manner he found so enchanting. "I'm glad." She was so delightful that Richard wanted to kiss her again, but he knew he must refrain. He'd done enough for one night—he must not ruin her reputation beyond repair.

Tina gave a furtive glance over her shoulder toward the house. "I must go in. My mother will be frantic, and if you are seen to be missing, too!" Her eyes sparkled, and she gave a giggle. "Imagine what she will be thinking."

"Imagine what Horace will be thinking," he said meaningfully. "He will be jealous, Tina. And you must make the most of it. Shrug indifferently if he begins to lecture you on your morals. He has no leg to stand on there. Give a secretive little smile if he asks you what you were doing."

Her smile faded a little. She glanced at him as they regained the path. "I know Horace is a man about town, but is he very bad? I mean, does he have a mistress? Or two? I don't know if I want to marry a man who has a mistress."

Richard wondered if he should enlighten her as to the state of most marriages in polite society but decided this was neither the place nor the time. "It is a fashionable affectation," he said with a shrug. "Once he marries you, he will change his ways."

"Yes, of course," Tina replied briskly, but he heard the doubt in her voice.

She'd told him that Horace was the love of her

life, her childhood sweetheart, and yet she was behaving as though this marriage was not for love at all. As if it was something she must do despite the fact that she didn't particularly want to do it.

Richard reminded himself he must speak to Archie and get to the bottom of all this.

They were nearly at the terrace now, and he stopped and moved back. "Go on alone, Tina. We mustn't be seen together. And come to see me tomorrow. Can you do that?"

She looked at him as if she didn't want to let him go. He felt his body responding to her and clamped down on his feelings. What he was imagining was madness, and a dangerous sort of madness. There was far too much at stake to muddy the waters with an ill-conceived passion.

"If I can, I will," she promised. "But don't you have any other clients to see? I wouldn't want to monopolize your time."

"At the moment, you are my most important client," he said gallantly, with a bow.

He watched as Tina hurried up the stairs and in through the open glass doors of the drawing room. There was a rise in sound, as though her entrance had caused a stir, and then her mother came to whisk her farther into the room and beyond his sight.

Richard found a cigar and lit it, spending some time deep in thought.

And, he admitted wryly, allowing his body to calm itself. Eventually he made his way back into the house, slipping unobtrusively inside and making certain to attach himself to Sir Henry, where he remained until it was time to leave.

Tina had known she wouldn't get off lightly, and as she'd feared, Lady Carol came to her room as she was preparing for bed.

"What on earth were you thinking! Going off into the garden like that. Horace was most concerned for you."

"Horace?" she said, taken aback.

"He said you had a little tiff. What was it about?"

Her mother had warned her about gentlemen like Horace taking advantage, and Tina used it to her own advantage now. "He tried to kiss me," she murmured, looking away as if the memory was a shameful one.

"A kiss?" Lady Carol declared. "Is that all? My dear, if you mean to marry the man, you will have to bear rather more than his kisses!"

Tina was startled, and so was her mother, so to Tina's relief no more was said.

When Maria came to brush her hair, Tina was so agitated that it took a while for her to realize that Maria seemed a little agitated herself. After the maid had pulled her hair for the third time, Tina took the brush from her, and said, "Maria, whatever is it?"

Maria twisted her hands together, her dark eyes anxious. "I heard Mr. Eversham was at dinner, miss. Is that true?"

"Yes, he was." Tina spoke evenly and tried not to remember kissing him, in case, she thought superstitiously, Maria saw it in her eyes. "Do you know him, Maria?"

"No, I don't know him. I . . . that is, I . . ." Maria was definitely worried about something.

"Tell me, for heaven's sake."

"I know his man, miss. Archie Jones."

"His man?" She knew Archie!

"His servant. Butler. Valet." Maria gave an uncharacteristically nervous laugh. "He's all three."

Tina blinked. "Archie Jones," she said cautiously. What had Archie told Maria? Did she know about her visits to Richard Eversham? She must not tell Lady Carol.

Now it was Tina's turn to be worried.

"We're, eh, walking out, miss. In a way. Nothing serious, just friends."

Tina turned to her reflection in the mirror and began to brush her own hair. "I don't understand. How did you meet him, Maria?"

"We just sort of bumped into each other, miss," Maria explained rather vaguely.

"He hasn't mentioned me?"

Maria started. "Goodness no, miss, why should he?"

Tina shrugged as if it were unimportant. "I-I know Mr. Eversham. A little. You must say nothing to anyone, Maria, it is entirely a business matter, and my parents would be sure to think the worst. Please, promise me you will say nothing to anyone."

"I promise, miss," Maria spoke with passion, and Tina believed her.

"Thank you, Maria."

The maid took the brush from Tina and began to resume her duties with more care. The sensation of the brush against Tina's scalp was soothing.

"Why did you ask about Mr. Eversham, Maria?" Tina asked dreamily. "Was it because of Archie?"

Maria seemed to be in a dream of her own and took a moment to answer. "Yes, miss, that was it. I knew he wasn't the sort of man to . . . well, from what Archie says, he's not known to be much in polite society."

Tina was satisfied with that, and soon she was tucked up in bed with the house silent about her. She was tired, and yet she couldn't seem to fall asleep for longer than a few moments.

She kept remembering her blunder with Horace, which made her prickly with dismay and embarrassment, and then her thoughts would turn to Richard's kissing her, and that made her feel warm and restless. She'd planned to visit him tomorrow. She wanted to. But she was beginning to wonder if that was a good idea.

Tina knew she was meant to be capturing Horace, to be concentrating solely on Horace, and here she was spending her time thinking about Richard. If she was going to succeed with her plan to marry Horace, then she really would have to stop allowing herself to be sidetracked into deliciously unknown territory.

Chapter 14

Richard opened the door of Sir Henry's office in Whitehall, obeying his instruction to enter. As usual the room was full of cigar smoke, and Sir Henry was frowning over a stack of papers.

"Ah, Richard, here you are. Well, what did you think of our candidates for the Captain?"

"I favor Gilfoyle although Little is an interesting character. Have you found out any more about him?"

Sir Henry was thoughtful. "I have made some inquiries, but he's a cagey fellow. It's as if he arrived in the tobacco-importing business fully formed. I can't find out very much about his early years, but he's certainly done well for himself since then. Keeps to himself, too. Doesn't seem to be much in the style of Gilfoyle, so their friendship, if that's what it is, appears odd."

Richard sat down, feeling his eyes begin to water from the smoke. He considered throwing open a window, but he knew that Sir Henry was particularly anxious about being overheard, and there were always listening ears in Whitehall.

"What do you think the state of play is with Miss Smythe and Gilfoyle?" Sir Henry asked curiously, glancing up at Richard from under his bushy eyebrows. "Can't see much sign of an impending marriage. What was all that fuss last night about Miss Smythe's vanishing into the garden after a tiff?"

"The man is a fool," Richard said shortly.

Sir Henry grunted.

"You know the Smythes well, sir?"

"I knew the father in the army, but it was a long time ago. We have remained friends, but I wouldn't say I knew him intimately. The wife was the one with the money—it was a love match. Lady Carol is rather fond of show, and she would be keen for her daughter to marry a man who could set her up in style, and Gilfoyle is that man."

"I know I asked you to get me an invitation, but I was surprised you managed it."

Sir Henry grinned wolfishly. "Jolly fun wasn't it? If they but knew the truth, eh? But, seriously, I hope you receive proper recognition for your work one day, Richard."

"I don't need recognition, sir, just let me have Anthony's killer."

Sir Henry fiddled with his papers. "There have been whispers—not loud ones mind, Sir Thomas keeps things close to his chest—but there have been whispers that he is in a hole, financially. Lost Lady Carol's fortune. But that might explain why the girl is so eager to marry Gilfoyle."

Richard had suspected this was so; it made sense. Now he wondered if Tina was a willing participant or whether this was an example of her being the dutiful daughter. After last night he was beginning to favor the latter.

"Isabelle is keen for a weekend country house party." While Richard was cogitating, Sir Henry had moved on. "She's younger than I, gets bored with nothing to do. Got to keep her busy. We'll be sending you an invitation, Richard. Don't worry, there'll be plenty for you to do. I'm asking Gilfoyle and Little, too. And the Smythes and their friends." He rubbed his hands together in anticipation. "Throw the whole lot of them together, eh, and see what happens? I wouldn't be surprised if something major crops up."

Richard tried not to shudder at the wasps' nest his commander was putting together. But Sir Henry's plans usually did work out, and if it meant they could flush out the Captain, then well and good. He just hoped there weren't repercussions.

"I still want you to go to Kent and take a reccy," Sir Henry went on, "but wait until after the weekend party, just in case we learn something more."

"Very well, sir: a reconnaissance to Kent."

"Nice girl."

"Pardon?"

Sir Henry looked up with assumed surprise. "Miss Smythe. Nice girl. Don't you think? Delightful."

"Yes."

Richard left it at that, but he could see his superior smirking to himself. Well, let him! Richard wasn't about to discuss with Sir Henry his feelings for Tina and the personal doubts that were beginning to afflict him. Once all he'd cared about was finding Anthony's killer, with no thought of what might happen next.

But Tina Smythe was forcing him to ask himself those questions. Uncomfortable questions. And with the questions came a tentative hope for the future.

It was early afternoon and Lady Carol and Sir Thomas had left the house for an appointment at the bank. Tina, who was waiting impatiently to fulfill her own appointment, changed quickly into her favorite blue dress with the matching bonnet. She'd been planning to go to Jasmine Square on her own, but now Maria knew about Mr. Eversham and was seeing Archie, it seemed prudent to take her, too. Then, if questions were asked, she could always say she was shopping with Maria.

They set off on foot. Lady Carol and Sir Thomas had taken the coach, but it was such a lovely day Tina was happy to walk. She noticed that Maria had taken some pains with her appearance and smiled to herself. She could not remember Maria's ever having a gentleman caller. Was that through choice, or was there some secret in Maria's past that stopped her from trusting men? Whatever the reason, Tina decided she would encourage this romance. At Maria's age this might be her last chance for happiness.

The door of Number Five opened so quickly, Tina was sure Archie had been lurking about inside, awaiting their arrival. "Miss Smythe," he said formally, and then his smile broadened. "And Miss Baez."

"Good morning, Archie," said Tina pleasantly.

"Would you mind keeping Maria company while I have my chat with Mr. Eversham?"

"Mr. Jones must be busy," interrupted an agitated Maria. "I'm quite able to occupy myself, miss."

"Actually, Miss Baez, I was about to go on a message for Mr. Eversham. It shouldn't take long, and we could walk. Would you care to join me?"

Maria glanced uncertainly at Tina. "Miss? Should I wait for you here?"

"Not at all, Maria. I am perfectly safe with Mr. Eversham. Go and enjoy your walk."

Archie stepped forward. "I'll just see you up first, Miss—"

"Nonsense," Tina interrupted Archie. "I'm quite capable of walking up a few steps on my own. Mr. Eversham is expecting me, is he not?"

"Yes, miss."

"Then you may go."

"Thank you, miss." He smiled at Maria, his eyes twinkling more than ever, and Tina couldn't help but smile herself at their obvious attraction to each other.

When they'd gone, Tina made her way up the narrow staircase. She felt curiously agitated and told herself it was because she knew that her mother would be horrified at her behavior. But that wasn't the real truth. She'd slept badly. Nothing seemed to be going as she'd expected and planned. And she found herself thinking more and more about Richard Eversham and less and less about Horace.

Richard opened the door to her gentle knock. "Tina," he said, holding out his hand.

Her heart gave a bump. She took his hand, as

always aware of his hard body radiating warmth close to her, and he drew her into the cozy room. The shades were drawn against the afternoon sunshine, making the light muted, and yet it felt bright and welcoming.

Was that because he was here?

Shaking off her abstraction, Tina accepted his offer of a seat on the sofa, removing her gloves and bonnet and setting them beside her. Tina's head had begun to ache, and she told herself it was from too much thinking. She had her plan, she must follow it. Horace was her target. Anything else was completely unacceptable.

But the words sounded like she was repeating them as a child repeats times tables, and they no longer held any meaning.

"You didn't tell me how you came to be there last night," she said, with a crease of her forehead.

"Didn't I?" His smile was bland, his expression unreadable. "I am a friend of Sir Henry. He knew my father. They were in the army together."

More army friends. That explained it then. Although not completely. It occurred to her that despite his charm and warmth, Richard was a man of secrets. She had placed her future and her reputation in the hands of a man she barely knew.

Aware of the silence, she looked up and found him watching her, that seductive, charming smile curving the corners of his lips. She wanted to trust him, she really did.

"I didn't do a very good job, did I?" she blurted out. "With Horace, I mean."

"These things take time, Tina. You mustn't give up yet."

"Is that what you tell your other clients? How

many actually succeed in marrying the person of their choice?"

"I've had one . . . no, *two* failures, and they were for reasons beyond my control. So you are in safe hands."

Instinctively, her gaze dropped to his hands. She remembered the heat of them against her bare skin, his confident, smooth touch, and the sound he'd made when she kissed him, as if he wasn't quite in control of himself after all.

Her mind was drifting again.

To pull herself back, she spoke briskly of the first thing that came to her head. "Maria, my maid, is walking out with Archie. Did you know that?"

"I did. Archie told me."

"It is strange that they should come together like this. Maria seems to think it was coincidence."

"An accident of fate."

"He won't hurt her, will he?" she said quickly. "She has been on her own for years—as long as she's been our maid."

"Archie isn't the sort of man to hurt a woman, and certainly not one he cares about. Even so, I'll have a word with him."

"Of course my mother will be horrified when she discovers he's your servant. I just hope she doesn't put a stop to it before it's had a chance to begin."

Richard raised a dark eyebrow. "My apologies for my scandalous reputation, but I can assure you Archie is entirely his own man. He's never come to me for advice where his love life is concerned."

She wondered if she'd hurt his feelings. He wasn't showing any emotion, but she sensed something beneath his urbane manner. And yet he had no reason to feel hurt; she'd only spoken the truth. His reputation *was* bad, and Lady Carol might well interfere if she thought her maid was in moral peril.

"Speaking of reputations, I'm surprised that Gilfoyle has never tried anything with you," Richard interrupted her thoughts. His gray eyes were watchful, almost brooding.

"What sort of anything?" she asked warily. "You mean has he attempted to seduce me?"

"Yes."

"No, he hasn't."

"Have you wondered why?"

"Perhaps because he has no interest in me. That *is* why I've come to you."

"So he has never tried to touch you? Never?"

Tina hesitated. She could change the subject now—that is what she should do—but Tina knew it wasn't what she wanted to do. There was a wicked creature stirring inside her, a temptress, and suddenly she gave in to it.

"Touch me?" she asked, being deliberately obtuse. "Touch me in what way, Mr. Eversham?"

But he was too cautious to be drawn on that.

"Your mother must have told you what liberties you should permit a gentleman?"

Tina waved a hand. "She mentioned something about it. Actually we discussed it recently. She said that although I must not let a gentleman touch me, I can let him look. Because, she says, a gentleman will not buy what he can have for free."

He chuckled.

"Surely that is a contradiction in terms?" she

added in a puzzled voice. "A *gentleman* should be beyond reproach in such matters."

"Tina, if you believe that, you have a lot to learn."

"That is what she said," Tina replied glumly.

Richard steepled his hands under his chin, as if, she thought, in amusement, he was about to impart to her the wisdom of the ages.

"In essence I agree with Lady Carol, particularly in Gilfoyle's case. Although a little touching can be good, too. Men like Gilfoyle, who are used to getting their own way, can be driven mad by a little touching if they're then refused the ultimate prize."

Tina wondered where he was going with this. She was beginning to feel very warm. *The ultimate prize.* She was tempted to ask him more about that but bailed out at the last moment.

"So what is acceptable?" she asked instead, wondering at her daring. "I am at a loss here, Mr. Eversham. I believed any contact, apart from a clasp of the hand, was unacceptable. But here you are telling me I can go further."

"I am indeed." His gaze was fixed on her with an intensity that set her skin prickling.

"I think you should demonstrate."

He went still, as if he, too, was making some inner decisions. Was he beginning to wonder, as she was, whether their meetings were no longer about business? Whether there was something much deeper happening between them?

"If you will permit me?"

At her abrupt nod, he rose and sat close beside her on the sofa. Reaching out, he gently stroked her cheek with the backs of his fingers. "This is quite acceptable. And here." He traced the delicate curve of her ear. "And here." He caressed her neck.

Tina felt herself becoming languid. She wanted to lean into him and kiss his mouth. She wanted him to touch her in other places, places she knew very well were unacceptable. She heard herself saying the words, shocked at her own forwardness.

"And where *shouldn't* he touch me?"

His eyes met hers, a strange glitter in them, and then he reached out and touched the pale skin directly above her décolletage. For a moment, he hesitated, as if waiting for her to tell him to stop, and then his hand slipped inside her dress and stroked the swell of her breast.

"This is a definite no-no," he rasped. His fingers lingered, brushing her soft skin, delving inside her chemise, until the tip of one finger actually came into contact with her nipple.

A river of heat ran through her, making her gasp. Reluctantly it seemed he removed his hand from her breast.

"I can see why," she managed in a curiously prim voice for one indulging in such wicked behavior. "Is there . . . is there anywhere else I must not let a gentleman touch me, Mr. Eversham?"

"Oh yes," he said with enthusiasm. "Most definitely."

"Then I think you had better show me."

"All of them?"

"It is important I know, don't you think? To protect myself?"

"Oh yes, extremely important."

His gaze swept over her, and again he hesitated. For an expert at seduction he was a little shy, Tina thought. He was supposed to be teaching her, and yet it was Tina who reached out to place her palm flat against his linen shirt and beneath that the hard heat of his chest.

"Richard," she murmured, "kiss me again. I really think I'm getting the hang of it."

For a moment, she thought he was going to refuse, the grand seducer refusing to seduce, but then she was in his arms, and he was kissing her with a passion that was savage and possessive and quite wonderful.

Chapter 15

The Serpentine had the sheen of glass, and Maria walked slowly by Archie's side, enjoying the warmth on her head beneath her straw bonnet and the dappled shade from the trees in Hyde Park. It was an oasis of calm here in the center of the busy city. London was a bustling place, and she loved it, so why did she still long for the baked plains and cool groves of her homeland?

Maria knew in her heart that was the reason she'd never put down roots here, why she'd remained single and alone. She'd always pictured herself returning home to Spain. She still did.

"You said you were surprised that your mistress knew my master," Archie said, breaking the companionable silence and returning to a topic of conversation they'd begun earlier.

"Yes, I was surprised. He is hardly respectable, and the Smythes are very respectable," she said. "When Miss Smythe told me she and Mr. Eversham were acquainted, I was concerned."

"You shouldn't listen to gossip."

She shot him an impatient look. "If her reputation is ruined, then she will never marry a gentleman. She will be a social outcast. You know how it is, Archie. You are no fool. My mistress's reputation is all she has to offer to her husband, and if it is soiled, then she has nothing."

Archie appeared uncomfortable at her reprimand, and she chose this moment, while he was off balance, to ask the question that had been niggling at her since they first met.

"Archie, was it Mr. Eversham who asked you to make the acquaintance of a member of the Smythe household?"

Her directness startled him and yet seemed to please him, too. "You are a very forthright woman, Maria," he said admiringly.

"I do not like liars, Archie."

He gave a grimace. "I'm sorry. Yes, it's true I bumped into you on purpose. How did you know?"

She made a scoffing sound. "I saw you from the window, walking back and forth, waiting. It intrigued me so I went out to see what you wanted. And then I decided I wanted to know you better, to find out what you were up to. You see, *I* am a spy."

He laughed at that as if he found it hilarious, while she glared at him.

"What is it, Archie? You must tell me the truth now or I will turn and walk away and you will never see me again. But perhaps that is what you want? Perhaps our friendship has never been more to you than a matter of expedience."

She wasn't sure her plan would work. Perhaps he really didn't care whether or not he saw her again. And yet despite her misgivings and her doubts about their future, in her heart she knew she would be sorry if this was their last meeting.

After a long, anxious moment he sighed, and said, "I can't tell you everything. There are reasons for that, and again I can't go into them. But yes, you're quite right, I needed someone inside Mallory Street so that I can discover why Miss Tina seems hell-bent on marrying Lord Horace Gilfoyle."

Maria pursed her lips. "The Smythes are almost bankrupt; Lord Horace is rich. Draw your own conclusion."

Again Archie was taken aback by her frankness.

"Well, that is what you want to know, isn't it? What your master had set you to find out? But now you must tell me why he is so interested in Miss Tina's doings. Perhaps he is in love with her himself."

Archie snorted. "Mr. Eversham in love? Now that would be a turn up." He grew serious. "Don't believe everything you hear about him, Maria. He has his reasons for what he's doing but believe me it's not Tina Smythe."

Maria eyed him warily. "You almost make me afraid, Archie, and not just for Miss Tina's virtue. What are his reasons? Please don't tell me he is a fortune hunter! Because if he is, he's chosen the wrong young lady."

"He has plenty of money of his own," Archie blurted out. "No, this is a government thing, Maria. A hush-hush thing. I can't tell you any more, honestly I can't, but he doesn't mean her any harm. Mr. Eversham's more likely to save her from danger than place her in it."

"But—"

"No, you'll just have to be satisfied with that. Now come"—and he slipped her hand through his arm—"enjoy the walk. Pretend we are without a care in the world, Maria."

She looked like she might continue to protest, but then she changed her mind and relaxed, giving him a tight little smile. "Very well, Archie. But the next time we meet I will have more questions, you know I will, and you must find a way of answering them."

They walked some more before she spoke again.

"I have told Miss Tina that we are 'walking out' together, Archie. I'm sorry but it seemed best. I wanted to continue to see you, to discover what you were up to, and I needed a subterfuge."

Archie chuckled in delight. "Walking out, Maria?"

"You can break it off with me if you wish," she said, gazing at the river in a studied manner. "I do not mind. It is all pretend anyway. My heart will not be broken."

"Is it? All pretend, I mean?"

His tone brought her head around. He was watching her almost shyly, and Maria didn't pretend not to understand.

"Perhaps it is not quite all pretend," she conceded. "And perhaps my heart would be a little bit broken, after all."

Archie smiled. "Then let's just carry on as we are, Maria. You help me with my spying, and I will help you with yours. Will we shake on it?" He held out his hand to her.

It was a typically masculine thing to do, but solemnly Maria shook his hand. "Here's to spying, Archie."

His smile broadened, and his eyes twinkled. "Here's to spying, Maria."

Richard knew he must stop. He wasn't sure what Tina's objective was, but she was playing a very dangerous game for a woman who wanted to marry someone else.

The reminder that she was to marry Gilfoyle was like a hot dagger in his brain. He wasn't sure whether that was because he wanted her for himself or because Gilfoyle might be the Captain, but if he kept kissing her like this, then all his plans would be undone.

Reluctantly he pulled away.

She lay against him, compliant, her breasts rising and falling quickly, her eyes closed, long, dark lashes lying against her flushed cheeks. Her mouth was pink and swollen from kissing.

Richard couldn't help but smile in pure male satisfaction. He hadn't lost his touch then.

He should be asking her questions about Gilfoyle, using her as a source of information, gathering all her secrets. But he wasn't. Instead he felt protective of her and he was reluctant to spoil their little idyll.

To feel that way made no sense at all.

He might tell himself she was just another woman, and he'd had plenty, but it wasn't the truth. There was something different about this one, something that was turning his usually sharp intelligence—his ability to make sacrifices for the greater good—to heroic mush. Tina was becoming his priority; Tina was what he thought of when he woke up, and it was Tina again when he went to bed.

"Tina? Sweetheart, wake up," he murmured gently. "Your maid will be back in a moment."

That brought her to her senses. Her eyes sprang open, and she sat up, a hand to her tumbled hair. She was a mess. Had he done that? Of course he had. Well, it must not happen again. With a new sense of resolve he began the search for her hair pins.

A moment later there was a quiet knock on the door, but by then they were ready to face the staff.

"Miss Tina? I'm very sorry we were so long," Maria spoke quickly. She was rather red in the face and short of breath, obviously more concerned about her own shortcomings than her mistress's.

"I'm afraid we lost track of time, sir," Archie added apologetically but didn't appear very sorry.

"Well you are here now," Tina said.

Richard watched admiringly as she rose calmly to her feet and held out her hand to him. She was so poised he doubted his own memory, but no, it was true; a few moments before they had been clasped in each other's arms on the verge of doing something irreversible. Damn it, but her acting was getting better by the day.

"Good-bye, Mr. Eversham," she said primly. "I shall be in t-touch with you soon."

Oh dear! Tina almost groaned aloud. Why did she stumble over that particular word? "Touch." Why was it that a word that had never had a secondary meaning before now have so many? The feel of his hands against her skin, the touch of his mouth against hers, against her throat, against every inch of her he could find without actually taking off her clothes. In fact, oh Lord, had she asked him to take them off? No, surely not. But yes, she remembered her breathless voice, pleading . . .

Tina swallowed and lifted her chin, hoping Maria hadn't noticed her agitation. Richard certainly had. His gray eyes sparkled with wicked laughter although his face was grave. Oh yes, he was a man who was good at keeping secrets.

"Good-bye, Miss Smythe," he said, holding her hand briefly, as a gentleman would. She turned and tried not to run down the stairs to the front door. Escape, it was all she wanted now. Escape from him . . . and herself.

The door to Number Five closed. She had taken two steps before Maria began to castigate her. Yes, yes, she knew she was behaving in a dangerous and reckless manner, yes, she knew she was risking her reputation, this was all fact, but it was for a purpose. That was her defense.

"Maria, I know you are worried about me, but please believe me when I tell you that I am perfectly safe. I know what I'm doing."

"Do you?" Maria replied with a note of desperation. "Miss, beg pardon, but I think you are being very, very foolish. This man is not to be trusted. What would Lady Carol say? Shall I tell her, is that what you want?"

Tina stopped walking and turned to face her maid. "Of course I don't want you to tell Lady Carol. Maria, I *must* marry Lord Horace. You know why. Do I have to speak it aloud, here, in the street?"

Maria calmed herself, as if suddenly aware of interested passersby. "No, miss, you don't have to do that. I know why. But that does not explain what has been happening between you and Mr. Eversham."

Mr. Eversham who, Maria now knew from Archie, was not at all what he seemed.

"I am learning from Mr. Eversham. He is teaching me how to win over a man like Horace. That is all. It is purely a business arrangement."

"And is that why your hair is all falling down and your cheeks all flushed? No, Miss Tina, do not try to flummox me."

Tina pursed her mouth into a stubborn line. "I am not trying to do anything of the sort. If I am a little flushed, it is because I am learning how to kiss. There! Now you are shocked. But how can I ever win a man like Horace, a man of the world, if I don't learn to be the sort of woman he wants?"

Maria thought that was probably true, but Lord Horace was a nasty piece of work, and she longed to tell Tina so. But what would that achieve? Even if Tina believed her—which was extremely doubtful—she would still feel she had to marry him, for her family's sake. No, Maria decided, best to keep that particular piece of information to herself for the moment. It might be useful later on, as a final effort to halt this madness.

"Miss Tina, I am still very worried."

"Well please don't be, Maria. I am perfectly able to take care of myself."

That brought a halt to the conversation, and they said no more on the journey home although Tina remained anxious and upset, and Maria remained anxious and troubled. Neither of them wanted to fall out with the other so it seemed better to remain silent.

When they reached Mallory Street, Tina learned that her father wanted to speak to her. With a warning glance at Maria, she removed her gloves and bonnet and went into her father's study.

Her first thought had been that he had somehow found out about her visits to Mr. Eversham, but thankfully his smile as she entered his domain put her mind at ease.

"Tina, come in, sit down."

She noticed there was a half-filled glass of brandy beside him. It wasn't her father's way to drink before the evening meal, and she cast a quick glance over his countenance.

He looked pale, and there was a worried frown on his face. But then there always was, these days.

"You had a pleasant afternoon out, Tina? You went to visit Anne, didn't you?"

Tina hadn't done anything of the sort, but she made some meaningless noises. It wasn't really a lie, and her father wasn't listening anyway; he was far too involved in his own thoughts.

"My dear," he said at last, "I think you know the straits we're in at the moment. All my fault. I was foolish enough to believe in someone who I thought was a friend. Now we are all but done for."

Shocked by his plain speaking, Tina reached for his hand. "Father, no! Surely everything will come about."

He shook his head although his fingers clasped hers. "Not a chance of it," he said with grim cheerfulness. "We are done for. Your mother's money is gone, most of it, and the house will have to go, and all the furniture. We will have to find somewhere smaller, cheaper, and well away from our friends. They probably won't want to know us anyway, and your mother won't want to run into them accidentally on the street. The shame would be too much for her to bear."

It sounded grim indeed, and for a moment, Tina could think of nothing to say.

"Your mother has mentioned something about your being keen on young Gilfoyle," he went on awkwardly. "I just wanted to hear the facts from your own lips. You know how she tends to muddle things up."

Tina felt her heart sink a little but forced herself to smile and sit up straighter. "I do have hopes in that direction, Father. He hasn't said anything yet, but I am determined to give him every hint that I am amenable to marriage."

Her father appeared relieved. "That is good news." He sighed. "And now Charles seems to have taken a shine to Anne. That would be a good match if her parents allow it. They are rather strict, and I'm not sure they approve of poor Charles. Still, both of you are making strides toward marriage with a, eh, suitable partner. I am very happy to hear it."

"I'm glad, Papa."

He shifted his brandy glass an inch to the left. "But Horace hasn't proposed, has he?"

"No, Papa. Not yet."

Her father sighed again. "Even if you were married tomorrow, it probably wouldn't make any difference, Tina; it is too late. Although in a month or so, if our debts were settled, we might be able to claw something back. But I can't get my hopes up. Very soon we will have to leave this house, where your mother was born and her father was born and his before him. What a mess."

"I'm so sorry, Papa."

"No, no, it's not your fault. I am the one who has failed you all. Your mother thinks so, and she is right."

He looked so miserable she didn't know what to say or do. In the end she simply kissed his forehead and left him alone.

Things were even worse than she'd thought. She must marry Horace, and without delay. There was no way out, no matter how interesting she found Richard Eversham or how enjoyable were his kisses. And she certainly couldn't rely on Charles to come to the rescue, even if Anne's parents did agree. No, this must be Tina's sacrifice and hers alone.

"Sacrifice." She turned the word over in her head. It made her think of a stone dropping into a pond, leaden, and that was how it felt. Tina had been telling herself for so long that Horace was her childhood sweetheart that she'd grown to accept it, and the fantasy had certainly made the idea of marrying him more palatable. But now it was time to face the truth, and it was Mr. Eversham who had shown her what that was.

She didn't love Horace. She liked him, she was fond of him, but to be his wife and grow old with him . . . No, that was not something that brought her paroxysms of joy. And she probably would never have come to that realization if she hadn't met Richard. To be with him, to be in his arms, to kiss him . . . their moments together had been a revelation.

Did she want to marry him? Tina didn't think so. Her practical soul reminded her that she hardly knew him. This was more to do with an attraction of the flesh, the sort of thing men indulged in all the time. Women weren't supposed to feel like this, and certainly they weren't supposed to admit to lust. But if it wasn't lust she was feeling, then what was it?

She sighed. Speculating was a waste of time. She was marrying Horace. The memory of her father's face just now was enough to strengthen her resolve. Marriages in her stratum of society were rarely for love, and she must not think herself hard done by. She was saving her family, and it wouldn't be so bad. She and Horace would rub along well enough.

Assuming he eventually proposed to her.

And for that Tina knew she needed Richard Eversham.

A treacherous shiver of pleasure curled in her stomach because she knew she had no choice but to see him again. And again. Until Horace proposed, Richard would be part of her life. Tina wondered how long Horace's proposal might take. Logically, going by recent events, it would probably take some time.

It was selfish of her—the curl of pleasure came again—but Tina was delighted.

Chapter 16

Richard heard the voices downstairs shortly after Tina left and thought for a moment she had returned. Dispassionately he noted, as if his own emotions were foreign to him, how his heart leaped, and his body hardened at the thought of seeing her again.

But it wasn't Tina.

Moments later Archie was opening the door to someone he very much *didn't* want to see. His sister-in-law, Anthony's wife.

"Evelyn, this is an unexpected surprise."

She was a beautiful woman, with her golden red hair and violet-blue eyes, but again Richard was able to observe this dispassionately. Long ago he hadn't been so cool in her presence, but then she'd married Anthony, and now his brother was dead.

"Dear Richard." She smiled as she took his hand, and only someone who knew her well would have been able to see the hint of petulance in her face. She was displeased with him because he was able to resist her charms. Evelyn would have preferred it if he had spent the last few years heartbroken and lovesick.

"What are you doing here in town?" he inquired, nodding at Archie to fetch some tea and cake.

"I can't stay forever at Eversham Manor, you know," she said with a hint of melancholy. "Beautiful as it is, I do need to seek out the gaiety of London now and again."

"No one is making you stay in Kent, Evelyn."

She made a moue. "On the small allowance I receive from you, Richard, there's nowhere else I can go."

"It isn't a small allowance, Evelyn, and it was left to you by your husband. Besides it is perfectly adequate."

"Well, we must disagree on that," she said with the hint of a snap.

Evelyn had been an actress before Anthony married her, but not a very good one. In fact, Richard thought with inner amusement, in his opinion Tina's abilities far exceeded hers already.

"You are up here to see your friends at the theater?" he said, carelessly, and received a savage look from her remarkable eyes.

"I have no friends, Richard. I gave all of that up when I married Anthony for love. Remember?"

"Oh, I remember," he said quietly.

She opened her mouth but didn't quite dare to say any more. Even her monumental ego wasn't quite steel plated enough for her to ignore the warning in his voice.

"Well," she said, seating herself on the sofa Tina had so recently left. "I was wondering when you might be coming home to Kent, Richard. There is a great deal needs doing on the estate, and I don't have the authority to tell Mr. Gregor whether or not to go ahead."

"Mr. Gregor is perfectly capable of writing to me, Evelyn."

"But it is so silly! You never visit. Anthony has been dead for two years, and still you stay away. I know it is because you feel you are to blame."

That tilt of her head, the bright malicious gleam in her eyes. He remembered it all so well. How could he have been such an idiot as to fall in love with her all those years ago? He had been utterly smitten. And then Anthony had met her, and Evelyn had realized which brother was the rich one. She'd set about acquiring Anthony, and soon they were married.

Richard hadn't spoken to his brother after that. He'd left for London and refused to return, despite Anthony's efforts to mend things. Of course he regretted his refusal now, bitterly, but it was too late. And Evelyn didn't help matters by inventing her own version of the past—and the future. She wanted Richard to tell her he was still in love with her, had never stopped loving her, and that he was seeking Anthony's killer for her sake, so that he could marry her with a clear conscience.

Such a perfect Evelyn ending!

All because he'd made the mistake at Anthony's funeral of telling her about his vow to find his brother's killer, and how he meant to deny himself his inheritance and any solace to be found in marriage until he did. She'd laughed at him, called him a silly, passionate boy.

"I'll marry you now," she'd said.

Shocked, he hadn't known what to say. He should have told her in no uncertain terms that he meant never to marry her, but he was reeling at his brother's death and all that had been left unresolved between them. She must know now that her hopes were nothing more than fantasies, and yet she persisted.

Evelyn was one reason he never visited Eversham Manor; Anthony's unsolved murder was the other.

" . . . A riot among some farmers, Mr. Gregor says, for no apparent reason than to show they could. Dreadful, isn't it?"

Richard snapped out of his reverie. "What did you say, Evelyn?"

She gave an exaggerated sigh. "I was talking about the Bossenden Wood riots in May, Richard. Mr. Gregor heard from . . . oh, someone or other, that there was a gentleman around at that time, gathering disgruntled farmers together to cause trouble. Evidently the ringleader was just a poor madman this gentleman had persuaded to act a part. And then, as soon as the men started rioting and the soldiers were called in, the gentleman vanished."

Her eyes were gleaming. She'd known he'd be interested, and by God, he was. "Do you know the name of this so-called gentleman, Evelyn?"

She pretended to give it a great deal of thought, and then Archie interrupted with the tray, and there was much ado about pouring tea and cutting cake. When they were finally alone again, Richard repeated his question.

"McGregor did not say," she said airily, "although he did mention he was medium height, with fair hair, and rather handsome. A toff, he said, from the north."

"From the north?"

"North of Kent, at any rate," Evelyn said, biting into her fruitcake with relish. She'd always had a good appetite, he remembered, even at Anthony's funeral.

A thought occurred to Richard, and he set down his cup. "Evelyn, did you know about Anthony? Did you know what he was doing when he died?"

She widened her eyes innocently, but he wasn't deceived.

"I might consider increasing your allowance, a little."

Those violet-blue eyes narrowed. "By how much?"

The figure was haggled over until she reluctantly agreed to an amount. "Yes, I knew what he was doing," she admitted coyly. "Anthony told me everything. He trusted me completely, unlike you, Richard."

"So you knew about the Guardians?"

"Sir Henry Arlington and his silly spy games? Of course I did. And I knew about the Captain. That was who killed him, wasn't it? Sir Henry had it put about that he'd been robbed and murdered by some ruffian, but I always knew that wasn't true. Sir Henry even secured me a little pension from the government, but it was really to keep me quiet," she said smugly. Then, seeing the shocked expression on his face, she hurriedly added, "Not that I would have said anything! But why refuse when one is a poor widow and desperate?"

"If you know who the Captain is, you'd better tell me," Richard said with soft menace.

Evelyn's lips trembled, and her eyes filled with tears. "R-richard? Do you think I would know the name of my husband's murderer and say nothing? I know I hurt you terribly, but surely you can't think such a dreadful thing of me?"

He felt ashamed, as she'd meant him to. He'd gone too far. Evelyn might be a greedy and unpleasant woman, but she wouldn't protect the man who'd killed Anthony. "I'm sorry," he said roughly. "I don't know what I was thinking."

By now her tears had turned to sobs, and reluctantly he came to sit beside her and put his arms about her to comfort her. Immediately she turned into his chest, clinging to him, shaking with grief. She was enjoying it, but he couldn't say that, and did he really know it for a fact? Perhaps it was time to set aside the ill feelings he had for her. Perhaps she was right, and in some corner of his heart he'd never forgiven her for throwing him aside because she preferred Anthony.

Evelyn raised her swimming gaze. "Richard, I am so alone," she said with trembling lips. "Come home, please come home."

He could have kissed her then. He could have taken her right here on the sofa, and he was fairly sure she would have let him. But Richard knew he would only be slaking his lust for Tina on Evelyn, and he couldn't do that. Whatever he felt about Evelyn, he was a gentleman at heart.

He set her away from him and handed her his handkerchief.

"I will come home when I have brought Anthony's murderer to justice," he said. "And if there is anything more you know about him, then you must tell me. Now."

Evelyn mopped her face, sending him pitiful little glances. "I don't know any more. When I heard about the gentleman and the riots I knew there might be a connection, and I came to tell you."

"I will write to Gregor."

"He will only confirm what I have said, Richard."

He watched her twisting the handkerchief in her fingers. "Did you really come all the way to London to tell me about the Captain, Evelyn?"

She took a breath and steadied herself. Her gaze was cool and clear, no tears and redness. Had she been crying at all, or was it all pretence with her? "Of course I did," she said. "I want Anthony's murderer caught just as much as you do, Richard. I know you will never forgive me until he is. And I want you to be happy. I want us both to be happy."

"Evelyn—"

"No, don't say anything. I know we can't speak of it, not yet. But when this man, the Captain, has been caught and hanged, then you must come to me at Eversham Manor, Richard. I will be waiting."

After she'd gone, Richard told himself it would have been cruel to tell her she could wait until hell froze over, that he would never trust her again with his heart, let alone love her. But the information she'd brought was valuable, and he sent off a letter immediately to Gregor to confirm it and discover anything more the land agent might know.

"Medium height, fair hair, and handsome,"

he murmured to himself. It could be Gilfoyle. It could be Little. It could be a hundred other men. But he felt as if he was getting closer to the end of his journey. "Nearly there, Anthony old chap," he said gently to his dead brother. "Nearly there."

"This had better be good," Lord Montague growled, as he sat down at the table. "I had to break an appointment at my club."

Sir Henry glanced about and nodded. "All present, the meeting will come to order," he announced, and turned at once to Richard. "Well, my boy, what was so important it couldn't wait?"

Richard began to tell them about Evelyn's visit and what Gregor had told her.

"Hearsay," Montague muttered. "And from a woman, by God."

"I believe her," Richard retorted, "and Gregor is a trustworthy fellow."

"The description could fit ten thousand men north of Kent," Sir Henry mused, "but it is interesting that it fits our latest two candidates for the Captain."

Will Jackson made some suggestions about following up the information, and notes were taken. Richard knew he would have to go to Kent, but first there was Sir Henry's country weekend. Interesting to see what Gilfoyle and Little got up to there. Interesting and dangerous.

"If the Captain finds out we are getting closer—"

"Closer!" Montague sneered.

"—he might take action. As he did last time with my brother."

Sir Henry nodded solemnly. "We are in a dangerous occupation, Richard. We take risks. But if not for us, then there would be anarchy. This man must be stopped, and if risks need to be taken, then they shall be."

A vote was taken to continue the course they were on, and the meeting broke up. Will Jackson followed Richard out. "Are you going to be at this weekend party, Eversham? Sir Henry has invited me. Perhaps we could travel down together?"

Richard agreed, and they made their arrangements.

As he walked away, Richard was remembering Gilfoyle's unpleasant smirk at the Smythe's dinner table and wondered again whether he was the Captain. It would give him great pleasure to see Gilfoyle dragged away by the authorities, but he admitted to himself it would give him even more pleasure to punch him square on the nose.

Archie had told him about Maria's admission. The Smythes were bankrupt, and Tina was marrying to save the family fortune and the family honor. If he could prove Gilfoyle was the Captain, he would save her from that fate. Although how that would help her family's financial woes wasn't exactly clear. Probably not, was the answer.

Well surely with Gilfoyle out of the way there could be someone more suitable found? Tina was a stunning girl, beautiful and clever. Richard was quite sure it would be a simple matter to find her a husband who could solve all her problems.

Of course, it would have to be someone of whom he approved.

What of Will Jackson? He'd considered him

before, and he was intelligent and honest, with a good family and with a reasonable fortune. Surely he was the perfect choice?

But the more Richard considered Will Jackson, the more he seemed to discover things about the man he didn't quite approve of. They were little things, but nevertheless Richard wanted perfection for Tina. There might be someone at Arlington Hall. Apart from himself, of course, because Richard had vowed not to marry, not until Anthony's murderer was brought to justice, and even then . . . well Evelyn had dampened his desire for marriage.

There would be the perfect someone for Tina, he reassured himself. He just had to keep looking.

Chapter 17

～～∽◯◯⌇～

Lady Carol had taken to her bed, and the household crept about like mice. The doctor was called to attend her. "She needs complete rest," he informed Sir Thomas. "No excitement of any kind, or I won't answer for the consequences."

Tina had a fair idea of the nature of the excitement that had sent her mother to her bed, and so did Sir Thomas. When the day's mail arrived and was carried in on the silver tray, they both pounced upon it as a way of diverting their thoughts.

Sir Thomas sifted through the letters, setting aside the bills, of which there were a great many, looking for anything to give his thoughts another direction. "Ah, here's an invitation for a weekend at Sir Henry and Lady Isabelle Arlington's country estate! Lovely spot. Right on the river and acres of woodland. Good hunting, as I recall."

"That should cheer Mama up. She loves the countryside."

He wouldn't meet her eyes. "Hmm. You and Charles are invited, too."

Tina waited a moment, and then said softly.

"Can we go, Father? I mean, is it possible for us to go just now, with things as they are?"

"Probably not," he muttered, throwing down the invitation. "I've arranged to sell the coach. How will we get there? And your mother will want new clothes, and how will we manage that?"

But when she heard of the invitation, Lady Carol had other ideas.

"You certainly will go! And Charles, too. Your father and I will make our excuses, but you and Charles *must* go."

"Mama, we don't need to, really, I understand that our circumstances have changed and—"

Lady Carol gave her a bleak look, and Tina's voice faltered and stopped. "The wretched bailiffs will be coming next week. You and Charles don't want to be here to see that, Tina."

"Oh, Mama!"

With an effort her mother rallied. "Never mind," she said, waving her hand as if to push the horror as far away as possible. "You must go, Tina. What if Horace chooses that weekend to propose to you? And I still have hopes for Charles and Anne although the Burgesses seem to have got wind of our dire circumstances and are warning her off him. Still if they aren't thrown together, then how can we expect a happy ending?"

Inwardly Tina sighed. Horace was their last hope. She must persuade him, somehow, that he loved her and wanted to marry her. The conversation played out in her head:

"Please make me the happiest man in the world, Tina, and marry me. I realize I can't live without you. How could I have been so blind all these years?"

"Yes, Horace, of course I will marry you."

"That's wonderful. Let's not wait. We must marry immediately."

"Yes, Horace, immediately. Uhm, by the way, my family are about to be turned out of their home onto the street. Can we borrow your fortune?"

Thankfully she never found out what Horace might have said in response, as her mother climbed from her bed with some of her old vigor.

"Ring for Maria, my dear! We must start planning your wardrobe. It was fortunate we had that new dress made for your visit to the theater, wasn't it? And somehow we must manage one or two more. There will be a ball, the Arlingtons always have a ball. You need a ball dress, Tina, something truly striking. I think I have one or two pieces of jewelry I won't miss too much, enough to pay the dressmaker at any rate."

"Mama, please don't—"

Lady Carol's mouth firmed. "No arguments. Ring the bell, Tina."

Tina went to ring the bell, trying not to let her mother see how her heart sank at the idea of wearing a dress that had been bought with her mother's precious jewelry.

"You have your dark blue dress for traveling," Lady Carol went on. "Does it still fit?"

"It is too short."

"Never mind, we'll manage. Perhaps a trim along the hem. At least we do not have to worry about your undergarments, even darned stockings will do at a pinch, no one will see them. Apart from the servants."

"Servants gossip," Tina reminded her wryly.

"Perhaps, but just remember that the next time they see you you will be Lady Tina Gilfoyle, and your underwear will be impeccable."

Tina wished she was as positive of the outcome as her mother, but as there was little she could do but agree, she set about making the best of it. And the country weekend away would be nice if she could forget that her parents were selling family heirlooms to pay for it.

"Father says he's arranged for the coach to be sold. How will we—?"

"We will hire one if necessary," Lady Carol said resolutely. "Your father has some rather nice bottles of wine put down in the cellar. I think they will fetch a fair price."

She gave a shudder as she said it, as if it was all too much to bear, then forced a ghastly smile. "Well, I'm sure it will all be worth it in the end, Tina. And I'm sure you will try your very best to secure Horace although I don't want you to feel as if you have failed us if he doesn't ask."

Oh no, Tina thought with miserable irony, *I mustn't feel that.*

"Should I tell him, Mama? About our troubles?"

Lady Carol eyes widened. "Good heavens, no! You must not say a word, not until he asks you and you say yes, and even then . . . No, leave all that to your father and me. We will broach it, very delicately, when the time is right. I'm sure Horace will be understanding. He is almost one of the family, after all, and Charles is his dearest friend. How could he not want to help?"

Tina could think of lots of reasons why Horace might be quite cross about the whole thing, but she wisely kept them to herself.

"I wonder who else will be there?" her mother was saying. "Lady Isabelle likes to play the gracious lady of the manor so there are sure to be lots of guests, some of them quite exotic, as well as more familiar faces. Mr. Little, perhaps? But I suppose it's no use thinking of him, not now that Margaret has her hooks in him. I do wish you would choose your friends more wisely, Tina," she added irritably.

"I don't think Mr. Little and I would have suited, Mama," Tina replied soothingly.

"A pity." Her expression hardened. "I hope that dreadful scoundrel Richard Eversham won't be there. Sir Henry has some very odd friends. I'm still not sure why he foisted him upon us, but I certainly don't want you in his company without me there to keep an eye on him. You will take care, won't you, Tina?"

Of course she would, she reassured her mother, and Mr. Eversham was unlikely to be there; surely he had better things to do? But in her heart she was hoping very much he would be there. At least that would give her one bright thing to look forward to among the shadows of worry and anxiety, and Horace.

Hunting Horace, capturing him, securing him. She'd already made one blunder. How was she to manage this time? And his proposing to her was only the beginning.

"You must take Maria, of course," Lady Carol was saying. "I will manage very well without her. I will have to manage, won't I? I doubt we will be able to afford more than one or two servants when we leave this-this house."

Her lip wobbled, and she bit down on it hard.

"Where is Maria?" she went on querulously. "Go and find her, Tina. I have so much to do."

Tina hesitated, but she could see that her mother didn't want her there while she indulged in her misery, so she went out quietly and closed the door.

She found Maria on the stairs. Her dark eyes widened when Tina explained about the weekend at the Arlington's country estate and Lady Carol's sudden ascension from her sickbed.

"She's asking for you," Tina said, as she continued down the stairs, leaving Maria to hurry up them. "I wonder if Mr. Eversham and Archie will be there," she added mischievously, over her shoulder.

"Hush, Miss Tina!" Maria whispered, glancing about her, but there was no one to overhear.

Maria wished Tina would understand the dangers of the game she was playing, or at least not pretend it was all a game. Did she really feel like that? Maria thought that she was probably playing a part, hiding her fears and doubts, while determined to do what was right for her family.

Miss Tina was like that, she always had been. If she wasn't very careful, she was going to end up being a martyr, and as far as Maria could recall from her childhood church attendance, they weren't a very happy lot. Marrying Horace might be her parents' answer to their problems, but Maria thought it a very bad idea for Tina.

Lady Carol would ask Maria to keep a watch on her daughter, and Maria would promise to do so, but there were forces at work that Lady Carol knew nothing about.

Mr. Eversham worried her. Just what was he up to? There might come a time when she would have to tell Tina what Archie had said although she'd prefer to wait until she knew the whole story herself. Would Archie be at the Arlington's country house with his master? If Maria was a woman who liked a wager, then she'd say yes.

Over the next week Tina found herself unable to do a thing without her mother by her side. There were fittings for the ball dress and such other items of clothing that Lady Carol deemed necessary, and as well as all that there was packing that needed to be done in preparation for the closing of the house. Although more was being sold than packed. There was a horrible incident when some burly looking bailiffs arrived and banged on the door and threatened them with eviction, but Sir Thomas went to speak to them and somehow managed to gain them another month.

"However did you do it?" Lady Carol demanded, trembling hands clasped to her bosom.

"I gave them your long case clock," he said shortly.

"With the paintings of the moon and stars?" she wailed.

"Yes."

"That belonged to my mother," his wife's eyes filled with tears.

"It was either the clock or us out on the street, my dear."

Tina held her breath as her mother struggled between her emotional attachment to the clock and her common sense. The latter won. She gave a brisk nod, before climbing the stairs again to her room, slowly, like an old woman.

Preparations for the weekend were now well under way. Charles was taking a valet, which was a tremendous expense but one Lady Carol felt could not be forgone. Often gentlemen visiting away used each others' valets or any available servants in the house they were staying in, but to do that seemed too penny-pinching and Lady Carol could not bear it.

"I don't know how we are going to afford this," she confided to Tina, as they sat in the parlor one morning, sipping tea from leaves which had been reused several times. It was barely tea now, more like hot water and milk.

The parlor looked quite bare. Most of the "good stuff," as Sir Thomas called it, had gone. Lady Carol still preferred to sit in here however and take her morning tea, with the view through the sash windows of the kitchen garden, now sadly neglected.

"Who will care for everything when we're gone?" she worried.

Charles blundering into the room was almost a relief. "Morning Mama, Tina." He blinked and looked about, as if suddenly realizing how many things were missing. "Had a clean out, Mama?"

"Yes, Charles." Lady Carol rallied at the sight of her son. She still persisted on keeping their true situation a secret from him, which Tina found ludicrous, but if it made her mother a little happier then it was best to go along with it. Although what Charles would think when he came home and home was no longer here, Tina couldn't imagine.

"Just popped in to say that Horace has offered me the use of his valet, so I won't need to worry on that front. And he's offered to take us in his coach, Tina. Nicely sprung, very comfortable, and his horse flesh are top notch." He beamed at them both, then closed the door behind him.

Lady Carol clapped her hands together. "That's marvelous!" she gasped. "You will be traveling with Horace and Charles. How many days' journey is that, Tina?"

"Three, Mama. So three days in the coach and then the weekend—although it is actually three or four days at the estate—and then three days back."

Lady Carol looked ecstatic. "Marvelous," she said again. Then her face fell. "Oh dear, we'd decided on the dark blue traveling dress, hadn't we? Because we thought no one would see you. I think we must find something a bit more flattering, Tina. Ring for Maria. We need to send for the seamstress."

Wearily Tina got to her feet. By the time Lady Carol was done she'd have more dresses than the queen, and certainly as many slippers and gloves and shawls. Not that she was ungrateful, she reminded herself. In fact she was very grateful, it was just that the reason for all this splendor was so daunting—the prospect of persuading Horace to marry her.

And as far as she could tell Horace seemed as little interested in her as he'd always been.

Horace's coach crept through the busy streets out of London. With Charles and Horace sprawled on the seat on one side, and Tina and Maria seated primly on the other, there was no room for Horace's valet, and he rode outside, with the coachman and the luggage. And Tina was self-consciously aware that most of the luggage belonged to her.

Horace was in a jolly mood, telling stories and making Charles laugh uproariously. Tina's head was aching already, and they'd hardly begun.

"I do hope there'll be people we know there," Charles said. "And at least someone under sixty!"

"Lady Isabelle is under sixty," was Horace's prompt reply.

"The delectable Lady Isabelle."

"Charles!" Tina reprimanded him.

He laughed a little wildly. "It's all right, Tina, I'm not about to seduce our hostess. I can't answer for Horace, though," he added with a sly sideways glance to their companion.

"Horace is a gentleman," Tina retorted, also looking to Horace, expecting him to say that seducing Lady Isabelle was a ridiculous idea.

Horace merely smiled benevolently upon them both. "Now, now, children, let's not argue. Tell me, Charles, did you stop by at our club the other night? I was otherwise engaged. Tell me, was—"

Tina was no longer listening. In truth she was disappointed. She didn't expect any better from her brother, but she'd hoped Horace might behave like a gentleman. Or perhaps she just wanted reassurance that even if she didn't love Horace, she wasn't making a terrible mistake about his character.

Instead she was, well, disappointed.

So she sat in silence, pretending to look out of the window as the countryside began to change. The narrow streets and buildings turned to single houses and then a house or two among the fields, until the world became green and leafy. She knew she should laugh and make conversation, show Horace what a perfect companion she was, but her heart wasn't in it.

She felt as if she were trapped in his coach, just as she was trapped into seeking their marriage. Her skin prickled, and her headache grew worse, until she began to find it hard to bear.

She tried to focus on the scenery outside. They had entered a forest, and it looked so dark and cool. She wondered if there was a stream nearby and how it would feel to dip her feet in the cool water. To sit in the silence and breathe the fresh air and forget all about the family expectations weighing her down.

"I say, Tina, are you all right? You've gone very pale."

It was Charles who spoke, and he looked worried. Perhaps he'd sensed her change of mood after all.

"No, I'm not," she said sharply. "I need to get out. Please ask the driver to stop."

The forest was as cool and shadowy as she'd hoped, and for a moment Tina took deep breaths, regaining her composure. The silence was actually not silence at all, but a choir of sweet birdsong.

"Miss, are you well now?" Maria was by her side, dark eyes anxious.

Tina sighed.

"It is just that the coachman is worried." She glanced back, and Tina could see the man in his coat, seated up high on the coach, peering through the trees. "He says there are robbers in these woods, miss, and we'd be wise to get through them as quickly as possible."

Horace had already taken up the subject, exclaiming loudly, "Robbers? Along here?" as if he found the idea of them daring to even think about robbing him infuriating. "We are armed, aren't we?" this aside to the coachman.

"Yes, my lord."

"Well then, I think any robbers who came upon us would be very sorry indeed."

"But, my lord—"

"Allow the lady to take the air, coachman, and we'll hear no more of robbers."

Tina found herself smiling at his sheer arrogance, and she reentered the coach in a much better frame of mind.

"Are you better now, miss?" asked Maria, as they settled themselves again on the comfortable seats.

"Yes, quite better. But I shall be happy to arrive. I'd forgotten how much I detest traveling in a coach. Even one as fine as this one," she added hastily, aware that Horace was listening.

"I should have brought my curricle," he said mildly, "and you could have had the wind in your face. Put some color into those pale cheeks, Tina."

"You could always sit up with the coachman," Charles added, a twinkle in his eye. "Get plenty of color in your cheeks up there, sis."

Suddenly their banter was comforting rather than irritating, and Tina was able to smile and say with perfect truth, "Thank you both, but I am quite content where I am."

Richard was making a similar journey, traveling with Will Jackson. He knew Will quite well although he had never considered him a friend, but this journey was proving a surprise for he found himself enjoying Will's company very much.

They didn't discuss Guardian matters, not with Archie in the coach with them, and had to find other topics. To Richard's surprise they seemed to find plenty of those. Still, he'd be glad when they reached Arlington Hall, Sir Henry and Lady Isabelle's country estate.

Archie spent most of the time dozing in the corner, or pretending to. Richard had found his manservant rather a disappointment when it came to his spying activities with Tina's maid. Archie had discovered very little, or at least he had told Richard very little. He had a suspicion that Archie was growing fond of Maria, and perhaps his emotion for her was affecting his job.

Richard frowned.

It just went to show, it did not do to allow one's emotions to interfere with one's work. He should remind Archie of it. And remind himself, he thought wryly. Emotion had no place in his life—not until he'd completed his mission.

Sir Thomas and Lady Carol had waited until their children had departed before setting out on their own journey. It was a final effort to find the funds to keep the house in Mallory Street, and it was a vain hope, but it was one they felt it necessary to make.

They were heading for Sir Thomas's brother, Harold Smythe.

Harold had already rejected the pleas for help Sir Thomas had made by letter, but he was confident—or so he told his wife—that a face-to-face meeting would do the trick. "Harold won't see me go down," he said, as their hired coach bumped out of London. "Turn on the waterworks when you see him, old girl. Harold could never abide women crying all over him."

His wife gave him a scathing look. It was the sort of look she'd been giving him a lot lately, and in his heart he couldn't blame her. This was all his fault. He'd lost everything. But the house, the material things, he could manage without them. It was his wife as she used to be that he missed, and he was beginning to wonder how he could live without her love.

Chapter 18

Arlington Hall sat in an undulating valley, surrounded by acres of grounds. There were wood-
lands behind the house, but the view from the
front was of manicured lawns, roses, lilies, and
all manner of other English flowers, as well as
some of the more exotic plants, with vistas over
a wide stretch of the river. As the coach drew up
on the circular entrance, under a wide, sheltering
portico, Tina could smell lavender from a central
bed where a fountain played.

It was lavish indeed. Sir Thomas had spoken
of Sir Henry Arlington's wealth, but Tina hadn't
really understood just how wealthy Sir Henry
really was. Until now. She stared up at the elegant
red Georgian house, with its chimneys and the
gleam of many windows, and tried to imagine
living in such a place.

Servants came out to help with the unloading of
the luggage, and Tina, Horace, and Charles were
ushered inside by the Arlington housekeeper,
who showed them upstairs to their rooms.

"Sir Henry and Lady Isabelle are in the salon with their other guests," she informed them, as they followed her around the curve of the grand staircase toward a bank of stained-glass windows.

"Many arrived yet?" asked Charles, who was never intimidated by anyone.

"You are the last," the housekeeper said, making it sound like a failing on their part.

Horace and Tina exchanged an amused glance. They'd always shared a sense of the ridiculous, and surely that was a good thing, if one were to marry? And yet these three days in the coach with Horace hadn't soothed her concerns as she'd hoped they might. She needed time to think when there was no time at all. She was being bustled along by her family and fate toward something that in her heart she did not want.

Tina's room was beautiful, the walls covered in hand-painted rose wallpaper and the furnishings light and feminine. There was a window seat under bay windows overlooking the vast gardens, which she saw were terraced all the way down to the river.

"Lady Isabelle chose this room especially for you, miss," said the housekeeper haughtily. "It's one of the nicest rooms in Arlington Hall."

"It is beautiful. I will tell Lady Isabelle so."

Her obvious pleasure seemed to pacify the housekeeper, who announced she'd send a servant to show Tina to the salon in half an hour.

Maria and the luggage arrived a short time afterward.

As they rushed about, changing Tina's traveling clothes for something more in keeping for a visit to the salon, and Maria brushed Tina's hair and arranged it into a loose knot with a profusion of ringlets, there didn't seem to be time to enjoy the peace and quiet of the country.

Tina stood in front of the looking glass, turning this way and that. "Will I do, do you think?" Tina asked her maid, suddenly uncertain. Perhaps it was the grandeur of the house or the haughty housekeeper, but she felt like an imposter. A young lady with very few prospects and no dowry, on the hunt for a rich husband.

"You look beautiful, miss," Maria reassured her. "Mr. Eversham is here, and Archie," she added, sounding breathless. "I passed him on the servants' stairs, on my way here."

Tina continued to examine her reflection, which seemed even less impressive than before.

"Did you hear what I said, Miss Tina? Archie and Mr. Eversham are here."

"I heard what you said," Tina said quietly, and left it at that.

After a servant girl had come to collect her and take her to the salon, Maria tidied up and began to put things away in their proper places. She felt a little shaky herself after meeting Archie on the stairs. He'd given her a wink, as if they were conspirators in a plot, and she couldn't help but smile back at him.

He had that effect on her. Life would never be dull with Archie if she chose to follow that road, but as yet she wasn't at all sure that she would. All these years, she had dreamed of saving up and returning home to Spain, and now she had enough to go. There was nothing stopping her, apart from Miss Tina and the Smythes, but that would not be forever.

No, Maria told herself decisively, there was nothing stopping her at all.

Charles and Horace were already in the salon with Sir Henry and Lady Isabelle and several other guests. Tina was relieved to see the familiar faces of both Anne Burgess and Margaret Allsop among them.

"Ah, Miss Smythe," boomed Sir Henry. "There you are. So pleased you could join our little party. The men are shooting tomorrow, if the weather holds. As for the women, I believe my wife has something planned, haven't you, my dear?"

Lady Isabelle had come over to greet Tina, her color a little hectic, her eyes a little bright. "Tina, here you are. I do hope you like your room?"

"It's delightful, Lady Isabelle. That wonderful view—it's as if the very walls are perfumed with roses."

Lady Isabelle was delighted with Tina's enthusiastic response. "Thank you, Tina. When I decorated the room, I thought it would be for my daughter . . . well, I am so glad you like it." Sadness drew down her mouth and doused the glow in her eyes.

"Time yet, my dear," her husband said bracingly. "Plenty of time."

"Of course there is," she agreed, rallying. "I am being maudlin again. I promise to be the life and soul of the party from now on."

Sir Henry looked as if he thought that was a worse idea, but he gave a dutiful smile.

Just then Anne and Margaret came to join her, and Tina engaged with them in some lively conversation about the journey. "Charles is here, somewhere," she added, looking about.

"I saw him," Anne said, and then blushed. "I mean, I saw Horace, too."

"I'm sure you did," Tina soothed her, but she couldn't help but smile. Was Anne still enamored of Charles despite her parents' warning? Whatever her own feelings in the matter, it seemed unlikely she would go against their wishes when it came to marriage. Anne was a practical girl—the sort of girl Tina had always believed herself to be—and romantic love would take second place to duty and practical considerations.

"Mr. Richard Eversham."

The name was announced by a footman at the door, and at once Tina went hot and cold. If she were being dramatic, she'd say those three words struck her like a sliver of lightning, lodging in the region of her heart. She actually couldn't find her breath and struggled to maintain a normal demeanor. When she finally felt able to, when she'd regained some control, she turned to look.

It was him. He was here, just as Maria had warned her.

He was wearing gray trousers and a well-fitted black jacket over a jade green silk vest and a gray cravat. His gaze caught Tina's, and a smile curved his mouth, almost as if the instinctive movement were beyond his control. Before she could stop herself, Tina was smiling back.

"Tina!" Margaret hissed. "Why are you smiling at the disreputable Mr. Eversham?"

"Was I?" Tina answered vaguely, but her heart was thumping in her chest.

"He is handsome. And charming. What a pity he's so unsuitable," said Anne.

"Is he really all that unsuitable?" asked Margaret, somewhat wistfully.

"Only if you value your reputation," Anne retorted.

If only they knew what she and Richard had done together! How very intimate they had become. Would her friends refuse to speak to her? Probably. Tina wondered if she would be cut off from society and branded a scarlet woman. Perhaps, she thought, watching Richard as he talked to Sir Henry and Lady Isabelle, but perhaps it might be worth it.

Tina half listened to her friends chattering and laughing, her thoughts miles away. For a practical girl, she was showing some alarming tendencies to daydream about matters that were most improper.

The last to arrive and be announced was John Little, who had, he explained, been delayed on business matters. He came and greeted Margaret with a solemn smile before turning to Tina.

"Miss Smythe, your parents aren't here?"

"No, they were unable to attend due to another engagement." Tina spoke the lie smoothly. She'd been telling a great many lies recently, and it was becoming easier each time.

"I must call upon them in London, to thank them again for their hospitality."

Tina smiled but couldn't help but wonder if he would find the house in Mallory Street closed up and shuttered, and no one home, and what he would think when he did. Would he seek them out at their hovel? Mr. Little did not seem like a snob, but he was a businessman, and if fraternizing with the bankrupt Smythes caused his business to suffer, she imagined he might make the hardheaded decision to drop them.

Tina glanced around, looking for Richard. There he was, by the windows. She thought about seeking him out, but every time she moved toward him, she was waylaid by her friends, until she finally gave up. Soon it was time to go upstairs to change for dinner.

Maria had laid out one of her new dresses, a deep buttercup taffeta with dropped puffed sleeves and a décolletage just short of scandalous—it was a sign of Lady Carol's desperation that she had not quibbled over it. With the new dress Tina wore her garnet necklace and earrings, presented to her by her parents on her eighteenth birthday. She fingered the stones, wondering if she should have offered to sell them. Well, if Horace didn't come up to scratch, she would have to, but for now she resolved to set aside her guilt and enjoy wearing them.

Maria was attending to her hair, watching her with a little frown, as if she was worried her young mistress might do something reckless.

She is right to be worried tonight, Tina decided, for she felt reckless. She felt as if she might set aside all the rules, everything she'd been taught about decorous behavior, and do exactly as she pleased.

"You were right, Mr. Eversham is here, Maria," she said. "I saw him in the salon although I didn't speak to him. I thought it might not appear proper to speak to him in front of all those people."

"His reputation—"

"I won't speak to him in public, and yet I am quite willing to kiss him in private. Don't you find that a little deceitful, Maria?"

"I find it very sensible, miss."

"He's a very good kisser, Maria."

Maria tightened her lips and said nothing.

Tina smiled. "Have you seen Archie yet?"

"I don't have time to worry about Archie," said Maria sharply.

"I envy you, Maria," Tina said dreamily. "You can marry whomever you want to, fall in love with whomever you want to. You don't have to worry about anything except your own wishes."

Maria smiled. "I am not quite as free and easy as you seem to think, Miss Tina. If I marry, I must find a man who will not take my savings and leave me without my shoes, or will not hit me when he has been drinking, or will not break my heart and then run off with another woman."

"But at least you can marry a man you want to marry, even if you make a mistake. You do not have to take into account family connections and the critical eyes of society, and wealth and lineage, and . . ." She ran out of breath and shook her head, making Maria cluck her tongue as a curl bounced free.

"I think you are seeing the life of a servant through rose-colored glasses, miss. And who said I intended to marry anyone? Come, you are ready to go down to dinner. You should put aside all your cares for this evening and enjoy yourself."

Tina smiled as she turned. "I will, Maria. And you must promise to enjoy yourself, too."

Maria nodded decisively. "I will, miss, so I will."

Chapter 19

After his third glance toward the door, Richard told himself not to be so stupid. He'd warned himself about getting emotionally involved; obviously, he thought wryly, he hadn't been listening. All the same, his reaction was surprising. What was it about this girl that made him feel so unlike himself? He thought about her more every day, and the taste he'd had, far from satisfying his desires, only made him want her more.

He chatted with Sir Henry and Will Jackson and Sir Henry's neighbor, Mr. Branson, waiting for her to appear, knowing that until she did, he couldn't think clearly. The glimpse he'd had of her earlier in the salon, the tantalizing smile she'd given him, had made him useless for work.

And then she was there. She wore a yellow dress that set off her dark hair and pale skin, and her beauty took his breath away. For an all-too-brief moment her eyes had met his, her expression startled, and then she'd turned away.

It had occurred to him that this frisson between

them might be as unnerving to her as it was to him, and now he was certain. And it was damned inconvenient! She was planning to marry Gilfoyle. Planning to kiss Gilfoyle, touch him, let him touch her. Let him have her in the most intimate of ways . . .

Richard grabbed a glass of champagne from a passing tray and swallowed it almost savagely. His hand was shaking, and he gripped the stem so hard he nearly broke it. This was utterly ridiculous. He must calm himself, he *must* put Tina out of his mind.

But if he was distracted, then so was Sir Henry, who kept glancing toward his wife. Lady Isabelle's voice rose above the chatter of their guests, and she flittered about, as if unable to keep still for even a moment. Once he beckoned a servant and murmured in his ear, and the servant scurried to her side to convey the message. Isabelle lifted her head, her smile mechanical, and waved her hand at her husband.

"I think we are ready to go in to dinner," he said to Richard. "Come along. And if my wife has put you next to my cousin Edith, then you have my sincere sympathy."

But thankfully Cousin Edith had been reserved for Will Jackson, and Richard was seated beside Tina's red-haired friend Margaret, a serious young woman, although he did his best to make her smile, and on her other side was Mr. Branson, a rather surly fellow. Tina was farther down the table, near Lady Isabelle, who appeared to have taken a great liking to the younger woman. Gilfoyle was there, too, and Richard struggled not to glare at the man as he chatted and laughed his way through the meal. As if, Richard thought darkly, he expected everyone to love him as much as he loved himself.

And yet he had to wonder if that was the real Lord Horace. It could just be an act. Perhaps the jolly lord was a role he played, to disguise the sinister truth.

That was one of the things Richard had come to Arlington Hall to find out.

"Enjoying your stay?" It was Branson, finally doing the polite with Margaret Allsop. "Nice spot this. My family owned it once—it was a working farm then—but prices dropped after the war, and we had to sell it off. Arlington got a bargain."

Margaret murmured something.

Branson responded a little less gloomily, and the conversation shifted to the weather, always a safe topic, thought Richard, his attention elsewhere.

Tina was laughing at something Gilfoyle had said, and now she put her hand on his arm. The minx! She was using the tricks he'd taught her. Well, of course she was. That was the whole point of his expert training, was it not?

It wasn't Tina's fault the idea no longer appealed to him—if it ever had.

His restless gaze slid over Will Jackson, the poor fellow desperately attempting to extract himself from Cousin Edith's endless discourse on birds. She told anyone who would listen, and even those who wouldn't, that she was a keen ornithologist. It was her only topic of conversation. Richard remembered thinking before about Will as a possible partner for Tina. He was a good man, honest and true, and he had some money of his own. Not the fortune that Gilfoyle had, of course, but adequate. Tina would be much better off with Will than Horace, and although Richard had previously found fault with his friend, he knew whom he'd prefer to marry Tina if it came to it.

Should he point her in that direction?

He shifted restlessly in his chair.

It would be the gentlemanly thing to do, and yet Richard wasn't feeling particularly gentlemanly tonight. He didn't want Tina to marry Gilfoyle or Will. He didn't want her to marry anyone. He wanted her unmarried and free, available to him whenever he wanted her. He missed her mouth, the warm sighs she gave when he held her in his arms, he missed the wonderful softness of her body beneath his hands.

The stark truth was he wanted her all for himself.

Lady Isabelle had arranged some entertainment for the evening, but before it could begin all the men must finish their cigars and brandy and join the women in the drawing room. Sir Henry was lingering over his after-dinner tipple with several of his cronies. Tina had found herself a seat near an open window, away from the chatter—and Horace, who seemed particularly irritating tonight—when Lady Isabelle found her.

"Lord Horace seems rather taken with you, Tina," she said at once, arranging the folds of her pale blue silk as she sat down.

"Do you think so?" Tina was genuinely surprised. She'd been thinking Horace an annoyance, but now, thinking back, she realized that at dinner there had been a difference in the way he looked at her, the way he spoke to her. Was he more attentive? She knew she ought to be thrilled that her plan was finally working, not so full of her own concerns that she had hardly noticed.

"I have known Horace since I was a little girl," she explained, aware of Lady Isabelle's curious gaze. "He is almost like a-a brother to me."

"He didn't seem to be looking at you in a very brotherly sort of way." Her hostess laughed.

"Oh." The ironic notion came to Tina that perhaps Horace suddenly found her attractive because she had lost interest in him—that her being unattainable had changed him.

A servant came scurrying over and murmured something to Lady Isabelle. Her face lit up. "Yes, yes, bring him in," she said breathlessly. Her eyes slid to Tina, and their pupils seemed enormous. "I have arranged for Signor Veruda to sing for us. He is a famous baritone. From Rome. We are very privileged to have him here at Arlington Hall."

Just then a dark-haired man came sauntering into the room, and not long afterward, he was followed by Sir Henry and the other dawdling gentlemen. Tina's eyes went straight to Richard, and she admitted with an awareness of regret that she was hunting the wrong man.

Signor Veruda came over to take Lady Isabelle's hand, his black eyes delving so shockingly into the shadows of her décolletage that Tina had to turn away. "My dearest lady, I have missed you unbearably. But I am here now, and I will sing to you."

"Yes, please do sing to me." Lady Isabelle placed her fingers in his and allowed him to lead her to the pianoforte. The pianist was Cousin Edith, who did have another talent besides watching birds.

With the chairs arranged and everyone seated, the music began. Vincenzo Veruda was not a tall man, and his middle was a little more rounded than it should be, but he would never go unnoticed among all these Englishmen. His dark eyes sought out the women in the room, and he smiled often, causing hearts to flutter and cheeks to flush.

"Damn poser." Horace had come to sit beside her while they listened.

"Who?"

"Him. Veruda."

"You're just jealous."

Horace snorted. "You don't find men like that attractive, do you?"

"Why not? He's charming and handsome, and obviously talented. I'm sure he would have a great deal to teach me."

Lord, why had she said that? To annoy him, she supposed. Only now, he would think the worst of her character.

His eyes narrowed, and she couldn't help but be nervously aware of his sideways glances in her direction. And Lady Isabelle had grown more and more shrill, with Sir Henry more and more anxious and protective of her. He hovered, which seemed to drive her to distraction.

"Go and talk to our guests, my dear," she told him testily.

"I am perfectly happy here," he rumbled.

"Then go and smoke a cigar in the garden."

"I am thinking of giving them up."

Angry tears sparkled in her eyes as she turned away.

There was definitely something not right at

Arlington Hall, thought Tina, as Signor Veruda launched into yet another song.

Eventually supper was served, and Tina was able to escape Horace, but she had to prowl about the room because every time she thought of settling she could see him, making his way toward her. It would have been amusing if it wasn't so awful.

"Are you enjoying the music, Miss Smythe?"

Richard had come up beside her, and his deep voice with its intimate tone played with her senses; if she'd been a harp, she would have quivered. With the smile she couldn't stop curving her lips, she turned to him, knowing she should be trying not to show how much his presence affected her and yet completely unable to help herself.

"I am. And you, Mr. Eversham? Are you musical?"

"Musical in the sense I enjoy listening to it, but I'm afraid I have no talent for playing any instrument."

It took her a moment to realize he had finished speaking and another to process what he had said. She floundered to think of something else to say, her normally easy conversation drying up. What on earth was wrong with her? She must pull herself together or he ... everyone ... *he* would notice.

He leaned closer, pretending to inspect a tray of meringues on the table in front of them. "Lord Horace seems to have changed his mind about you." His voice was grave, as though he was delivering bad news.

"Has he?" She glanced in Horace's direction and saw to her dismay that he was watching her. He didn't look pleased.

"He isn't looking at you like an old friend, Tina."

Suddenly she felt as if she were the one being hunted. She stood up, her shawl sliding from her shoulders before she could stop it. He bent and retrieved it for her. She reached out to take it, but instead he slid it about her shoulders, his fingers brushing bare skin.

Tina gave a gasp; she couldn't prevent it.

He was very close, and she wanted him even closer.

"Tina . . ." he half groaned.

"I beg your pardon, Eversham. Sir Henry wants a word." It was Horace, eyes narrowed, clearly suspicious that something was going on. Richard gave him a look as if he'd like to strangle him, then with a bow to Tina, turned and walked away. Horace took her arm in a proprietary grip.

"Don't like that fellow," he said in a voice that was far too loud. "Don't know why Sir Henry keeps inviting him."

Tina opened her mouth to argue and then changed her mind. What was the use of increasing Horace's suspicions? Instead she said, "I am rather tired, Horace, and Signor Veruda is giving me a headache. I think I will retire. Good night."

He looked put out, as if he'd expected a gushing thank-you for rescuing her from the awful Mr. Eversham, but suddenly she didn't care what he thought. She just wanted to be alone, to sleep away her fears and anxieties.

And to dream of a totally impractical future that was all about Richard Eversham.

Chapter 20

Lady Carol was pretending to be asleep. Her head was badly cushioned by the worn squabs, and every time there was a bump it jolted her, so that now she had the beginnings of a headache. Still it was better to pretend to be asleep than watch Sir Thomas scowling to himself on the opposite seat of the hired coach.

The visit to his brother Harold had not gone well.

There had been the usual recriminations and mutterings about Sir Thomas's shortcomings as a responsible adult, but they'd been prepared for that. And to give him credit, Harold had agreed to pay some of their more pressing bills. It was the manner in which he'd done it that rankled with his brother.

Harold hadn't handed Thomas the money—he'd refused point-blank, saying his brother could not be trusted. Instead, he'd directed his steward to pay the bills, humiliating enough in itself but even more so when he gave the man his instructions right there in front of them, using it as another chance to belittle Thomas's money-management skills.

No wonder he was scowling.

Lady Carol wriggled to try to get more comfortable, wishing she were home in her bed. At least now they would be spared losing the house for a little longer, but they would still lose it. Harold had made it clear he would not be coming to their assistance again, no matter how dire things became or how much they groveled. This was it.

She'd tried hard not to blame her husband for their mess, but she couldn't help it. It was his fault they'd lost everything, and it gave her a dark, achy feeling in her heart. She might never be able to forgive him. Worse, she might never be able to love him again. Theirs had been a happy marriage—oh, they'd had their good and bad times, the same as anyone else, but compared to some other unions she'd witnessed, theirs was a truly happy one.

Or it had been until now.

She glanced out of the window at the passing forest. Ironically, they were only a few miles away from Arlington Hall, where Tina and Charles were staying. Lady Carol sighed, wondering how they were managing and whether either of them had secured a proposal of marriage yet. She hated herself for thinking of it, but she couldn't help it—she'd never intended to be the sort of mother who pushed her children in the path of rich partners and marriages of convenience, and here she was, doing exactly that.

And she blamed Sir Thomas for that, too.

The sudden jerking stop of the coach brought

her out of her dark thoughts. Sir Thomas reared up like an angry serpent. "What is happening?" he roared, reaching to open the door.

Before he could touch it, however, it was opened for him from the outside, and Lady Carol gave a muffled scream.

A man stood there wearing a black hat and a mask hiding all of his face apart from his cold, pale blue eyes. He wore black gloves and in one of his hands he held a long-barreled pistol, which he pointed at her husband.

For a heart stopping moment Lady Carol thought he was going to discharge the weapon, and that Sir Thomas was going to die right in front of her shocked gaze. The whole world seemed to slow and solidify, and in that instant she knew that if he were to die, then life for her would also cease.

The highwayman laughed, a dry, dead sound, and said, "What's happening? Why, a spot of highway robbery, that's what!"

Lady Carol heard another laugh and looked up from the awful sight in front of her. There were two other men, sitting astride their horses. They both wore the same black masks covering most of their faces, and they both held pistols, and their coachman lay on the ground, unconscious or dead.

The highwayman laughed again as he noticed the expression on her face. "Sorry, lovely, I wish I had time to play." He looked her up and down and she cringed. "Very nice for an old 'un," he said softly.

"Leave my wife alone!" Sir Thomas shouted. "Just take our belongings and go."

"Shut up, old man," the robber said quietly.

Lady Carol shivered and reached for her husband, clinging to him. She had never been so terrified and never felt so helpless in her life. She needed Sir Thomas, she knew now how much she needed him, just as this man was threatening to take him away from her.

"Hand over all your valuables. Now!"

Lady Carol whimpered as Sir Thomas handed his fob watch to the masked man. "That's all I have," he said angrily although he had stopped shouting and was trying to remain calm. The highwayman frightened him, too, but mainly because of the way in which he was looking at his wife. "You've held up the wrong coach. We're bankrupt."

"So they all say. Out of the coach!"

Sir Thomas assisted his frightened wife down from the coach.

"Jewelry," demanded the highwayman.

With shaking hands Lady Carol fumbled with her pearl necklace and when she couldn't open it burst into tears. Just as it seemed the highwayman was about to rip it from her throat, Sir Thomas gently undid the clasp and handed the pearls over.

"Blunt?" asked the man.

Sir Thomas handed over some coins. "I told you, we're bankrupt. We have no more."

One of the other men got down from his horse and began to search Sir Thomas. He checked his pockets and patted him down, then he climbed into the coach and searched there but found nothing. Finally, he'd turned to Lady Carol and seeing she was next to be searched she began to scream.

"Be quiet, woman!" the highwayman growled, but Lady Carol was beyond reasoning now. She screamed louder and louder and even Sir Thomas could do nothing to stop her. With a nervous glance over his shoulder, the highwayman muttered, "We'd better be off before her screeching brings the law down on us."

"Yeah, they ain't got nuffink anyways," said one of the other men. "Not worf swingin' for."

The next moment they were gone.

It took Sir Thomas some time to calm his hysterical wife, and then he checked on the coachman, who was unconscious and thankfully not dead. The road they were on seemed very quiet, and despite the noise Lady Carol had been making, no one had come to their rescue.

"Looks like we're going to have to rescue ourselves, my dear," Sir Thomas said with a wry smile. "Can you help me with this fellow? We'll get him into the coach."

Lady Carol tottered over, and the two of them began to drag the coachman toward the coach. He was heavy but thankfully not a large man, and with much huffing and puffing, they got him up and into the coach and made him as comfortable as possible. When they were done, Sir Thomas found his silver brandy flask still in its spot in a pocket of the seat and drew it out triumphantly. He was about to take a swig when he saw his wife, white-faced, slumped on the ground, and sank down beside her.

"Here, my dear, have a sip of brandy."

For once she did not protest, and took a sip and then another. By the time Sir Thomas had taken his gulp of the fiery stuff, she was looking a little better, and her cheeks had some color in them.

"What are we going to do, Thomas?" she said, her green eyes wide.

He slipped an arm about her and gave her a comforting squeeze. "Looks like we'll have to drive ourselves, my dear. It's been a good while since I drove my phaeton. Do you remember it? Marvelous vehicle. I used to bowl along with you at my side."

Lady Carol smiled reminiscently. "I remember. We were very dashing, weren't we?"

"We'll just have to pretend this lumbering coach is a phaeton. Come on, my dear"—and he helped her up—"the sooner we get on, the sooner we will find an inn. Do you know," he added, as his wife took his arm, "I never thought I'd be glad of Harold's miserly ways, but I am today. If he'd given me the blunt to pay my own bills, we'd have lost the lot."

Lady Carol stretched up to kiss his cheek. "I'm sorry I've been horrid, my love. It takes something like highway robbery to make one realize what is important to one. Things are just things, but if I'd lost you . . . it doesn't bear thinking."

Sir Thomas smiled. "We have each other, and whatever becomes of us, we must remember that."

"We must."

There was a sparkle in Lady Carol's eyes he hadn't seen for some time, and Sir Thomas felt an enormous weight lifted from his shoulders. The world had turned topsy-turvy, but he had his beloved wife back again.

Chapter 21

The following day, the men set off early for their shooting, and the women rose late. Maria brought Tina a tray with tea and toast and then began to prepare her clothing for the morning at Arlington Hall. Outside it was turning into a sunny day, despite Sir Henry's fears the weather might turn nasty, and Tina sat up in bed on a mountain of soft pillows and gazed at the view from her window.

Irrational as it might seem, she had a sense that this day was going to be important to her, that there was something momentous fast approaching, and she'd best prepare for it.

After she'd washed and dressed in a cream-colored day dress with a pastel print, Maria brushed her hair and pinned it up. Satisfied with her appearance, Tina went downstairs to breakfast.

Lady Isabelle greeted her cheerfully enough, but she looked weary, and her spirits were clearly not as high as they had been the night before. A couple times she lapsed into silence, staring at nothing, and smiling to herself. As if she was replaying some memory in her head. When it happened Tina exchanged glances with her friends and couldn't help but wonder what pleasant thoughts Lady Isabelle was indulging in.

Eventually it was decided that those who wished to could come on a stroll in the gardens and down to the river, while the less active guests could remain in the house to read or doze or whatever else took their fancy.

By now it was a glorious day, the sun warm but not yet hot and the air clear and pure. As they walked, Lady Isabelle spoke, and she appeared to know the names of all the plants in her garden and waxed quite lyrical about them. It was an unexpected side to her.

"When I married Sir Henry and came to Arlington Hall the garden was very overgrown. I replanted the entire garden and restored many of the stone walls and pathways. Sometimes we allow the public in to visit and they picnic on the lawns or stroll about the borders. Only when we're not in residence, of course. Sir Henry grumbles about my spending so much time out here in the garden, but I know he's glad I've found something with which to occupy myself. We had hoped for children, but I am beginning to lose hope."

She looked sad for a moment but then seemed to shake it off. Turning to the other women, who were lagging behind, she called rather testily, "Come along, ladies. Catch up. Do you see this shrub?" The shrub was covered in purple flowers, and the perfume was beautiful and exotic. "It comes from India. And this one over here, with the red flowers that look rather like brushes? All the way from Australia. Can you imagine?"

While they were admiring these specimens a familiar voice interrupted their tour.

"My dear Lady Isabelle, here you are!"

Signor Veruda was striding purposefully in their direction, smartly dressed in beige trousers with a well-tailored chocolate brown jacket and a matching brown waistcoat with gold-and-beige swirls. His starched white cravat was high beneath his chin, and his jet-black hair shone in the weak English sunshine while his black eyes glittered with mischief and warmth.

Suddenly Lady Isabelle was all aflutter. "Signor! I thought you might join the gentlemen for shooting?"

He pulled a face. "I am not one for the bang-bang."

The women tittered, but Lady Isabelle could only gaze at him with adoring eyes. It was quite embarrassing really, Tina thought afterward. And it was becoming very clear that Lady Isabelle and her Italian baritone were more than just friends.

They turned back, meandering along the paths, chatting and laughing and keeping an eye on their hostess and the signor. He was certainly a fascinating character, every bit as exotic as the plants in the garden, and every woman there was drawn to him. The house was in sight when suddenly they could hear dogs barking and voices shouting, and Tina could see Charles hurrying toward them. Something in his manner struck her with fear—was this the momentous happening she'd been expecting? Lady Isabelle's face went white, and Signor Veruda held her arm to support her.

"Lady Isabelle." Charles was breathless and flustered. "Beg pardon. There has been an accident. Sir Henry . . ."

Lady Isabelle swayed and clutched at the signor's coat. "What has happened?" she cried.

Charles, belatedly realizing he should have put things less bluntly, opened and closed his mouth.

"Charles, what is it?" Tina said sharply, stepping up to him. "What's happened?"

"Oh. Tina? There you are. Eh, someone tried to . . . no, no, I'm quite sure it was an accident, it must have been."

"Charles, for goodness' sake!"

"Tina, Sir Henry was very nearly shot! The bullet made a groove across his scalp above his ear. He hit his head when he fell, and now he's unconscious. We carried him back to the house, and Eversham has sent posthaste for the doctor."

Lady Isabelle was already hurrying to the house, her skirts rustling furiously about her, Signor Veruda at her side, whispering in a mixture of English and Italian. Tina took Charles's arm, about to follow, when Anne came up to them, her blue eyes wide.

"How awful, Charles," her gentle voice was trembling. "Will he . . . do you think he might . . ."

"Steady on, Anne," Charles said. "Sir Henry is a tough old bird. It'd take more than a bullet and a fall to finish him off."

Tina thought her brother's reassurance rather rough-and-ready, but Anne was gazing at him as if he were perfection itself. She left them to it, going ahead to the house, where she found Horace standing alone in the vast entrance hall, staring thoughtfully into space.

"Horace? Charles has just told us what happened."

Horace pulled a face. "An unpleasant business. He's unconscious. Not a peep out of him. They've sent for the doctor, and Eversham's thrown us all out of the room." His face darkened, but Tina hurried on before he could start down that particular well-worn track.

"I don't understand how anyone could shoot Sir Henry by mistake. He doesn't look like a pigeon."

"A gun might have gone off accidentally."

"Has anyone owned up to that?"

"No, and I don't imagine anyone will, do you? No one wants to admit to being such a fool."

"But surely someone else must have seen something? You were all together, weren't you?" asked Tina.

"Here and there." For a moment, he looked uncomfortable, as if he'd prefer not to answer her questions. He took her hand tightly and squeezed it almost painfully. "Lady Isabelle was in a state. Guilty conscience."

"Guilty conscience?"

"That singer fellow. It's obvious, isn't it? Lady Isabelle is a great deal younger than Sir Henry and looking for diversion, and she's found it in Signor Veruda. She probably thinks it's all her fault her husband is at death's door."

"Horace, is she really . . . ?"

"What, having an affair with the Italian? Yes, I should say so."

Tina felt uncomfortable with the idea, despite the fact she'd suspected it herself, but she was far more uncomfortable with the suddenly lascivious look in Horace's blue eyes. "Tina," he said, his voice dropping to an intimate pitch, "I've been meaning to talk to you."

Thankfully just then Charles and Anne came upon them, and he had to let her hand go and move away. A moment later the hall was full of people, and Lady Isabelle appeared, pale and fragile, at the head of the stairs.

"I'm so sorry," she said shakily, "but Sir Henry will have to spend the rest of the day in bed. Please, you must all continue with the picnic luncheon. No, I insist," she hurried on, as protests were raised. "Sir Henry would insist. All is in hand, and my housekeeper will show you the way. Now, if you will excuse me," and she was gone again.

"Eversham is making the most of it," Horace muttered, and, following his gaze, Tina saw Richard in the shadows behind where Lady Isabelle had been standing. He was looking pensive, gazing down into the hall, but she couldn't see who he was looking at.

Herself? Or perhaps Horace?

A moment later he was gone, and despite herself she felt the loss.

The picnic was to be held by the river, where there was a wooden pavilion set up with tables and chairs. Hardly a picnic then, Tina thought wryly, more like an outdoor dining room. The guests had a choice of strolling down or being driven, and Tina had decided to walk.

"Will we be safe?" Anne whispered, still shaken from the morning's events.

Charles heard her and laughed. "Perfectly safe, Miss Burgess. Sir Henry had an accident, he wasn't attacked by outlaws. And *I'll* be here to watch out for you."

Anne reached for her parasol, but Tina noticed the color in her cheeks that always seemed to appear when Charles was about her. "Thank you, Charles."

He held out his arm for her, and Tina smiled to herself. She'd be delighted if her brother settled down with Anne, and not only because such a rich bride would take some of the pressure off her to marry a wealthy man. Charles needed a steadying influence, and Anne was certainly that. And, Tina admitted uncomfortably to herself, it would do him good to see less of his great friend Horace, who always seemed to bring out the worst in him.

In fact both Charles and Horace seemed decidedly lacking in character when she compared them to a man like Richard Eversham.

Branson and his wife were in an open carriage, rather rudely calling for everyone to hurry along, as they bowled past them. Charles explained to Anne that the Bransons had once owned Arlington Hall, before it was Arlington Hall, so perhaps they still felt proprietary about the place.

"Excuse me, Miss Smythe?"

She turned to find a young man she'd been briefly introduced to last night as Will Jackson. He was gazing at her a little shyly, but his smile

was pleasant, and she found herself smiling back.
"Miss Smythe, I wonder if I might escort you to
the picnic? Richard . . . that is Mr. Eversham asked
that I take particular care of you."

She wasn't quite sure why Mr. Eversham would
think it his place to ask anyone to look after her,
but as Will Jackson seemed sincere she simply
nodded and took his arm. They spoke about the
weather and the countryside, anything but Sir
Henry's accident, and after a time Tina had the
feeling that he was deliberately steering her away
from the topic. She couldn't help but wonder
whether there was a reason for that and what that
reason might be.

The pavilion was big enough to seat them all,
and waiting servants bustled about, serving the
food and drink, catering to their every need.
Through the open doorways and windows the
river appeared idyllic, the blue sky reflected in it,
but a chilly breeze was beginning to strengthen,
and Tina began to wish she'd dressed more
warmly.

"Lady Isabelle comes here to bathe," the neighbor, Mrs. Branson, seated to one side of her, was
saying. "There is a bathing house that can be
pushed out into the river, for the sake of discretion."

Horace, seated beside Tina despite all her at-
tempts to escape him, nudged her. "Lady Isabelle
and discretion, surely that's an oxymoron."

Tina shot him a look.

"Don't slay me with your eyes, Tina, you know
very well what I mean."

"I notice you don't condemn Signor Veruda."

"The vile seducer? Come, Tina, all men are vile seducers. That is the way we're made."

"All of you?" she retorted, uneasy, willing it to be a jest.

"Do you really think Signor Veruda is the first?" he leaned to whisper in her ear. "Lady Isabelle is incredibly generous with her favors."

Tina shuddered. She felt a little sick. "I don't believe you," she said bluntly.

"You should believe me. Tina. If anyone should know, then it is I."

It was as if he were boasting, as if he thought she would be impressed by his confidences, but Tina was repulsed. Why must all men be vile seducers? Was that the truth or simply Horace's own belief?

Tina did her best to ignore him after that, eating her cold chicken and salad, listening to the others enjoying themselves. His words ate at her, eroding away any sort of feeling she'd had for him.

Richard had done all he could for Sir Henry. The sight of the older gentleman lying on the ground, bleeding from the bullet wound, had shocked Richard more than he had let on. He hadn't seen his brother immediately after he'd been shot, but Anthony must have appeared much like that.

Sir Henry was resting comfortably, according to the doctor, and it was best to leave him sleep. Healing came through sleep, and if Sir Henry had damaged his brain, then he needed to rest and heal himself.

And if he didn't wake up?

It was Isabelle's trembling question that caused the doctor to hesitate and then reassure her that in nine times out of ten, the patient woke up.

"I couldn't say in front of Her Ladyship," the doctor murmured later, when he was alone with Richard, "but I have grave fears for her husband. He's sustained a very nasty injury. We must pray he wakes soon."

Will Jackson had returned from the picnic, and he and Richard shut themselves into the library.

"You need to question all the men who were out this morning," Richard said seriously.

"You don't think this was an accident then?"

"I don't know, but Sir Henry told me he was looking into the lives of John Little and Lord Horace Gilfoyle. They are both here. Perhaps they decided to put an end to his inquiries."

"Or perhaps it was a simple accident," Will Jackson soothed. "However I will begin to ask some questions."

"Be subtle about it, Will. Tell them Lady Isabelle wants to know."

"I'll be subtle, Richard."

Richard lapsed into thought for a moment. "If someone was trying to shoot him, then there's a good chance our Captain *is* one of the guests."

"Good point. Perhaps we should create an opportunity for him to take a shot at me and catch him in the act!"

Richard smiled despite his gravity. "One wounded Guardian at a time, Will. Did you find Miss Smythe?" he asked. "You're back awfully quickly."

"I found her. I tried to sit with her at luncheon,

but Gilfoyle pushed in. Didn't seem much point hanging around after that, so I came back here."

Richard had hoped that Will and Tina might find some sort of common ground, but it seemed that Gilfoyle had other ideas. For a man who'd been indifferent to Tina, calling her an innocent and boring, he'd certainly changed his opinion of her. Richard had the uncomfortable feeling that it had been his lessons that had brought the change about, the absolute opposite of what he'd intended.

"I'll go and join them at the river," he said abruptly. "Stay here with Sir Henry, and let's just hope he wakes soon. Perhaps he saw who shot him? That would solve all our problems."

"There is another possibility," Will began tentatively. "Lady Isabelle and Signor Veruda."

Richard sighed and shook his head. "I know what you're thinking, but I can't see it. Despite her behavior last night Lady Isabelle loves her husband. They have an awkward relationship; well awkward on her part anyway. Sir Henry is the calming influence, he's her rock. She would never leave him, and certainly never harm him. And as for Signor Veruda . . . can you see him lurking in the woods with a loaded gun, taking aim, then melting into the trees? He wouldn't be able to help launching into an aria."

Will grinned. "Put like that, perhaps not."

Chapter 22

The picnic luncheon was finally over. It had been uncomfortable and distressing for her, sitting next to Horace. His behavior toward her was on the verge of insolent, and she was certain he'd said several things that were far too risqué for her ears—not that she understood them but she could tell by the glint in his eyes.

Was this her doing? Had she given him cause to believe she was eager to be his mistress? How could her plans have gone so awry!

Escaping Horace—he'd become embroiled in a conversation with some other guests—Tina made haste to join Charles and Anne at the riverside, where a jetty jutted out into the water. Several rowing boats were tied up and awaiting those who wished to partake, and already groups of guests were setting out, making a pretty scene of bright gowns and waistcoats and ribbons on straw bonnets, while parasols cast shade over delicate complexions.

Anne was being assisted into a boat by Charles, when Tina touched her brother's arm and, drawing him aside, murmured that she wanted to speak to him.

"Speak to me about what?" Charles said grumpily, watching Anne being rowed away without him.

"Charles, you know Horace better than anyone. Is it true? Have he and Lady Isabelle been lovers?"

Charles stilled. "Who told you that?" he said quietly.

"Horace told me."

He looked momentarily too surprised to speak, and then his face darkened. "He shouldn't have. A lady's reputation is sacrosanct and . . . well, he shouldn't be talking like that to you. I'm going to have a word with him." He turned about, seeking Horace among the crowd.

Tina was pleasantly surprised at his protective attitude—she'd been afraid her brother might take Horace's side and disregard her feelings. But then again, she couldn't allow him to become embroiled in anything he didn't properly understand, not without explaining matters to him, no matter how difficult and embarrassing that explanation may be for herself.

"Charles, wait. I-I think I may have given him the wrong impression," she said woodenly with a sideways glance. "Lately I've been . . . it's just that he might have thought I was angling to be his lover, too."

Charles stared at her as if she'd lost her mind.

"Actually, I was trying to persuade him that I would make him a perfect wife, but he seems to have got it into his head that I want to be the perfect mistress."

He shook his head at her. "Why would you want Horace to marry you?"

"I love him," she said.

"No, you don't! And besides, Horace would make a terrible husband. He would never be faithful, Tina, and he has mistresses and women . . ." His mouth closed in a prudish line. "I think I've said enough."

Tina blinked. "No, I don't love him, you're right, but I do have to marry him, Charles. The family . . . that is, Father . . ." Her voice trailed off. How could she explain to Charles that they were destitute? He would be shocked and horrified, and apart from that, she'd been told not to tell him, that he wouldn't be able to cope with the news.

However the Charles facing her now was no callow youth. He was a man. And he looked as if he would shake the truth from her if she didn't speak it very soon.

The words came bubbling from her lips, all about Father's money problems and their having to sell the heirlooms and then Tina's decision to marry Horace, and Lady Carol's encouragement. The cold hard fact that this weekend was to be her last chance to secure him before it was too late for them all. By the time they returned home there would be no home to return to.

Charles listened, his face turning to the color of ash, and when she was finished he stared at her with eyes that were far older and wiser than they'd been a moment before.

"They should have told me." He groaned. "I've been going off to clubs, thinking everything was all right, when . . . Good God, how could I not have known!" He turned away but turned back almost immediately. "Do you really think marrying Horace will put everything right, Tina? If you do, then you're a fool. He might be my best friend, but I would never let you marry him. He would make you miserable, and nothing is worth that."

Tina watched him walk away, feeling sick and upset, the beginnings of another headache drumming against her skull. Suddenly she couldn't bear to be here with everyone enjoying themselves. She wanted to be alone. She wanted to be completely and utterly alone.

She turned and began to run along the path by the river, losing herself in a grove of shady trees, running until she could no longer hear the voices or the careless laughter.

Richard saw her running from his position up on the pathway that looped down to the river. Immediately he cut off the path and across the lawn, in the direction she was going, hoping to reach her before she got too far ahead.

What on earth had sent her into such a mad dash? Was she in danger, or had Gilfoyle hurt her in some way?

Richard lengthened his stride. Tina's pale gown appeared between the trees, gone one moment and back again the next, and he began to worry she might vanish completely. He began to run, too, his heart thumping, his blood pumping, his jaw clenched so tightly his teeth hurt.

There she was!

She'd slowed down to a walk, and then she stopped altogether, standing disconsolately, with her head bowed. She looked absolutely despairing, and with a burst he made the final sprint to reach her. She must have heard his approach because suddenly she spun around.

"Tina," he breathed, and then she was in his arms, her mouth on his, her face hot and damp with tears. He wasn't sure who made the first move, and he didn't care. This felt so right he couldn't have stopped himself if they had had an audience of hundreds. They clung together, and she was returning his kisses, passionately, as if she couldn't stop herself, either. As if she didn't want to.

When at last they drew apart, they were both breathless and shaking.

"What is it?" he gasped, staring at her frantic expression and teary eyes. "Sweetheart, what has happened?"

She opened her mouth as if to tell him, but just then they heard voices drawing closer along the path, beyond the trees, and she shook her head and pulled away. "I'm sorry," she said huskily. "I shouldn't have done that. I'm sorry, Richard. I've ruined everything; I can't do anything right."

"Tina, please, there's nothing to be sorry about. Let me help you."

"You can't help me."

He could see that she believed it, and he wanted to kiss her again until she capitulated, but those blasted voices were getting louder and closer, and, any moment, they would be seen. Suddenly an audience didn't seem such a good idea.

"I'll come to your room." He said the words instinctively, without thought, only knowing he must. "Tonight. Tell me then."

She went still. She probably couldn't believe he'd said something so indecent; he could hardly believe it himself. But what else could he do? They needed privacy, and he needed to know what was going on.

"I just want to talk," he said to reassure her, with a quick glance at the strolling guests fast approaching. "Tina?"

She nodded, just once, and then she was walking away from him, her pace quickening, and he let her go.

Richard felt frustrated and angry. He was a man who was in total control of his life, but somehow that urge to control had grown to also include Tina. He wanted to protect her, help her, cherish her, and he wouldn't be denied. Thinking of her tear-stained face again, he wondered what in God's name had happened to upset her.

Was it Gilfoyle?

His face darkened.

Of course it must be Gilfoyle. He'd hurt her or-or insulted her. Richard began walking purposefully toward the pavilion until he came within sight of it and the milling guests. There he was, laughing with a group of his admirers, blond hair bright in the sunshine.

Richard stood and stared at him and it took an immense effort of will not to keep walking, drag Gilfoyle away from his friends, and punch him in his smug mouth. He squeezed his hands into fists, rigid with fury, trying to regain his reason. There was a violence inside him, a recklessness, that threatened to overcome the current need for calm common sense.

He reminded himself that Gilfoyle was not going to get away with his behavior. He was a liar and quite possibly a murderer, and soon, very soon, Richard was going to unleash his vengeance upon Lord Horace in a way he would never forget.

One of Arlington Hall's upper footmen had been hanging about Maria, but Archie followed them to the landing on the servants' stairs and soon saw him off. Maria stood in the sunshine that glinted through the window and smiled.

"You frightened him with your fierce expression," she said.

"Good. He's too young for you."

Maria lost her smile. "Too young?"

"You need a more mature sort of man."

She laughed then, quietly, intimately.

Archie had hardly seen her since they reached Arlington Hall. The servants here were strictly regimented, men in one area and women in the other, and although they all ate together, there was also a strict precedence when it came to seating arrangements. And that blasted upper footman was always putting his nose in where it wasn't wanted.

He also suspected Maria had been avoiding him, and he suspected he knew why. He'd been keeping secrets from her, and she didn't approve.

"I was hoping to speak to you," she said, interrupting his thoughts. "I was going to come and find you in the men's quarters if I had to."

"That's very bold."

"It was necessary. I'm worried about Sir Henry's being shot."

Archie felt his expression go tense and a little cagey. He knew Mr. Eversham wouldn't like him talking about this, and yet Maria had a way of wheedling things out of him, and he was beginning to think she was far better at wheedling than he. Besides, he preferred to be honest with her.

"Is your master involved in this, Archie?"

"In the shooting?" he hedged.

"No, foolish man, I don't think he would have shot Sir Henry," she mocked. "I meant, is this something to do with his work. With your work? I'm asking not through idle curiosity but because I need to know whether Miss Tina is in danger."

Archie scratched his chin. "I'm sure—"

"Don't make excuses, Archie. Or I will leave you here all alone and go and find that nice young man you just chased away."

He sighed and knew he was beaten, and seeing it, her smile grew wider.

"Mr. Eversham *is* worried about the shooting, but your mistress isn't in danger. If anyone is in danger it's probably Mr. Eversham."

"Oh. Why is that?"

"He is seeking a particular gentleman, someone who has evil intentions for the country and the government. Someone he also has a personal grudge against. He suspects this gentleman might be here at Arlington Hall."

Maria's eyes were round. "But surely that is very dangerous, Archie? Who is this man? I need to know so that I can take care around him."

Archie hesitated and then made his decision. He'd already said far too much, but in for a penny, in for a pound. If he was going to ask Maria to share her life with him, he had to trust her, and she had to trust him. "He thinks the gentleman he's seeking may be Lord Horace Gilfoyle."

Now Maria was very worried. "But he is the friend of Mr. Charles and Miss Tina! You must warn them at once, Archie."

"Most definitely not. If we warn them, then

he will hear of it, and the next thing he'll flee the country. We must stay quiet, Maria. Do you understand? We must trust Mr. Eversham to deal with this."

"But Archie—"

"Maria, I have said things I should not, but you cannot repeat them. I will lose my job."

Reluctantly she nodded, but now Archie could see that Maria's priorities weren't the same as his. She didn't care much for the government, but she did care for her mistress. And her mistress seemed to have got herself into a bit of a bother with Gilfoyle and Mr. Eversham. Archie could appreciate that being the personal maid to Miss Tina could be a very worrying thing, and the sooner this mess was sorted out—hopefully by Mr. Eversham—the sooner he could take Maria away from it all and look after her properly.

"Mr. Eversham will make sure she is safe," he went on confidently, hoping she'd believe him. "I think he's got a bit of a soft spot for Miss Tina."

Her dark eyes narrowed as they fastened on him. "He'd better take very good care of her, or I'll deal with him myself."

And looking at her, Archie knew she meant it. His Maria was a loyal and wonderful firebrand of a woman, and he was pretty certain he was in love with her. As to whether she was in love with him? Well, that was another problem, and he wasn't sure yet how to solve it.

Chapter 23

❧

The two men met in the gloomy woods behind the hall. They would be unlucky if anyone noticed they were missing. Everyone else was otherwise engaged, either resting before dinner or taking afternoon tea in the salon.

"You idiot! What on earth possessed you to take a shot at Sir Henry in front of everyone?"

Branson, with a sullen curl to his lip and a rebellious glint to his eyes, looked as if he might say something rash, but common sense prevailed, and at the last moment he bit it back.

"Well? Answer me, damn you, Branson!"

"It was just to give him a scare," he muttered, chastened. "I had no intention of killing him, or he'd be dead. I'm a good shot, you know."

"Why on earth would you want to give him a scare? Are you sure you weren't having your own little revenge on the man? Everyone knows you're sick with jealousy because he owns Arlington Hall."

Branson couldn't think of anything to say.

"And you do realize that because of you Sir

Henry knows that we are among his little group—that someone here is most likely the very man he's been looking for?" He threw up his hands in an excess of frustrated emotion. "I can't believe you could be so stupid."

"He'll never think it was me!"

His companion stared at him in amazed disgust. "No, probably not, but he has no reason to trust me, has he?"

Branson scrambled to dig himself out of his own mess. "Someone must have noticed you in the shooting party among the others. They'll say you were there in plain sight when Sir Henry was shot. You're safe. There's no harm done."

The other man sighed and shook his head, beginning to calm down, beginning to think. One of the Captain's main strengths was a cool head. "You are a fool. But I suppose now we'll find out who else here is in Sir Henry's little team. No doubt someone will be questioning us all in the morning."

"Eversham" was Branson's prompt reply. "He and Sir Henry are thick as thieves."

"Well, we shall know soon enough. Now I'd better get back to the house in case they're watching me. And don't do anything else without consulting me first."

He didn't wait for Branson's reply but strode off. As he neared the stables at the back of the hall, he began whistling nonchalantly, hands in his pockets, as if he'd been out for a pleasant afternoon stroll.

Branson was a complete fool, and he would no longer trust him. In fact he would never have taken him on, but at the time the man's disaffection with Sir Henry had made it expedient. And now what if Sir Henry died? There'd be hell to pay, but he'd make certain Branson was the one who hanged. It shouldn't be too hard to point the finger in his direction.

For a moment he let his thoughts wander back, to Anthony Eversham's face as he put the bullet into him. He gave a satisfied smile. Anthony had found out about him, but luckily he'd decided to keep his information to himself, play the lone hero. He'd nearly caught the Captain, but his luck had held.

It would hold this time. He wouldn't believe otherwise. And if Anthony's brother got too close; well, he'd go the same way.

Chapter 24

Tina felt as if she were at the center of a growing storm. Charles knew about their financial circumstances, Horace thought she was eager to be his mistress, and Richard Eversham was coming to her room tonight to talk to her.

She bit her lip on a hysterical giggle, hastily composing herself as she came under Maria's suspicious gaze. Her maid knew there was something happening, but Tina had made certain she didn't have a chance to question her by keeping her busy, or chattering nonsense whenever there was a silence.

She didn't want to discuss any of it. In fact she didn't even want to think about it.

Her evening dress was laid out. Rose silk, the color of freshly opened petals, with short sleeves ending in a flounce and a matching flounce on the bottom of the skirt. The décolletage was scooped quite low but made respectable by a smidgeon of white French lace. Maria fastened her corset and enveloped her in petticoats and then eased on the ball gown. Despite her day outdoors, Tina's complexion was flawless, and her pale skin emphasized her green eyes and dark lashes. Once again, she wore the garnets about her throat and the matching earrings.

She felt buffeted by circumstance, no longer certain in which direction to turn. Which direction to run. Her husband-hunting plan with Horace had gone horribly wrong, and now she'd broken her parents' confidence and told Charles the secret family shame, and he was so upset . . . Her breath caught, but she disguised her sudden emotion by reaching for her long evening gloves and drawing them smoothly on. Maria buttoned the tiny seed-pearl buttons and clipped a pearl bracelet about Tina's wrist.

She glanced in the mirror again, feeling the cool air coming through the inch of open window, the scent of the garden and the river, the sounds of bird life settling down to sleep.

"Have you heard any more about Sir Henry?" she asked her maid. "It seems wrong to be going to a ball when he is in his bed and perhaps very ill."

"Only that Lady Isabelle insists everything go ahead as planned and that Sir Henry would want it that way."

Tina wondered if she would be that stoic if her husband were at death's door. She couldn't imagine it. But then she couldn't imagine herself married, not now that Horace had proved to be such a disappointment.

"You look beautiful, Miss Tina."

Maria was smiling at her from the candlelit shadows.

"Thank you, Maria."

A moment later, she was descending the stairs to join the other guests. The ballroom was a vision, and she paused to take it in.

Flowers were displayed in huge vases along the walls; an abundance of roses, lavender and lilies perfumed the air with their fragrance. There were chairs around the sides of the room and several musicians on a platform at the far end. It was very elegant, not a hint that the master of the house lay upstairs, unconscious, perhaps dying, although perhaps it was that fact that gave the whole occasion a sense of frenetic energy.

Tina strongly felt as if she must seize her happiness with both hands and not let it slip away, that life was finite, and she might never have this chance again.

Once more Richard found himself standing in a crowded room, waiting for Tina. He nodded as Will detailed to him the security measures he had taken for Sir Henry, and he listened carefully and smiled as other guests spoke to him, but his mind was elsewhere. He was restless, looking up every few moments, incomplete.

Until she entered the room.

As if on cue the music started.

Richard moved toward her, determined to have the first dance, only to be thwarted by Lady Isabelle, who placed a large middle-aged man in Tina's path. As he watched, there was some conversation, Tina smiled, and the two of them were off in a whirl of other couples.

He stood feeling ridiculously wretched.

Lady Isabelle observed the couple, a little smile playing about her mouth, and as she turned away, she noticed him.

"Richard," she said, and he had no option but to bow over her hand and ask how Sir Henry did.

Her smile dimmed. "He is sitting up and eating broth," she murmured, "but that is not what you want me to say, is it? He is meant to be unconscious, close to death." Her eyes searched his.

"Yes, that is what you must say," he agreed quietly. "He is well guarded in his room. If anyone tries again, we'll catch him."

"He can't stay there indefinitely."

"No. I think he will wake tomorrow," Richard said thoughtfully.

"This is all so awful," she began, but caught herself and gave a little shake of her head. "Never mind. You must enjoy yourself, Richard. I have gone to a great deal of trouble to make this ball a success and so it must be. There are people from all over the county, and Mr. Freer, who is dancing with Miss Smythe, is from America!"

Richard looked over at the couple, who appeared to be enjoying each other's company. He found himself wishing they were miserable.

"Really, America?" he repeated, as she'd meant him to.

"In confidence, Richard, he is here to find an English wife. He is rather taken with the English and says only an English wife will do. So I am on the lookout. I wondered whether Tina might be the one for him. Though she is very beautiful, and I'm sure she has many admirers. A middle-aged

American might not be what she wants, despite his being obscenely rich."

"Has she many admirers?" he said idly, as if the idea were new to him and of no real interest.

But something must have given him away because Isabelle's gaze sharpened, and her tone grew tart. "Why Richard! Are you jealous? I always thought your heart was made of stone."

He bowed again. "And so it is," he assured her. "Granite, in fact."

Her laughter followed him as he went to seek a partner from among the other women. He was wearing his heart on his sleeve indeed if Lady Isabelle had noticed; he must be more careful. Sir Henry was upstairs as bait, and Richard must have his wits about him tonight, just in case another attempt was made on his commander's life.

Tina had hoped Richard might dance with her, but so far he seemed to have made it his mission to partner all the wallflowers. It was very gentlemanly of him, of course, but she wished he'd come and ask her. Not that she'd lacked for partners, and most of them very pleasant.

Apart from one.

She hadn't wanted to dance with Horace, but there he was, and after so much had passed between them she felt she could not refuse him without causing a scene.

"It has been quite an exciting weekend in the country, Tina, don't you think?"

"That depends on what you find exciting, Horace."

He smiled, but it was not a nice smile. Suddenly, Horace did not seem like a very nice person.

"I noticed you beside the river after luncheon. You were running, Tina. Is that a new fashion for ladies?"

Startled, Tina met his eyes. She felt her heart begin to thud uncomfortably. "Running?"

"And I'm sure I saw Mr. Eversham running after you. It was very odd, but perhaps I was mistaken."

"Perhaps you were."

But his skeptical expression told her he knew he wasn't and that he wasn't happy with what he'd seen, and he could make mischief for her if he wished. "You know," he said, suddenly serious as the final strains of their dance were played, "you can always come to me if you need help, Tina. We have known each other a very long time, haven't we?"

"We have, Horace. I'll bear it in mind."

Tina was very glad to leave him behind and walk away. She must tell Richard. He might be able to do something to stop Horace from spreading rumors. But then she remembered that this was all her fault, she'd caused this mess, and it wasn't really fair to ask Richard to fix it.

"Ah, Tina!" It was Lady Isabelle again, bright-eyed, cheeks flushed. She caught Tina's arm and led her out of the crush. "I have been remiss. There is someone here you *must* dance with."

Although Tina put a bright smile on her face, she went with her hostess reluctantly. Who now? She'd been so looking forward to the ball, to dancing with Richard, and it was all going awry.

"Tina? Here he is."

She looked up and found herself face-to-face with Richard, who seemed as surprised as she. "Richard," Lady Isabelle exclaimed, like a conjurer who has performed a magic trick, and then bending close to murmur in his ear, she said "My gift to you, for protecting Henry. I really am grateful, you know."

Richard took Tina's hand in his as if it was something utterly priceless. Isabelle was speaking again, something about Mr. Freer being rather smitten with Margaret Allsop, but her voice seemed to fade into the far distance, and next thing Richard had led her onto the floor, and they were swirling around in a haze of candlelight and color.

"You are the most beautiful woman in the room." It was no polite compliment; he meant it, she could tell, and her heart fluttered.

When he held her close, Tina felt like the most beautiful woman in the room—in the world. She flowed into his arms. She felt overpowered by emotion and longing; surely, everyone here could see how she felt? And yet she didn't care, she wanted to stay like this forever, encircled by his arms, their bodies together and moving with the music.

Tina had danced with many men tonight but not like this. This one felt right. This was perfection.

And all too brief. Moments later the dance was over, and John Little claimed her, and she had no choice but to thank Richard and walk away from him as if she weren't miserable about it.

She had seen less of Mr. Little this weekend than she'd expected, and on the occasions she had seen him, he'd appeared preoccupied. But now he was his usual quiet and polite self, a little too quiet perhaps, as if he were counting his dance steps.

"I'm sorry Sir Thomas and Lady Carol aren't here, Miss Smythe."

"No, they are otherwise engaged."

Dealing with the bailiffs.

"So you said. I enjoyed their hospitality. I am not always shown such kindness."

"But sir, surely no one is ever *un*kind to you?"

He smiled. "You are a sweet young lady, but you must know there is a great deal of unkindness in polite society. Particularly to someone of my standing."

"Mr. Little, you are a gentleman."

"I am, but I am also in trade, and the two are not considered compatible. And although I was born a gentleman, my circumstances have not always been as I might have wished."

The music stopped and he looked so sad and Tina felt so sorry for him that instead of walking away she lingered.

They were near the doors leading to the garden. "Perhaps some fresh air, Miss Smythe?" he asked hopefully.

Tina allowed herself to be led outside.

"I didn't mean to distress you with old grievances, Miss Smythe," he said. "The past is just that. I have moved on."

They walked along the terrace. An urn stood on the steps, and a fountain twinkled. Tina caught sight of a couple in the shadows, and noted Lady Isabelle's bright hair. The next moment she heard her hostess's voice, rising shrilly in the still evening air.

"No, Vincenzo, I cannot. You know I cannot."

John Little had heard too and was looking in the same direction.

They could see Signor Veruda hovering over her, trying to hold her back, but the next moment Isabelle broke free and ran, blundering between them as if she didn't even know they were there, her face a white and tear-stained blur. Behind her Signor Veruda stood staring after her, his expression one of terrible unhappiness, and then he seemed to collect himself. He gave a brief bow in their direction, before he turned and vanished into the shadows.

"Unfortunate," John Little said. He had taken out a cigar and was making moves to light it. The scene had made Tina uncomfortable, and she decided it was time to go back inside. "I think we might return to the ballroom, Mr. Little."

"Are you sure?" He sounded disappointed.

"I believe it's almost time for supper."

She was pleased to see her brother and Anne approaching and moved to join them.

"Nearly time for food, sis. I could eat a horse."

"I do hope they won't serve up the horses, Charles."

He laughed. "No, probably not, but I *am* hungry. All that dancing."

"I'm glad you're feeling better, Charles," Tina said meaningfully, slipping her arm through his.

He shrugged philosophically. "Fiddle while

Rome burns. Time enough to be miserable when I get back to Mallory Street."

If Mallory Street still belongs to us.

They exchanged a meaningful glance.

The supper was an enormous spread, as if once again Lady Isabelle had set out to impress. Tina and Charles and Anne sat together, enjoying the various treats before them. A waiter filled their glasses, and Tina allowed herself two glasses of champagne.

Why not? she thought. *Charles is right. Fiddle while Rome burns indeed!*

After this weekend she might have to take some dreadful post as a governess or a companion or work in a factory. She shuddered. It didn't bear thinking of, but she would have to think of it. Not yet, though, not tonight.

Joseph Freer, she noticed, was proudly leading Margaret around the room as if they were already engaged. She pointed them out to Anne, who sat between her and Charles. "Just look at those two."

"He seems quite taken with her, doesn't he?"

"Besotted, I would say," added Charles.

"Isn't he a little old to be besotted?" Anne giggled.

"Never too old to be besotted." Charles grinned.

"Well, I wish them both the best," said Anne. "Although I did think it was Mr. Little Margaret had her eye on, I believe that is now quite finished."

"Finished?" Tina asked curiously.

"Mr. Little is not to be relied upon, at least that is what she told me."

"In what way isn't he to be relied upon?"

Anne picked up her spoon and dug it into her dessert. "I think he offered to take her to the theater and then had to cancel at the last moment. And it wasn't just the once. Margaret is very keen on keeping one's word, you know."

"Poor Mr. Little," Charles muttered, his mouth full.

Tina was watching Margaret and her American. "It's just—he's so old, I can't imagine . . ."

"You can't imagine what?" asked Charles, one eyebrow raised.

Kissing him!

"Never mind. I'm sure he'll make a very good husband."

Richard had been upstairs to check on Sir Henry. He'd encountered Branson lurking about outside the door, but the neighbor seemed merely curious about the current state of Sir Henry's health.

"Terrible accident, terrible," he kept saying, shaking his head.

Richard agreed and suggested he return to the ballroom. Something about the way the man glanced at him as he scuttled away struck him as odd, but he couldn't decide why that was. Branson hadn't been on his list of suspects, but now he remembered overhearing some comments made by the man and the cloak of bitterness that seemed to envelop him.

Mr. Branson might bear further investigation.

Sir Henry was propped up in his bed and restless, wanting to get up and take part in the entertainments—keep an eye on Isabelle, more likely—but he knew he had to stay here if they were to spring the trap they'd laid to catch his attacker.

"Have you found any clues?" he asked grumpily.

"Will is going to question the other shooters in the morning, sir. We might know more then."

"Humph. What fool would take a shot at me on my own dung heap? I'd have thought the Captain was smarter than that, Richard."

Richard agreed, but as he explained to his superior, they couldn't take any chances.

Downstairs again, Richard seemed to have caught Sir Henry's restlessness. He wandered about, and eventually found himself in the supper room. There was Tina and her brother, enjoying themselves, laughing. He liked watching Tina laugh.

She has the most exquisite mouth, he thought.

He wanted to walk over and kiss her there and then. In front of everyone. Claim her so that no other male in the room could have her. He leaned against the wall and wished he could have a brandy, but he'd denied himself any drink until later tonight. For now he needed his wits about him.

How in God's name was he going to come to her room and keep his hands off her? Was he deceiving himself even imagining he could? He'd be better staying away; he could make some excuse.

Then she looked over and caught him watching. She smiled, and he knew that nothing was going to stop him coming to her tonight, no matter the risks he was taking. It was fate or destiny or whatever you wanted to call it.

It was simply meant to be.

Chapter 25

Tina sat on the window seat in her room, drinking in the perfumed night air. There was a sliver of moon hanging low in the sky, reflected in the ripples of the river. She'd been watching it move slowly against the arc of velvet darkness and knew that soon it would slip below the horizon, leaving her alone.

It was very late now, and he still hadn't come.

Perhaps he'd had second thoughts? Well she couldn't blame him for that, but she would forever regret the loss of their one night together. Because she knew he wasn't coming to her to talk, things had gone too far for talking, and if he did come, then there would be no going back.

Tina wrapped her robe more closely about her and tried not to shiver. Maria had removed Tina's ball gown and helped her into her nightgown with the darned sleeve, and now she wondered if she would ever wear the ball gown again or whether it would become a ghost in the attic, full of lavender bags and memories.

Or more likely it would be sold to pay some outstanding bill.

Maria had brushed and braided her hair before leaving her to sleep—as she thought. Tina glanced over at the comfortable bed, considered retiring, but didn't move. She knew she wouldn't sleep. The day had been a long and exhausting one, but excitement hummed through her, tingling over her skin, making her nerves jump. Without her corset and underwear, she felt free, her body unrestrained by convention, and with the shedding of her grand clothing had come a similar shedding of her doubts about Richard.

Where was he? Please come, please . . .

She wriggled against the cushions on the window seat, trying to get comfortable, and then froze.

There was someone out there.

A light flickered in the darkness, darting like a firefly among the shrubs of the garden. Tina watched it, leaning forward intently. Surely it was the lighted tip of a cigar? One of the gentlemen enjoying the night air, that must be it.

With a soft release of breath, she relaxed and leaned back. And nearly let out a scream.

A hand had closed over the nape of her neck. Warm and strong, it held her as she tried to turn, and then with a mere whisper of sound he stepped even closer, his thighs hard against her back.

"Richard?" she sounded uncertain as it occurred to her it might not be him.

"Who else were you expecting?" His soft teasing caused her to slump with relief. Gently his fingers caressed her nape, and she felt as if she might melt like butter.

"You took so long," she said, and then silently reprimanded herself for giving herself away.

"I had a great deal to do."

"What did you have to do?"

He began to release her braid, fingers raking out her hair until it lay in soft, dark tresses over her back and shoulders. "I cleared the ballroom, and then I tidied the supper room and washed up the crystal and crockery, but Lady Isabelle said the glasses weren't clean enough so I did it again, and—"

"Richard," she said between laughter and irritation.

"What? Don't you believe me, Miss Smythe?"

She tilted back her head, and this time he let her. He was without his waistcoat or jacket, the buttons of his shirt undone at his throat, his hair rumpled. Rather like he'd been the first time she had seen him.

"Kiss me," she commanded.

He bent down, taking his time, closer and closer. His gray eyes were warm and smiling beneath his dark brows, and she could smell fire smoke and brandy on him. Where had he been?

He stopped just before his smiling mouth reached hers.

"Richard"—she sighed—"don't be cruel."

"Aren't you supposed to pretend you're indifferent to me? To increase my ardor?"

"I don't need a lesson. This isn't part of our business arrangement," she retorted, and turning on the seat slid her arms about his neck and pulled him down beside her.

He did kiss her then, their lips clinging, their mouths hot and eager. But it wasn't enough. He slipped his hand inside her robe and enclosed her breast in his big, warm palm.

Tina gasped, aware of sensations she'd only dreamed about until now, and a hot, tight feeling building low in her belly.

"May I?" he said huskily, and before she could find the wits to answer he drew the edges of her robe apart and bared her upper body to his gaze.

Tina made no attempt to cover herself or play the coy innocent. She *was* innocent, but this seemed so right she didn't feel the need to act any part but being herself.

"Beautiful," he groaned.

He bent to press his mouth to the curve of one breast while his hand was busy with the other. His lips trailed down until he was able to envelop an engorged nipple, his finger flicking the other one, stroking her over and over again until it felt more pain than pleasure, but she did not want him to stop.

Tina's gasps turned to soft cries. She pressed his head to her hot skin, wanting more, much more, because something was building within her, and she could not go back now. The need, the sensation of his mouth on her made her frantic, and she tugged his shirt from his trousers, her hands exploring his bare chest and hard belly. His skin was so warm, and different from her own soft curves, and she licked her tongue over it, tasting him, unable to resist.

But there was more, there must be more, and she wanted to experience it all. She must know what it was his body was promising to show her.

"Tina," he said hoarsely, catching her hands as they moved lower to the fastening of his trousers. "No, stop it."

She looked at him as if he were insane, still completely immersed in her desire. "Stop?"

"I will not take your virginity."

The bluntness of his words confused her even more, and she blinked up at him. "I thought you . . . I thought we . . ."

"Not because I don't want to," he added, answering the unspoken question in her eyes, "but because I have made a promise. I've sworn I will not marry until I have fulfilled that promise."

She shook her head with a spurt of anger. "But what has that to do with us? I don't care about marrying you, Richard. Don't you understand? I am sick to the stomach of spending my every waking moment trying to make men marry me!"

His eyes lit with laughter, but he bit his lip to stop it spilling from him. Just as well, Tina thought darkly. She wouldn't be laughed at, not tonight.

"Tina, I don't want to compromise you, do you understand?"

"No, I don't understand."

"I don't want to take your virginity until I know I can secure our future—if that is what you want. If that is what we both want."

Their future? Promises? What did any of that matter to her now? Tina shook her head, her long, dark hair whipping wildly about her. "I don't care about that," she told him decisively. "You don't understand, Richard. It was all a lie. I have nothing to offer you or any man, nothing apart from myself. I am poor, my family is bankrupt. We have lost everything, and by the time I go home, we will have lost our home. No one will want me when that is known. I will vanish into the shadows. This night . . ." Her mouth trembled, but she firmed it, refusing to feel sorry for herself. "This night is all I have."

She would have climbed to her feet then, brushing by him, fleeing with her misery to some small, quiet place. But he caught her and held her, gripping one of her hands firmly in his and placing it against his body. Her surprise at the touch of that hard piece of flesh contained by only a thin piece of cloth made her stop.

"Oh." She looked back at him, eyes wide and dark in the moonlight from the window, her face full of amazement. "Does that mean . . . ?"

"That I want you?" he rasped. "Yes it does. I want you more than anything else in the world. But I won't take your virginity, Tina, not until I know I can offer you a future you deserve."

"Then how?"

"There are other ways."

Tina tried to read his face, and he smiled a smile that made her heart turn over. "Show me," she whispered. Slowly, his fingers still entwined with hers, he drew her toward him.

It seemed natural to kiss him, and when his hand brushed aside her robe and skimmed over the curve of her belly and down between her legs, she groaned into his mouth. She was hot and achy, and his fingers played with her, teasing another groan from her as they slid deep inside her slick body.

For a moment she lost herself in sensation, aware of nothing but his mouth on hers and his fingers inside her. Was this it? Was this what drove women like Lady Isabelle to madness? Well, no wonder . . .

"Touch me, too," Richard said hoarsely, bringing her back to herself, and Tina didn't need him to ask twice. Her hand reached down between them and pressed against him, eagerly exploring, and when she didn't find that satisfactory, she unfastened his trousers and slipped her fingers inside, causing him to catch his breath.

He was big and hard, but with a velvety softness. She wanted to lick the tip of him, where she could feel a drop of moisture, but when she tried he jerked against her and pulled her away, his hands shaking as he held her upright. "My willpower is growing weaker by the moment," he said.

"Good."

He laughed breathlessly, then laid her down on the window seat, kneeling before her open thighs, and began to use his tongue on her in exactly the same way. The sensation was so exquisite. The pleasure building inside her rose like a bright light, and she almost touched the stars, but he stopped before she could reach them and lay down beside her.

"Touch me now," he whispered against her ear, his fingers replacing his tongue. She could smell her own scent on him, and, somehow, that was exciting, too. His own touch between her legs grew more deliberate, stroking her, flicking the hard little bud so swollen and aching for attention. Tina could feel excitement building again, but she didn't stop her own attentions to him, and he placed his hand over hers and taught her how to hold him, how to apply just the right pressure around his shaft.

Her lack of experience didn't matter, they were both caught up in the heat and need of the moment, and when the pleasure lifted them high, they both cried out, mouths fusing, bodies rocking, as if they really were joined as one.

Chapter 26

"**Y**ou did what?" The Captain's voice rose in fury, and he only just managed to stifle the shout that would give away their meeting place in the garden at Arlington Hall. There was no one about, but he couldn't take the risk.

"I held up their coach and took their blunt. A nice pearl necklace, too."

"I don't believe I'm hearing this. You robbed Sir Thomas and Lady Carol Smythe?"

Sutton rolled his eyes. "I rob lots of folk, Captain. It's how we finance our little rebellion, remember?"

The Captain strode forward a few steps and then back again, hands clenched in fury at his sides. He felt as if he might do Sutton some serious violence, and he was capable of it. He always had been, but he had learned over the years to hide it behind his affable face.

"Bring it to me," he said, "so I can return it."

Sutton laughed as if he didn't believe him. The Captain slapped his face, swinging the oaf's head around with the power of the blow. Sutton put a hand to the reddening mark, his pale blue eyes full of hatred.

"You'll regret that," he said icily.

"I regret I can't cut your head off so I don't have to look at your stupid face anymore. Now do as I say."

Sutton slunk off through the shrubs and down to the river, where he'd moored his boat. The Captain waited a moment, trying to still the fury in his heart. He seemed to be surrounded by fools. It wasn't like that in the early days—then they'd all been fired by righteous zeal—but something had changed. Sometimes he wondered whether they would ever succeed. Well, when Sir Henry's fate was clear, he would be able to plan his next step. He had no fears about the interview with Will Jackson in the morning—he'd shot no one—but there was still Branson.

The Captain yawned. He needed to sleep, to keep a clear head. He began to make his way back to the house, lighting up another cigar as he went.

"Hush, they will hear us," Archie whispered, as he drew Maria deeper into the garden, tugging her along by her hand as she tried not to giggle.

They had arranged to meet at midnight, sneaking from their separate quarters and into the moonlit night. Maria found her heart beating with excitement and more, a desire she had not felt in a very long time. It was almost as strong as her desire for home, and suddenly she was afraid that Archie would become more important to her, that she would wake up one day and feel trapped.

"What is it?"

He'd sensed her unease.

They were at the river now, and dark and smooth, it flowed past them. A fish jumped and vanished again beneath the surface with barely a ripple.

"Maria?"

"Nothing," she whispered.

He waited a moment more, then sat down on the path and began to take off his shoes and stockings. Maria watched in bemusement and when he removed his jacket and began to pull his shirt over his head, she realized what he was intending and laughed.

"Can you swim, Archie?"

"Like that fish," he said, and began to unfasten his trousers. "Can you?"

"A little," she admitted.

"I will hold you up," he said.

It seemed that he was saying one thing and meaning another, and for a moment she gazed into his eyes, trying to understand. "Why not?" she said at last, suddenly reckless. She might not get this chance again, to swim in a river with a man she had come to love.

And she did love him.

But did she love him enough?

Archie unfastened her dress, helping her to remove it and her petticoats. Her corset was barely laced—she hadn't wanted to wear it at all but convention had caused her to put it on. And then she was as naked as he, and they looked at each other in the moonlight and liked what they saw.

Archie reached for her hand again, his fingers entwining with hers.

"Come on," he said, "swim with me."

Maria smiled and let him lead her into the water.

Tina woke to the sound of birds singing outside the bedroom window. She was in her bed, and Richard was beside her, his arm heavy across her body, a curl of his hair hanging over his eyes, and his mouth slightly open as he slept.

As she watched him she remembered the things they had done, things she could hardly believe, and how much she had enjoyed them. There was a delicious ache throughout her body, a sensation of languid completion. When he had kissed her in the juncture of her thighs, using his tongue and his mouth, he had brought her to such delight, and then he had showed her how to do the same to him.

Tina shivered at the memory, and when she glanced at Richard again she saw that his eyes were open, and he was remembering, too. He smiled that smile that promised her so much pleasure. It had been there all along, that promise, she just hadn't been able to read it.

"I should go back to my own room," he said, his voice deep and husky.

"Yes," she said, and waited.

He reached for her instead, and with a gasp, she went into his arms, naked as he was. Her body was already opening for him like a flower, and her heart fluttered as he began to work his way down with lips and tongue. By the time he reached the place she wanted him, she could hardly bear it, and her body jolted with the shock of contact.

"Richard," she moaned, and then cried out with a shockingly fast climax.

But it wasn't enough for him. He kissed her and delved into her, working leisurely, until her excitement had built all over again, and this time when she came it was long and intense, with ripples of sheer bliss that spread through her body. Finally she opened her eyes, and he was grinning down at her from where he knelt at her side, and his cock was clearly begging for her to lean over and take it into her mouth.

This time it was Richard who groaned and begged and shuddered. And afterward, they lay, exhausted and very pleased with themselves, gazing into each other's eyes until they fell asleep.

When Maria came to wake her mistress an hour later, she found them both still asleep, bold as brass, in the big bed. She froze inside the doorway, her hand over her mouth as if to keep her heart from jumping right out of her throat.

Lady Carol would be furious, and Maria would more than likely get the blame for not protecting her darling adequately. But even so, Maria was more concerned for her young mistress than herself—she was very fond of Tina, and what she was seeing here was not a good thing.

Eventually, when she felt her emotions were under control, she crept to the bed and bent to whisper in her mistress's ear. "Miss Tina? Wake up!"

Tina smiled, the naughty puss, and then opened her eyes. When she realized what was happening, she sat up like a jack-in-the-box, but although she tried to appear ashamed and repentant before Maria, Maria could see she was neither.

"Oh dear, is it morning already?"

"The household are up and about, Miss Tina. What have you done?"

"Richard?" She was shaking him, and he blinked and yawned and then with a curse leaped from the bed. Maria might have laughed if the situation was not so precarious.

"I must get back to my room," he said, holding his clothing before him as if Maria had never seen a man's body before. And quite recently, she thought, with a warm inner tremble, remembering Archie's arms about her. Perhaps that was why she couldn't quite castigate her young mistress as she should.

But their cases were entirely different. Miss Tina's whole life could be destroyed if this was discovered, and Maria would do everything in her power to prevent that from happening.

"I'll see if anyone is out there," she said, and hurried to the door, opening it to peer out.

Behind her she could hear them whispering to each other and a kiss or two. Then she saw someone coming and jumped back inside the room, shutting the door behind her.

"Mr. Charles is out there!"

Tina's green eyes grew very big, and Richard Eversham began to pull on his clothing with incredible speed. Maria thought she must tell Archie about this when she saw him again and wondered if he'd be shocked or whether he would laugh. Both, perhaps.

There was a knock on the door, and a familiar voice called, "Tina?"

Now Tina tumbled out of bed and pulled

her gown around her. She went to the door and cracked it open an inch or two. "Charles? What on earth are you doing here?"

"Anne and I are going sailing and we wondered if you wanted to come. Oh, and Sir Henry is awake and calling for his breakfast."

"Thank goodness he's all right," Tina said, genuinely relieved.

"Yes. What about the sailing? I've been questioned about the hunt so I'm free to go. No prison for me," he added jovially.

Tina thought it was too early in the morning for Charles's jokes. "I don't think I'll come, Charles. You and Anne go. I'm sure you'll enjoy being alone together."

Charles looked thoughtful. "Do you think it's proper if we go alone? I wouldn't want to ruin her reputation."

"You are guests at a country weekend party, Charles. It is perfectly proper to go sailing together." Tina wasn't certain of this, but it seemed the right thing to say, and Charles was pleased to hear it. Besides, who was she to offer advice on what was proper after last night?

"I'll be off then," he said, and strode away.

Tina closed the door, but a moment later Richard set her to one side and opened it again, peering out nervously. As he slipped out and closed the door behind him, he caught Tina's eye, and she felt the thrill of being with him. It didn't matter if he meant it when he spoke about a future with her. She didn't care. For now, just being with him was enough.

"Miss Tina, what are we going to do?" Maria said worriedly.

"Don't worry, Maria. I'm not."

Maria sighed. "You have lost your wits, Miss Tina. This is a dreadful situation. You will be completely ruined and never allowed into society again."

Tina went back to the bed and lay down, pressing her face into Richard's pillow and breathing him in, before turning with a smile to her maid. "Do you know, Maria, I couldn't care less. I am ruined already and poor as a church mouse. I have nothing left to lose, and I like it."

Maria threw up her hands in despair and went to fetch warm water for her mistress to wash in before she started the day.

Chapter 27

Richard hastily washed and changed. He couldn't remember ever being caught out like this and felt slightly ridiculous, but he only had to remember Tina in his arms, and he knew being with her was worth any small embarrassment he might be experiencing right now.

Did he really mean to make his future with her?

When the words had come spilling from his mouth he'd wondered whether he was losing his mind, but they had seemed so right. His life had been full of nothing but his work with the Guardians and the search for Anthony's killer—he'd been driven and hadn't had time for anything else—but now suddenly he was imagining what it would be like to have more. A woman and one day children—most men his age were already burdened by several of the little blighters. He could call his first son Anthony, after his brother.

Recently he'd realized how rarely he had a conversation that wasn't related to his job. Now he imagined discussing the mundane with Tina, lounging by the fire with her sitting on his lap while they dreamed of their future. Sharing things that might seem boring to others but were intimate and special to them.

Blast it, he wanted to marry her!

All this time he'd been looking around—not very hard he had to admit—for the perfect partner for Tina, and no one had come up to the mark. Well, of course not. Obviously, in his heart, he'd meant her for himself all along, and it'd just taken some time for his intellect to catch up.

"Brown jacket, sir? Or the gray?"

Archie was being very disapproving. He'd probably been talking with Maria, and they'd decided he was a wicked seducer.

Richard pointed to the brown jacket. Archie held it out and silently assisted him into it. As Archie turned to put away the other jacket Richard noticed a mark on his valet's neck, just above his collar. To one of Richard's experience it was unmistakable.

He smiled.

"Seen Maria, Archie?"

His manservant raised a supercilious eyebrow. "I beg your pardon, sir?"

"Not my business, eh?" Richard guessed, straightening his sleeves with sharp tugs. "If you don't want people to know you are seeing Maria, you might want to wear a higher collar," he said with a grin, and strode to the door, leaving Archie fumbling at his clothing and peering at his reflection in the mirror.

Feeling more like his old self, Richard made his way to Sir Henry's rooms to make sure all had gone to plan. Will Jackson was outside the door, awaiting Lord Horace Gilfoyle, who was the last of the shooters to be questioned and had inexplicably gone off somewhere.

"Any possibilities yet?"

"Not really. There was one thing. Mr. Branson said something odd, about Sir Henry's deserving to be brought down a peg or two. If I didn't know better, I'd almost believe he was glad Sir Henry was shot."

Richard nodded, thoughtful. "He's an odd chap. Seems to resent Sir Henry's occupying the house that used to belong to him. Well, I suppose we can understand it, but why accept an invitation from a man he hates?"

"Unless he wanted to see him 'brought down a peg or two,'" Will quoted.

"Yes, good point. You'd better go find Lord Horace and see what he has to say," said Richard. "Then we can begin to put it all together."

"**A**nd who did you see nearby when Sir Henry was shot?"

Horace held up his hands and counted on his fingers. "I saw Charles Smythe, John Little, Richard Eversham, Sir Henry of course, and a couple of local chaps he was employing as gamekeepers, whose names escape me. I didn't see you." He looked smug.

Will was writing down the names. So far no two witnesses remembered the scene in the same way although there were some consistencies. He sighed and put down his pen. "Thank you, Lord Horace. I think we're finished here for now."

After Horace had left, Will looked over the list in front of him. There was one man whose name had been missing from all of the accounts, and now here it was again. Mr. Branson. Lord Horace hadn't mentioned seeing him, but then he'd made a point of saying Will himself wasn't there, and Will definitely had been.

Will shuffled back through the statements, looking for Branson's. Yes, here it was. He glanced over it. Branson claimed to have seen everyone else in the shooting party and, according to him, he'd never been apart from them at any stage.

So why hadn't they seen him?

The sun was streaming in the window when Tina woke again, to the smell of tea and toast as Maria put a tray down on the side table.

"Oh, Maria, what time is it?"

"It's eleven o'clock, miss. Most of the ladies are having a late breakfast after the ball last night although Miss Allsop was asking for you."

"Margaret? Oh Lord, now what? First it was Mr. Little, and now Mr. Freer. Perhaps she's found a new man."

Maria ignored her levity. "Lady Isabelle is celebrating Sir Henry's recovery and is planning an afternoon tea on the terrace."

"Will Signor Veruda be singing?" Tina asked, remembering the scene she'd been a witness to last night.

"I think Signor Veruda has gone. I saw him with all his bags on the carriageway this morning waiting for his coach."

So Lady Isabelle had made her choice between love and duty. Duty, was that what marriage was all about?

Richard had spoken of the possibility of marriage last night although he hadn't actually said the word "marriage." *Secure your future,* he'd said, or some such thing. *If that is what you want.*

Well Tina wasn't sure she wanted to marry anyone just now. The thought of being at someone else's beck and call, being obliged to act in a manner that wasn't to her liking, well, suddenly she didn't want to do it. She'd escaped Horace—imagine being married to him with all those other women!—and she wasn't keen to consider stepping up to the altar again. Did that make her improper?

Tina smiled to herself.

She was beginning to like being improper. What was the point in being a perfectly behaved lady when she was poor? Surely the best part of being poor was doing exactly as one pleased. She'd heard that the lower classes lived their lives to a different set of rules than everyone else, and Tina was beginning to think she might enjoy that.

She stretched and yawned. "I must get up and dress. Everyone will think I'm a slugabed."

"I'm quite sure they all think you're a well-brought-up young lady, miss, who behaves just as her parents would wish."

The tone of disapproval was obvious.

"You won't tell, will you, Maria?"

Maria lost her starchy attitude and sighed. "No, miss."

"Then no one else will ever know."

"Take care, Miss Tina. Mr. Eversham may not be quite as he seems."

Tina sat up. "Of course he is as he seems. He's perfect. I wonder if Charles has proposed to Anne yet. Wouldn't that be wonderful! Unless her parents refuse the banns when they find out just how badly in debt we are."

Maria gave her a doubtful look. "Are you in debt, miss?"

Tina grimaced. "Yes, we are. Surely you've noticed? You must have, all the darning and patching you've been doing lately. And all those pigs' trotters for supper, ugh. Can you marry Archie immediately? At least then we won't have to give you notice, Maria, when we get home. If we have a home."

Maria had paled. "It is that bad, miss? I knew . . . that is, I was aware, of course, but not how serious it had become."

"Now you see why I am a little reckless suddenly, Maria. I had hoped to marry Horace and save us all, but that has gone terribly wrong, so I have decided to enjoy myself as much as I can before I have to take some dreadful position as a companion or a governess. I suppose my education at Miss Debenham's will help with that. Someone will snap me up, you wait and see."

Even to herself, she sounded breathless and overwrought.

"If they find out about last night, miss, no one will snap you up."

Tina waved a hand. "Nonsense. That will never come out. You wait and see, Maria, all will be well."

Maria wished she shared her young mistress's

optimism. She'd been worried about Tina's plans to marry Horace, knowing what sort of man he was, but now those worries seemed minor in comparison. Richard Eversham! According to Archie he was a dangerous man who led a dangerous life. She could not help but fret for any woman who fell under his spell. Perfect, indeed!

Miss Tina must be told, but telling her would mean breaking her promise to Archie. Maria was in a bind.

Archie would forgive her, of course he would, especially after last night. Wouldn't he?

Miss Tina's life was at stake here, and Maria had cared for the girl for too long to see her hurt because of something she failed to do. She could never live with herself if anything happened to her young mistress.

Richard had hoped to seek out Tina, but he found himself busy with the statements Will had taken from the shooters, as well as soothing Sir Henry's frustration at their lack of progress.

At one point he happened to glance out of the window and saw her in the garden. She was wearing a dark blue muslin dress and a straw hat with a matching ribbon. She also carried a parasol to protect her skin, although—and Richard smiled to himself—he'd detected a hint of gold to her complexion last night, so perhaps the parasol wasn't working very well.

His smile faded.

She was walking with her brother and Anne Burgess, but Gilfoyle was lurking behind them.

He kept thinking it was madness to consider marrying her—even if she'd have him—not before he'd found Anthony's killer and kept his promise to his dead brother. But he couldn't let her go. What if Gilfoyle got hold of her, promised her his fortune to help her family? She'd feel obliged to agree. No, he mustn't let that happen. And he might have the Captain in his grasp today. Tomorrow? But then again he'd been hoping that for two years now. How long would Tina wait for him? She was young, beautiful, and he couldn't expect her to believe in him and be patient forever.

And speaking of being patient . . . Richard wondered how long he could hold back from the ultimate act of physical pleasure. Last night had been exceptional, even for a man as experienced as he, but because of that experience he knew his limitations. One night he would lose control, and then . . . For her sake, he couldn't risk the scandal of a pregnancy. He would have to marry her and set aside his promise.

The promise that had meant so much to him, that had directed the course of his life for two years.

Anthony's face rose before him as he'd last seen it, but Richard dismissed it with a shake of his head and turned back into the room, where Will and Sir Henry were frowning over a mass of papers spread across the latter's desk.

"I can't believe it," Sir Henry growled. He'd thrown a brightly colored robe over his night attire, but his skin was yellowish, his cheeks appeared sunken from his brush with death, and his mustache was untrimmed. The wound on his head was covered by a thick bandage, which only added to his disreputable appearance.

"I know Branson is a miserable old bugger, but would he attempt to shoot me? I can't believe it."

"He's the main suspect," Will said stubbornly. "I think we need to talk to him again."

Sir Henry continued to shake his head in disbelief.

"What about Little or Gilfoyle?" Richard interrupted. "Did you find anything in either of their stories to make you doubt their word?"

Will shook his head. "They were where they said they were. Too many people saw them, even allowing for confusion."

"This Captain chap is clever," Sir Henry mused, "too clever to fire off a shot. I just don't believe he'd do something to draw attention to himself."

It was what Richard had thought all along.

"Get Branson in," Richard instructed Will. "If he's the one who shot Sir Henry, we need to break him."

And if they did it quickly enough, then perhaps Richard could spend some time with Tina.

Chapter 28

⁓⚬⚬⁓

Anne and Charles were strolling alongside the river, and Tina dropped behind to give them some privacy. The way Charles hardly took his eyes off Anne made her wonder if at last he was about to propose; she just wished he'd get on with it. At that point Horace, somewhat to her alarm, joined them.

"Not too warm for you, Tina?" he said, adjusting the tilt of her parasol with a frown. "This weather can't last much longer."

Tina hoped he was wrong. Her time at Arlington Hall had been something she would never forget, and when she let her memory wander back along these paths, it was to a backdrop of blue skies and sunshine. Perfect days without a hint of rain.

As they walked she found herself relaxing in his company, returning to the way she used to feel long ago, when they were friends, and before she made her husband-hunting plans. Perhaps it was her own fault everything had changed, and she couldn't entirely blame Horace.

"Do you think we can be friends again, Tina?"

he said, as if he'd read her mind. "I miss our friendship."

Tina met his blue eyes. He was a handsome man, but his good looks left her unmoved. She knew now she'd never marry him, even if he asked, but that did not mean they could not still be friends.

"I hope we can," she said.

"I haven't been quite myself these past days. I don't know what got into me, but I'm sorry if I've caused you any upset. We've been friends for so long, and I don't want to lose you."

He sounded sincere, and she was touched. She reached out to take his hand, squeezing it warmly. "I don't want to lose you either, Horace. We are almost like brother and sister."

Something in his eyes told her that wasn't quite what he wanted to hear, but he smiled anyway and returned the pressure on her hand.

"Can I confide in you, Tina? I want you to understand the reason I haven't been quite myself. I met a woman, a married woman." He grimaced at her shocked expression. "I suppose this isn't the sort of thing I should be telling you, but I want you to understand. I visited her several times while her husband was away, and then she came to see me. Do you remember the night of my soiree?"

Tina remembered only too well. That was the night she tried to make Horace notice her by behaving rather recklessly, and the same night she had drunk too much champagne and met Mr. Little. There had been a moment when Horace *had* seemed uncharacteristically upset, now she came to think of it.

"She came to tell me that she was having a child. My child. She had barely left my house when I had to go and play host and pretend nothing was wrong."

Tina's eyes grew big. "You have a child, Horace?"

"Yes." He sighed. "But I will never see him—I think of it as a son. She's made that plain."

"Do you want to see him?" Tina said curiously. Horace a father? Well, stranger things had happened.

"At first I didn't but now . . . Well, it is my own fault, I suppose, that I have been separated from him. I've learned my lesson."

Had he? Somehow Tina doubted that Horace would ever change. Her temptation to tell him all about her own problems faded. What was the point in sharing disasters? Horace must sort out his own life, and so must she, and besides, she didn't want to dwell on that today. She wanted to enjoy herself before it was time to leave tomorrow.

One more day of freedom. One more day of Richard.

Before she faced the bleak reality of her situation.

Charles and Anne had stopped and were watching as Lady Isabelle directed some servants to wheel the bathing machine out into the river. She noticed them, and called, "If anyone wants to bathe, there are costumes in the pavilion. Do give it a try, it is very invigorating."

Horace shuddered, but Margaret Allsop and her American beau had paused to watch, too, and he was encouraging her to join him in the water. In no time they were splashing about, teeth gritted, and when Margaret climbed out she looked blue. The ever-attentive Joseph Freer bundled her up in a blanket.

"You aren't bathing, Miss Smythe?" It was Mr. Little, who had been standing behind her, also observing the happy couple. His smile appeared genuine enough, as if Margaret's fickle heart did not bother him one bit, but Tina could not help but wonder if it was a veneer. Surely any man would be wounded to see the woman he'd begun to think was his own enjoying herself with another.

"No, Mr. Little, but what of you? Do you like to bathe?"

He shook his head, his gaze drifting back to Margaret and Mr. Freer, as if he couldn't help himself. "I knew a fellow once, went bathing when the water was too cold and became cramped. He drowned."

He said it with such relish, as if he was wishing the same fate upon the American. Tina was glad when Horace offered her his arm again, and they began the slow stroll up through the garden toward the terrace, where afternoon tea was awaiting them.

Lady Isabelle had excelled herself, and if her color was a little high and her eyes a little bright, Tina felt she could be forgiven her show of emotion. Sir Henry was there, too, as the guest of honor, seated in a large, comfortable chair that had been carried out of his library for the occasion. Although he looked drawn, and his head was still bandaged, he was chatting freely with his guests and accepting their congratulations on his recovery.

"Marvelous to see him up and about," Lady Isabelle declared, reaching for his hand and lifting it to her lips. Tears sparkled in her eyes. "I don't know what I would have done if he'd . . . Well, I shall not go there."

Sir Henry gave her an adoring smile. "I hope I may be around for a good many years yet, my dear. Perhaps we can go on that trip to the Continent you're always banging on about. Our very own Grand Tour."

"To Italy to see Signor Veruda," Horace whispered in Tina's ear.

She gave him a warning glance and moved away from him, only to find herself within range of Mr. Little. Not wanting to speak with him either she slipped through the guests toward the steps that led down from the terrace into the garden.

A warm breeze had sprung up, and with it a few clouds to cover the sun. If anyone asked her where she was going, she could say she'd forgotten her shawl and was going to fetch it. With a smile she reached up and removed the scrap of paper from inside her bodice. The note had been delivered to her by Archie a moment ago, and now she read it with a thrill of excitement.

Meet me at the folly,

R

The folly was an Italianate building on a manmade hill, designed by Lady Isabelle. Tina had not visited it before, and Lady Isabelle had not encouraged her guests to do so, saying it was being repaired. Now she quickened her step, wending her way through the shrub borders and flower gardens, toward the white columns she could see through the trees on the rise above her.

Eventually she was able to see the folly in its entirety; the circular building with its outer shell of columns seemed to float above her like an ancient temple. There were several low steps, also constructed in a circle, leading up to it. When she reached the top she saw that it was actually like a large open room, with bright cushions and furnishings. A place to relax and contemplate the garden, perhaps.

Or a place to make love.

Was that why Lady Isabelle had discouraged them from coming here? Was it her own personal hideaway?

Someone had left a sketch pad and pencil upon a table, and Tina flipped through the drawings, recognizing Vincenzo Veruda in varying stages of undress. She dropped the pages, and they scattered onto the floor.

"What is it?"

Richard had come up behind her without her hearing him—he was good at that—but she was so glad to see him that she didn't mind. For a moment she simply smiled at him, enjoying the moment, but as she moved toward him, her foot sent one of the pages sailing across the marble floor.

Richard bent to retrieve it.

"Good God," he muttered, when he saw what it was.

"This must have been their special place," Tina said, glancing about, feeling a hint of sadness. "Where they had their trysts."

"At least the signor has gone, and for now Sir Henry can have his wife back."

Tina gave him a curious look. "You make it sound as if it is a story you have heard before."

"I have. I'm afraid Lady Isabelle is not a faithful wife, Tina. Signor Veruda was just one in a long line of lovers she has chosen to bestow her favors upon."

Tina put a hand to her heart. "But that is awful! Does Sir Henry know?"

"Of course he does."

"And yet he condones it?"

"He loves her, so he puts up with it."

Tina shook her head. "I can't imagine it, Richard. I would not put up with it. Marriage . . . love . . . they are forever. That is one thing your lessons have taught me. While I was learning how to pretend to love, I discovered I would never be very good at pretending, not for long. One should choose a partner carefully, and if one is not sure, then one should say no."

He touched her cheek gently, and smiled. "That is good. Do not lose that, my dearest."

But his reaction wasn't what she wanted. He was treating her like a silly innocent, and Tina was neither. She might be young, but she had grown up a great deal lately, and now that she'd formed her opinion she didn't believe she would change it.

The heart, once given, would be given forever.

Behind her Richard was still speaking. "My brother was married to a woman who was unfaithful to him." She heard him crumpling up Lady Isabelle's sketches, one by one. "He never knew, but others did. They looked upon him like a fool, a dupe. I cannot forgive that. He did not deserve that."

"I'm sorry."

Richard threw the crumpled pages into a pile on the floor and wiped his hands on his trousers, as if he felt soiled. Tina realized that it mattered to him, too, that loving someone, marrying someone, was a serious business to Richard Eversham. Not something he would take on lightly.

Remembering his words from last night, she wondered if that was how he felt about her. Did he really want to spend the rest of his life with her? But surely, if he did, he wouldn't let this promise, whatever it was, get in the way. *Men*, she thought with a touch of scorn. *Why did they have to complicate everything?*

"I'll be leaving in the morning," she told him, watching him carefully, but he didn't react. "Charles and I will be going back to Mallory Street . . . or wherever we are to live. I'm sorry I won't be able to pay you for your lessons, Richard."

"I didn't want to be paid; well, only if you succeeded in capturing Gilfoyle. Remember? That was our bargain. And frankly I was hoping you would fail."

Tina smiled—that was better. "The strange thing is that now I don't want him, Horace suddenly seems to be finding me fascinating. But I know I would be miserable with him. I'm sorry to disappoint my parents, but actually in an odd sort of way I'm looking forward to being poor."

He laughed. "Tina, do you have any idea what being poor means?"

She pursed her lips, pretending to be serious. "I will have to dress myself and fetch my own breakfast, I suppose."

"Minx," he growled, and came toward her.

Chapter 29

Tina tried to run but he caught her around the waist and swung her into his arms. She gasped, and the next moment they were tangled together on the sofa, lying among the soft, colorful cushions.

"I will dress you and fetch your breakfast," Richard said, leaning over her, his warm gray eyes smiling into hers.

Tina ran a fingertip over his lips, tracing their shape. He cupped her face, smoothing his thumb against her skin, and then he leaned into her and began to kiss her.

The passion she had felt last night, that she always felt when she was with him, instantly caught fire inside her, brighter than ever. His tongue delved into her mouth, teasing her, while his fingers slipped beneath her bodice and found the hard nub of her nipple.

"I thought that was one of the places I shouldn't allow a gentleman to touch me," she managed breathlessly.

"I'm not a gentleman," he said.

"Oh, I think you are," Tina whispered. "You are

very much a gentleman despite what you want people to believe."

"Would a gentleman do this?" he retorted, reaching down to draw up her skirts into a bundle so that his hand could find her stockinged calf and caress her knee. Tina thought of the darns in the woolen cloth, wondered whether he would notice, and then didn't care as his fingers found the bare skin where her stocking ended.

She slid her own hands over his chest and down to his belly, finding the hard shape of him beneath the fine cloth of his trousers. Already, she was familiar with his body, wanting to touch him, explore him. And then his fingers found her moist center and he pressed deeper, and she cried out in pleasure and anticipation.

He lifted his face from the crook of her neck, which he'd been kissing, and met her eyes. His own were glittering with desire, and as her hand closed around him, he groaned deep in his throat.

"I want you," he said, and she could tell he meant it.

His fingers slid into her heat, confident, sure, giving her pleasure. She moved with him, pretending it was his body inside hers, that they were joined together. But they weren't, and suddenly it wasn't enough. With an urgent whimper, she pushed him away and sat up, her hair coming loose about her, her breasts bare through the half-open bodice of her dress.

He rolled onto his back and reached for her again, settling her on top of him so that she was straddling him, her hot nakedness pressing against his hard bulge through his trousers. Despite their not being skin to skin, the pressure was exquisite, and she moved against him, hearing her voice deep in her throat, crying out with the pleasure of it.

He gripped her hips, holding her, urging her on, guiding her, until their passion reached its crescendo and tipped into ecstasy.

The first thing Richard thought, when he could think again, was: *I won't have to break my promise. I didn't lose control although by God it was a close thing.*

His arms were full of woman, soft and glorious, and he could feel himself growing aroused again already at the memory of what they had just done. If he didn't get up and put some distance between them . . . well, how much longer could he trust himself?

And yet he didn't move.

She stirred, pushing her hair out of her face, and propped herself up on one slender arm to gaze down at him with sleepy green eyes. She looked utterly magnificent, and he reached up to tuck a long, tangled strand of hair behind her ear. She turned her head to lick his hand with the tip of her pink tongue and then smiled.

"Is it always like this?" she said, and made him laugh with joy. Tina was never afraid to say what she was thinking, and he hoped she'd never change.

"No," he admitted, "it isn't. This is . . . exceptional."

She seemed pleased with that. Her green eyes glowed, and her lips curled into a smile that was tempting him to reach up and kiss her. He wanted to. He wanted to stay here all afternoon and make love to her over and over again. But he had work to do, Sir Henry needed him at his most alert, and when he was with Tina he found his wits too easily went wandering.

While they were wandering this time, she'd begun to unbutton his shirt, and now she slipped her fingers inside it to continue an exploration of his chest. She circled his nipples and raked her fingertips through the line of dark hair that ran down over his belly and disappeared inside his trousers. From the rapt expression on her face she was enjoying what she was finding, and he knew it would only be a matter of moments before those clever fingers were tugging at his buttons, caressing his erection until he was hard to bursting.

He groaned.

She bent to lick his skin. "You taste of . . ."

"Ambrosia?" he managed thickly.

She smiled. "Cigar smoke."

Unfortunately, that was one of the drawbacks of working for Sir Henry.

"Was that you, last night, in the garden?" she murmured, returning to her work. Her finger circled his nipple and watched it go hard. "But it couldn't have been, could it, because you were with me? Unless you ran very fast."

He'd been so intent on enjoying her touch that he hadn't really been listening to her, but suddenly the words penetrated his pleasure-sodden brain. "Was someone outside in the garden last night?"

She nodded. "I saw the glow of a cigar. One of

the men going for a stroll, I expect. Does it matter?" She glanced at him, resting her cheek against his skin, her eyelids heavy over her green eyes. Her naked breast brushed his arm, and he reached out to cup the soft, heavy flesh in his palm. Her eyelashes fluttered, and she made a little sound, half pleasure and half longing for more.

He shook his head. The man in the garden could have been the Captain, plotting, and he'd been playing at seduction with Tina. At one time he would never have allowed anything like that to escape him, and now here he was, too weak to climb out from beneath the woman.

But not just any woman, the voice in his head mocked him. *Tina Smythe is certainly not just any woman.*

What was she doing now? He made to sit up, just as her hand closed over the hard shape tenting his trousers.

"Sshh," she whispered, as he groaned, "let me make it better."

She began to unbutton his trousers, slowly, so that he wanted to shout at her to hurry up. He could tell she was enjoying herself, making him suffer, so he bit his lip and said nothing, letting her have her way.

At last she finished with the buttons and with a smile slipped her hand inside the flap and found him. "Tina," he said, "you are playing with fire."

"Am I?"

She held him a moment, then began to stroke him, finally encircling him with her hand and giving a gasp of admiration.

"So big," she breathed. "I wish . . ." But whatever it was she wished for was never uttered. Instead she showed him with actions rather than words.

He moved involuntarily in her grip, his hips jerking, and this time when she straddled him he was her slave. He could feel her moist heat above him, so hot and tempting, and for a moment he almost stopped her. But then she smiled down at him, her dark hair lying over her shoulders and playing peekaboo with her breasts, and began to slowly, carefully, lower herself onto him.

It was her first time—she was a virgin—but she was determined. She was a goddess, and she wanted him, and he was only a mortal, how could he resist? Richard could see her determination in the set of her mouth and hear it in her little gasps of pleasure and pain. Miss Tina Smythe was going to have her way.

"Tina," he warned, but he'd left it too late.

His will, always fragile where she was concerned, gave way.

She bit her lip as she felt resistance—her blasted maidenhead—but now it was his turn, and with a jerk of his hips he'd pushed through the thin membrane and lodged deep inside her. She cried out, but almost at once she was moving against him, her expression utterly rapt at the sensation created.

"I feel you . . . inside me . . ." she panted.

He guided her movements, quickening his thrusts, deeper, and then her body began to contract about him.

She cried out, her climax rippling through her, and he grasped her hips, driving up into her, and giving his own cry of pleasure. And despair.

He'd broken his promise.

Or at least he soon would.

Richard pulled her down into his arms, so that she couldn't see his face, and held her, both of them gasping for breath. He tried to examine how he felt emotionally, and knew he should be feeling guilty. But he couldn't feel guilt or dismay or even sadness. He was too busy feeling like the luckiest man in England.

As if to berate him for his lack of remorse, there was the rumble of thunder outside as a storm began to build.

The perfect weather had finally broken.

Chapter 30

Tina had reached her room and begun to wash and change for the evening. She'd taken a circuitous route back to the hall and was confident no one had seen her. She'd left Richard at the folly.

He'd been very quiet, as if he had something on his mind. Or perhaps, she thought with a smile, he was simply worn-out from their lovemaking. Her own body had a slight ache where he had joined with her, but she didn't regret it for a moment. And he hadn't protested despite his promise.

Should she feel guilty about his breaking it? Surely, if it had been important, he would have explained what it was and why he needed to keep it? Tina was inclined to think that if he really hadn't wanted to break it, then he wouldn't have. Or was it a bit like her "promise" to marry Horace, something that waxed and waned with the changing situation.

And now that they were physical lovers would Richard try to persuade her to marry him? Well, she wasn't at all certain she wanted to marry him. Richard was obviously not a wealthy man—no one with money would have a job teaching seduction—so if they wed, they would both be poor. Where was the point in that?

No, much better to stay free and live life as they pleased. They could come together—she was looking forward to visits from Richard and secret trysts, rather like Lady Isabelle. That sounded far more romantic, and just now, after all she'd been through, Tina was rather keen on filling her life with romance. She didn't think she loved Richard—she'd thought she loved Horace, but now she was sure she didn't. What she needed was more time to come to a conclusion, and that meant more time in Richard's arms. Oh yes, she was looking forward to that.

Tina had stripped off her clothing and was carefully dressing in another of her new gowns when Maria opened the door.

"Miss? Why didn't you call me to help?"

Tina avoided her maid's suspicious eyes. "I have to learn to dress myself, Maria."

She hoped Maria might leave again, but the maid came closer, casting a narrowed glance over the pile of clothing on the floor. She picked up a hairbrush and lifted some loose strands of Tina's dark hair, inspecting it.

"There are a great many knots in your hair, miss."

"Are there?"

"And it is damp. Were you out in the storm?"

Tina smiled. "Yes, I was. I ran back through the rain. It was very exciting, with the thunder crashing and the lightning flashing. I suppose that is the last of the sunshine now. Oh well."

Even as she spoke, the wind blew a patter of water against the window, and the view of the garden and the river was now smeary with rain.

"You've been with him, haven't you? Mr. Eversham."

She thought about denying it but decided there was no point. And what did it matter what Maria thought now? Everything was about to change, and Maria would no longer be a part of her life. She felt a twinge of sadness at the thought; she and Maria had been together a long time. But, hopefully, her maid would find her own happiness with Archie.

"Yes, we met in the folly. Lady Isabelle's folly."

Tina had never thought Maria was a hand-wringing sort of person, but now here she was, wringing her hands. "Miss Tina, don't you realize how dangerous this behavior is? And Mr. Eversham is not a man to be trusted."

Tina was on the verge of dismissing this comment when something in Maria's expression caught her attention. She took a step toward her, staring into her face. "What do you know, Maria? Has Archie told you something? Come, you'd better tell me."

Maria shook her head, stepping backward as Tina came forward, the brush in front of her as if it might protect her.

"Is he a fortune hunter?" Tina demanded.

"No. That was what I thought, but Archie says he has a great deal of money."

Tina took another step and almost stumbled. Richard was rich? Then why . . . ? But she put that fact aside and concentrated on Maria. If she wanted her questions answered, then she would have to force her maid—who'd suddenly developed an uncharacteristic reticence—to answer them.

"Then what is it you know? Come, Maria, you'd better tell me. I didn't think we had any secrets."

Maria gave her a skeptical look. "You are the one with secrets, Miss Tina."

"Well I don't have any now, do I? Come, Maria, please."

Her maid wavered. "I promised Archie," she said with a shake of her head, and then sighed and capitulated. "He works for Sir Henry."

"Archie?"

"No, Mr. Eversham. Well, Archie too, but Mr. Eversham is an important man to the government. He hunts out anarchists and the like, people who might wish England badly. Archie says he's a hero, but I don't think he would be a very safe man to fall in love with, miss. And he's dedicated himself to his work, so he won't be getting married or setting up house. In fact he's made some silly sort of promise swearing to remain unattached."

"Oh."

Maria eyed her mistress cautiously as Tina walked rather stiffly over to the window seat and sat down, heavily, as if her strings had been cut, and stared out of the room.

"So he isn't really what he says he is? That charming, careless attitude . . . it's all a lie? The work he does helping gentlemen seduce ladies . . . is that a lie, too?"

"I think it is a way of discovering people's secrets, so he can use them to do his work."

Tina felt herself go hot and then cold.

So he'd used her. How he must have enjoyed it when she came to him for help, believing he was what he said he was, believing *him*. And he was still lying to her. What had he said? He'd made a promise and he couldn't marry until it was fulfilled, so he couldn't take her virginity.

Well that was a lie because he had taken her virginity. And anyway he was married to his work.

Not that she wanted to marry him. He could be as rich as Midas, and she wouldn't marry him, not now, not ever. He'd lied to her, toyed with her, and she'd trusted him.

"Thank you for telling me, Maria," she said calmly, as if her heart weren't one big ache in her chest. "I hope Archie isn't cross with you."

Maria was watching her anxiously. "I should have told you before . . . before things went so far, miss. I'm sorry."

"Well, never mind."

"Miss"—Maria put a gentle hand on Tina's shoulder—"you must not think this is the end of the world. Men, they are like dandelion fluff, they come and go, and there will always be more of them to blow away on the breeze."

Tina managed a smile. "I'm sure you're right. Now, I might just spend a moment alone before I go down to supper. Thank you, Maria, I'll call you if I need you."

Maria hesitated, clearly wanting to stay, and then she nodded and hurried from the room, closing the door behind her.

Tina allowed her body to slump a little, bowing her head, feeling the pain spreading from her heart to her throat and her head, where a headache was forming.

It had been a wonderful weekend, and she should remember that, remember the good things and not the bad. In years to come, it would not even matter that Richard Eversham had played her for a silly fool, and she would look back on this moment with the wisdom of age and . . .

Cry?

That wasn't what she'd planned, but the tears were already filling her eyes and spilling over her lashes to trickle down her cheeks. It seemed pointless to fight them, so she let them come and even indulged in some sobbing and wailing and pounding the cushions with clenched fists. Eventually she felt a little better and composed herself.

After a time she felt able to go downstairs. She didn't think she'd appear at supper after all, that would be asking too much, but she might search out the library and find a good book she could bring back to her room and lose herself in.

Something to take her away from her problems and make her forget she ever knew a man called Richard Eversham.

It occurred to her that might not even be his name. If he was working for the government, he might be using a false name and actually be called something like Ogden. Or Aloysius Hogfish. She managed a weak smile, but at least that was better than more tears.

"I thought you'd gone!"

Branson came a few steps into the library, glancing nervously over his shoulder, before turning back to Sutton.

"What are you doing here? If *he* sees you . . ."

"I don't care if he sees me," Sutton growled. He picked up a snuffbox from a collection on a side table and tossed it into the air, catching it neatly and then slipping it into his pocket. "He's a bastard who thinks he can treat me as he pleases, well he can't. This started off as an equal partnership, and now he's the one giving all the orders. Too bad. I don't take orders."

Branson couldn't believe he was hearing this, but at the same time he was deriving a certain enjoyment from it. He'd also been on the receiving end of the Captain's fury so he understood all too well the effect it had.

"Heard you took a potshot at that bastard Arlington," Sutton added with a vicious smile. "Pity you missed."

"I didn't miss," Branson retorted. "I mean, I didn't want to kill him, just give him a scare."

Sutton shook his head in disgust. "And he says I'm a fool. Who are you going to shoot at next? The wife? I hear she's a nice piece, not averse to a bit of rough."

"I wouldn't harm a lady," Branson protested huffily.

"Come on then; you've started now, who's next? I'd love to see *his* face when you do it. Finish off the lot of them, I reckon, then we wouldn't have the bother, would we?"

Branson had turned thoughtful. "I might take a shot at Eversham, he's a swine. Had me in for more questions before, threatening me, shouting in my face. What gives him the right to treat me like that, eh? Yes," he smiled sourly, "I'd like to put a bullet between his eyes."

There was a sound over near the bookshelves,

and both men froze, staring in that direction, but a moment later a gust of wind rattled the windows and a draft set the pages of an open book on a nearby table fluttering. They relaxed, and Sutton pocketed another snuffbox.

"I'm going," he said. "His Highness wants me to return the pearls I stole. Seems that these days it goes against his moral code to steal. As I'm going to have to give them back, I needed to be reimbursed." He patted his bulging pocket.

Branson snorted a laugh. "How are you going to get out?" he asked.

"Same way I got in, through the window."

Sutton opened it and slipped out, vanishing into the darkness and the rain. Branson waited a moment, and then he left by the door.

Tina's heart was beating so hard she had been terrified they would hear it. She'd knelt down to pull out a book from the bottom shelf and then became immersed in its pages, sinking down onto the Turkish rug and forgetting where she was.

Until the men began speaking.

At first she'd thought Mr. Branson was speaking to another guest, but then she'd heard what they were saying. Understanding had come at once. Mr. Branson had shot Sir Henry, and now he was planning to shoot Richard. Her aching heart was momentarily forgotten—she might not *like* him very much anymore, but she wasn't about to stand by and see him killed.

The book had slipped from her hands and the two men had stopped and she was certain they would find her. As she waited, trembling, she thought of her family and, yes, she did think of Richard. Would he be sorry when her body was discovered lying over a copy of *A Sultan's Harem*?

But then the windows had rattled, and everything was all right again. The men had left, and the room was empty. But still she took her time. She inched her way cautiously around the bookshelves to the door. With a sigh of relief she glanced behind her, just to be sure.

He was standing outside the window, his wet hair plastered to his head, his cold pale blue eyes staring in at her. Like a nightmare. He was the most frightening person she'd ever seen, and as she stood, frozen to the spot, he began to open the window.

With a scream, Tina turned and flung herself at the door, fumbling at the knob and managing to open it and then running. She hardly noticed Branson, his face white and shocked in the shadows; all she could think of was the nightmare creature at the window. He could be behind her, and there was only one person she could think of who would save her—it didn't even occur to her that her savior was now a cheat and a liar, and she hated him. Clinging to the banister she hurled herself up the staircase toward Sir Henry's rooms and the safety of Richard's arms.

Chapter 31

〘∽〙

"Sir Henry and Mr. Eversham are in the study, miss."

The footman gave her a curious look. Tina knew she wasn't at her best but tried to keep her emotions inside just a little bit longer. She hid her trembling hands behind her back.

"I need to see them."

"They asked not to be disturbed," the footman said, with the air of one used to diverting pesky visitors from his master.

Tina decided then that she would have to be rude, very rude. She gave him a push, catching him by surprise, and flung open the door before he could stop her, bursting in. Three men were gathered about a huge oak desk and they looked up, startled, at her abrupt entry.

"Tina?" Frowning, Richard moved toward her.

Distraught, Tina tried to speak, but she was suddenly too breathless to get a word out and leaned against the back of a chair, feeling faint.

She felt his hand on her arm, warm, supporting her. It felt wonderful, and all she wanted to do was curl into his chest and cling there like a limpet. Unfortunately, due to her recent discoveries about him, she felt obliged to shake his hand off. And that was his fault, too.

Behind her the footman nodded at a gesture from Sir Henry and closed the door. "My dear Miss Smythe, whatever is the matter? Sit down and catch your breath. Will, get some brandy, would you?"

Will Jackson placed a glass into her hand and Tina sipped at the brandy. As it warmed her insides she began to recover herself a little. Richard was still by the door, watching her, his slanting brows drawn down over eyes that were uncharacteristically serious.

"There was a man in the library," she spoke at last. "Two men. One of them was Mr. Branson, and one of them was . . ." She shuddered violently.

"Tina, what happened?"

Richard came to stand at her side, but she turned her face away so she didn't have to see him and so wasn't confused by her feelings.

"Let the girl alone, Richard," Sir Henry said quietly. "Go on, Miss Smythe. Take your time. Tell us what you saw and heard."

Tina had a good memory, and she repeated the conversation almost word perfectly, unable to help glancing at Richard when she recounted Branson's vow to kill him. *Shoot him right between the eyes.* The glass shook violently in her hand, and Will removed it with a sympathetic smile.

"He saw me through the window," she burst out.

"Branson?" Sir Henry said quickly. He nodded

at Will, and the young man slipped from the room.

But Tina shook her head. "No, the other one. The thief. The one with the cold eyes. Pale blue eyes."

Sir Henry and Richard looked at one another, exchanging a wealth of meaning without speaking. Tina found it irritating, as if they were keeping something secret from her—which, of course, they were.

"Branson," said Sir Henry with a frown.

"No real surprise there," answered Richard. "I know you didn't want to believe he'd tried to kill you, but it looks like we have the truth from his own mouth."

"And he wasn't working alone," said Sir Henry. "Is this other man the Captain? Sounds more like another member of the gang. You didn't recognize him?" Sir Henry turned to Tina, eyes piercing beneath his bushy brows, his bandage pushed up at one side like a strange sort of hat. "Are you sure?"

"I'd never seen him before, sir."

"And he saw you?"

She nodded uncomfortably, remembering those cold eyes and the nightmare face through the window.

Sir Henry leaned closer to Richard, his murmuring too low for Tina to hear more than a word here and there. They seemed to be making plans. Why couldn't they say it aloud, so she could hear? It was very annoying, especially when their conversation probably concerned her.

Eventually Richard came and took her hand, raising her to her feet. She was too surprised to shake him off this time and stood, gazing up at his face and waiting to hear what he had to say. He certainly looked very serious.

"You are in danger, Miss Smythe," he said.

She turned to Sir Henry for confirmation, but he only gave a nod.

"The man at the window . . ." she asked, but it was Richard who answered.

"He is part of a group headed by a man called the Captain. A dangerous man who has caused trouble all over England, and more than one death."

Richard didn't sound like himself. He was no longer charming and careless with laughing eyes, no longer the man who'd held her in his arms and whispered her name in the throes of passion.

This man was a stranger.

"So you think I am in danger?" she asked him cautiously.

"I don't think they would hesitate to silence you, Miss Smythe, if they thought you could point one of them out in a court of law."

Remembering again the face at the window, Tina believed him utterly. "What should I do?" She was visualizing fleeing to somewhere isolated, like the Lake District, living in a small cottage with several burly guards. It wasn't a pleasant idea, but if it was necessary . . .

Richard sighed and squeezed the hand he was still holding. "I will have to take you under my protection."

Her heart leaped and almost immediately sank again.

Under his protection? Being by his side, constantly? After what had passed between them and what she now knew about him? Tina wasn't sure she could bear it, even for the sake of staying alive. "I don't think—"

But before she could continue her protest there was a commotion outside, and the door was flung open.

Mr. Branson was there, his arms pulled behind his back, being manhandled by Will Jackson into the room. Richard hurried over to help, and between the two of them they got the struggling Branson into a chair in front of the desk, facing Sir Henry, who sat on the other side. Mr. Branson looked flushed and furious, but there was something in his eyes that gave lie to his protests.

He knew why he was here, and when his gaze fell on Tina, he suddenly deflated like a pricked balloon, all of the hot air going out of him. Tina watched in fascination as he began to make excuses for his actions, telling the very man he'd tried to shoot that it was his fault.

"This was all mine, Arlington, until you took it from me." He waved his arm about the room. "Stole it from me."

"I paid you a good price, Branson."

"A pittance."

"You sold because you could no longer afford to hold on to it. I don't say you were careless with your money or that it was your fault, but neither was it mine that you had to sell."

Branson opened his mouth to continue the argument, but Richard put a stop to it.

"Enough! Miss Smythe saw you in the library with another man. What is his name?"

Branson's expression became sly. "I don't know what you're talking about." But with Richard and Will firing questions at him it didn't take long for him to give them the answer they wanted. "Sutton. His name is Sutton. I don't know where he lives—a hole in the ground probably. He's a thug and a thief, he'll do anything the Captain wants him to do."

Richard smiled a nasty smile. "Oh yes? Well now we want to talk to you about the Captain."

"Don't know any Captain."

"Oh come on!" Richard roared.

Tina jumped.

"Do you know what it's like to spend twenty years in a tiny cell in a filthy gaol, Branson? Or would you prefer the gallows? The noose and the crowds jeering and laughing, the smell of fear as you step out of the cart and climb the steps. Just imagine that's your last moment on earth; just imagine that's the shameful legacy you're leaving your wife."

Will murmured at her side, "It is vitally important we discover this man's name, Miss Smythe," as if he feared she might be shocked.

Richard shot a glance at her, but there was no smile. This was deadly serious stuff. "Tell us who he is, and things might go easier for you, Branson. I might ask for the firing squad instead of the noose."

"We already have a fair idea of the Captain's identity," Will added, and managed to crease his usually amiable features into a fearsome mask.

"Do you now?" Branson muttered.

"Tell us, old chap," Sir Henry put in, "and I'll see your name is kept out of this. I know you didn't mean to shoot at me. I'm quite prepared to let bygones be bygones."

"Oh God, what a mess." Branson put his hands

over his face, his shoulders slumped, but Tina suspected this was more to give himself time to think than because he was in any way repentant.

Outside they could hear laughter as some of the guests took part in a game of croquet between showers. Horace's voice rose above the others, declaring himself hopelessly beaten, followed by Charles's protests.

Branson took his hands away. "I have your word?" he demanded of Sir Henry. "I will not be punished or brought to any kind of justice?"

"My word," Sir Henry agreed.

Branson nodded. "Very well. The Captain is here, you're right. His name is Lord Horace Gilfoyle."

Tina gasped aloud, she couldn't help it. "Horace?" she cried, her tone shrill with shock and disbelief. "Horace would *never*—"

"Thank you, Miss Smythe," Richard cut her off.

Branson was smirking, and Tina had absolutely no doubt he was lying again. Why didn't the others demand the truth from him? How could they believe such nonsense without a single protest?

And yet it seemed that they could.

A moment later Branson was hustled from the room, and Richard was escorting Tina back to her room. They walked in silence, hers angry and sullen, and his . . . well, she no longer knew him well enough to guess what he was thinking.

"I'm sorry if I frightened you in there," he said at last, not looking at her. "We needed that name. *I* needed that name if I'm to protect you."

"I'd prefer someone else protect me if it's really necessary."

He shot her a glance that was more frustration than anger. "Your life is in danger, Tina. This man is a murderer. He killed—"

"Horace is innocent, Mr. Eversham. He would never hurt anyone."

"Perhaps you should marry him then."

She glared at him. "I was intending to, remember?"

She thought she heard him sigh, but a moment later they reached her room, and he said, "Stay here," in a voice that did not invite argument. "I am going to lock the door. I'll send your maid to you."

"Richard, please, just *listen* to me!"

But he wouldn't meet her eyes. He was angry with her, she could feel it, see it in his face. She'd made him break his promise, and he hated her for it.

With a sinking heart she heard the lock turn, and a moment later he walked away.

Richard was angry. Very angry. But he wasn't angry at Tina, he was angry with himself. What on earth had possessed them all to think it was a good idea to combine a social weekend with their hunt for the elusive Captain? Certainly it had been Sir Henry's plan, but he might have persuaded him otherwise had he been thinking with his brain instead of his cock. Now Tina was at risk, and if anything happened to her, he could never forgive himself.

And she was out of sorts with him, and he was yet to learn why.

Was it because of what had happened in the

folly—despite her being a willing participant—or was it because of his belief in Gilfoyle's guilt? But she'd been angry before Branson gave up her friend. And the way she'd snatched her hand from his had nothing to do with modesty or fear of their relationship's being discovered.

Her green eyes had been glittering with emotion.

He shook his head to clear his thoughts. No time now to worry about Tina and what the future might hold, he had to concentrate on his job. Gilfoyle would be brought to Sir Henry's study and questioned, and if Sutton, the man Tina was so frightened of, could not be found, then he would have to protect her until he was.

No matter how repellent she found that prospect.

When he reached the study he could hear loud voices from within, mostly Horace's aristocratic tones. The man was furious, and if he was guilty of being the Captain, then he was putting on a good show of outraged innocence, but then Richard had always suspected Horace of being a fine actor.

Gilfoyle turned to face him when he opened the door, and his face darkened, blue eyes narrowing. In that moment he seemed to be blaming everything that was happening to him on Richard, and his words confirmed it.

"Eversham! I might have known it. What the bloody blazes do you think you're doing? I am Lord Horace Gilfoyle and I will not be treated like this. I have friends in the House of Lords, and they will see you thrashed."

Sir Henry cleared his throat. "We do not

answer to the House of Lords, Lord Horace. We are a select group with complete autonomy. In other words, we act as we think fit."

Horace looked as if he might fly at them and attack them, but a moment later he regained control of himself. He sat down and glared at Richard, still choosing to blame him. His tone was scathing.

"What is this ridiculous rubbish you're spouting? I know nothing about any Captain, and I'm certainly not he. You know who I am. Ask Miss Smythe. We've been friends for years and . . . well, I am hoping to marry her."

Richard gave a snort of laughter, which didn't help the situation.

"Stop it the both of you!" Sir Henry roared. "Now," he went on, when all was quiet and everyone paying attention, "we have a reliable witness who has identified you as the Captain, Lord Horace. I won't listen to any more of your lies. Give yourself up, and it will be the better for you."

Gilfoyle sat sullenly, his chin on his chest, his arms folded, rather like a naughty schoolboy, thought Richard. He leaned over the chair, into the other man's face, and said, "Give yourself up, Gilfoyle. My brother died at your hands, and I'm not going to let you get away without punishment. I've spent the last two years pursuing you, and here you are. I'm going to enjoy watching you hang."

Gilfoyle's chin jerked up, and he stared back at him, reading the hard truth in Richard's eyes. "You're insane," he spat. "Completely and utterly insane. And to think I was contemplating using your services to win Tina over. By God, what a narrow escape!"

Richard straightened in amazement. "Using my services to marry Tina? She wouldn't marry you, Gilfoyle! A woman would have to be desperate to even consider it, and she'd still say no."

Gilfoyle launched himself up out of the chair, and they grappled furiously. Richard managed to get a glancing blow to Gilfoyle's nose, while Gilfoyle struck him in the eye. Sir Henry roared again, "Enough, I say!" and Will forced them apart. Richard stepped back, panting, wishing he'd landed another good punch on that smug mouth, but there'd been satisfaction in making his nose bleed. Gilfoyle shook himself free of Will and sat back into his chair, snatching the handkerchief the other man offered and dabbing gingerly at his nose.

"You'll be sorry for this," he threatened, breathless. "All of you. I won't say any more until I see Lord Montague. He's one of you, isn't he? Yes, I thought so. Well, he was a friend of my late father."

And with that he closed his mouth.

Richard wondered why Lord Montague had never mentioned his friendship with the Gilfoyles. Well, they would find out soon enough. His eye was aching, and he knew from experience that soon it would begin to swell and close. He should put something cold on it, but there was no time to indulge himself, no time to do anything but find the Captain and his man Sutton, before they found Tina.

"You were at the Great Southern Inn in May,"

Will began. "You were on your way to Kent for the Bossenden Wood riots."

Silence.

"You were traveling with John Little. Isn't that so?"

Gilfoyle looked surprised, then thoughtful, but he still would not speak.

They continued to question him, but the silence went on, and eventually Sir Henry decided it would be best to take him under guard back to Whitehall and question him there.

"At least tell us where your henchman Sutton is hiding?" Richard demanded, as Gilfoyle was led to the door. "He's going to hurt Miss Smythe if he remains on the loose. Give him up for her sake, if you really love her."

Gilfoyle turned his head to stare at him. "You are an idiot, Eversham. I know nothing of this. If Tina is in danger, then it is entirely your fault, and if any harm comes to her, then I shall blame you for it."

The door closed. Richard swore and went to the window, then back again, restless and anxious and unable to do anything about it.

"If he's guilty, he's giving a good impression of an innocent man," Sir Henry said quietly.

Richard threw him an angry look. "He's not innocent. Don't let him gull you into believing that, sir. He's a consummate liar."

"Humph. Well, we shall see," Sir Henry said.

Will returned, having given instructions to the trusted servants Sir Henry was using to keep watch over Gilfoyle until he was transported to London. He looked from one to the other of them and decided it was safer to hold his tongue.

"I'll take her to Kent," Richard said suddenly, almost as if he were talking to himself. "She'll be safe there, and I can watch over her."

"It'd be an easy enough matter for Sutton to follow you," Will blurted out, and then wished he hadn't as Richard shot him a nasty look. "However, I'm sure you've thought of that," he added hastily.

"This friendship between Miss Smythe and Lord Horace," Sir Henry said thoughtfully. "You don't think they're in this together? Not the first time a beautiful woman has made a fool of us men, eh?"

Richard took a breath as if he were about to explode, and then calmed himself, to the relief of the others. "Miss Smythe has nothing to do with the Captain, I'd stake my life on it. Gilfoyle has duped her just as he has everyone else."

"Very well then." Sir Henry rubbed his hands together. "I'll get ready to return to London with Lord Horace. I'll take Branson, too; give him a bit of a scare in case he hasn't told us everything. You and Will here go to Kent with the young lady, and stay there until we consider it safe. I'll keep in touch."

Sir Henry came over to shake hands with them both. "Congratulations. This has been a difficult mission, but we are finally nearing its end. Your brother can rest peacefully at last, eh, Richard?"

As Richard agreed he realized with a sense of shock that he hadn't been thinking of Anthony at all when he fought with Gilfoyle just now. He'd been thinking of Tina.

Chapter 32

Tina sat on the bed in her undergarments and watched as Maria packed her belongings carefully in her trunk and boxes, ready for the journey to Kent. All those expensive and precious gowns and bits and pieces, teamed with the worn and patched petticoats and darned stockings. It told the story of her life better than any words. She couldn't believe so little time had elapsed since she had arrived here at Arlington Hall, and yet so much had happened.

The woman she'd been then was someone she barely recognized now. She'd been weighed down with her concerns, certainly, but she'd also been dreaming of Richard Eversham and enjoying the relative freedom of Arlington Hall. They'd walked in the sunshine and dined in the pavilion by the river, and although her plans in regard to Horace had been unsuccessful, she'd seen her brother Charles in an entirely new light.

"Charles!" She started up. "Maria, we must tell Charles what is happening. He'll be worried and what will he tell my parents?"

Maria soothed her. "He's been told, Miss Tina. Mr. Eversham and Sir Henry explained matters to him. He's going to return to Mallory Street tomorrow in Lord Horace's coach."

"But the bailiffs!" she wailed, and put her hands to her face. "I can't go to Kent. It's impossible. There's too much to do at home."

Maria put an arm about her waist and led her toward the bed. "Lie down, miss, and rest. We will be leaving this evening, and it is a long journey without, I'm sure, many stops. Please, close your eyes and sleep. You are making yourself ill with worry."

Tina wondered how she was meant to sleep with all this going on, but she didn't have the heart to argue, and lay down, abandoning herself to the soft feather mattress, and let Maria draw the covers over her and tuck her in. The fragrance of roses drifted in from the open windows—the storm had blown itself out, and the air was still and calm once again.

To her surprise she did sleep, but it was a restless slumber, with snatches of nightmares interrupting memories of the folly and Richard's arms. When the face of the man in the library suddenly jumped into a dream about swimming with Richard in the river, Tina sat up with wide-open eyes.

The room was in darkness apart from a flickering lamp, and someone was knocking on her bedroom door. Maria, who also looked to have been dozing, hurried over to answer it.

"Who is it?" she demanded.

"Lady Isabelle. May I come in and speak with Miss Smythe for a moment?"

Tina nodded to Maria and, climbing out of bed, draped a robe about herself to cover her underclothing. Lady Isabelle came into the room as Maria hastened to turn up the lamp to brighten the gloom.

"My dear Miss Smythe, is there anything I can do?"

Tina, allowing her hands to be taken in her hostess's warm grip, looked into her compassionate eyes and felt like weeping.

"Sir Henry has told me the whole story. I find it difficult to believe that such dreadful things have been happening here, in my home."

"Lord Horace," Tina whispered, a lump still in her throat.

"Horace, yes?"

"He would never . . . Lady Isabelle, believe me, Horace may be unpleasant sometimes and . . . and arrogant, but he would never do the things they are saying he has done."

Lady Isabelle squeezed her hands. "My dear, I, too, find it difficult to believe Lord Horace guilty, but my husband assures me he will get to the bottom of this situation. If your Horace is innocent, then he will be found to be so. My husband is an honest man, and I'd trust him with my life."

Tina tried to take comfort from what she was saying.

Lady Isabelle led her to the window seat, and they sat down facing each other with the darkening garden and river behind them.

"I am more worried about you, Miss Smythe. This person you saw in the library, the man who frightened you so, I hope he may be far away by now, but if not . . . well, we must put our faith in

Mr. Eversham and Mr. Jackson. My husband tells me they are both extremely capable men and will keep you safe from harm."

"Yes. I just hope it will not be for very long," Tina said in a little voice. "I want to go home. There are reasons I cannot . . . my mother needs me."

"Well, I'm sure she will understand why you are prevented from returning just now."

Tina wished she was as confident, but she thought it more likely Lady Carol had taken to her bed again and, in her darker moments, imagined she was being moved, bed and all, to the family's new location—probably a nasty little hovel by the docks.

Lady Isabelle glanced over at Maria, but the maid was busy at the hearth, stoking the coals into a warm blaze. Lady Isabelle lowered her voice and leaned closer. "Mr. Eversham cares for you, Tina. I don't know whether that is of interest to you, but I think it is. There are rumors that you have already given your heart to Lord Horace, and if so . . . But I wanted to say this to you, in case you are in a quandary. Women marry for many reasons: security and duty and familiarity. And love. I think if I had been able to, I would have married for love. Not that I don't admire my husband and have a great affection for him, for I do. But there has always been something lacking in my life, and my search for it has made Sir Henry, and I, miserable at times."

She sighed, and Tina was aware Lady Isabelle was generously sharing something that was important to her in the hope it would help Tina.

"I did think I was in love with Mr. Eversham,"

Tina admitted at last, "but now . . . I don't know. He isn't the man I thought him. How could I have been so wrong, believing I understood him so well, and yet he was a different man altogether? That frightens me, Lady Isabelle, and makes me wonder what else I might have got wrong about him."

"My dear, I think you will find you *do* know him."

Tina shook her head wildly. "No, I don't. And now, with Horace . . . I can't abandon him, can I? Even if I don't love him in the same way as . . . well, we have been friends forever."

"Hush, Tina, calm yourself. You are too over-wrought at the moment to make a decision about anything. Give yourself time to reflect. That has always been my mistake, rushing into a thing in the heat of passion and repenting at leisure."

Tina had never been one to rush into anything in the heat of passion. She was the practical one, the sensible one. And yet lately she seemed to have lost her no-nonsense air completely. "I will try, my lady."

"Well then. I hope you will avoid the same mistakes as I. We are both passionate women, Tina, and I think that is why we must marry for love."

She leaned forward to kiss Tina's cheek and rose to her feet, turning to the maid. "Maria, Mr. Eversham asked me to tell you that he is ready to leave now. I will send some servants up to collect Miss Smythe's luggage." And then she was gone, the fragrance of her perfume lingering a moment after the door closed.

Maria began to hurry about, helping Tina into

her traveling dress and cloak, gathering together
her own belongings. Shortly afterward the servants came for the luggage, and Tina and Maria
followed them down the stairs.

The coach rattled down the long carriageway,
leaving the brightly lit Arlington Hall in its wake.
Richard and Will sat opposite Tina and Maria,
but Archie was outside, rugged up, riding with
the coach driver. There were also several outriders Sir Henry had arranged to accompany them,
as an added precaution. He'd had another word
with Richard before they left.

"You know, don't you, that this fellow Sutton
may follow you to Kent?"

"I'm aware of that, sir."

"All right, don't get testy, Richard. I'm sure you
are perfectly capable of protecting this girl, but I
need to be sure you're cognizant of the full picture.
The girl has become the bait, hasn't she? Where
she goes, this fellow will follow, and when he de-
cides to strike, we will have him." He clapped his
hands together like a man squashing a fly.

"I don't want to think of Miss Smythe as bait for
this thug," Richard said grimly, "but I understand
what you're saying. I will be protecting her with
my life, Sir Henry, believe me."

Sir Henry gave him a curious look and then
smiled. "I believe you will, Richard. Good, good.
But don't let that blind you to the possibilities. If
you lay your trap carefully and lure him in . . ."

Richard shifted restlessly. "I don't like to think—"

"Well you'll have to. This fellow will be very

valuable to us, together with Branson and Lord Horace. And if Lord Horace is the Captain, then we'll have taken the head of this particular snake. I don't think it will be able to function without his brains."

"*If* he is the Captain?"

"I know you dislike him, but I'm of a cooler disposition, and I'm not entirely certain of it, not yet. Wouldn't want to get it wrong and let the real Captain go free, would we? By the way, have you seen Mr. Little?"

"He is leaving in the morning."

"Yes, he came up to me and expressed his shock. Of course gossip is rife now, all sorts of strange stories flying about the Hall as to what's going on, but I think I said enough to put his mind at rest. He thinks Lord Horace was heading up a ring of poachers."

Richard laughed.

"Unlikely but people will believe anything if you say it with enough panache."

"Did you manage to get the reason why he was going to Kent in May, before the riots?"

"Without resorting to fisticuffs do you mean? I did. He was rather surprised, but he said he had relatives he was visiting, and it was his bumping into Lord Horace that day that brought them together in what has been an unlikely friendship. He sounded sincere, so I let him go. For now. We know where to find him if we need him, Richard. He's a businessman with an importing business to run. He couldn't just vanish even if he wanted to."

Just before Richard left he remembered something else. "You told Branson you'd let him go, and now you're taking him to London. I thought you were a man of your word, Sir Henry?"

Sir Henry smiled a crafty smile. "One's word is a flexible thing, Richard. There are times when it can stretch to include all sorts of half-truths. Oh I'll let him go, if he gives me everything he has, but first I want to make sure he never involves himself in anything like this again."

The coach hit a rut in the road and brought Richard back to the here and now. In the gloomy interior, lit by a single light, his companions looked like strangers, even Tina. A beautiful stranger. He glanced at her, but she was looking down at her folded hands, smoothing her gloved fingers one by one, deep in her own thoughts.

And he would not be able to fathom those thoughts until they could speak alone, and that would probably not be until they reached Kent. He was certain Tina would not seek him out before then, and if he tried to seek her out, she would avoid him.

He caught sight of one of the outriders beyond the window and was glad of the extra protection. At least he wouldn't have to worry about Tina's safety on the journey. When they reached Eversham Manor he would have two choices: to keep the men about them, making certain no one got near her, or to let them go and leave Tina seemingly unprotected. To use her, as Sir Henry had said, for bait, to once and for all capture this threat to her safety.

He hadn't decided yet. He'd always been a man of decisive actions, but this time he was having difficulty.

Once more Richard settled his gaze on Tina,

the soft downward curve of her mouth, her dark lashes hiding her green eyes, the dark curl that had come loose from beneath her bonnet and kissed her cheek. He knew his feelings hadn't changed; he still wanted her, to be with her, to spend his life with her.

As if she sensed him watching, she looked up and caught him. Surprise widened her eyes, but a moment later other emotions hardened her beautiful face. Distrust and suspicion. And quite possibly disgust—his eye was swollen and bruised from Gilfoyle's ministrations.

"Get some rest, Miss Smythe," he said evenly. "It is a long journey."

Resolutely she turned away and rested her head against the seat, closing her eyes, shutting him out.

Oh yes, she had changed her opinion of him all right, but it was up to him to win her back.

A lesser man might give up, but Richard had spent the past two years teaching gentlemen how to win the ladies of their dreams. He was confident he could win back Tina. At least, he wasn't about to give up without a fight.

Chapter 33

⁓ ∞ ⁓

"Oh, Archie!" Maria chuckled sympathetically. His curly hair was standing on end from the force of the wind, and his cheeks were bright red. Traveling outside the coach was rather closer to the elements than he was used to. Still, he gave her a grin and, with a glance over his shoulder to make sure they were not being observed, a hug.

They were in the stable yard of a coaching inn, awaiting a change of horses. The others were inside the inn partaking of some refreshments but Maria and Archie had quickly scoffed down their own food and drink so that they could spend a moment together, alone.

"My mistress is unhappy." Maria sighed, speaking aloud the worry that was concerning her the most. "Your master has broken her heart, and I don't think she'll ever forgive him. And now Lord Horace's being hauled off like a criminal. It is not right, Archie."

"Maria, I know you told Miss Smythe about Mr. Eversham."

Maria's eyes widened, and then she gave a little

fatalistic shrug. "I'm sorry. I had to tell her. I didn't want to break my word to you, but—"

"No, no, I think I knew you'd have to tell her, eventually."

Maria nodded unhappily, expecting him to accuse her of choosing Tina over him, thinking he wouldn't understand.

Instead he surprised her.

"This is something they will have to sort out themselves. It isn't up to us to mend it for them—if it can be mended."

"I have looked after Miss Tina for many years, Archie."

"And has she ever asked for your advice? Has she always listened to it?"

"Well . . . not always. She is a strong-willed young woman."

"I thought so. Maria, let her make her own mistakes. You can't always be there; you won't always be there. You have your own life to lead now."

She opened her mouth to argue, then met his eyes and decided against it. Archie was right. Miss Tina must travel her own path in life.

"I will not have a position as maid after this is over," she informed him with a little wobble in her voice. "They cannot afford me any longer, so I will have to find another position, or . . . or I can go home. To Spain."

There, she'd spoken the words that for so long she'd held close to her heart. Home. After all these years.

And yet, strangely, it didn't have the same appeal as it used to. The vision in her head was still there, the shady groves and the baked plains, but they had the air of something a little old, a little tarnished. And here was Archie in front of her, alive and solid and so very real.

He touched her hand and lifted it to his lips.

"I love you, Maria. I know our relationship started as a job, a way of getting information, but I only had to look into your eyes and all that changed. I want to marry you."

"Archie . . ."

"No, there's no need to answer now. I know you want to go home. I wish I could go with you. Perhaps I will. Thumb my nose at the authorities, eh?"

Maria shook her head. She knew if she allowed him to go to Spain, she would be leading him into danger, and she couldn't do that. This decision was one she alone had to make.

The silence between them lengthened, and soon it was time to climb back inside the coach.

Richard looked up as Tina entered the private parlor, she having been upstairs to the room he'd engaged, to brush her hair and tidy herself. He was alone now, with Will having returned to the coach, and Archie and Maria slipping off somewhere together.

Seeing him she started, made as if to turn and leave again, then changed her mind. Slowly she came to the fire and held out her hands. He could see the shadows under her eyes, the unhappy droop to her mouth, and wished he could make it all better. But that wasn't going to happen, and he very much doubted she would allow him to try.

You are an expert in situations like this, Richard, a voice in his head chastened him. *Who do gentlemen turn to when they have all but given up? You! And why do they come to you? Because you are an expert!*

Richard wasn't quite sure it was the same when it was the expert himself who was seeking to win his ladylove, but in one respect the inner voice was right: What did he have to lose?

"I'm sorry," he said.

First rule of winning your ladylove: apologize. It doesn't matter what you are apologizing for, or whether or not you've done anything wrong, just apologize, and keep apologizing.

"I'm so sorry, Tina."

She gave him a suspicious glance before turning back to the fire. "What are you sorry for?"

"Everything."

"I'd prefer to hear specifics," she said coldly.

Perhaps this wasn't going to be as easy as he'd hoped, but then if it were easy, wouldn't everyone be deliriously happy all the time? She was watching him surreptitiously, trying to read his thoughts, and he put on his most charming and dependable face, aware it was spoiled a little by his black eye. Her response wasn't promising.

"You lied to me, Richard. You've been lying to me from the first day we met. I find that impossible to forgive."

Ah, so that was the problem. And he didn't like the way she said "impossible." Still, he wasn't going to be put off by an adjective.

"I didn't know you then, Tina. I was doing a job, a difficult and important job, a job I'd been doing two years. I couldn't have imagined that

the day you came to see me I was going to meet
the woman who would mean more to me than . . .
than anything else."

Richard knew his ending was lame; he could
have done better there. But Tina had that effect on
him, turning his wits to water.

"I love you," he blurted out.

Her eyebrows lifted, and she curled her lip. "*You
love me?* I doubt it. I don't think you have a clue
what love means. And if I ever believed myself in
love with you, then I've learned the error of my
ways. You are a stranger, Richard."

And with that she stalked from the room, leaving him sitting there by the fire, alone.

Richard groaned and rubbed his hands over
his face, wincing when he touched his sore eye.
Obviously he'd overestimated his expert abilities. This wasn't going to be easy. But he refused
to give up. He would win her back . . . after he'd
saved her life.

Sutton watched the group at the inn from the
shelter of the trees, eyes narrowed, sitting very
still upon his horse, as if he were part of the land-
scape. Earlier he'd lured one of the stable boys into
a quiet spot with a couple of shillings and asked
questions; as he expected they were heading for
Eversham's estate in Kent. He intended to leave
them now and ride on alone, taking the shorter
cross-country route.

He had plans to make.

The woman had seen him, and he knew it
would be her testimony that would hang him. He

dismissed any threat offered by Branson—he was a fool, and everyone knew it—and as for the other one, the gent—Sutton smirked with derision. No, it was the woman he had to get rid of before the truth came out, and as soon as possible.

He turned his horse and began to ride.

Sutton decided he'd kill her slowly, take his time. He might even kidnap her and hide her away somewhere, taking out his frustrations on her body—she was a beauty. Remembering her now, standing in the library, the shape of her body, her dark hair and white skin, the brilliance of her eyes. A real lady, she was, and Sutton hadn't had a real lady for a while.

Oh yes, he was going to enjoy himself, and afterward, the devil could have him, he didn't care. His time was probably up anyway. But just in case it wasn't, he might head toward Faversham. He had a sister there, who'd always been fond of him, and he of her. She'd look after him and scold him and tell him to behave himself.

Sutton smiled. His soul may be beyond redemption but it was still nice to have someone who loved him.

Chapter 34

Tina opened her eyes, complaining as the shaking continued, and realized someone was trying to wake her. It was Richard, so close to her that she could feel his warm breath against her skin. The bruise around the eye Horace had punched was finally fading, but she wanted to reach out and stroke it gently. He smiled, and just for a moment she smiled back, forgetting everything that had come between them, and then she remembered and sat up abruptly. He moved away with a nod to Maria, who came to help her from the coach.

"We are here, miss!" Maria said in a cheerful tone belied by her tired eyes and pale face. "This is Mr. Eversham's house."

Tina blinked at the building lit by the setting sun. It was built of mellow pink brick, and with its turrets and gables and arched windows, looked rather like a magical castle. And then the front door opened, and the most beautiful woman she had ever seen came to greet them—a magical princess for the magical castle. Her glorious red hair shone in the lingering sunlight, and her violet-blue eyes were matched by the dress she wore.

"Richard!" she cried, hands outstretched to grasp his. "You have come home."

Richard seemed to hesitate, then took her hands briefly, and turned toward Tina. But the woman clung to his arm, hurrying along beside him, as if they were . . . well, Tina—wide-awake now—couldn't help but wonder just how close a relationship these two had.

"Evelyn, this is Miss Smythe, and this is Will Jackson, an associate of mine. This is Evelyn, my brother's widow."

Ah, the widow, thought Tina, as Evelyn gave her another of her perfect smiles. The *unfaithful* widow. Lady Isabelle Arlington might be described in a similar manner, but Tina didn't get the same warm sense of liking with this woman. Despite her beauty and her welcoming smile there was something cold and off-putting about Evelyn Eversham.

"We get so few visitors here, don't we, Richard?" she was burbling on, glancing at him as if they were in league. A couple. "Are you staying? Richard, are they staying with us?"

Richard had grown more and more uncomfortable, and now he removed his arm from Evelyn although not without a forceful effort, Tina noted, hiding her smile behind her hand. "Miss Smythe's life is in danger," he said gravely.

Evelyn gave a gurgle of laughter. "Her life in danger? My goodness, Richard, that is dramatic."

Richard opened his mouth, probably to reprimand her, but Tina had had enough of this little scene and decided to answer for herself.

"I was unfortunate enough to come face-to-face with a dangerous man, Mrs. Eversham, and he knows that if he is caught and I identify him, then he will be hanged. I imagine he will do anything in his power to prevent that."

Her quietly serious tone froze Evelyn's smile.

"I see," she said, changing tack. "Then you are most welcome at Eversham Manor, Miss Smythe. Richard was right to bring you here."

She turned to lead the way inside, and Maria murmured in Tina's ear, "As if it all belongs to her, miss! The cheek of her."

But Tina was thinking that perhaps it did belong to Evelyn, and Richard, too. He'd lied to her about other things, why not about his sister-in-law? She was a beautiful woman, and his brother was dead. Was it not entirely possibly they were lovers?

And why oh why did the thought of it hurt so much!

Inside the manor the entrance hall was paneled in dark oak, with a vaulted ceiling in the Tudor style. Tina looked about her, wondering how old it was and how long Richard's family had been in possession of it. Maria had said he was wealthy—not that Tina cared a jot about that—and yet the house didn't look as if it had had much care taken of it.

Will, following along behind her, almost ran into her. It was because he couldn't take his eyes off Evelyn, she was amused to see. "Do you live here the year round, Mrs. Eversham?" he asked, probably hoping he might see her in town at some point.

"I very rarely leave," she said pensively. "An occasional visit to London to see old friends, but I am unused to all the noise these days. I am afraid I've become quite the country bumpkin."

Richard raised his eyebrows. "You were in London the other week, Evelyn, so don't play the poor widow. My sister-in-law," he said to Will, "was an actress before she married my brother and has many friends."

Evelyn didn't look pleased to have her version of the story routed, and her response was to pretend not to hear as she instructed a servant to bring tea and refreshments to the sitting room.

"Afterward, I will see you to your rooms," she said, her smile once more in place. "You are all staying, I presume?"

"Yes, Evelyn, they are all staying. Excuse me for a moment"—it was Tina he looked to—"I need to speak to some of the household. Will?"

The two men went out, and for a moment silence reigned.

"What a very nice room." Tina made the effort to be polite, and it *was* a nice room, feminine, with a great many flowery fabrics.

"Yes, I believe it was Richard's mother's favorite room," Evelyn said dismissively. With the gentlemen gone, Tina noticed that the other woman's appealing manner was no longer quite so appealing.

"Do you have any children, Mrs. Eversham?"

Evelyn gave a playful little smile. "Unfortunately not, Miss Smythe." She made a show of looking about her. "This house is so big, it needs children. Perhaps one day Richard and I . . ." But she chose not to end the sentence, leaving that to Tina's imagination.

The tea tray arrived, and Tina was glad to sip the hot liquid and partake of several sandwiches, as well as a large slice of fruitcake She'd been feeling queasy from the coach, but now hunger had taken its place.

"Have you many friends in the area?" Tina tried again, when she was feeling more the thing. "You must be always out visiting."

Evelyn waved a delicate white hand. "When Anthony, my husband, was alive we were always out and about, but since he died I do not seem to get many invitations. They do not want to share their table with a widow in mourning."

That didn't sound likely, but Tina thought she knew the real reason Evelyn was not invited, and decided to be frank. "Pardon me, Mrs. Eversham, but I think it is because they do not want a beautiful widow at their table."

Evelyn appeared pleased with her observation. "Well, perhaps," she acknowledged with her playful smile.

"Was your husband a young man when he died, Mrs. Eversham?"

Evelyn looked at her impatiently. "Goodness, what a great many questions you ask, Miss Smythe. Yes, he was young. He was murdered."

Tina was so shocked she almost choked on her fruitcake.

"Oh yes," Evelyn went on, having got the reaction she'd hoped for. "Shot in the chest, not far from the house. In the woods, in fact. Hasn't Richard told you?" she added sourly. "I'm surprised. He's made it his life's mission to find Anthony's killer."

"I didn't know that. I'm very sorry to hear such a thing, Mrs. Eversham."

SIN WITH A SCOUNDREL   317

"Yes, well." Evelyn lapsed into silence.

Tina wondered if she still grieved for her husband or whether she was too busy grieving for herself. That might sound unkind, but it was understandable. Evelyn was a young and beautiful woman, trapped here in a country manor, with few friends—if her comments could be believed. It was hardly surprising she had fixed her sights on Richard as an escape.

Or am I being too generous to them? Tina asked herself. *Perhaps she and Richard are already lovers and intend to marry one day. Perhaps that was just another lie he told me.*

"I'm surprised Richard hasn't mentioned me to you before," Evelyn said airily, choosing a slice of cake for herself. "He must be keeping me a secret." And she laughed. "Honestly, I don't know what I'd do without him. I am so lonely here when he is in town, and I know he is very busy so I don't like to bother him, but he visits when he can."

Tina was beginning to feel queasy again, and this time it had nothing to do with riding in a coach. Where Evelyn was concerned it seemed impossible to pin down the fact from the fiction. But one thing was certain—the widow considered Richard her property and was doing her best to warn Tina off.

She didn't like to admit it to herself, but she was relieved when Richard returned, with Will Jackson, from whatever they'd been doing.

Richard saw immediately from Evelyn's smug expression and Tina's disheartened one that things were not going well between them. If he'd had any other option, he would not have brought her here, but he was desperate to protect her, and because he knew his own estate and trusted his servants, this was the best place to be. He'd also wanted to talk with Gregor, his estate manager, to follow up the letter he'd sent. Luckily the man was in his office, but as Evelyn had warned him, Mr. Gregor knew nothing more about the "toff from the north."

It was just a shame Evelyn was in residence, like a spider at the center of her web. Good Lord, he wouldn't even put it past her to tell Tina about their ancient affair. Well, there was only one way to head off Evelyn's nasty tricks, and that was to tell Tina the truth from his own lips.

If she would stay in his company long enough to listen.

"Are the rooms ready for our guests, Evelyn?" he said coolly. "We've had a long journey and need to rest."

Evelyn gave him a hurt look. "I'll go and see, Richard."

When she had left the room, Will said, "I hope we're not putting her to any trouble, Eversham."

"She only has to order the servants, Will, not too strenuous, even for Evelyn."

"I say, you're being rather harsh on her, aren't you?"

"Oh, Will"—Richard sighed—"please don't set your cap in that direction. You will only be hurt, believe me."

"And you're the expert on setting one's cap, aren't you?" Tina said tartly, and stood up. "If you don't mind, I *am* rather weary, so I will go to my room now and rest." She'd reached the door when she stopped and turned back to face them. "Are there any instructions? Should I lock and bolt my door and windows? Should I hide in a cupboard? Up the chimney? I need to know what to do if this man comes upon me unaware."

Her green eyes were bright with malice, and he wanted to go to her and shake her and then kiss her until she stopped hating him and started loving him again. But unfortunately that wasn't possible, not yet.

Richard sipped his tea, leaning back in his chair and crossing one leg over the other. He could see his relaxed attitude was infuriating her. "You don't need to do anything, Miss Smythe. The situation is completely under *my* control."

She gave him one more glare and then marched out.

Will shifted in his seat. "You upset her on purpose, old chap."

"I did, didn't I?"

"And that's not entirely true, is it? About the situation being under your control. "

"Isn't it?"

"Sutton is out there somewhere, watching and waiting."

"I am more than capable of protecting Miss Smythe, Will. We wait, we pounce, and we catch him."

Will still looked doubtful. "You do seem a bit distracted, Richard. You have been ever since you met her."

"Have I? Why do you think that is, Will?"

Will pondered. "Well, I don't like to speak ill

of any woman, but she seems to me to be a rather willful sort of girl. Rather a handful."

Richard grinned. "She is, isn't she? And damned if I don't like that in a woman."

Will gave his head a puzzled shake and went off to find his own bed.

Chapter 35

Lady Carol hadn't taken to her bed, as Tina had feared. In fact she was quite chirpy since the highway robbery; it seemed to have put things into perspective for her in a way nothing else had. And Sir Thomas had a look in his eyes when he smiled at her that made her heart beat just a little bit faster, as it used to when they were young.

Silly really, she knew, but she couldn't seem to help the way she felt. It was as if they had fallen in love all over again.

"My dear, my dear!"

Her husband's voice brought her from her reverie, and Lady Carol hurried from her parlor and into the study. She could run quite fast now there was barely any furniture to impede her journey, for although they were still in their home in Mallory Street, the house itself was almost empty.

Sir Thomas was standing at his desk, the day's post before him. There were several discarded bills, but that was commonplace nowadays. It was the open parcel that caught Lady Carol's eye, and the gleaming booty within its nest of brown paper wrapping.

"Is that . . . ?"

She came closer, hands clasped, and peered down at her necklace of pearls within the packaging.

"Your pearls, my dear. And my old fob watch, too. Who on earth sent them back to us?"

She stared at him with wide eyes. "The highwayman? But no, he was a repulsive fellow! Those horrid eyes. Such a pale blue color. Like ice. I don't believe he would do anything so charitable."

Charles, hearing the commotion, had also arrived in the study, and now he expressed his wonder at the arrival of the parcel. But he'd overheard his mother's final remarks, and something about them struck a chord in his memory.

"Mama, you haven't mentioned that fellow's eyes before."

"I try not to think about him, Charles," she retorted.

"Yes, but, Mama I think . . . that is, he sounds very like . . . oh dash it, perhaps I'm making a mountain out of a badger hill."

"Mole hill, my boy," Sir Thomas corrected him fondly. "Just tell us what you're thinking, and we will tell you whether it is important."

Relieved, Charles proceeded to remind them about Tina's meeting with the thief in the library at Arlington Hall and what he had since heard of the man's description.

"Sir Henry spoke to me about it when I went to talk to him about Horace."

"Poor Horace"—Lady Carol sighed—"but he will go associating with undesirables. Perhaps he has learned his lesson now."

"Lord Montague is doing his best to free him, but Sir Henry seems to have more power than the prime minister," Charles grumbled.

"Yes, yes, but what is it about this highwayman that reminded you of Tina's man?" Sir Thomas interrupted. "Do stick to the point, Charles."

"His eyes!" Charles burst out. "She said he had cold pale blue eyes. A killer's eyes."

Lady Carol shuddered violently, and Sir Thomas had to take her into his arms to comfort her. Charles looked on dubiously.

"I think we should tell Sir Henry," he said, when he thought his elderly parents had indulged themselves enough in this hugging nonsense. "And that the pearls and fob watch have been returned. It is very odd, and he'll want to know. It's the sort of thing that might happen if the thief was sorry and wanted to make amends."

"That creature who robbed us wouldn't want to make amends," Lady Carol said.

"No, but his master might. And from what Sir Henry said there is a chap in charge of Branson and this thief, someone they call the Captain."

Sir Thomas nodded. "Very well, Charles, tell Sir Henry if you think it will help to catch this Captain and clear Horace's name."

"And bring Tina home!" his wife wailed. "I want my little girl here, safe, with me."

"Sir Henry says—" began Charles, only to stop as his parents turned to glare at him. "As you please," he muttered, and retreated from the room. Sir Henry would be very interested in what he had to say, and with luck he might visit Horace at the same time.

Sir Henry *was* interested, and afterward, with Sir Henry's permission, Charles did manage to get in to see his friend.

Poor Horace was being kept prisoner at a house not far from Whitehall, and although it was a nice house and certainly not a prison cell, he was still being prevented from leaving.

"It is John Little," he said as soon as Charles explained about the highwayman.

"But the eyes—"

"No, you fool, not the highwayman. The fellow in charge. I've told them, but they won't listen. I remember seeing him at that inn on the way to Kent. I was going to see that pretty ladybird I was fond of at the time. Her husband was out of the country, and it was the only chance we had. And now the doxy refuses to admit I was with her!"

Horace pulled at his hair in such a way Charles feared he might make himself bald.

"Now, now," he soothed, "you know we're all on your side, old chap. Just stay calm, and we'll get you out of here."

Horace's face darkened. "It's that swine Eversham. He wants Tina, and he thinks with me locked up his way is clear."

Charles frowned. "Steady on, Horace. Eversham seemed genuinely concerned about Tina, and even Sir Henry believes she is in real danger."

Horace muttered something his friend chose

not to hear. For a time they sat in silence while a clock ticked on the mantel.

"I've asked Anne to marry me," he said at last, a little shyly. "Haven't told anyone else yet. I'm going to see her father when this business is all over, and I hope he'll give me his permission."

Horace eyed him sourly. "Well good luck with that. Maybe I'll be out of this gaol by the time you have your fortieth wedding anniversary."

Horace wasn't himself these days, Charles decided, but he wouldn't hold it against him. Besides, Charles was far too happy at the moment to spend any time being miserable. He was in love, and if luck was on his side, then soon he would be married to the most beautiful woman in the world.

Sir Henry was mulling over the information Charles Smythe had brought to him. It sounded very strange, and yet his instincts told him there was a connection. Sutton the highwayman had been hanging about the Hall for a reason, and that could well be a meeting with the Captain. Branson had admitted as much although he still insisted the Captain was Lord Horace Gilfoyle. Lord Montague—suddenly Lord Horace's best friend—was furious and threatening all sorts of action, but so far Sir Henry had managed to keep the reins in his own hands.

Not for long, though. Lord Horace knew some powerful people, and they were all lobbying on his behalf.

He sat down and picked up a pen, dipping it

into a pot of ink. He would write at once to Richard in Kent, warning him of the latest developments. Sir Henry just hoped everything down there was going to plan. And from now on, he was going to keep a very close eye on John Little.

Chapter 36

Evelyn Eversham popped her head into Tina's room after knocking and being asked to enter. "I hope everything is all right, Miss Smythe?"

"Yes, thank you. I am very tired so I will retire now."

Maria was turning back the covers on the bed, and Tina longed to climb in and close her eyes. Her head was aching, and she wanted nothing more than to forget all her troubles in deep and untroubled sleep.

"You may borrow my personal maid, if you have need of her," Evelyn went on.

Tina glanced at Maria, aware of her maid's stiffened back and stony silence. "Thank you, Mrs. Eversham, but Maria has been my maid for many years now."

"Oh." Evelyn's gaze lingered on Tina, as if judging her and finding her wanting. "Well, if you change your mind, my maid always relishes a challenge."

"Thank you." Tina didn't even have the energy to be insulted.

"I will see you in the morning then, Miss Smythe. Oh, by the way, you were asking about Anthony, my husband . . . I should have mentioned that before I married Anthony, I was engaged to Richard, in case he forgets to do so. He has always loved me, but, of course, when Anthony and I were together, there was no question of Richard's interfering. It is only now that Anthony is dead that Richard has felt able to declare his love for me once more."

And she was gone, the door closing gently behind her.

"She's utterly poisonous," Maria muttered.

Tina was still too stunned to say anything. A bubble of laughter welled up in her throat, but when it came out it was actually a sob. She covered her mouth to stop it, swallowing hard.

"Miss Tina, please don't listen to her. Archie says she is a terrible woman, and Mr. Eversham is always having trouble with her. He does not love her. It is quite clear to anyone with eyes that he loves you!"

"Maria, I really don't care. Mr. Eversham and I are nothing to each other. Now I am going to bed."

And she climbed between the covers and shut her eyes.

She could hear Maria hovering, but eventually her maid drifted off, folding clothing and putting it away, turning down the lamp, and setting the fire screen about the fireplace. Tina was beginning to float into her longed-for sleep when she heard the faint click of the door closing as Maria left the room.

Tina sighed. At last she was alone. Now she could cry all she wanted to. But strangely enough she no longer wanted to. She was sick and tired of the Evershams, and she had more pride than to allow them to make her cry. From now on, she would maintain a dignified disinterest.

Her eyes fluttered closed and she relaxed into the soft mattress, and in another moment she was asleep.

Sutton stood a moment, listening to the world around him, but there was nothing that shouldn't be there. He'd seen the outriders leaving earlier but didn't find anything suspicious in it. Doubtless Eversham believed himself safe here and was not expecting Sutton to have followed him from Arlington Hall. There were servants watching the entrances to the house, but they were easy meat to a man like him.

With a cruel twist of his lips, Sutton approached Eversham Manor.

Tina woke in an instant. There was no confusion, no in-between moment when she imagined she was dreaming. She was awake, lying frozen in her bed, a hand hard across her mouth.

She screamed, except she barely made a sound, and then she flung herself about, arms trying to strike out, legs kicking.

He lay on top of her, his heavy weight bearing her down into the soft mattress until it seemed to be swallowing her up like quicksand.

"Tina, in God's name . . . it's me . . . it's *Richard* . . ."

She stopped, uncertain, peering at him through the gloom.

"Sshh, don't wake Evelyn, please. She's still up, creeping around, watching us. That's why I had to wait so long to come to you. Tina? Can I remove my hand? Will you be quiet now?"

She waited until he took his hand away, and then she wriggled out from under him, as far as possible to the side of the mattress. She was breathing quickly, and her heart was thudding heavily, but that was anger rather than fear.

"What do you think you're doing?" she whispered furiously. "I thought it was *him*. Sutton."

"I'm sorry," he said regretfully. "I just need to talk to you, Tina, and Evelyn hasn't left us alone together for a moment since we arrived."

She was tempted, very tempted, to order him from the room. How dare he frighten her like this? But common sense prevailed. She knew they needed to talk, that he probably had official things to say to her, and Evelyn had been very evident.

"What did you want to talk to me about?" she said at last, with a trace of huffiness, to let him know she still wasn't completely appeased.

Richard turned onto his side, facing her, and she found herself doing the same, although there was still a safe distance between them. Just as well, because Tina had no intention of doing anything other than talk.

"I don't know what Evelyn's told you—"

"Your sister-in-law and I have no secrets," she assured him.

Richard gave a groan. "I was afraid of that."

She watched him, trying to read his expression in the darkness, preparing herself for more lies. She wouldn't believe him this time, no matter how plausible he was, she'd not be hurt by him again. And yet, as he began to speak, Tina found herself listening despite herself, caught up in his spell.

"I grew up here at Eversham Manor. My brother, Anthony, was three years older than I, and we were the best of friends. We didn't realize at the time of course, but our life was idyllic until our mother died. She was a great believer in freedom; we played outside—had no lessons until I was six—no formal lessons. In fact our mother was teaching us constantly—we went for long walks on the weald, and she taught us the names of the plants and birds—she was the daughter of a bishop and a very well educated woman. She would read to us every night."

"Your life *does* sound idyllic," Tina said, and found herself smiling before she remembered they were no longer friends and stopped.

"Father would join in at times, but even then he was a rather distant figure. We didn't realize that it was our mother who made us a family until she died. It was sudden, she didn't suffer, a failure of her heart the doctor thought. We missed her terribly, but it was worse than that. With her gone everything changed."

Despite herself Tina found her heart aching for the little boy he'd been then.

"We needed our father, but he just became more distant. Mother was the most important person in our lives, but to him she was his whole life. As time went on and the grief lifted, Anthony and I learned to look to the servants and each other for comfort. We became closer than ever and, being the elder, he took it upon himself to look after me.

"It was the same at school. He protected me from the bullies, made sure I wasn't too homesick. I relied on him . . . too much. When we came home again, nothing had changed, our father was probably more distant than ever, and spent most of his time reading in his study or walking the countryside. He didn't need us, barely acknowledged us.

"Anthony stayed down here, running the estate, quite happy with country life. When our father died, I was off in London, enjoying myself. I had a substantial allowance and saw no need to spend it wisely, and I found plenty of people who were only too willing to help me spend it. I was a fool, but I was a happy fool, or so I thought.

"Then I met Evelyn."

Tina waited while he sought a starting point to the next part of his story. She was not surprised to hear about his wild years—it was part of his current reputation as a rake, and the reason he was an expert on what women wanted from their men. *Not an expert on me, though.*

"Evelyn was an actress. Not a famous one but she had a number of parts in famous plays and musicals. The gentlemen flocked to see her, as you can imagine. She was just as beautiful then as she is now, and hard not to notice. I set her up in her own little house, paid her bills, bought her clothing and jewelry. She seemed content with the arrangement—I think she'd done the same before with several other men.

"She just happened to be in my rooms one day when Anthony turned up, and he was smitten. She gave the impression that she was, too."

"That must have hurt you."

Richard gave a humorless laugh. "I was jealous and hurt. My own brother—the brother I looked on more as a father—had taken the woman I believed myself in love with. I see now that it wasn't as simple as that. Evelyn later admitted that she'd been interested in Anthony all along, he was the heir and had more to offer her than I, and when she had the chance she made her move."

"She still believes you are her property, you do know that?" Tina said dryly. "She warned me off. Do you have an understanding with her?"

Tina didn't know what she expected him to say but she squeezed her hands into fists as she waited.

"Tina"—and his voice sounded weary—"Evelyn is the most entirely self-centered person I have ever had the misfortune to encounter, and I will celebrate the day I finally get her out of my life."

Her tension eased, and she found herself tucking a hand under her cheek, moving a little closer to where Richard was lying.

"But I have an obligation," he went on, choosing his words carefully. "If not to Evelyn, then to my brother. He loved her, poor fool, and he would want me to look after her."

Richard was an honorable man, Tina already knew that, but it was a shame he couldn't be a little *less* honorable where Evelyn was concerned.

Although if he had been, Tina admitted to herself, she wouldn't love him.

She sighed. Yes, difficult as it was to acknowledge, she *did* love him. Did that make her a fool, too, like Anthony?

"When he confessed to me that he and Evelyn were going to be married, Anthony tried to make it up to me. He knew how betrayed I felt—I was a selfish creature, I admit it, but I suppose I'd only ever had my brother to look up to and to care for me. To have him suddenly betray me, as I saw it, was desperately painful. He apologized over and over again and said he would do anything to make up for his action. But he was unable to give me the one thing I really wanted. So I turned my back on him and refused to see him.

"I didn't know it then, but Anthony had been recruited by a group called the Guardians; they work for the government in matters that require secrecy."

"You mean spies?" she said ironically. "I think I gathered that."

"Anthony had a mission to find a man known only as the Captain. I think he did find him and was following him, but the Captain found out and, his identity under threat, struck out and killed Anthony. He was found here, not far from the house. They brought him home, and incredibly he was still alive. His wife didn't send word to me, so I never knew. He lived for three days and never regained consciousness. He died here without my being able to tell him how much he meant to me and how sorry I was. I know he was unconscious but . . . it would have meant a great deal to me to see him once more."

Tina was shocked. It was obvious Evelyn wasn't a nice person but to do such a thing was cruel. She felt angry tears stinging her eyes and wiped them away with her sleeve.

"The servants were here, too, and were like family to him, after our mother died. You mustn't think he was alone with no one but Evelyn. They made his last days as comfortable and bearable as possible. I know, because they told me."

"What happened next?" Tina demanded huskily.

"When Anthony died, I was recruited by Sir Henry into the Guardians, and I learned that his death was probably due to the Captain. I vowed then that I would not claim any part of his legacy—the house, the rights as heir—and I would not make a happy life for myself by marrying—I knew I didn't deserve to be happy—until I found the man who had killed my brother and brought him to justice."

"Oh," she said softly. "The promise. Now I understand."

She was ashamed to think how she'd disregarded his promise, thought it nothing important, and persuaded him to break his vow for her own pleasure. He hadn't been lying to her, not then at least. He'd been frank and honest. If anyone should feel mortified, then it was Tina.

"I couldn't tell you everything. I've never spoken of my work outside the Guardians. Can you forgive me, Tina? I know I'm asking a great deal, I know I've hurt you and made you distrust me, but I want us to be friends again, at least."

If she were Evelyn, no doubt she would use this moment to her full advantage, extracting all sorts of promises from him, making him beg and grovel, but Tina wasn't Evelyn. And she didn't want revenge. She just wanted him.

With a soft cry, Tina threw herself into his arms.

Chapter 37

〜〜◯◯〜〜

Richard began to kiss her, desperate to return to the heady days he'd spent with her at Arlington Hall, when his life finally looked to be sailing out of rougher seas and into calmer waters. She seemed more than willing to oblige him, and as he cupped her breast through her nightgown, stroking the taut nipple, she moaned softly.

Suddenly neither of them was able to bear clothing between them, and he was tugging at her nightgown while she was tearing at his shirt, both frantic in their efforts to be naked. Their mouths fused, hot and needy, and he grasped the soft globes of her bottom and drew her against him, so that she could feel the rigid length of his erection.

She was already wet and ready for him, and moments later he was entering her. She welcomed him in, hooking her leg over his hip and pushing against him. The sideways position was new to her, but she didn't seem to be fazed by it, not his Tina.

"Marvelous girl," he gasped, his mouth open against her breast, suckling her as she let her head fall back and moaned in ecstasy.

"Splendid man," she managed, and then one more thrust and she was shattering around him, her body quivering while he groaned into the soft place between her shoulder and neck, one of the places he'd been dreaming of these past few days.

It was over all too soon for Richard's liking.

She curled against him, as if she wished she could enter his skin, and although her unbound hair was tickling his nose, he didn't move. Not an inch. He loved her, and she loved him, and all he needed now was to capture Sutton, bring the Captain to justice, and take possession of his home from Evelyn.

Not a great deal to ask.

Sutton crept toward the bed, and it wasn't until he'd reached it and stood, staring down on the shape under the covers that he realized he'd been tricked. It was too late then of course. He felt the barrel of a pistol pressing painfully into his kidneys.

"Who are you?" a voice rasped, but even so he could tell it was a woman. Was this the little lady he'd come for? He didn't think so. He couldn't imagine her with a gun at his back.

"I'm a friend of Miss Smythe," he said with a rough laugh. "Didn't she tell you I'd be visiting her tonight?"

The gun pressed harder, but he remained still, and then it was withdrawn. He heard her step back but wasn't inclined to try to overpower her, not until he knew what he was dealing with.

"Turn around," she hissed.

Slowly, carefully, he turned to face her and wondered if his surprise was evident on his face. It was the beautiful lady of the house, her bright hair like flame around her shoulders, a shawl over her nightdress, her feet bare on the bedroom floor. He spent a moment in silent admiration before raising his gaze to hers and found her eyes as cold and heartless as he knew his own to be.

It seemed they were well matched.

"You're no friend of Miss Smythe. You're the one they've been talking about, the one who's come to kidnap her. Or kill her."

It wasn't a question.

Sutton gave a little bow, expecting any moment to hear her call out for help or to feel a bullet plowing through his flesh and bone. But neither happened.

"I don't like Miss Smythe," she said at last. "She is interfering with my own plans. I'm not going to stop you taking her. But you might want to try the room at the end there." She nodded over her shoulder toward the farther part of the house. "And you might want to wait until my brother-in-law has finished with her." And then she smiled at him.

He felt his body harden instantly and made a move toward her, but the pistol came up, perfectly steady, aimed with deadly accuracy.

"I'm not interested," she said. "I've always found intercourse overvalued. Make use of Miss Smythe instead, I'm sure she won't mind."

Sutton gave a guffaw. "I think I could make you interested, but another time." He moved sideways, toward the door, and she followed his movement, the pistol trained on him. He knew he'd be back one day. She'd said she wasn't interested in him, but she was thinking of pleasure, and he guessed she might be more interested in pain. Like him.

With a regretful smile he closed the door.

The corridor was lit by a candle behind glass, flickering slightly in the movement of air. Sutton made his way silently toward the room at the end, aware of sounds coming from inside, familiar sounds.

Good. It was just as she'd said. The woman was in there with Eversham. Well, that was useful; he could deal with them both at the same time.

"**I**'m sorry I made you break your promise," Tina whispered, her cheek pressed to his. He pulled her closer. He wasn't quite sure how he'd achieved it, and he accepted that when it came to his own ladylove he was no expert, but he was enjoying the sensation of having her compliant in his arms once more.

"Tina, I wanted to break my promise. You were just too delicious, and I couldn't play the martyr any longer."

She giggled. "And now we've broken it again."

"Have we?" he said with pretended horror.

She smiled against his skin. "I love you. Can I say that? You told me you loved me, and I was horrible to you. With reason," she added, lifting her face to look at him sternly. "But I do love you, and I want to tell you so every day and every night."

"Only if I can make love to you every day and every night." He stroked her cheek, tucking her hair behind her ear. "This business with the Captain is nearly over anyway, but even if it weren't . . . I want to marry you. Anthony would think I'm insane refusing to be happy until his killer is caught, he'd laugh at me. I just . . . I had to . . . for his sake . . ."

She gently kissed his lips. "I know you had to, Richard, and I love you all the more for the man you are."

He was thinking of making love to her again, only this time slowly, bringing her to her climax again and again, but suddenly she stiffened and her eyes opened wide in shock. She was looking at something just beyond his head, and sensing another person in the room, but too late to react, he tried to leap from the bed.

The blow was savage and took him hard on the crown of his head, and the next thing he knew he was drowning in darkness.

He fought against it, struggling to the surface again and again, only to be dragged back down. But slowly, through waves of pain and nausea, Richard fought his way one last time to the surface and pulled himself onto land.

He opened his eyes.

Someone was holding his hand and his head and shoulders were resting in someone's lap, with a very feminine bosom pressed to his face. Just for a moment he thought it was Tina, that she was safe, that everything was all right. And then Evelyn said:

"Richard, oh Richard, something terrible has happened!"

And he knew everything wasn't all right after all.

Chapter 38

Tina woke to complete blackness. As if all the light had gone out of the world and she'd been left without a candle. Was she still in her bedroom at Eversham Manor? It was when she struggled to sit up that she realized her error.

Her hands were tied behind her back, and she was having trouble breathing—there was something over her head. She deliberately slowed her breathing, calming herself, and found with her mouth open she was able to get enough air into her lungs. Gradually memory returned—the man had been in her room, the man with the cold eyes and nightmare face, and he'd struck Richard.

Richard had gone limp, without a sound, and lain in her arms like one dead, and although she'd tried to help him, tried to fight for them both, a sack had been placed over her head, and she'd been carried away.

For a time lack of air, shock, or sheer terror had made her lose consciousness.

It wouldn't happen again, she told herself determinedly, and began to tug at her wrists to see how tightly she was bound. She must escape and get back to Richard; she mustn't let this nightmare man destroy her happiness.

"So you're awake at last."

The voice was unfamiliar and close. Tina jumped.

"I thought I'd kidnapped Sleeping Beauty."

"What do you want?" she said, and found her voice a hoarse whisper. "My family has no money!"

"I don't want your money."

She didn't want to ask, she really didn't, but the words spilled out anyway. "What do you want then?"

She heard him take a step, and now he was so close she could hear him breathing. Something cold, like metal, scraped across the soft curve of her breast above her bodice, and she flinched away.

"Very nice," the man whispered, "very nice indeed."

"Leave me alone. Mr. Eversham will come for me, and if you hurt me, he will punish you."

"I'm terrified." A breathy laugh accompanied the mocking words, but at least his footsteps moved away.

Tina slumped in relief, leaning back against the hard surface where she lay—it felt like a wooden settle or bench, and when she stretched out her foot, there was a definite gap between herself and the floor below. At least her ankles weren't bound, and if she got the chance, then she could run, although running with a sack over her head and her wrists tied wasn't ideal.

Just then there was a pounding on the far side of the room; it sounded like a fist on a door. She heard Sutton cursing and then a shout. Richard? Had he come to save her so soon? But it wasn't Richard. Her hopes were dashed when the door was pulled open, and Sutton and the newcomer, obviously familiar with each other, began to argue.

She could catch a few words here and there, enough for her to understand they had had a serious falling-out. Her hopes lifted; any falling-out between these villains was surely a good sign for her.

"You fool . . . I knew I'd find you here . . . predictable . . . you'll get us all caught and . . ."

She was finding it difficult to breathe again, there didn't seem to be enough air in the sack, and there were dark specks floating before her eyes. In a moment she would faint, and then she would be helpless to stop them if they wanted to harm her.

Tina cried out, struggling to sit up. And then, so suddenly she was blinded by the candlelight, the sack was swept from her head, and she could breathe. And see.

Her gaze focused on the man before her. He was holding a candle, the flame flickering and smoking, but it seemed brilliantly bright after such darkness. His features were familiar but she couldn't . . . Tina blinked and then cried out in relief.

"Mr. Little! Oh thank goodness!"

But in the next instant she realized her joy was premature. This man was not her savior. He was just another of her enemies.

The words spilled out of her aching throat, even though she knew they'd be better left unspoken. "You're the Captain, not Horace. You're the Captain, and now you'll kill me just as you killed Richard's brother."

Little stared at her and then threw an order over his shoulder to Sutton. "Get her some water." Sutton did his bidding, but Little took the water from him and squatted down beside her. Gently he lifted the mug to her lips and held it while she sipped, only then realizing how very thirsty she was. At last she leaned away with a sigh. "Better?" he asked with his familiar smile.

Tina did not smile back, even though it would have been simple to do so, to fall into believing him her friend. Perhaps she could pretend that all of this was a terrible mistake, just like Horace's arrest, and after a moment all would be explained, and she could go home.

And then she remembered Richard, hurt, perhaps dead, and her eyes filled with tears.

John Little's brow creased with concern, and he began to search in his waistcoat pocket until he found a handkerchief, using it to dab at her cheeks where the tears were trickling. "I'm not going to hurt you," he assured her. "I know you're afraid, but there's no need to be. And I won't let Sutton hurt you, either," he added, with a savage glare in the direction of the other man.

"Don't untie her," Sutton warned. "She's not the helpless creature she pretends to be."

But John Little ignored his advice and began to saw at Tina's bindings with a pocketknife he'd also produced from his waistcoat. He was leaning close to her, and she could see how weary he looked and the stubble on his cheeks where he hadn't shaved. She'd never known Mr. Little less than perfectly turned out, and it was a shock to see him so disheveled.

"Are you hungry?" he asked her kindly.

Tina considered refusing to answer but decided it was better to remain friends with him, outwardly at least. They were being so polite, and yet she remembered the look in his eyes when he'd imagined Margaret's American drowning in the cold river water.

"Yes, thank you, I am a little hungry."

"She's hungry. Get her some bread and cheese," Little snarled over his shoulder to the other man.

Sutton didn't argue, and that told Tina a lot about John Little's true character. He'd hidden that ruthless side behind a bland exterior, but he was a chameleon, someone who could show a different self to fit in with the company he was keeping. Her skin prickled. This man was playing at being her friend, but it wouldn't last; soon he would turn on her. She must get away from him.

Startled, Tina felt his fingers brush her cheek and she flinched away before she could stop herself. She heard him give a regretful sigh.

"There was a time, Miss Smythe, when I thought I might persuade you to marry me. And then dear Margaret seemed a better prospect, and she was very keen. Oh well, water under the bridge now."

"What are you going to do to me?"

"What do you think?" He smiled in anticipation. "Come, Miss Smythe, make a guess."

She didn't answer, and suddenly she didn't

really want to know, but it was too late. She'd
stirred the sleeping beast, and he was leaning
over her, his fingers touching her again. "Please
don't," she begged.

"Why not?" he snapped. "You're a beautiful
woman. Don't you want men to admire you?
I've seen the way Eversham looks at you and the
way you look at him, so don't play the innocent
with me."

"They were in bed together," Sutton interrupted, satisfaction in his voice. "That's how I
managed to get her. Eversham was too busy to
notice me until I walloped him."

Little took his hand away from her skin with
a look of distaste. "Shame," he said. "I don't like
spoiled goods."

Tina gave him a defiant stare. She'd rather be
spoiled by Richard than pampered by a man like
John Little, and she wanted him to know it.

Sutton came to hand her a rough metal plate
with a hunk of bread and some dry-looking
cheese. Tina took it from him and began to eat,
to distract herself from their stares and the dread
that was growing inside her with each passing
moment. She hardly tasted a bite and was surprised when she looked down at the plate to find
it empty.

"Good girl," Little said, taking the plate from
her and rising to his feet. "Get some rest now,
Miss Smythe. You have my word you are safe for
now."

As if, thought Tina, his promises were worth
anything. But she thought it best to give an obedi-
ent nod and lie down on the hard settle, closing

her eyes. She felt him placing something warm over her, and when she dared to look, saw it was his cloak.

But at least they hadn't tied her up again although there was no chance of her escaping with the two men in the same room. They sat by the far side, closer to the fire, and she could hear the murmur of their conversation although she couldn't make out what they said apart from once or twice when one of them raised his voice.

She sensed they were arguing about her. They were trying to decide what to do with her. Sutton would kill her now, but Little still had a conscience about it, perhaps because he knew her. He'd want to at least pretend she wouldn't suffer.

Tina found herself dozing off despite her efforts to stay awake, and when she woke again the bag was back over her head and her wrists were being bound roughly. She cried out, struggling, but it was useless, and she finally subsided. Someone was tearing holes in the covering over her face, and she was relieved to find they were airholes and, something her captors didn't realize, they gave her some vision.

"Come now, Miss Smythe, don't make this difficult."

Why not? she thought wildly. Why shouldn't she make it difficult?

They forced her to her feet and held her up and she stumbled along between them, out into the darkness. She tried to see where she was, but there were only snatches of shapes and colors—a cottage and a faint light, the wrinkled face of an old woman pressed to the dirty windowpane. She

opened her mouth to cry out, but the curtain fell
back into place, and it was too late. Perhaps she'd
imagined the face, perhaps she was losing her
mind.

There was a coach waiting, and they pushed
her into it and onto the seat. Then the door
slammed, and she was alone. It seemed that John
Little didn't even want to ride inside with her now
that she was damaged goods. After a moment the
vehicle started to move, and as it traveled away
from Richard, she began to lose all hope of seeing
him again.

Chapter 39

Richard felt as if his head might come right off, but he couldn't give in to the pain, he simply refused. Tina was out there somewhere in the hands of a killer, and he had to find her. He couldn't face another loss like Anthony, and this time he wouldn't get over it. He already understood that Tina's death would be his destruction.

"How did he get inside?" he muttered, pushing away Evelyn's hands as she tried to minister to him with warm water and bandages. "Why didn't anyone see him?"

"You sent the outriders away," she reminded him maliciously.

"But I set watches!" he shouted, and then groaned and wished he hadn't.

"Richard!" Will, who'd already been outside searching, came pounding into the room. "Pardon, Mrs. Eversham," he said to Evelyn. She gave him a little smile, and Richard saw she found his infatuation amusing and wanted to shout again.

"Get on with it, man."

"One of the men on watch took a knock, too,

but his head can't be as hard as yours. He's unconscious, and I've sent for the doctor."

"Good." So that was how he got in. He'd believed the men were up to the task, but clearly Sutton was too cunning for them. Richard wanted to rant and rave and blame himself for being distracted, but there was no point in that. He had work to do, and he must remain calm and in control.

"There's more," Will added with a triumphant grin. "A fellow from the nearby town saw Sutton go by—I didn't ask him what he was doing out so late at night on your estate, but I suspect he's been poaching. Anyway he must be a brave fellow because he didn't pretend to be blind deaf and dumb, as they usually do when they're caught. He said he recognized the wagon. It belongs to the timber merchant in the town, and he knows where the merchant lives. He's waiting outside to take us there now."

"Well done, Will." Despite Evelyn's tearful protests, Richard staggered to his feet and headed for the door.

"What about me?" she cried. "What if that man comes back, and I'm here all alone?"

"You're not alone," he retorted. "You have the entire household on guard."

"Richard, please don't leave me . . ."

"I don't have time for your nonsense now, Evelyn," he said, white-faced, swaying slightly from his head wound. "Tina is in grave danger, and I have to find her."

And then he was gone.

"I'm going with Mr. Eversham," Archie explained, glancing up at Maria as he quickly saddled his horse. All around them the grooms and stable boys were hurrying to help, eager to do anything they could for their master. Mr. Eversham, he had discovered since he arrived, was well loved. It was the hope of the staff of the manor that the universally loathed Evelyn would leave and Mr. Richard would marry and live here in her stead.

Maria had wrapped a thick woolen shawl about her nightdress, but her dark hair was loose about her shoulders, shining with blue lights in the gloomy stable, and her eyes were big with worry.

"You must find Miss Tina," she said. "If she were to be . . . I could not live a happy life without knowing she was safe, Archie."

Archie nodded gravely. "I will do my best, Maria."

Maria reached out and clasped his arm, leaning close so that her hair made a screen between them and the other men. "You do not understand," she whispered. "My happiness—"

He almost shrugged her off. Suddenly he felt empty. He knew it was selfish, with Miss Tina missing and Mr. Eversham hurt and in despair, but Archie was in despair, too. He wanted this woman, he wanted to spend his life with her just as much as Mr. Eversham wanted to marry Tina.

"I know you are going home to Spain," he began.

Maria cut him short. "No, that is not what I am doing, Archie. I have dreamed of home for so long that it no longer seems quite real. A child's dream because I was a child when I left. I have made my choice. I want you, Archie. I want to stay here in England and marry you. That is what I want."

He looked astonished at his good fortune, causing her to give a muffled laugh and reach to stroke his cheek.

"But our happiness could not be complete, if Miss Tina . . ." she said, her eyes delving into his.

He nodded and turning his face kissed her hand. "I will bring her back, Maria."

Maria sighed and stepped away, but she was smiling.

And so was Archie.

They took horses, Richard and Will and Archie, with the poacher—a lad rather than a man—riding behind the latter. Soon they'd reached the small town some miles beyond the Eversham estate and found themselves riding through darkened streets, with not even a lamp to show them the way. Everyone was in bed, or so it seemed.

When they reached the timber merchant's establishment they found it was closed, but his wagon was standing outside a cottage on the opposite side of the road, the horse still in harness and cropping grass. After knocking on the door of the cottage and receiving no answer, Richard tried not to lose hope.

He wouldn't give up on her. He refused to give up on her.

"Look!" Archie pointed to the dwelling next door. It was a derelict building that barely appeared capable of sheltering anyone, but there was a flicker of candlelight in the thinly covered window.

An old crone answered their pounding on her door. She was wrapped in a patched shawl with rags tied about her feet instead of shoes, and behind her the room told a story of poverty.

"Aye, gents?" she said, her mouth full of blackened teeth. "I was 'aving a little rest but always available to gents like you." The smile left her face, and she peered at Richard. "I know you. Squire Eversham isn't it? I knew you from when you were a babby. Your mother, she was a wonderful woman, sir." She peered at him again. "You haven't come about the workhouse? I don't need the workhouse, I can support meself."

Richard tried not to show his impatience. "Ma'am, I have nothing to do with the workhouse. We're looking for some men who were in the cottage next to yours and left this wagon here. Did you see them?"

"I know when to close my curtains, squire," she said, tapping her nose in the sign for minding her own business. She wrapped her scrap of a shawl tightly around her scrawny body and made to shut the door, but Archie already had his foot planted firmly in the way.

Richard dug some coins from his pocket and held them out. "Please, ma'am—it's very important—you could be saving the life of a beautiful young lady."

"Oh, aye," she said without any particular interest.

"My betrothed," Richard added desperately.

"The soon to be Mrs. Eversham. You are certainly invited to the wedding."

"Steady on, old chap," muttered Will.

But the old woman's eyes brightened although whether because of the wedding invitation or the coins in his palm, he wasn't certain. "Aye, well, if that's the case that's different. I seen those men, one of them was dressed like a gent, the other was a real ruffian—funny he looked like someone I used to know, that one. And then there was a third one, with som'it over the head, like a prisoner goin' to the gallows. That couldn't 'ave been no beautiful lady, could it, squire?"

"When did they leave? Where did they go? Speak up, woman!" Will had lost his patience.

The crone put a hand to her head. "Don't shout at me. Now I need to sit down and rest a bit. I don't get enough to eat, see. Perhaps a few more pieces o' silver, sir?" She gave Richard a plaintive look.

Richard held out another handful of coins, accompanied by Will's humph of disgust. "She's just going to spend it on gin, Richard."

"I don't give a damn," Richard retorted through gritted teeth. "I want Tina back."

The crone smiled her horrible black smile. "They woke me up an hour ago, they was headin' off in a real hurry in a big black coach, they was, with four horses. I think they was black, too. Gave me a fright, I can tell you, rushin' down the street in the dead of night. I was afeared the grim reaper was comin' for me. It's a wonder I didn't die of fright."

"You recognized them as the same men who'd been in the cottage?"

"Aye. I recognized one of them. He looked up at me window, and he had the coldest eyes I've ever seen." She shivered. "Dead man eyes."

"Where were they going?"

"Ain't a mind reader! But they was goin' that way along 'ere, that's all I can say." She indicated the direction with a long, gnarled finger.

"They're going toward the coast," said Will, as they walked away. "They might have a boat. We should get after them straightaway. Richard?"

Richard had swayed and for a moment seemed about to collapse, but he held himself up with a hand on his horse's saddle. "Yes, there's no time to lose," he agreed.

"Hey, you there! Squire Eversham!" It was the old woman again; she'd followed them out. "I remembered som'it. The one with the cold eyes. I do know him. His name is Ben Sutton, and he has a sister, in Faversham, on the coast. I remember the two of 'em as kiddies, they lived right here in that cottage—their mother wasn't much use, and they was always in trouble. Your father, the old squire, had Ben up before the magistrate a few times for stealin'. Still, he must 'ave done well for hisself, because he bought that cottage for his mother to spend her last years in. He's been home last few months, since his mother died, but I thought the cottage had been sold. He musta hung on to it."

Richard tipped all that remained of his coins into her hand.

"Do you know the sister's name?" Will said, with a frown of disapproval at Richard.

"Peggy, sir, Peggy Sutton."

Richard heard her answer, but he was already

preparing to mount his horse although he needed Archie's help to steady him. "We'll catch them, sir," he murmured reassuringly, "never you worry. We have to. Maria will turn me into a Spanish omelet if I don't get her mistress back to her."

Richard managed a grunt of laughter. He knew he was looking as if he were at death's door, his face chalk white, while he could feel a trickle of blood running down the back of his neck. But he couldn't play the invalid, and nor would he. He'd been in plenty of scrapes before, and he'd not let them stop him, and this was far more important than any mission he'd ever worked on for the Guardians.

"We can take the main road," Will was saying, when the poacher lad spoke over him, "No, sir, there's a quicker way. I know it. I can show you."

Richard nodded, making his head pound, and then they were off along the road, their horses' hooves pounding, the stars showing them the way.

He tried to concentrate on staying on the horse and not think of Tina in the hands of his enemies and the evil things they might do to her. They would kill her eventually, he knew that, because to keep her alive when she could identify them and send them to the gallows was sheer foolhardiness. But it was the things they would do before they killed her that caused the terrible pain in his chest.

He must save Tina, he must bring her home. He'd been a fool to let her go once, and now he swore he'd never do so again. He'd not had a family since Anthony died, he'd been alone, and he knew what it was to be alone. Tina had changed that, she'd shown him how good life could be.

Richard knew he couldn't go back.

Tina had wrenched at her bounds and struggled to free herself, but they were tied too tightly to budge, and now her wrists were raw and bleeding although the pain had faded to numbness. Her whole body felt numb. Perhaps, she told herself, that was a good thing. If she was numb, then she wouldn't feel the final death blow.

A tear trickled down her cheek and tasted salty on her lips, but there was only one. She had no more tears to cry. Richard was far away now, probably too injured to follow. She could still remember the sickening crack of Sutton's blackjack on his head. By the time he was able to pursue her captors, she would be long gone . . . or dead.

It was so unfair that just as she had finally discovered exactly what she wanted, that she had finally found true happiness, it was to be taken from her. No more holding Richard in her arms, no chance of a happy ending. And what of her parents, and Charles? Their lives would change and move on, but she wouldn't be there to see it.

There was a shout.

Alert now, her misery forgotten, she listened intently. She felt the coach begin to rumble to a halt. Once it stopped she could hear voices. The old leather seating smelled beneath her head, but she ignored that, straining to catch what the voices were saying, wondering if she might be able to escape before they opened the door and dragged her out.

"Ah, Peggy, don't be like that," Sutton whined.

"What do you mean you want to stay here?" It was a woman's voice, sharp and querulous. "What are you up to now, Ben? I don't want this gentleman getting you into any trouble. You know I don't like trouble. You could be a good man if only others would let you be."

"He's not getting me into no trouble," Sutton replied. "This is just a favor. Just for tonight. We'll be off again in the morning."

"I'll pay you well," John Little's voice came in, and his words seemed to do the trick. Peggy, whoever she was, still complained, but it was more for show.

"I'll have to sort out the kiddies," she said. "I don't want 'em to see. Leave her out here until I sort the kiddies, and then you can put her in the cellar. But you're to be gone in the morning, mind."

"I told you, Peggy, we have a boat."

"Is Miss Smythe well secured?" Little asked, and he sounded anxious, as if he wasn't at all sure this was a good idea.

"Tied up good and proper," Sutton replied. "She's not going anywhere, Captain."

Their footsteps faded away, and then there was silence. Tina was just working up her courage to try to open the coach door, bound and blinded as she was, when it was jerked open and the coach dipped as someone heavy stepped inside.

Oddly, she could smell the sea, just a faint tang of salty air. And then she could smell tobacco smoke. Instantly she thought of John Little, and that it must be him returned. A heavy hand pressed down on her shoulder, making her cry out with despair.

"Be quiet," came an urgent whisper in a voice that was definitely not Little's. "Get her out, over into those bushes. Quickly and quietly."

Shocked, Tina felt herself lifted quite gently and carried, her head dangling down toward the ground, so that all she could see were snatches of boots and trouser legs. She didn't speak, she couldn't, because the voice she had just heard sounded very much like that of Sir Henry Arlington.

Perhaps, she thought dizzily, she was going insane. Because how could Sir Henry be here?

But it was Sir Henry, for now they were removing the covering over her head, and his face was peering down at her in the starlight, that bandage still wound around his head beneath his hat.

"We've been following Little," he explained gruffly. "Told Richard a man like that couldn't disappear completely, even if he wanted to, and when he set off for Kent, I knew he was up to no good. Sorry to take so long, Miss Smythe. We wanted to make sure we got the whole lot of them in one fell swoop."

"Richard?" she whispered.

Sir Henry smiled. "My spies tell me he's on his way."

For a moment she couldn't think of anything else to say, she was so relieved to hear her beloved gentleman wasn't dead.

"Where are they?" Sir Henry was speaking to one of his men.

Tina managed to sit up, some of the pain returning to her injured hands now that they were free, and there also seemed to be bruises all over her body if her soreness was anything to go by. Through the shrubs and trees she could see a largish house, set back from where the coach had stopped on the road. Lights were shining from its windows, and there was a dark plume of smoke coming from the chimney.

"Little is in there with Sutton and his sister?" Sir Henry said gruffly.

"He is, sir."

Something occurred to Tina, and she said in a muffled cry, "Don't let Mr. Little escape, please, Sir Henry. Richard has made a vow to capture his brother's murderer, and if he gets away, we won't be able to get married."

Sir Henry's mouth twitched. "Oh has he now? That sounds like our romantic Richard, doesn't it? Well, we'd better capture him then, hadn't we, Miss Smythe? For the sake of a happy ending, eh?"

Chapter 40

"This is it." Will pointed toward the narrow track that led off the road. "The lodge will be down there."

They'd knocked at an inn in Faversham and got directions to Sutton's sister's house—Peggy, a widow with two children, owned an old hunting lodge outside the town. The innkeeper seemed to think the goings-on there were less than law-abiding, but no one had been brave enough to have her charged. "She has a brother," he explained, "puts the fear o' God into anyone who threatens to haul her up before the magistrate."

The men urged their horses forward.

"It could be a trap, sir," Archie said nervously.

"Not if they don't know we're onto them," Richard reminded him. "And if it is . . . we'll just have to take that chance, won't we?"

"Please be careful, sir," Archie said anxiously.

Richard met his gaze. "Still taking care of me, Archie? Well, I thank you for it, and the years we've been together. You've always been a friend to me."

He was almost saying good-bye, and Archie seemed to know it. Richard knew he was being reckless again, but he had to save Tina, and if he couldn't . . . he'd rather die with her than go on alone. He turned away from Archie's understanding gaze.

"Come on," he said, and led them down the track.

"**S**omeone coming," one of Sir Henry's men gave a loud whisper, pointing down the track. But before they could do more than look, the door to the house itself was opened, and Sutton came striding out, heading toward the coach. Sir Henry edged forward under cover of the bushes, and when Sutton opened the coach door and climbed inside, the men rushed out and trapped him.

Sutton gave one shout, loud enough to be heard inside the house, because a moment later Little ran out, making a run for the trees.

Just as Richard rode up with Will and Archie.

"Sir Henry?" he blurted out, as if he couldn't believe his eyes. "What are . . . ?"

"No time for questions, Richard."

A woman was screaming, more with rage than fear, and being dragged from the lodge. At the sight of her, Sutton began to shout and swear, fighting as he was hauled from the coach, and when Richard dismounted to help, he felt a light touch on his arm.

"Richard."

He turned, and she was in his arms, warm and alive. He could have stood there holding her forever, but in the end he set her away, eyes searching her face for marks, for signs of hurt or suffering, but apart from a weary cast to her features, she looked remarkably well. And she was smiling.

"Your head?" she said softly, reaching as if to touch him.

"My head hurts," he said, forgoing any heroics.

He saw her hands then and clasped them, turning them over, scowling at the injuries made by her struggles with her bonds.

"They will heal," she said. "There is nothing wrong with me that will not heal."

Her meaning was clear to him and despite seeing her hurt like this, Richard felt an overwhelming relief. He swayed and might have fallen, but Sir Henry's shout reminded him that his night's work was not finished.

"Richard!" Sir Henry repeated impatiently. "Little is getting away. I thought you'd made a vow to capture him?"

Richard gave Tina's hands one last squeeze and turned to go, but Tina wouldn't release him.

"I want to come," she said frantically. "I need to come."

He read her eyes, seeing the pain she'd suffered and, more, the desperate need she had to see his promise fulfilled. And then he did something totally unprofessional. Richard threw her up into the saddle, mounted himself, and, ignoring the shouts behind him, set off at a gallop toward the trees where Little had vanished.

At first he couldn't see him, for although the moon had risen, it was still too dark among the trees. But just as he was considering returning for more men, they reached a clearing. "There!" Tina pointed, and he caught a glimpse of Little disappearing into the trees on the other side. Spurring his horse on, Tina's arms around him, Richard made short work of reaching the spot.

Now that she saw how close these trees were growing together, Tina gasped and clung tighter in anticipation, but Richard wasn't going to risk following on horseback. He drew his mount to a halt and jumped to the ground. Reaching up, he caught Tina, already scrambling down after him, and held her against him, feeling the rapid beat of her heart.

"You should stay here," he said, his eyes dark and solemn in the faint light. "You know what sort of man he is."

"That's why I have to come with you," she insisted. "We have to do this together. And then you will give up the Guardians."

He smiled at the sound of her issuing orders, just like Sir Henry, but, inside, he agreed with her wholeheartedly. Richard was ready to give up his secret life and settle down.

"Show me the way then," he said, and it was Tina who cautiously stepped into the trees.

The quiet was suffocating, but up ahead they could hear the crackling of running footsteps and once a faint cry, as if someone had fallen. John Little didn't have much of a lead, and they quickened their pace as best they could.

Once Richard murmured, "Hush," and drew her back against him, holding her still, listening. Her heart was thudding in her breast, and for a moment she couldn't hear anything but the whoosh of her own blood, and then she did. Some movement close by, but it had slowed considerably.

Richard's words were a breath in her ear. "I think he's injured."

Tina nodded to show she understood, and then they were moving forward again, guardedly, watchful for Little's tricks. A moment later he came into sight, just ahead of them. He was stooped over, one hand clutched to his side, the other grasping at the passing tree trunks as if to hold himself upright.

"Little! Stop!"

Richard's shouted order made him jump, and Tina could see his white face as he turned to stare back at them. He looked from side to side, as if searching for a way out, but there wasn't one, and he must have known it, accepted it, because he stopped and waited for them to approach him.

"You recruit women in the Guardians now?" he mocked, his voice breathy and thin. "Why am I not surprised?"

"You're injured, Mr. Little," Tina said, taking a step forward.

He gave her a blank look and then glanced down at the hand he had clutched to his side. Tina saw to her horror that there was blood all over it.

"Sutton's sister," he croaked. "Attacked me when she saw her brother had been taken. The bread knife. She was preparing us some food. I had a boat ready, but we needed to wait for the tide," he added, and gave a despairing cry, as if only just appreciating how close he'd been to escape.

"Mr. Little, you need a doctor."

"Do I?" He looked down at his injury again and grimaced. "Perhaps it would be better if I died. I'm going to be hanged anyway. Aren't I, Eversham?"

Richard met his gaze, his own sober. "Yes. You killed my brother in cold blood, Little; you must have known that one day I'd catch up with you."

Little nodded, as if in acceptance of his sentence.

"Why did you do it?" Richard asked him, and he meant everything, all of it.

Little shrugged and grimaced with pain. "My father killed himself when I was a boy. Lost everything, though not for lack of trying. Some lord or other decided he wanted what we had and took it—he could, you know, the law is always on their side. My father committed suicide and left my mother and me to fend for ourselves. I always had great respect for the poor, the struggling disadvantaged, fighting against the wealthy and privileged. What would the world be like if it were controlled by the little man?" He gave a painful laugh at the pun. "Imagine, Eversham, if you and your friends had to scrape and bow to the laborers and farmers and bakers and butchers? I think it would be a better place, and I tried to make it happen."

Richard looked skeptical. "Did you? With all your money you could have really helped those in need, but instead you persuaded them to riot, had them killed and sent to prison, and for what? For the sake of your own sense of superiority. To be pulling strings made you feel important. You didn't care about the little man. My brother was a kind and generous person, loved by everyone who knew him, and you shot him in cold blood to save your own skin. Sorry, Little, I have no sympathy for you."

Tina reached for Richard's hand, squeezing it. Little's expression was implacable, and Tina wondered if he found it impossible to understand any point of view but his own. And then with a gasp, his knees gave way, and he collapsed in a heap on the ground.

He looked up as Tina knelt beside him, his face ghastly. "I sent them back," he gasped. "The pearls and the watch. They were kind to me. I sent them back."

Little did not live to see the doctor. Tina didn't know whether she was glad or sorry that he wouldn't be hanged after all, but she supposed Little himself would have been glad. Sutton, in response to Peggy's insistence he make a clean breast of everything, and before he was wrestled into the coach to be returned to London, admitted that it was Evelyn who had told him where to go, to kidnap Tina.

Evelyn's days were numbered, thought Tina, with a glance at her beloved's uncompromising expression. Just as well. She couldn't imagine sharing Eversham Manor with that woman. She wanted to live there with Richard and make it into the sort of happy place it had once been, when his mother was alive. For now, Evelyn had been restricted to her own rooms, under the close watch of the servants, while Richard and Tina took possession of the manor.

"I wonder if my parents will have to live with us," Tina said uneasily. Now that she was safe and they were together, it was time to consider the future. And her future meant bankrupt parents.

He gave her a startled look. "Your parents?"

"They may not have a home any longer, Richard."

"Good God. Well, they can stay until we find them somewhere else, Tina, but I will not live with your mother. She hates me."

"I'm sure she will grow to love you. How could she not?"

She was teasing him, and he smiled. They were in the sitting room at Eversham Manor, just her and Richard, gazing out at the garden. It wasn't as exotic as Lady Isabelle's garden, nor so extensive, but Tina already loved it. And, she promised Richard, she had no intention of turning it into a showpiece.

"Although I may want a folly," she said, and then giggled when he caught her up and swung her onto his lap.

"We don't need a folly," he said. "But you should feel free to change anything you like. It has been so long since I've lived here, I feel it's time for a new start. A fresh start for a new line of Evershams."

"A new line?" She raised her eyebrows, and tapped her fingertip against his chin. "Are you planning on creating a dynasty, Richard?"

"Of course. At least ten children, I think."

Tina smiled and kissed him. "If we start with one, we can go on from there," she suggested practically.

"I am, as ever, putty in your hands, my love."

Tina doubted that, but she loved him for the man he was, and she knew he loved her. Everything felt right, and although she knew they would argue and disagree, they would always make up their differences.

She'd planned to marry Horace only to discover he was all wrong for her, but in hunting him, she had found someone else. Someone who was perfect.

"Kiss me, Mr. Eversham," she murmured.

His eyes warmed. "Why?"

"Because I feel in need of more lessons."

His mouth hovered over hers, teasing. "How many lessons do you think you'll need, Miss Smythe? You do realize there is a price to be paid at the end of them?"

"As many as possible. I intend to be your only pupil from this moment on. And, Mr. Eversham, I am quite willing to pay any price you may ask of me."

"Well then," he said, "I'd better get started."

Epilogue

Tina was nearly ready. Her dress, a simple, cream-colored satin with ruching about the hem and the sparkle of pearls sewn into the bodice, was quite simply beautiful. She went to the window and looked out at the garden at Eversham Manor, where she had decided to be married. It was a glorious day, and the white rosebushes had been trimmed into neat balls by enthusiastic gardeners, while the fountain, with its dolphin statue, was splashing water, droplets glittering like stars in the sunlight.

Down below her, Tina could see the guests moving about, awaiting her arrival. The wedding was larger than Richard had expected, but Tina had just laughed at his astonishment. "They love you, Richard," she'd told him, when he understood how many guests would be coming from the surrounding countryside. "They want you here at Eversham Manor, creating your dynasty."

Archie and Maria had come from London, where they now owned the tearoom in Camden that specialized in Spanish sweets. A big change for Archie, although he seemed happy with his new life. Maria said it was as good as being in Spain. Better, because she didn't have to leave Archie.

They did seem very happy, Tina thought with a smile.

Her parents were thrilled at her happy union once they'd heard the full story, and Lady Carol and Richard seemed to have overcome their rocky beginnings. Sir Thomas was even more thrilled when Charles announced his engagement to the wealthy Anne Burgess, and it seemed as if they wouldn't have to leave Mallory Street after all.

Thinking of her parents reminded Tina of John Little, and his last words to her. She hadn't understood until later what he meant, about *sending them back*. His last good deed to her parents. It had been a sad life, but Tina agreed with Richard, Mr. Little's early misfortune shouldn't be an excuse for what he had done later on.

Below, in the garden, she thought she caught sight of someone with red-gold hair in a violet dress, and grimaced. But Evelyn wasn't here. She was moving to London and talking about taking up her acting career again.

Tina had a feeling Richard was behind the offer of roles Evelyn received—he still had a great many contacts with the Guardians, and Sir Henry would always look after his favorite spy. She knew Richard still mourned his brother, but the pain had faded, and she knew he now felt that he had kept his promise. And he wanted Evelyn gone from his life.

"You are ready, miss?"

Tina nodded to her maid. One more glance below . . . ah, there they were, her friends from Miss Debenham's. They were gathered together, chattering away, with so much to catch up on. Suddenly, she wanted to be with them, to learn how their own husband-hunting exploits had gone, and to tell them about her own.

Just then there was a tap on her door. Behind her, the maid opened it, there was a murmur, and then it closed once more.

"I was beginning to wonder if you'd changed your mind," said a familiar, deep voice.

Tina turned and found her beloved standing in the room behind her, contemplating her in her finery.

"You look beautiful," he added, "just as I knew you would."

"I was watching the guests from the window," she admitted. "You were right, there are a great many of them."

He came and took her hands, his gray eyes warm and smiling beneath his slashing dark brows, his hair a little tussled, but that was fine by Tina, that was how she liked him.

"We could have been married privately," he reminded her. "I did suggest it."

"I know, but it wouldn't have been the same, would it? I want everyone to be there, to share in our happiness."

He moved closer and bent his head to kiss her lips, a gentle kiss but with the promise of passion. Later. When it was all over.

"Come on, Tina," he said, drawing her toward the door. "If we wait any longer there'll be talk that the expert on making matches can't make his own."

She laughed and squeezed his hand. "I will have to talk to you about that one day. Your education when it comes to women is rather lacking."

"Minx," he said lovingly.

And Tina and Richard went down to the garden, where their friends and families were waiting, to make new promises. This time to each other.

*Next month, don't miss these exciting
new love stories only from
Avon Books*

Kiss of Surrender by Sandra Hill

Trond is a thousand-year-old Viking vampire angel who's undercover as a Navy SEAL. But it's not all bad. Working out with SEALs like Nicole Tasso is a perk. Nicole knows Trond is hiding something strange, but it's not easy figuring out a man she finds as attractive as she does annoying. Will Trond and Nicole get their stories straight . . . before it's too late?

King of the Damned by Juliana Stone

Given a chance to atone for his past, Azaiel, the Fallen, must find out if the League has been breached. What he doesn't foresee is the lovely Rowan James, a powerful witch out for vengeance and in need of an ally. Wanting Rowan means risking salvation, but will these desperate souls find love...or be forever damned?

The Importance of Being Wicked by Miranda Neville

Thomas, Duke of Castleton, has every intention of wedding a prim and proper heiress. That is, until he sets eyes on the heiress's troublesome cousin. Caroline Townsend has no patience for the oh-so-suitable men of the *ton*. Suddenly Caro finds herself falling for a stuffy duke . . . while Thomas discovers there's a great deal of fun in a little wickedness.

How to Deceive a Duke by Lecia Cornwall

When her sister runs off the night before her arranged marriage, Meg Lynton saves her family by marrying the devilish Nicholas Hartley herself. Nicholas never wanted to change his wicked ways for a wife—until he discovers Meg's deception. Now, the Duke will have to teach the scheming beauty how to be a duchess, kiss by devastating kiss . . .

Visit www.AuthorTracker.com for exclusive
information on your favorite HarperCollins authors.

Available wherever books are sold or please call 1-800-331-3761 to order.

REL 1112

605

*G*ive in to your Impulses!

These unforgettable stories only take a second to buy and give you hours of reading pleasure!

Go to *www.AvonImpulse.com* and see what we have to offer.

Available wherever e-books are sold.

AVONIMPULSE

IMP 0811